INNOCENCE

Also by David Hosp

Dark Harbor
The Betrayed

INNOCENCE

David Hosp

WARNER BOOKS

NEW YORK   BOSTON

Copyright © 2007 by Richard David Hosp
All rights reserved. Except as permitted under the U.S. Copyright Act of 1976, no part of this publication may be reproduced, distributed, or transmitted in any form or by any means, or stored in a database or retrieval system, without the prior written permission of the publisher.

Warner Books
Hachette Book Group USA
237 Park Avenue
New York, NY 10017

Visit our Web site at www.HachetteBookGroupUSA.com.

Warner Books and the "W" logo are trademarks of Time Warner Inc. or an affiliated company. Used under license by Hachette Book Group USA, which is not affiliated with Time Warner Inc.

Printed in the United States of America

First Edition: July 2007
10 9 8 7 6 5 4 3 2

Library of Congress Cataloging-in-Publication Data
Hosp, David.
   Innocence / David Hosp. — 1st ed.
      p. cm.
   ISBN: 978-0-446-58014-4
   I. Title.
   PS3608.O79I56 2007
   813'.6—dc22   2007000452

For Joanie, with all my love.
Thank you for all you do, and all you have given me.

Acknowledgments

I would like to thank and acknowledge:

All those who volunteer their time, effort, and dedication to the New England Innocence Project and similar organizations across the country;

The lawyers I have had the privilege of working with on civil rights matters stemming from the wrongful conviction of Stephan Cowans, including: Joe Savage, Sheryl Koval, Michelle Gonnam, and Rob Feldman;

Stephan Cowans;

The partners, lawyers, and professionals at Goodwin Procter LLP, for their dedication to pro bono causes like the New England Innocence Project, and for the support they have given me as both a lawyer and a writer;

Lynne Sollis and Jill Piedrahita, for their invaluable assistance over the years;

Joanie Hosp, Richard Hosp, Martha Hosp, Ted Hosp, and Joan McCormick, for giving helpful comments on early drafts;

Shane DiGiovanna, who is an inspiration and a terrific young writer;

ACKNOWLEDGMENTS

Richard and Laura Salazar, for encouraging my writing years ago (and for the use of your last name);

Karen Thomas, for your help on this book, and others to come;

Elly Weisenberg, Jamie Raab, Latoya Smith, Michele Bidelspach, Beth Thomas, Celia Johnson, and the entire group at Warner Books and Hachette, for all your wonderful assistance;

A special thanks to Maureen Egen—thank you for everything, I will miss working with you;

Aaron Priest, Lisa Erbach-Vance, and everyone at the Aaron Priest Literary Agency;

Finally, as always, my children, Reid and Samantha, as well as family and friends too numerous to mention, but too important to forget—thank you all for your love and support.

INNOCENCE

Prologue

September 1992

Madeline Steele looked out through the rain-spotted glass toward the bodega on Columbus Avenue in Roxbury, pressing the pay-phone handset hard against her ear so she could hear over the thunder of her own heartbeat. One ring. Two. Five. Where was he? Finally, on the seventh ring, a voice came over the line.

"What?"

"It's me."

"What's happening?"

"They're here. I think we've got them nailed." She looked out at the storefront, making sure no one was going in and no one was coming out.

"Not to make a bust, but it's a start."

"It's more than a start, Koz," she said. "What else could they be doing here? Do you know how many people must be involved? How much money? If it's what it looks like, it's bigger than I ever thought." There was no answer on the other end of the line. "Koz?" Still nothing. "Koz, you still there?"

"Get out of there, Maddy," came the reply.

"Why?"

"You're undercover, and you haven't been trained for it. We'll deal with this in the morning, but right now I want you out of there."

"Are you kidding? I have to wait and see who else shows up. See who else comes out."

"Get out of there. That's an order."

"You're not my boss on this, Koz."

"No, but I'm your friend. Get out of there. Now."

She sucked in a breath, watching the raindrops splinter the colored lights from the sign on the liquor store across the street. "Fine. But this is still my case. I did the legwork; I deserve it."

"It's your case," he reassured her. "Let's just make sure we get it right. We'll talk in the morning, okay?"

"You got it. And, Koz?"

"Yeah?"

"Thanks."

She hung up but stayed in the phone booth for a couple of minutes, looking out at the tiny storefront, desperate to know what was going on behind the neon signs hawking tobacco, lottery tickets, and beer. Then she slid the door open and walked out into the storm.

She crossed the street and walked up the block, slowing as she passed the storefront, looking in, trying to see through the cracks in the dirty cardboard advertisements. Anyone catching sight of her would think she was merely window-shopping. She'd been careful not to attract any attention.

Once she cleared the window, she picked up speed. She was convinced she hadn't been followed, but she kept her concentration focused behind her nonetheless, making sure no one was coming out of the store to find out why she was there.

She smiled to herself. There was no one back there, and that meant she'd done her job well. Her father and her brothers had always questioned whether she could handle it. Tonight, if nothing else, she'd proved that she belonged to the job, and the job belonged to her.

She was still smiling, her head inclined just slightly behind her, when *she passed the alley off Columbus. She never saw the dark figure behind the stack of boxes at the alley's entrance; never saw the man move toward her; never saw his hand raised as he swung quickly, the handle of a long blade coming down on her head.*

Vincente Salazar climbed the stairs to the fourth-floor apartment on the edge of Dorchester near the Roxbury line. The place smelled like home to him, the aromas of *platanos rellenos* and *nuegados en miel* mixing with the ubiquitous *pupusas* from different apartments, swirling in the hallways.

He opened the door and walked into the apartment, pulling off his jacket and hanging it on the back of the door.

"*Hola*," his mother greeted him from the sink. She was elbow-deep in pots, and the stove was covered with sweet-smelling pans full of stuffed peppers. "*¿Cómo te fue tu día?*"

"English, Mama," he reprimanded her gently. "We speak English in this house."

"Ahh," she grunted, waving her hand dismissively at him. "How was your day?" she repeated in heavily accented English.

"It was fine," he replied, nodding in appreciation of her linguistic surrender. "The store manager says I am to have more responsibility."

"Good. More pay, too?"

He shook his head. "It is good, though, to be trusted."

"Trust should pay more."

He said nothing as he made his way over to the battered crib by the window and picked up his daughter. "And how are you, little one?" he asked as he held her above his face. She beamed down at him, and he brought her in toward his body, hugging her and kissing her cheek as she gurgled and drooled through her smile. "Did you hear that, Rosita? Your papa is getting more respect now."

"Respect should pay more, too," his mother said from the stove, her back toward him still.

"We are better off here, Mama. Here, we can have a life."

"In El Salvador you were respected. There you were important."

"In El Salvador I was hunted. It was only a matter of time. Besides, my daughter is an American. She will grow up in America."

"If we can stay."

"Don't worry, Mama. I said I would take care of it, didn't I?"

"*Sí*. Yes."

"Is Miguel home from school yet?" he asked.

"No. He seems bad. I think he is worried about school. You should talk to him."

"I will. Has the baby eaten?"

His mother shook her head.

"Well, then," he said to his daughter, "you must eat." He smiled and kissed her again before wedging her into her high chair and snapping a bib around her neck. He was mixing her baby food when the knock came at the door.

"Vincente Salazar?" a voice yelled from the stairwell.

He went to the door and listened. "Yes?" he answered without opening it.

"It's the police! Open up!"

A wave of terror swept over him, and all of a sudden the smell of the sweet peppers frying on the stove made him feel ill. "What do you want?"

———— ·❧· ————

It couldn't be happening. Not to her.

Panic ripped through Madeline Steele as she regained consciousness and felt her forehead pushed into the cement. The stink of oil and dirt and asphalt from the Roxbury alley burned her nostrils, and the pounding of the rain filled her ears.

"Please! No!"

"Cállete, la ramoa!" the voice behind her hissed. "Ahora sentirá el poder de Trece!" He had her by the hair, and he pulled her head up hard, bending her neck back to the point where she was sure it would break. "Abra tus ojos!"

She looked up and saw the quicksilver gleam before her eyes, raindrops dancing on a long, thick blade as it was drawn slowly in front of her face. Then it was pressed to her throat, and she felt a sting that paralyzed her as the machete slid lightly over her skin.

An eternal moment passed, and then she was facedown on the pavement again as she felt her skirt pushed up from behind and her underwear ripped off. In the rain, she found it difficult to tell: Was she crying? And if she was, did it matter anymore?

She found the answer with her eyes closed in the faces of her family dancing before her. It mattered. It mattered because of who she was. It mattered because she was the person they'd made her.

She choked back a breath and forced herself to focus. Out of the corner of her eye, she could see her purse lying a few feet away, where it must have fallen when the first blow took her on the back of her head. If she could only reach it . . .

The animal behind her was distracted, lost in his determination to position himself to enter her. She wouldn't let that happen.

Without warning, she spun on him, her arm shooting out, fingernails clawing at him, glancing off his face and digging fast into the flesh where his shoulder met his neck. He screamed, and she gripped him tighter, feeling her fingernails sliding into his skin.

He screamed again, louder this time, and pulled away. It might just be enough. She rolled to her side, grasping at her bag. She could feel her gun; she pulled it out, spinning back on her attacker, trying to aim and get a shot off before he could react.

He was too fast, though. He brought the handle of his machete down on her wrist, knocking her arm wide. Then he grabbed her hand and the two of them struggled. It was hopeless, she knew. He was bigger and stronger, and on top of her, he had all the leverage. Slowly, the gun turned inward on her, toward her abdomen.

When the shot rang out, she wasn't even sure which of them had pulled the trigger. All she felt was the searing in her stomach and the numbness in her legs. She heard footsteps and felt the warmth spreading out underneath her as she caught an unmistakable whiff of iron swimming in the rainwater.

This was better, she thought. As the feeling ebbed from her extremities and the numbness spread to her torso, she was secretly relieved. She wouldn't have lived well with the shame, and her family wouldn't have lived with it at all. They were all prepared for death. But shame?

She closed her eyes and let herself drift off as she heard the sirens approaching. Yes, she thought, this was definitely better.

"We want to talk. Open the door!"

Vincente Salazar stood at his front door for a moment, running through his options until he concluded there were none. He unhooked the safety chain and opened the door a crack. "Show me your badge," he said.

They unleashed the whirlwind without warning. The door was kicked in hard, blowing him back into the rattrap apartment, knocking him into the high chair, spilling the baby onto the floor. He stumbled and fell, watching as his daughter's head slammed into the wooden floor. He looked up and saw the flood of armored policemen washing into the room, then turned again to find his Rosita screaming in pain and fear. At that moment he felt the first set of boots on his ribs, hurling him against the wall.

"Please! My daughter!" he pleaded, but it was no use. The boots came again.

"Police! Freeze, motherfucker!"

He heard his mother scream, "Rosita!" and saw her moving toward the baby, but one of the storm troopers cut her off, throwing her back into the heated stove. "Stay where you are!" the man commanded, pointing a gun into her face.

The baby continued to cry on the floor.

"Please, I don't understand!" Salazar begged, but he was kicked again, this time in the face.

"I said freeze, asshole!"

In his pain, Vincente reached out toward the sound of his daughter's wails, his fingers groping for her in desperation until a heel connected with his forearm and he heard a bone snap. All around him there was screaming. He could hear his mother, but he couldn't make out what she was saying.

One of the policemen knelt next to him as Salazar struggled in agony to his knees. "You're in a shitload of trouble, cocksucker," the cop hissed, grabbing a fistful of Vincente's hair and yanking his head back.

"Please! Let me help my daughter! I'm a doctor! There's been a mistake!"

"Oh yeah, there's been a mistake, all right. And you made it." The man laughed. "He doesn't look so tough now, does he, boys?"

Vincente tried to turn his head to see if Rosita was okay, but the man held fast to his hair.

"You know the woman you attacked last night?" the man asked, leaning in close and breathing in his ear.

"No, please—"

"The woman you shot and left to die in an alley?"

"No—"

"She was a cop!" The man slammed Vincente's face down into the kitchen floor, grinding his hand into the back of his head.

Vincente struggled back to his knees, but the policeman was behind him now, riding him as he grabbed his hair again. He pulled Vincente's head all the way back. "You like that, motherfucker?" he screamed as he pushed Vincente's face down to the ground again.

"Easy, Mac," came another voice from behind them.

Vincente could feel the blood running down his face, and all sensation had deserted his arm, but he didn't care. All he could think about was his daughter; all he heard now was her crying.

He felt his head pulled back up and slammed down again, and he could taste the blood and mucus in his sinuses. "You like treating a woman like that?" the man screamed from behind him.

"C'mon, Mac, that's enough!" Salazar heard a tinge of desperation in the other cop's voice, and it scared him.

"Motherfucker!" the cop yelled as he pulverized Vincente's face into the floorboards one last time.

Vincente lay on the floor, semiconscious. He wasn't sure for how long, but it didn't matter anymore. He could hear his mother still screaming, but she sounded eerily distant. There were voices, too, male voices thick with anger and indifference. And as he lay there, unable to move or speak, he realized in all the pandemonium around him that something was missing: a sound as familiar to him as his own heartbeat, its absence horrifying. He sobbed as the tears ran down his face, tears not for himself but for the sound he no longer heard.

Rosita was no longer crying.

PART I

Chapter One

Mark Dobson sat on the hard wooden bench in the back of the small courtroom on the twelfth floor of the Suffolk County Courthouse. His bow tie was tight around his thin thirty-year-old neck, and his wool double-stitched Oxxford suit was buttoned against the cold of the out dated building. The courthouse was never comfortable in winter. The heat was either off, allowing icicles to form on the insides of the windows, or blasting, leaving those who'd dressed for December in Boston sweating. On balance, he'd take the cold, he decided.

Sitting several feet away from him in the gallery was an old, disheveled refugee from the streets. An oily newspaper from the day before was spread out next to him as he shifted his attention between the previous day's headlines and the proceedings at the front of the courtroom.

"Haven't seen you here before," the old man whispered to Dobson during a break.

"I don't get to court very often," Dobson replied. He was trying to be polite, but as the old man leaned in toward him, a foul odor attacked Dobson's nostrils, and he realized it was probably a mistake to encourage him.

The man jabbed a dirty thumb into his own chest. "I'm here every day," he said. "Got a bed at the Vets' Home over on State Street, but I come here every morning. Bailiffs know me and know I'm not lookin' for trouble, so they leave me alone. I served my country, so I figure I got the right to admire the fruits of my labor. Plus, it beats the streets; warm in here, at least usually."

"There are probably other courtrooms where the heat is on," Dobson suggested, trying at once to be helpful and to rid himself of the distraction.

"Sure there are," the man agreed. "But I check the docket every morning." He pointed to one of the lawyers at the front of the room. "His name's Finn. When he's due in court, I go where he goes. I been comin' here the better part of ten years now, and I bet I seen every lawyer that's stepped up to the bar in this city. He's one of the few I ever seen worth a fuck."

Dobson nodded. "He's the man I'm here to see." He stared at the homeless vet for another moment before turning his attention back to the front of the courtroom, where Scott Finn was questioning a witness.

"You were fifty-two when you married Mrs. Slocum, isn't that right, sir?" Finn asked the bald, thick-necked man on the witness stand. The tall, dark-haired lawyer was looking over his notes, pretending he didn't already know the answer. He was street-thin, and there was a quiet confidence in the way he questioned the witness. It was a preliminary hearing in a divorce case, and from what Dobson could tell, it had been a nasty split. Because the matter was set down for only a hearing on a pretrial motion, the jury box was empty.

"I was," the man testified.

Finn walked behind counsel's table and touched his client, an attractive woman who looked to be around thirty, on the shoulder. "And Mrs. Slocum was twenty-six?"

"That sounds about right."

"Half your age."

The witness's lawyer jumped to his feet. "Objection, Your Honor. Is that a question?"

Finn considered it. "More of a mathematical observation, Your Honor, but I'll take a response if the witness has one to offer."

Judge Harold Maycomber leaned back comfortably in his chair and smirked. He was a potbellied man with unfortunate hair that had inspired the popular courthouse nickname "Judge Comb-over." "Overruled, Mr. Dumonds. It's close enough to a question for the witness to respond."

Slocum, the witness, flushed as his eyes slashed out at Finn. "Yes, she was half my age," he answered at last.

Finn ignored the look and continued. "You were already wealthy when you married, were you not?"

A conceited grin poked through the older man's bulbous lips. "I suppose that depends on your perspective."

"Oh, don't be modest," Finn encouraged him. "You were already known as the 'Cement King' of Massachusetts, weren't you? In fact, you've been the top supplier of cement to construction projects in the Commonwealth for over a decade, isn't that right?"

"I was wealthy," Slocum admitted.

Finn walked back up to the podium. "And because you were already a wealthy man, you demanded that your wife sign a prenuptial agreement, isn't that right?"

"I'm too old to be naive, sir," Slocum responded, folding his arms in front of his sagging chest.

"Can I take that as a yes, Mr. Slocum?"

The eyes flashed again, and Dobson could sense violence in them. "Yes. I asked her to sign a prenuptial agreement, as any prudent man in my position would."

"Thank you. Did she draft the agreement?"

Slocum scoffed. "Don't be an idiot. I had my lawyers draw up the agreement to make sure there were no loopholes."

"I apologize; I'll try to keep the idiocy to a minimum. Did Mrs. Slocum at least have a lawyer review it on her behalf?"

"No, she couldn't afford a lawyer. Besides, she said she wasn't marrying me for my money, so she didn't care what it said. At least that's what she told me at the time." Slocum's focus shifted to Finn's client, but the look of hatred remained.

"Of course, I understand," Finn said. "Love can make people do some foolish things."

"Objection." Slocum's attorney got to his feet again.

"Move along, Mr. Finn," Judge Maycomber prodded, though he looked more amused than annoyed.

Finn nodded. "Just one more question, Your Honor." He picked up a document. "May I approach?" Getting a wave of the hand from the judge, Finn walked up to the witness stand. "This document has previously been marked and identified as the prenuptial agreement you had your wife sign. Looking on the second page at section thirteen, you'll see that the agreement is null and void if you had sexual relations with anyone other than your wife during the course of the marriage." He let his preamble linger for a moment, building suspense as the man on the stand was caught in an indignant stasis. At last Finn asked the question: "Did you?"

The crimson that had tinged Slocum's face throughout the questioning blossomed to purple. "I beg your goddamned pardon!" he growled.

"I'm sorry, was my question unclear?" Finn moved toward the witness stand, to within a few feet of Slocum, and spoke with exaggerated clarity. "Did you have sexual relations with anyone other than your wife during the marriage?"

Slocum looked as though he might leap off the witness stand and attack Finn. "No," he said at last, his voice quivering through the last threads of self-control. "No, I did not."

Finn smiled as though they were close friends concluding a hard-fought chess match. "Thank you, Mr. Slocum. Nothing further."

At the back of the courtroom, the old man with the newspaper chortled next to Dobson. "That was the setup," he whispered. "The kill's gotta be just around the corner."

The judge looked at Slocum's lawyer, a diminutive man with a pinched nose and shoulders so bony they looked as though they might slice through his suit. "Mr. Dumonds, any questions?"

"None, Your Honor."

"Fine, Mr. Finn?"

"Yes, Your Honor; one final witness. We'd like to call Abigail Prudet."

Scott Finn loved creating drama in the courtroom; always had. Even now, with no jury present, he knew that to keep the judge's attention, he had to be part entertainer. It was one of the things that separated him from other attorneys—what made him truly one of the most effective courtroom lawyers in Boston: his ability to draw his audience in and keep them interested. As he'd often explained to his clients, *An argument can't be effective if people aren't listening to it.*

That was one of the reasons he enjoyed being on his own as a solo practitioner. Out here, he could fight his battles alone and push the limits as he saw fit. He'd spent several years in the respected white-shoe law firm of Howery, Black & Longbothum, and the training had served him well. He could have stayed if he'd wanted, but he'd decided to take a risk. Sometimes, when he ran into a stretch where work was hard to come by and he found himself living off petty drug cases, slip-and-falls, or trumped-up disability claims, he wondered whether he'd done the right thing in turning down a partnership at his old firm. He'd be making well over half a million a year by now were he still there, living without any financial pressures other than those self-inflicted. Instead, he spent much of his time scraping and struggling to stay ahead of each month's expenses—both personal and professional.

And yet the work he'd done at Howery had been stifling in many ways, and it had never provided the drama he was able to feed off of in his solo practice. Like the drama he hoped to create now.

The doors at the back of the courtroom swung open on cue, and Abigail Prudet was led into the courtroom by Tom Kozlowski. They made quite a pair. She was young and pretty, with a brand-new designer suit and a sway to her walk that made even Judge Comb-over straighten in his chair. Kozlowski, on the other hand, was nearing fifty, wearing a suit so old only the shine on the elbows hid his shirtsleeves. He was an intimidating presence nonetheless, with his broad shoulders, solid torso, and thick scar running the length of the right side of his face. He peeled off as he neared the front of the courtroom, directing Prudet toward the stand.

Slocum put his head down as she passed him; then he turned toward Dumonds, grabbing his lawyer's lapels and pulling him over, whispering frantically into his ear.

Prudet shimmied her way up into the witness box and was sworn in.

"Would you please state your name for the record," Finn directed her.

"Abigail Suellen Prudet," she replied, her voice ringing with a sharp, trashy, sexy Southwestern twang.

"Ms. Prudet, would you tell the court what you do for a living?"

She crossed her legs. "I'm a personal escort."

"You're a prostitute," Finn corrected her.

"I prefer 'personal escort,'" she replied, frowning at Finn. "But that's right."

Dumonds, who had been released momentarily by his client, stood again. "Your Honor, I hope that Mr. Finn isn't going to ask this young lady questions that might implicate her in criminal activity. She has rights, even if Mr. Finn isn't willing to apprise her of them."

"Wouldn't dream of it, Your Honor," Finn replied. "If I might proceed?"

Comb-over was leaning forward in his chair, practically drooling as he looked down at the young woman on the witness stand. Was he actually looking down her shirt? "Please," the judge encouraged Finn.

"Ms. Prudet, where do you work?"

"I work at Sylvester's Cathouse in Pahrump, Nevada."

"And to your knowledge, is prostitution legal in Nevada?"

"It is in eleven counties," she replied defiantly. "I work only in licensed brothels, and I get tested every week for sexually transmitted diseases. I've never failed once; I'm clean."

"Thank you." Finn turned and looked at Dumonds, raising his eyebrows as if to ask whether the little man had any other objection. Dumonds sat down only to be grabbed by his agitated client once more.

Finn turned back to Abigail Prudet. "Have you ever met Mr. Slocum, that man over there at the table?" he asked her, pointing toward Slocum.

"I have."

"Will you tell the court under what circumstances you met him?"

She nodded. "He came to Sylvester's. Couldn't have been more than a couple months ago. He came in lookin' for a party, an' after a while he took me back to a room, and we had sexual relations." Finn cringed as Abigail Prudet spoke. She pronounced her words with an exaggerated precision and formality, unsuccessfully calculated to convey a sense of class and education. The words came out in a synthetic cadence—"sex-you-all rela-she-uns"—that would never play to a jury. It probably wouldn't matter in front of Maycomber, who was so focused on the woman's chest as it heaved up and down with her speech that he likely wasn't listening to a word she said. But if the case went to trial, Finn would have to work with her.

"Ms. Prudet, just to be clear, you have sex with a lot of men for money, right?"

"That's right," she answered, sounding defensive.

"So what makes Mr. Slocum stand out in your memory?"

"He was a specialty customer," she replied. "They're easy to remember; they pay more."

"A specialty customer? What does that mean?"

"He wanted somethin' unusual."

"Can you define 'unusual' for us?" Finn asked. He thought Combover might actually fall forward off the bench.

"You know, *unusual*. Some of the girls say 'weird,' but I don't judge like that. He wanted to be tied up, and then he wanted me to wear a vibrator, an' he had this—"

"Objection!" It looked like the veins on Dumonds's head might actually burst. "This is outrageous! What possible relevance, Your Honor—"

Finn leaped in to cut him off. "That's quite all right, Your Honor; I have no interest at the moment in causing any embarrassment. I'll rephrase the question. Ms. Prudet, is it fair to say that your experience with Mr. Slocum was unusual enough to have left an impression such that you're sure that the man sitting over there was the same man you met at the Cathouse?"

She took a long look at Slocum. "That's fair to say. Yes."

"Nothing further, Your Honor," Finn said, walking back to counsel table. "Your witness," he said to Dumonds as he passed the man. He couldn't resist tweaking him. Dumonds didn't even notice; he was busy listening to his client, who was hissing into his face.

"Mr. Dumonds?" Maycomber said after a moment. "Do you have any questions?"

Dumonds looked up. "Yes, Your Honor. One moment." He listened to his client rasping away, then finally got to his feet. "Ms. Prudet, just a few questions. You indicated that this alleged encounter took place a couple of months ago, correct?"

"That's right."

"Can you be more specific?"

"No. But I'm pretty sure he paid with a credit card, so there's probably records."

"That won't be necessary," Dumonds said quickly, flushing red. "Did the man you were with—assuming it was, in fact, Mr. Slocum—indicate that he was separated from his wife and had been for quite a while?"

"I don't remember him bein' much of a talker. He was very preoccupied; wanted to get right down to business. Seemed like he'd done this before."

"Objection, Your Honor, nonresponsive. Move to strike." Dumonds looked flustered again.

"Strike away," Maycomber said, his full attention still directed toward Abigail Prudet.

"No further questions," Dumonds said, sitting down.

"Redirect?" the judge asked Finn, a suggestion of hope in his tone.

"None, Your Honor," Finn replied. She'd already served her purpose.

Prudet stood up and walked out into the gallery, taking a seat halfway back in the courtroom. Maycomber paused for a moment to watch her walk before addressing the lawyers. "Any other witnesses?"

"That's all we have, Your Honor," Finn said. Dumonds just shook his head.

"Very well," Maycomber replied. "Mr. Finn, this is your motion to have the prenuptial agreement excluded. Do you want to argue the issue first?"

"Certainly, Your Honor," Finn said, rising out of his chair. "I don't want to waste too much of your time with this. The language of the prenuptial contract is clear: The agreement is null and void if Mr. Slocum slept with anyone other than Mrs. Slocum. He did. As a result, the agreement should be kept out, and Mrs. Slocum is entitled by statute to half of the marital estate and alimony sufficient to support her in her current lifestyle. By our calculations, that's eleven million dollars in marital assets, and monthly alimony of twenty thousand dollars."

Maycomber looked at Dumonds. "Counsel, I assume you disagree?"

"We do, Your Honor. The Slocums have been separated for over six months. Even if you credit Ms. Prudet's testimony, the encounter in question took place four months into the separation. Nothing in the agreement suggests that the fidelity clause was meant to apply after divorce proceedings had been instituted. The agreement stands, and Ms. Prudet is entitled only to those assets she brought to the marriage, along with the two-thousand-dollar-per-month stipend, as specified in the agreement."

"Excuse me, Your Honor," Finn said. "If I might? The agreement is clear that it is null and void if Mr. Slocum has sex with anyone other than his wife 'during the life of the marriage.' As you well know, they are still legally married today. Whether this particular encounter took place two months ago or two hours ago, it still nullifies the agreement. To the extent that there's any ambiguity, Mr. Slocum admitted that his lawyers drew up the agreement, and it's well established that any ambiguity in a contract is construed against the party that drafted the agreement. They lose, Your Honor. Either way, they lose."

"Your Honor, that's absurd!" Dumonds exploded. "You can't honestly think that the contract was intended—"

"Enough!" Maycomber bellowed. "I've heard enough." He looked at the two lawyers with weary disgust. "Here's what I'm going to do," he said. "I'm going to take this under advisement and issue a ruling in a few weeks. In the meantime, Mr. Dumonds, if there is a reasonable settlement offer on the table, I'd advise your client to consider it very seriously. There's every chance that you're not going to like my ruling."

"Your Honor, you can't—"

"Oh, but I can, Mr. Dumonds. Think about it. Any reasonable offer." Maycomber put his hands to his face and shook his head. Then he picked up his gavel and brought it down on the tabletop. "Court is in recess."

Chapter Two

FINN WALKED OUT through the doors at the back of the courtroom and led his client to the elevator bay. The soon-to-be-former Mrs. Slocum was beaming. "Thank you," she said, kissing Finn on the corner of his mouth as she stepped into the elevator. He tasted a hint of strawberry in her lipstick.

"Don't thank me yet," Finn replied, watching his client disappear as the elevator doors closed. "We still have a long way to go," he said to himself.

Meghan Slocum was hardly the doe-eyed victim she portrayed so well in the courtroom, he knew. In all likelihood, she'd ranked Slocum's bank account highly in considering his marriage proposal, and Finn had serious concerns about what he'd see crawling around if he cared to lift the sheets on Mrs. Slocum's own personal life. She had a legitimate case, though, and he couldn't afford the luxury of impartiality. Besides, it wasn't as though Slocum had married a bombshell half his age for her wit or personality. As long as the sleaze dripped on both sides of the courtroom, Finn felt justified.

"Mr. Finn!"

He turned and saw a nattily dressed man hurrying after him. He looked to be seven or eight years younger than Finn—late twenties or early thirties from the look of him—and his face seemed familiar, but Finn could put neither a name nor a context to it.

"Scott Finn," the man said. "Mark Dobson." Finn nodded and held out his hand without a word. "From Howery, Black," Dobson continued. "I'm an associate in the Trial Department; we never worked together, but I was a third-year when you left."

"Of course," Finn said, feigning recollection. "I think we met at some point."

Dobson nodded. "Once at a firm dinner. It's nice to be remembered."

"Well, there was usually a fair amount of drinking at those dinners," Finn said. The young man nodded again without saying anything, and Finn began to feel awkward. "So, what brings you up here? If you were a third-year when I left, you must be a fifth-year now. Aren't you still a little young to be let out of the library without a partner's supervision?" It was a targeted poke at the lack of responsibility junior associates were given at large firms, and Dobson's expression told Finn it had struck its mark.

"I've been dealing with a pro bono matter" was all he said. "Do you have a minute to talk?"

Before Finn could respond, Slocum and his lawyer came around the corner. Slocum saw Finn and headed straight for him, like a journeyman heavyweight coming out of his corner at the sound of the bell. Dumonds put a hand in front of his client as if to restrain him, but the size differential between the two was too great for the gesture to have any impact. "Do you have any idea who you're fucking with?" Slocum yelled, getting right into Finn's face.

Finn remained calm. He was used to dealing with angry litigants—both those he represented and those he didn't. He gave a crooked smile. "Sure. You're the cement head, right?"

"Do you have any fucking idea who I'm friends with?" It sounded like a threat to Finn. He turned to Dumonds, who had caught up to his client.

"Counselor," Finn said, "would you explain to your client that it would be inappropriate for me to engage him in conversation, please? You can also remind him that you have our latest offer to resolve this for eight million, and we'll be waiting for your response shortly."

"You arrogant asshole!" Slocum bellowed. "You want my fucking response? I'll cram my fucking response up your ass right now!"

Dumonds was pulling at his client. "Sal," he was saying, "this isn't helping. Let me deal with this."

"Yeah, Sal," Finn agreed. "Let Marty handle this."

Slocum allowed Dumonds to pull him away, but before they headed for the elevators, the large man turned back to Finn and wagged a finger at him. Finn responded with a curt wave. Then he turned back to Dobson. "Sorry about that," he said. "You were talking about a criminal matter?"

"I was. It's a criminal matter I've been handling for a little while."

Finn frowned. "Are you really qualified to handle a criminal case?"

Dobson's expression shaded toward defensiveness. "I've been a member of the bar for over four years, Mr. Finn. That means I'm licensed to handle criminal matters in court."

"Licensed and qualified are two different things."

Dobson tried to hold his indignant look, but Finn could see fear there, too, and after a moment Dobson dropped all pretense. "That's why I'm here. It's a matter I'd like some help with—I'll even refer it to you officially, as long as I can stay involved in some capacity."

Finn smiled. "What's wrong? Don't the partners at Howery still go to court? When I left, there were over a hundred attorneys in the Trial Department."

"They do, but . . ." Dobson seemed to be searching for an answer that Finn would buy, and Finn guessed what that meant.

"But no one over there wants to take on a dog of a pro bono criminal matter that's going to cost them hundreds of hours, right?" Finn guessed.

"No," Dobson protested. "It's just that some of the people at the firm said this might be more up your alley."

"I'm guessing they didn't intend that as a compliment."

"Please, Mr. Finn, you're wrong. Howery would be willing to provide some support, but the consensus is that you'd be more appropriate as trial counsel."

Finn looked Dobson over carefully, trying to gauge the man's motivations. Before he had a chance to respond, Abigail Prudet approached him with Tom Kozlowski in tow. "Where's my money?" she demanded. Her voice was quiet but determined.

"She wanted to see you," Kozlowski said. "I tried to explain it to her."

Finn turned, embarrassed, toward Dobson. "Mark, I'd like you to meet Abigail Prudet. And this is Tom Kozlowski, a private investigator I work with on many of my cases. Koz, Abigail, this is Mark Dobson, a lawyer at the firm where I used to work." He hoped a formal introduction might convince Abigail to alter her tone. He was wrong.

"Where's my money?" she seethed again.

Finn took her by the elbow. "Did Detective Kozlowski explain to you how this works?"

Dobson cleared his throat. "Perhaps I should give you folks a minute alone," he suggested. "I wouldn't want to get involved . . ." His voice trailed off.

Abigail Prudet shot a glare at him, her brow drawn in indignation at the perceived slight. "I don't lie, mister." She spoke clearly and met Dobson's surprised eyes. "But I don't tell the truth for free, either."

"Go back to your hotel, Abigail," Finn said. "Enjoy the evening. Have a good dinner; maybe see a show. Then, tomorrow, you bring all your receipts by the office. I'll need the records, though—legally, I can't pay you a dime without them. I'll cut you a check for your out-of-pocket costs, and another for your appearance fee." He looked back at Dobson. "We wouldn't want anyone to get the wrong idea, would we?"

Prudet's frown deepened. "You don't want to fuck with me," she said quietly.

"Seems to be a trend today," Finn agreed. "Besides, I don't think it would be legal outside of Nevada." He nodded to Kozlowski, and the detective hooked her under her arm and escorted her to the elevator. The elevator doors opened and she stepped in, turning to look at Finn.

"Tomorrow," she said.

"Wouldn't miss it for anything," Finn replied. The three men watched as the elevator doors closed slowly. The woman's eyes never left Finn's before she disappeared. Now it was Finn's turn to clear his throat. "My practice has become more colorful since I left the firm, as you can tell," he said to Dobson. "Now, I believe you wanted to talk to me about a referral?"

"I did." Dobson nodded. He looked at Finn with a combination of envy and revulsion. "Yes, I think you're exactly the lawyer I'm looking for."

Chapter Three

"His name is Vincente Salazar."

Dobson took a file out of his briefcase and slid it across the table toward Finn. They had moved to one of the courthouse conference rooms reserved for lawyers and their clients. It was a bare cell with plain, dim green walls, solid wooden chairs, and a sturdy laminate table: designed in all respects for the endless stress and abuse suffered by those caught in the gears of the legal system. Finn, who was sitting next to Kozlowski and opposite Dobson, flipped open the file.

"You may remember the case," Dobson continued. "It was big news back in the early nineties. Salazar was an illegal from El Salvador, part of a wave of immigrants who poured into the country during the final years of the war down there. A sizable community grew along the Dorchester-Roxbury border. A task force was formed in 1992 to root out many of those who were in the country illegally. It was a joint enforcement program between the INS and the Boston Police Department. Salazar's name hit the list, and he was targeted for deportation."

"I remember." Finn nodded. "He shot a cop, right? A woman?"

"That's what he was convicted of," Dobson replied. "Allegedly, he tried to rape her, and then he shot her with her own gun. Madeline Steele was her name; she was part of the task force, stationed out of

B-2, and she was the one going after Salazar—that was the motive provided at trial. She identified him, and they had his fingerprints on her gun—that was the evidence that put him away. He was sentenced to fifty years, no parole."

Finn turned to look at Kozlowski. "You were stationed out of B-2 for a while, weren't you?"

Kozlowski nodded, his features granite.

"You know Steele at all?"

Kozlowski nodded again.

Finn turned back to Dobson. "Sounds like a pretty clean case. So what's the problem?"

"The problem is that a lot of the other evidence doesn't line up. Salazar had an alibi—a solid one. Plus, another witness saw the perp running from the scene and said it wasn't Salazar."

Finn shrugged. "That's why we have juries, right? If the jury saw it differently, who am I to argue?"

"There was a rape kit done at the time. No fluids turned up, but they apparently took scrapings of blood and skin from underneath the Steele woman's fingernails."

"And?"

"They never tested it. Never even told the defense it existed."

"I'm still not seeing a basis for a new trial," Finn said. "DNA or not, it seems like this guy was most likely right for the shooting. Why would I want to get involved now, fifteen years later? Why would you, for that matter?"

Dobson leaned back in his chair. "I do a lot of pro bono work with an organization called the New England Innocence Project."

Finn rolled his eyes. "I've heard of it. A bunch of do-gooders trying to get felons out of jail, right?"

"Wrong, Mr. Finn. It's a bunch of do-gooders trying to get innocent people out of jail. We identify cases where physical evidence exists that could prove definitively the guilt or innocence of people who have been convicted of a crime. If the evidence shows that the person is guilty, we close the books on that case. If it shows they're innocent, though . . .”

“And in this case, the skin and blood recovered from under Officer Steele's fingernails prove Salazar is innocent?”

Dobson shrugged. “We won't know until it's tested.”

Finn pushed the file back at the attorney across the table. “So test it. What do you need me for?”

“We'd love to, but the DA's office and the city refuse to give us the samples to be tested. They say that the case has been decided, and they won't open up the investigation again. We're going in front of the judge in two days to argue our motion to force them to give us the evidence so we can run the tests ourselves.”

Finn shook his head. “I still don't see why you need me.”

Dobson heaved a heavy sigh, folding his fingers together. “The motion's going to be heard by Judge Cavanaugh.”

“Ah,” Finn said. It had suddenly become clear why Dobson had come to him. “Are you going to try and act surprised when I tell you that Cavanaugh was my mentor when he was teaching at Suffolk Law School?”

Dobson shook his head. “I wouldn't insult your intelligence that way.”

“You think the argument will be better received by Judge Cavanaugh if it's coming from someone he knows? Someone he trusts?”

“The thought had occurred to me.”

Finn waved his hand dismissively. “You don't know Cavanaugh, then. He'll see right through this. If anything, he'd be harder on me than he would on someone he doesn't know. He'll probably be so insulted, he'll bounce me right out of the courtroom.”

“In which case, what have you really got to lose?” Dobson asked.

“You mean besides my credibility?” Finn responded. “I think the more relevant question is: What have I got to gain?”

“A chance to do something good?” Dobson offered.

The laugh that came from his throat almost choked Finn. "You clearly didn't do enough research on me."

Dobson considered this for a moment. "You're still friends with Preston Holland, right?" Finn gave a noncommittal tilt of his head. "He was the one who sent me to you. He retired last year, but he still does some work in the legal community. He said he hadn't talked to you in a while, but he claimed you were one of the best trial lawyers he'd ever seen. Preston isn't someone given to overstatement. He said that with the right case, you could be one of the all-time greats." Dobson looked around the plain conference room. "Are you happy doing what you're doing now? Paying hookers to rat out husbands in divorce cases so your gold-digging clients can keep their homes in Weston? Getting drug dealers and thugs out on bail so they can run their scams while waiting to go up to the pen at Concord? Cleaning up some fat cats' DUIs? Is this really what you were meant to do?"

Finn felt as if he'd been slapped, and he reacted angrily. "I'm not at Howery, Black anymore," he spat out. "Principles can be expensive, and I've got to eat."

Dobson's look hardened. "Fine," he said. "If it turns out Salazar's innocent, I'll give you the inside track on his civil rights case against the city for false imprisonment and deprivation of liberty. Cases like that seem to be settling out at up to five hundred thousand dollars for every year spent in jail. Salazar's been in for fifteen. That could come to over seven million. Maybe more if you win at trial instead of settling. On contingency, you'd net well over two million. Not a bad take." He pushed the file back toward Finn.

Finn opened the file and flipped through it once more, scratching his head. He was tempted, he had to admit; not just by the money but by the challenge. On the other hand, he recognized that it could be a rabbit hole, and he would likely spend endless hours running through a blind maze without anything to show for it. He couldn't afford to give away his services with quite the abandon lawyers from the large firms could. And then there was Kozlowski. The private detective hadn't spoken during the meeting, but he had acknowledged knowing Madeline Steele. Kozlowski was practically Finn's partner, and Finn couldn't risk upsetting his close working relationship with the man lightly. More than that, while neither of them would ever admit it, they were friends, and Finn had precious few real friends.

He looked up from the file. "One question," he said.

"Shoot," Dobson replied.

"Why do you care so much?"

"I told you, I do work with the Innocence Proj—"

"Don't give me that bullshit," Finn cut him off. "There must be hundreds of cases like this, where all you've got is a mere possibility of innocence. Why spend so much time and effort on this one case when you could just move on to the next?"

Dobson thought for a long moment. Then he stood up, put on his coat, and picked up his briefcase. He walked to the door and opened it. Looking back at Finn, he said, "You can answer that question for yourself tomorrow."

"How?" Finn asked.

"It's visiting day at Billerica. I'm taking you to meet Vincente Salazar."

———

"You pissed?"

Finn was guiding his battered MG convertible through the streets of downtown Boston, toward the river and out onto Monsignor O'Brien Highway, headed toward Charlestown. It was gray out—the kind of deep, penetrating gray that only New Englanders know. The buildings and the streets and the sky blended together in a wall of slate as the impossibly impractical car dodged frozen puddles and potholes in the road, the darkened slush clinging to its wheels.

"About what?" Kozlowski asked, looking out the passenger window.

Finn knew he hated riding in the miniature vehicle, which could barely contain his large, square frame. The ratted soft top felt like it might actually give way to his shoulders, and the wind whistled through gaps where the canvas didn't quite reach the steel.

"Okay," Finn said. "I won't take the case."

"Your call."

Finn took his eyes off the road for a moment and looked over at the man sitting next to him. The thick scar that ran down his face was hidden from Finn's view, and seeing him in profile, Finn realized that the private investigator must have been handsome once. "I'm assuming you remember the Steele shooting?"

"Yeah," Kozlowski replied, his eyes still scanning the streets outside his window. Then he went silent again.

"That's it?" Finn asked. "'Yeah'? That's all I'm gonna get out of you? Any chance you want to elaborate a little?"

Kozlowski folded his arms. "It was a bad time for the department. Maddy—Officer Steele—was popular. She was a good young cop. She was a woman."

"And?"

"As a cop, you can't let that stand—particularly not with a woman. No one gets away with shooting one of your own. It'd be rough on the department if Salazar got out; it'd open a lot of old wounds."

"So you want me to leave it alone?"

"Didn't say that. I'm not in the department anymore; they forced me out, remember? The only person I'd feel bad for would be Maddy. The rest of them can fuck themselves, for all I care."

"She lived, right?"

"She did. It was a long fight for her, and it wasn't fun. The bullet hit the spine; she's in a wheelchair now, and that's where she'll be for the rest of her life. It wasn't the easiest thing to come to grips with."

Finn raised his eyebrows. "Sounds like you knew her pretty well."

"We were friends."

"Friends?"

Kozlowski glared at him. "Just friends."

"Okay. So what do you want me to do?"

"Like I said, it's not my call."

Finn pulled the little car into a parking space in front of a small two-story brick structure on Warren Street. The pointing was chipping away between the clay squares, and the entire building listed uneasily to one side. A small Historical Society plaque on the bottom corner near the doorway read CIRCA 1769; a larger sign to the side of the entryway advertised SCOTT T. FINN, ATTORNEY AT LAW, and below that, KOZLOWSKI INVESTIGATIONS.

Finn pulled up on the hand brake and looked at Kozlowski again. "That's bullshit, Koz, and you know it. I don't have a dog in this fight—not yet. Could be an interesting case; lucrative, too, if Salazar's actually innocent. But I can walk away just as easily. I've got no interest in pissing you off, particularly when I'd probably need your help with the legwork on the case if I take it. So you tell me, what should I do?"

Kozlowski opened the door and got out; Finn did the same. The older man leaned against the car's top, and Finn worried briefly that it would collapse. "Meet the man," Kozlowski said after a moment. "See what you think."

Finn looked long and hard at Kozlowski, trying to read him. "You think I should talk to him?"

Kozlowski nodded. "Just one thing."

Finn listened for the sound of the other shoe hitting the cobblestone. "What's that?"

"I want to meet the man, too."

———※———

Finn opened the door to his apartment, stepped in, and dropped his briefcase on the floor. It landed with a weary thud. As was his custom, he debated leaving the lights off and stumbling his way to bed in the dark. He had no plans to eat anything, and the thought of facing the apartment depressed him. He knew, though, that living in a world of denial and avoidance depressed him more.

The lights came on eagerly as he flipped the switch, as though they'd been waiting to torment him. They threw shadows off those items that hurt him most: the couch he had purchased with her and struggled to cram up the narrow staircase and into the apartment, laughing through the entire ordeal; the antique globe she'd had since college, on which they'd traced the paths of all the trips they'd planned to take together; the water-color she'd bought on their first vacation together down on the Cape. He faced them all as adversaries now, with the respect and grim determination owed worthy opponents. He'd considered getting rid of them, taking them to Goodwill or putting them out on the street . . . or burning them. But that would constitute an admission that it was over, and he refused to wave that white flag.

The sharp metallic cry of the phone on the wall interrupted his internal tug-of-war, and he turned to regard it with suspicion. He knew who it was without checking the caller ID. Somehow it rang differently when it was her.

After the fourth ring, his ancient answering machine picked up. The greeting finished and the tone sounded. Finn held his breath, wondering whether she would leave a message. His apartment was quiet for several seconds, and he thought she might have hung up. Then, finally, she spoke.

"Finn? It's Linda." There was another stretch of silence. "Finn, please pick up. I want to talk to you."

Chapter Four

THE BILLERICA HOUSE OF CORRECTION lay in uneven humps of brick and concrete, like architectural roadkill by the side of a dead-end offshoot near Route 3 in a secluded part of the suburban enclave twenty miles northwest of Boston. Originally built in the 1920s to house three hundred inmates, it was one of Massachusetts's oldest prisons, now home to nearly twelve hundred convicts. Those unfortunate enough to become well acquainted with the correctional system regarded Billerica as one of the worst places to be sent following conviction, and its buildings sprawled brown and red and seemingly lifeless across several acres well removed from the eyesight of what was, otherwise, a picturesque middle-class New England town. The locals had grown accustomed to their nervous disregard of the prison, acknowledging the institution only when pressed. It was the uneasy trade all prison towns made in exchange for good jobs and state funding.

Dobson led Finn and Kozlowski through the security check. The process was eased somewhat by the fact that both Dobson and Finn carried state bar cards identifying them as attorneys, and Kozlowski

34

carried the ID of a retired detective. A trip through a metal detector and a brief pat-down were all that was required, and because Kozlowski had locked his gun in the glove compartment, there was no trouble.

The visiting room was large and crowded, with prisoners and their families sitting at open tables, watched over by several guards around the room. There before him, Finn saw a panoply of human emotions played out on a dim concrete palette. Wives and girlfriends leaned across tables to touch the hands of men in prison garb, holding on with all their might to tamp down their desperation, and anger, and loneliness. Children, some shy, some scared, some seemingly carefree, sat on the laps of the fathers they saw only on rare occasions, and only under the careful eyes of armed guards. Parents and grandparents of the incarcerated forced small talk, trying to feign normalcy with the grown children they would always love, regardless of their transgressions.

"He's over there," Dobson said, pointing to the far corner of the room.

Finn looked over and saw him. At first glance, there was little to set him apart from most of the other prisoners. His long black hair was better kept than most, brushed back from a severe widow's peak at the top of his almond-brown forehead, and the shirttail of his prison fatigues was tucked in neatly, but other than that, he appeared to blend in. With a longer look, though, a sense of strength and confidence emanated from the man. Finn couldn't put his finger on what it was about him, but there was something in the set of his shoulders, or in his posture, that was compelling.

Beside him, a teenage girl was leaning in toward him as they spoke. On the other side of the table, an older woman, heavier in both carriage and countenance than her two companions, sat watching quietly as Salazar talked with the young girl.

Finn took a step toward the table, but Dobson put a hand in front of him, holding him back. "It's his mother and his daughter," he said. "He gets only forty-five minutes with them each month. As his attorneys, we can stay later. Let's give him a few more minutes."

"I'm not his attorney yet," Finn pointed out, and then regretted it.

Dobson scowled at him. "Just a few more minutes."

Finn looked at Kozlowski, who nodded, and the three of them eased their backs against the wall to wait. From that spot, Finn watched the ongoing exchange between Salazar and his daughter. Finn easily saw that, young though she was, she would soon be a beautiful woman. She was still caught in the awkward shadow of adolescence, and she held her head low, at an angle that made her look painfully shy and disinterested, but her face had a refined Spanish grace to it, and her features were nearly flawless. Once she gained the confidence to meet the world with greater poise, he thought, there would be few young men who would be able to resist her looks.

After a few more moments of observation, Finn realized that his initial impressions were off. It wasn't awkwardness in her he had noted; it was something else, something more defined. Her movements were cautious and narrow, and she seemed disconnected from everything around her except her father.

Finn frowned. "What's wrong with her?"

Dobson looked Finn over carefully. Then he turned back to the table where three generations of the Salazar family sat in the one conversation they would have that month, caught in an awkward, synthetic, longing moment. Finn looked back also, and as he turned his attention to Salazar, the only thing that seemed clear about the man was the love and tenderness he expressed for his daughter in every movement he made.

Dobson let Finn watch for another moment before he answered. "She's blind."

"My wife, Maria, was the most beautiful woman in the world."

Salazar spoke English better than most of the lawyers Finn dealt with on a regular basis. He carried only a slight accent, and it gave him an air more of continental sophistication than of second-language hesitation.

"When she smiled at me, or when I looked into her eyes, it felt as though everything made sense—as if my life had purpose and meaning, because she was in it." He sat up in his chair, gathering himself back from the moment of introspection before continuing.

"Her family was part of the elite in El Salvador—the ruling oligarchy—that traced its lineage back to the first wave of Europeans who conquered the natives and settled on their land. Land has always been the central resource in my country. I was the son of a prominent merchant who had done well in the fifties and sixties, exporting coffee and timber. But my lineage traced back to the conquered. For all the education my parents were able to give me, I would never be accepted by Maria's family or their peers, and our romance was a scandal for them. I was a doctor, and I thought that might help, but it didn't. Still, she was stubborn and in love, and she agreed to marry me when I asked. Her father, one of the wealthiest landowners in the country, agreed reluctantly, only because he knew it was pointless to argue with his daughter. He threw us a fine wedding and even provided a dowry of sorts—a new house in a respectable neighborhood a comfortable distance from them—but made clear that we would be largely cut off from the family and its money thereafter."

"Nice in-laws," Finn commented.

Salazar shook his head. "It made sense," he said. "And I expected nothing more. You wouldn't understand, but El Salvador is still largely a segregated country at the highest levels, both socially and racially. Besides, it wasn't a hardship. I was happy to be spared the whispers I would have been subjected to if I'd been allowed into her family's clubs. I was a young doctor, and I was making a decent living. Maria and I were together, and she said that was all she cared about—that was enough for me."

"If it was so good, why did you leave?" The question came from Kozlowski, and there was an air of challenge to it.

"In my country, all happiness is an illusion."

"The war?" Finn asked.

"The war," Salazar confirmed. "I was never political, but I was a doctor. I treated the sick. I treated the injured. I never asked my patients about their political affiliations. I thought I was uninvolved; I was naive."

"You treated the wrong people?"

"I treated all people. There were no right or wrong people, as far as I was concerned." Salazar's gaze grew intense as he spoke, and Finn could feel, for the first time, a hint of anger in his tone. Then, as quickly as it had appeared, the resentment was gone. "I never turned anyone away, and that meant I was treating partisans on both sides." He looked at Finn. "How much do you know about the war in my country?"

Finn considered the question. "Not much, really," he admitted. In fact, he realized as he thought about it, he knew very little. His head was filled with vague recollections of headlines but little actual information.

"In the eighties, the government was effectively controlled by a combination of the military and the wealthy elite. There were attempts at the time to prop up a government operating under the pretense of reform, but it was always a facade."

"Another illusion?" Finn asked.

"Exactly so. The rebels were Marxist Communists, supported largely by the rural peasants and the small educated middle class. They lacked the resources to mount a coherent frontal attack, so they relied on kidnappings and sporadic brutal attacks, aimed largely at the elites in the urban areas like San Salvador to make their point."

"Terrorism," Kozlowski grunted derisively.

"Yes, terrorism," Salazar readily concurred. He looked directly at Kozlowski for the first time. "I neither excuse nor condone the tactics employed by both sides in the war. I merely tried to save those who were injured."

Finn inserted himself back into the conversation, sensing the tension between Salazar and Kozlowski. "I assume the military was particularly brutal in putting down the insurgency?"

Salazar continued to stare at Kozlowski. "Somewhat," he said at last. "Though the government tried to keep as low a profile as possible in going after the leftists. You see, the vast majority of the El Salvadoran population lived in poverty—over ninety percent—and many of them harbored sympathy for the rebellion. The government recognized that it was sitting on a powder keg, and it understood that it always ran a significant risk of lighting a match that would blow apart everything those with wealth and power were working to preserve. To avoid that, the government farmed out much of its dirty work."

"To who?" Finn asked, genuinely interested now.

"To the death squads."

"Death squads?"

Salazar nodded. "Small paramilitary groups—mercenaries, thugs, and common criminals—recruited for the grimmest tasks. They were directed by the military and funded by the wealthy landowners: the elites who wanted to keep the leftist insurgents from gaining a stronghold."

"I remember reading something about them," Finn commented.

"You would have. In 1980 they killed three American nuns who were working with relief efforts in the countryside. It caused a great deal of trouble for the American government, because the administration was supporting the government that everyone knew was allied with the death squads."

"Nuns?" Finn was repulsed. "Why would they kill nuns?"

Salazar's laugh was humorless. "You can't be that sheltered, can you,

Mr. Finn? War knows no decency, even in dealing with the devout. Besides, the Catholic Church in El Salvador supported the insurgents, or at least significant reform. Many of those who came to do missionary work recognized that reform—or even revolution—was the only way to raise the vast majority of the population out of squalor. Even the archbishop of San Salvador was an outspoken critic of the government, pushing for real reform—until he was assassinated." Finn realized that his face must have betrayed his horror. "Yes, Mr. Finn; you see, this was El Salvador, and no one was beyond death."

"So what happened to you?" Kozlowski asked, sounding unimpressed.

"One night there was a knock on my door. When I opened it, I found an old friend of mine, Alberto Duerte, leaning against my entryway. There was a stream of blood running from his shoulder. He said he'd been mugged and he needed help. I knew he was lying, but I asked no questions, as was my practice. I took him to my clinic, and I treated his wounds. He left that night, and I never saw him again."

"And?" Finn prodded.

"I found out later he'd been injured in a bombing—a terrorist bombing, as I'm sure your friend will point out," Salazar said, motioning to Kozlowski. "Alberto was the one who planted the bomb that killed a wealthy industrialist and his wife. He miscalculated, though, and was not far enough away from the blast to avoid catching some shrapnel. The death squads tracked him down within the week."

"That couldn't have been pleasant for him," Kozlowski observed.

"No, Mr. Kozlowski, I'm sure it wasn't." Salazar turned back to Finn. "A few days later, my father-in-law appeared at my clinic. I hadn't seen him in several months, so I knew something was wrong when I saw him. He told me to go home, get his daughter, pack a few things, and leave. He told me that Alberto had been tortured before he'd been killed, and he'd given up the names of many of the people he'd worked with. He'd also told them that I was the one who had treated his wounds. As a result, I had been targeted by the death squads—they were coming that night."

"What did you do?" Finn asked.

"First I tried to explain to my father-in-law that I knew nothing of Alberto's activities—that I wasn't interested in politics. I think he understood, but he told me he was powerless to intervene. To do so would put the rest of his family in danger. He told me that his only concern was for his daughter, and he had arranged for us to get out of the country."

"How could he do that if the government knew that you were targeted?" Kozlowski pressed.

Salazar shrugged. "It wasn't difficult. My father-in-law knew people who could help. In the early eighties, when the gangs in Los Angeles were at their height—the Crips and the Bloods—a new criminal organization was born in an East L.A. neighborhood populated largely by El Salvadoran refugees—many of them former members of the death squads. It was called Venganza del Salvadoran, and while it was smaller than some of the other gangs, it quickly developed a reputation as the most vicious of all the groups. Over time, some of the members were deported back to El Salvador, and once there, they formed an affiliate gang in my old country. They recruited new members and continued doing work for the death squads. As they became more sophisticated, they started branching out into other areas. Drug production and smuggling; weapons; extortion, both here and in other countries. They used their gang connections in the United States to establish a pipeline to run drugs from El Salvador and other countries through Central America and Mexico to America. My father-in-law knew these people, and he knew that they would do anything for money—their motivation was never politically based. He paid them well to get me and Maria out of the country and safely to America."

"Illegally," Kozlowski noted.

"Yes," Salazar agreed. "Did I have a choice? What would you have done?"

"And once you got here, you figured you were safe," Finn said.

"I did." Salazar sat up and looked around. Then he hung his head and sighed heavily. "I was wrong."

———◆———

Josiah "Mac" Macintyre sat at his desk on the third floor of the Boston Police Headquarters building in Roxbury. The building, which had been completed in 1997, was a monument to modern police practices, with a computer infrastructure that put those of most police departments to shame, and offices for psychologists and sociologists to aid them in solving crimes and dealing with the impact.

Mac hated the place. He'd never found comfort in or use for modern police tactics; he was old-school through and through. He missed the days when cops were given free rein to get their job done.

And now look at me, he thought. He was pushing fifty sitting behind his desk, his gut falling farther and farther over his belt every day. His hair, which he'd always kept at military length, was nearly gone on top. His barber still passed the clippers over his crown, but it was more a courtesy than a necessity, and Mac suspected the man would have dispensed with all pretense if he hadn't been so afraid. Was this really what Mac had fought and clawed so hard to get?

"Sergeant?" a female voice called from across the roomful of desks. It was Detective Sarah Koontz, whose surname had thrilled Mac when she'd joined the squad because it allowed him to make clear his distaste for chick cops through a minor mispronunciation for which he'd never be reported. "You've got a call that was misdirected to my line," she said. "I'm transferring it." That was fine with Mac; handling incoming calls was the extent of what women should be doing for the police department anyway.

He pushed a button on his phone and hoisted the handset to his ear. "Mac here," he said.

"Mac, it's Dave Johnson."

"Johnson," Mac grunted. The two of them had worked together years ago. Mac had always regarded Johnson as soft, and they'd never been friends. "How's retirement treating you?" Johnson had taken his pension at twenty years, a decision Mac considered a betrayal. He was pretty sure Johnson had taken another job, as most ex-cops did after finding that the pension wouldn't support a man in his forties for long.

"Retirement." Johnson laughed nervously. "Right. It'd be great if it wasn't for my job. You still got a weekly poker game? I could use the cash."

"More like every other week, but yeah." Mac stopped short of inviting Johnson to join. As far as he was concerned, cop poker was for cops.

"Gimme a shout the next time you get together. It'd be good to see you guys, and like I said, I could use your money."

"What d'you want, Johnson?" Mac didn't even try to feign civility.

Johnson said nothing for a moment. Then he forced a laugh. "Same old Mac. Listen, you were one of the point people on the Madeline Steele shooting back in the nineties, right?"

Mac's ears perked up. "It was before I made sergeant, so it wasn't my case," he said. "But yeah, I was involved in the investigation."

"I thought so. That's why I'm calling. I'm up here at Billerica. I'm an assistant supervisor of the corrections officers now."

He said it as though Mac should be impressed. He wasn't. But Johnson did have his full attention. "Yeah?"

"Yeah. It's not too bad. Beats the streets for me. At least it's easier to tell who the bad guys are; they're usually the ones wearing prison fatigues."

"That's a good one." There was no laughter in Mac's voice, only impatience. "I'll have to remember that."

"Anyways, listen, Vincente Salazar's got some people up here visiting. Lawyers, looks like. Word on the block is he's trying to get himself a new trial."

"Every con wants a new trial," Mac commented cautiously.

"Yeah, I know. Salazar's been writing to anyone he thinks'll listen to him for fifteen years, right? So it's probably nothing. But it looks like a couple of people are listening. I just thought you'd want to know. It'd be a damn shame if some spic could put a cop on wheels for life and walk free, you know?"

Mac considered this. "Yeah, it would," he agreed. Every synapse in his brain was firing, but he kept his voice even. "It's probably nothing, though. No court's gonna let a guy like Salazar back on the street, not after what he did."

"Yeah, you're probably right." Johnson sounded like he suddenly regretted calling. "I just thought you'd wanna know, being as you were involved in the investigation and all. I didn't mean to give you any headaches."

"No headaches, Johnson," Mac said. "I always appreciate hearing what's going on with any of my old cases—particularly when they involve a guy who shot one of ours."

"Yeah. Well, that's all I figured. Like you said, it's probably nothing."

"Probably not."

"Okay. Well, it was good to talk to you again, Mac. It's not too bad up here, but it's not the same as being on the job. I sometimes miss the guys at the station, y'know? Tell them I said hello, would you?"

"Tell 'em yourself," Mac said. "We're playing poker over at Henderson's next Wednesday. I'm sure no one would mind if you sat in."

"Really?" The schmuck actually sounded excited. Pathetic. "That'd be great. I'll see you there."

"Looking forward to it." Mac hung up the phone before Johnson could say anything else. He couldn't listen to the man anymore.

He sat quietly at his desk, mulling over the information. Most of what he'd said to Johnson was true. It probably was nothing. Convicts were always looking to get a new trial; hell, they had nothing else to do with their time. And the likelihood that a court would ever listen to a plea from a guy with the kind of conviction for which Salazar was serving time was almost nonexistent. So there really wasn't anything for him to be concerned about.

And yet he was concerned. He had the kind of feeling that cops get when they know something's going bad. Intuition. Fuck the computers; silicone would never have hunches, and hunches were what made a cop effective.

He picked up the phone and dialed a number from memory. "We gotta talk," he said when the line was picked up on the other end.

———

"Maria was pregnant when we arrived in this country," Salazar said. "She was so happy. It was difficult for both of us to leave our home, but we were excited to be in America, to have a fresh start away from the violence."

As Salazar spoke, Finn was captivated. From his own experience growing up shuttled from state homes to foster care to the streets, Finn knew about hardship. He'd made something of his life, to be sure, but he still felt alone. Salazar, on the other hand, had gone through a different sort of hell: Ripped from his home and stuck in a tin can for a decade and a half, and yet he seemed at peace. There was no hint of loneliness about him, only evidence of an invincible spirit. The difference, Finn suspected, was family. Salazar had one; Finn didn't.

"When Maria's father told us we had to leave, I asked him to make arrangements for my mother and my brother, Miguel, as well. If I'd left them, the death squads would have hunted them down. My father died the year after Maria and I married, and my brother was still only seventeen, so he and my mother were living with me and Maria.

"VDS, the criminal gang that arranged for our escape through Mexico and across the border, is very organized. It controls much of the drug smuggling from Central America. It has contacts in many of America's cities: Los Angeles, New York, Washington, Boston. With some of my own money, I arranged for them to take us here."

"Why Boston?" Finn asked.

"There is a significant El Salvadoran community here. Besides, I am a doctor, and Boston's reputation as a center for the medical profession was familiar to me. In honesty, I was young and foolish. I thought I would be able to get a job in a hospital, maybe even find a patron who would be a sponsor of sorts and help me get a license to practice as a doctor here."

Kozlowski laughed derisively. "You have to be a citizen, or at least a legal alien, to practice medicine here."

"As I said, Mr. Kozlowski, I was foolish. You see, in places like El Salvador, America is still viewed with a sense of romanticism; there are few stories about the hardships immigrants encounter here. Of course, I hadn't realized that hospitals are very careful about who they hire. They want records, and without them, it is impossible to get a job, even as a janitor. As a result, I had to accept employment at a convenience store for less than minimum wage." He looked at Kozlowski. "At least I didn't have to pay taxes."

Kozlowski nodded. "Touché."

"We lived in a small apartment in Roxbury, but we were excited about the baby, and I made some extra money treating other immigrants in the neighborhood."

"Practicing medicine without a license is a crime," Kozlowski pointed out. Finn frowned; he was beginning to wonder whether bringing the detective had been a good idea.

"And failing to treat the sick is a sin," Salazar replied. "Besides, I wasn't dispensing any prescription drugs. I only examined people; handed out over-the-counter medications; sometimes delivered babies. If someone needed more treatment than I could provide, I told them to go to an emergency room." He sighed. "They never did, of course. If you are an illegal and you go to the emergency room, there is always a chance that you will be reported. You risk deportation. Many felt that they had a better chance of surviving with disease than deportation."

"Mark told us that's how the police found you—when you took Maria to the hospital," Finn said.

"Yes. Things were going well in many respects. Between my job at the convenience store and the small amounts I made treating poor people, we were getting by. My brother, Miguel, was doing well in school—one of the few places where immigrants seem to be able to participate without repercussion. He had learned English, like me, in a private school in El Salvador, and he was always the smartest in his classes. Things started to fall apart when Maria went into labor."

Salazar took a deep breath before continuing. "In her thirty-seventh week, Maria began experiencing pain. It isn't so unusual at that point in a pregnancy, so I wasn't concerned. I told her to stay off her feet, but we didn't want to go to the hospital because we were afraid. I thought everything would be all right. I didn't know it, but she had a fibroid tumor that was blocking the birth canal. Shortly after she went into labor, her womb ruptured. There was so much blood . . ." His voice trailed off, and he went quiet. No one spoke.

"I rushed her to the emergency room, but it was too late. She lived through the cesarean section and even heard Rosita cry before she bled to death. I suppose I take some small comfort from that."

"And your daughter was born blind?" Finn asked.

"No, she was fine when she was born."

"So what happened?"

"That happened when I was arrested," Salazar explained. "You see, when I took Maria to the hospital, the authorities learned that we were in the country illegally. Nothing came of it for several months, but then the police began a program to identify and deport illegal immigrants— South and Central American immigrants in particular. My name was put on a list, and an investigation was started. The goal was to have us deported. Officer Steele, the woman who was attacked, was the officer in charge of my case."

"So you had a good idea that your time in this country was limited unless Steele's investigation was stopped," Kozlowski pointed out. "That's one hell of a good motive to take her out."

"That was the argument that the prosecution made," Salazar confirmed. "Except that I probably wouldn't have been deported in the end. I was going through the process of applying for asylum in this country. As long as I could prove that I faced the risk of political retribution if I was forced to go back to El Salvador, I would have been permitted to stay here in America. Given my circumstances, I believe I would have been successful."

Finn was skeptical. "I don't know. My understanding is that the standards for asylum are very strict. Getting the evidence necessary to prove that you were in real danger would have been difficult."

"Perhaps," Salazar admitted. "But the legal process can take a very long time, I was told. Besides, what good would it do to 'take out' Officer Steele, as Mr. Kozlowski puts it so colorfully? Do you really think her cases wouldn't be reassigned?"

"It's a fair point."

"In any event, I was going through the process legally, and I hadn't even heard of the attack on Officer Steele. Then one evening the police broke into our apartment. Miguel wasn't there, fortunately. He was eighteen and full of adolescent anger. He probably would have fought back, and that would have only made things worse. As it was, they broke my arm and my nose and beat me very badly. But it was Rosita who suffered most."

"What happened?"

Salazar hung his head and rubbed his temples. When he looked up again, his eyes were red. "She was just a baby at the time. When they came in, they knocked her high chair over, and her head slammed into the floor. I tried to get to her. I tried to tell them that I was a doctor, that she needed help, but they wouldn't listen." He wiped his eyes and cleared his throat before he continued. "She suffered a traumatic brain injury similar to what happens when you shake a baby violently. She lost her vision, and she's had some learning disabilities. She is wonderful, though, and for the most part she is happy, thank God."

"How did your family get by after you were arrested?" Finn asked. "With a child who needed that kind of care, and with no money?"

"That was the great irony. You see, Rosita was born in this country—she's an American. Because of that, she could get benefits under Medicaid and other social services. When the social workers found out what had happened, they worked with immigration officials to keep my mother and my brother in this country. And then there was Miguel. He was always the smartest in the family. He worked two jobs while finishing school and graduated at the top of his class. He even got a scholarship to the University of Massachusetts, and he excelled there as well, all the time supporting my mother and Rosita. He has essentially been her father while I've been in jail. He's a doctor now—and a naturalized American citizen." Salazar beamed as he spoke about his brother. "He is a great American success story."

"You must be bitter," Kozlowski said.

Salazar frowned. "Why do you say that?"

Kozlowski looked at Finn, and it was Finn who answered. "When you think of everything you could have been—everything that's happened to you and your daughter—how could you help but be angry?"

Salazar looked back and forth between the two of them. "You don't have children, do you?" Both men shook their heads. "When the police stormed my apartment, I watched Rosita's head hit the floor. I heard her scream and then heard her go quiet. I'm a doctor, and I know what kind of damage a fall like that can do to an infant. I thought she was dead."

Finn and Kozlowski continued to look at him, not comprehending his point.

"You see, when you are a parent, and you believe that your child has been killed, you die as well. I couldn't imagine my life without my daughter; everything lost meaning to me in an instant. When I found out that she was alive—that she would survive—it was like being reborn. Am I angry at the men who blinded my daughter? Yes. Am I angry at the men who put me here? Yes. But bitter?" He shook his head. "My daughter is alive. Blind, yes, but a happy, healthy, beautiful girl. She is safe, and she knows how much I love her. As long as I know that, the bitterness will not swallow me."

He leaned forward, staring hard at Finn. Finn thought Salazar's eyes might bore a hole through him with their intensity. "Now, Mr. Finn," he said slowly. "Would you like to hear more about the specifics of my case?"

Finn could feel Kozlowski stiffen in the chair next to him, but he refused to look at him. He didn't hesitate in his answer. "Yes, Mr. Salazar," he replied. "I think I would."

Chapter Five

"HE'S A REMARKABLE MAN, isn't he?" Dobson asked as he emerged from the Billerica House of Correction with Finn and Kozlowski.

"He's different, I'll give you that," Finn replied.

"On the inside, because he's got a medical background, he was assigned a work detail as an orderly in the infirmary. Doctors in there say he's one of the best physicians they've seen. They obviously have to 'oversee' everything he does because he's a prisoner and because he never got his license in the U.S., but there isn't one of the doctors who wouldn't want him treating them."

"I'm impressed."

"Impressed enough to take the case?"

Finn looked at Kozlowski, who hadn't said a word since they'd left Salazar. "I gotta think about it a little," Finn said. "I'll give you a call one way or another later this afternoon."

Dobson looked disappointed but held his tongue. "I'll wait for your call" was all he said before heading over to his car.

Finn turned in the other direction, toward the far end of the large parking lot where he'd left his car. The wind whipped across the open fields that surrounded the prison, stinging Finn's eyes. Kozlowski fell into step with him silently. "What'd you think?" Finn asked.

Kozlowski said nothing; he just kept walking next to Finn, not even looking at him.

"I mean, you gotta admit, the guy seemed to have his shit together. I know that doesn't mean he didn't do some bad things in the past, but you ask me now whether I think this guy tried to rape and kill a cop? I'm not buying it. And it sure sounds like the investigation had some significant holes in it." Finn's eyes darted over toward the large detective. "You said you were friends with Steele, right?"

"That's what I said."

Finn waited to see if there were any additional thoughts Kozlowski cared to reveal, but trying to get information out of the man was like trying to get money from an old-line Brahmin. "Right. So you may have a different view of the guy. Me? I'm just trying to figure out whether this is worth my time. I mean, if the guy's innocent, I'd like to help him. Plus, if I get him out, we could really hit the jackpot on a civil rights lawsuit against the city. I mean, fifteen years in that hellhole? What's a jury gonna value that at? Ten million? Maybe fifteen?"

Finn paused again, to see if Kozlowski would fill the silence: nothing. "Of course, if he's guilty and I take the case, and then the DNA evidence comes back as a match, we can drop the guy right then and there. That way, we can feel pretty good that we know the cops got the right guy on this—everybody's a winner." Finn wondered whether it was obvious to Kozlowski how badly he wanted to take the case.

Kozlowski flipped up the collar on his raincoat. It was an old, shapeless khaki rag that was great for Columbo impersonations but useless against the New England winter. Finn had gotten Kozlowski a new coat for Christmas the year before—a nice wool/cashmere blend in charcoal—but it had never been out of the detective's front hall closet. He shoved his hands into his pockets as he arrived at the passenger side of Finn's car.

Finn unlocked the driver's side and then paused, looking at Kozlowski drawn up tight against a mean winter breeze. "I'm not taking the case,"

Finn said. "It's pretty clear that this is bothering you. I'm not sure what it is, exactly, but it's not worth it to me. Besides, I'd need your help on it, and if your heart isn't in it, it isn't fair to Salazar. Better that he have people behind him who are invested."

"Take the case," Kozlowski said.

Finn was silent for a moment. "You sure?"

"Yeah. Open the friggin' door, it's cold."

"Why?"

"I told you, it's friggin' cold."

"No. Why do you want me to take the case?"

Kozlowski shook his head. "I'm not buyin' this guy the way you are. Yeah, he seems okay now, but even if he didn't shoot Maddy, he's been in for fifteen years, and nobody spends that kind of time in a place like this and keeps his shit the way Salazar claims to have. He's conning us, no matter what, at some level."

"But . . . ?"

"But I was friends with Maddy Steele. I may not be convinced that Salazar is innocent, but I'm not convinced that he's guilty, either. And if Salazar didn't shoot Maddy, then the asshole who did is still out walkin' the streets. That doesn't sit well with me, and it won't until I get some answers." He punctuated his point with his eyes, daring Finn to ask any further questions. "Now open this fucking door before I peel off this ratty piece-of-shit cloth you call a roof and open it myself."

Finn slipped into the driver's seat and reached over to unlock Kozlowski's door, pulling on the handle to open it. Kozlowski grunted loudly as he folded his bulk into the low, narrow passenger seat. "You know," Finn said as he turned the key and the engine sputtered to life, "you're really very strange."

"No," Kozlowski replied, "mainly, I'm really very cold."

Finn and Kozlowski stopped for lunch on the way back to the office: bangers and mash for Kozlowski and a Reuben for Finn at a local pub in Charlestown. The food was great, but the service left something to be desired, and it was nearly two o'clock by the time they pushed open the door to the old building that housed their offices. Finn had put a down payment on the brownstone with the generous severance he'd taken from the partners at Howery; Kozlowski paid a nominal rent for the use of two rooms in the back.

"Jesus fucking Christ, where have you been?" Lissa Krantz accosted them as they walked through the door. Finn was still adjusting to the way she littered her language with creative obscenities. It wasn't unusual for the older legal practitioners to season every sentence with a pungent curse or two, but it shocked Finn, coming from Lissa. She was a petite thirty-two-year-old law student at Northeastern, with a lithe body toned from endless hours on treadmills and StairMasters, dark hair and olive skin carefully maintained through regular trips to high-end Newbury Street salons, and shoes and clothes that he was sure cost more than his car. She'd been interning with Finn for eight months, and her legal and organizational effort had been astounding, so Finn was beginning to get over the swearing.

"Lunch, thanks," Finn replied. "Why, did you miss us?"

"Always." She fluttered her eyes in flirtatious ridicule. Kozlowski nodded to her and headed back to his office to hang up his coat, closing the door behind him.

"Problem with your contact lenses again?" Finn asked.

"Just trying to be demure," she replied.

"Try harder, I'm spoken for."

"Wonder Woman down in D.C., right? Good for you; that seems to be going really fucking well—eight months and I haven't even met her."

Finn's gut clenched, and he hid his gaze in the mail on his desk. "I'm spoken for, all the same."

"Like I said, good for you. It's awfully egotistical of you to assume I'd bat my eyes at you in the first place. You're not my type."

Finn looked up from his mail. He pointed his finger at himself, then tilted his head and turned his finger around so that it was aimed at the door leading to Kozlowski's office. "No way," Finn said. "You're kidding, right?"

She shrugged. "Some girls like older men."

"Yeah, but he's not a man. He's some sort of prehistoric creature the police thawed out of a glacier in the Arctic Circle a few decades ago and brought back to life to fight bad guys in Boston."

"Stop it, you're just turning me on. Besides, scars are sexy."

"Don't get me wrong, he's the closest thing I've got to a friend at this point, and I'd take a bullet for him if I thought bullets would actually hurt him. But Tom Kozlowski and romance? We're not exactly talking about chocolate and peanut butter."

"Whatever," Lissa said, turning to her desk, picking up a stack of papers, and dropping them on Finn's desk. "Here's the research you wanted."

"Already done? That was fast."

She raised an eyebrow at him. "You expected less?" She turned and walked back to her desk, then swung around again. "Are you really gonna take this guy on as a client? Do you have any idea how hard it is to set aside a jury conviction in a criminal case?"

"Not really. That's why I wanted you to do the research."

"And I did. It's really fucking hard. You have to show manifest injustice. Do you know how fucking hard it is to show manifest injustice?"

"Really fucking hard?"

Kozlowski reemerged from his office. Lissa looked at him. "You agree with what the boss is doing?"

"He's not my boss," Kozlowski replied.

"Fine," she said. "Who am I to complain? I'm guessing I'm the most liberal person in the room by a pretty wide margin. I just wouldn't have pegged you two to be the type to tilt at windmills."

Finn looked at Lissa, then at Kozlowski, and then back at Lissa. He raised one eyebrow. "I guess we're all full of surprises today."

"Fuck off," Lissa said.

"That's all I'm saying," Finn said.

"Jesus fucking H. Christ, that's all *I'm* saying."

Finn went back to flipping through his mail. "You should be a little more careful, taking the name of someone else's lord in vain. God forbid I was Muslim. How'd you like it if I started taking Moses' name in vain?"

"Moses is Old Testament and, technically speaking, belongs to both of us, so you'd probably be okay."

Finn tore open a letter. "Barbra Streisand, then?"

"Bite your fucking tongue."

"See what I mean?"

"Fine. You should just understand you've got an uphill battle. Like Everest kind of uphill. I've looked through every case Cavanaugh has been asked to reopen. He's ruled on twelve of these motions in other cases. Guess how many times he's let in additional evidence."

"I don't want to know, do I?"

"That's right. Zero. Never."

"Good thing thirteen's my lucky number."

"It'd better be." She grabbed her purse. "I'm going to get something to eat. Some of us didn't get a long, leisurely lunch today. I'll be back . . . if you're lucky."

The door banged behind her as Finn picked up the stack of research she'd handed him. "She does good work," he said to Kozlowski after a moment.

"I'm sure," Kozlowski replied. "She's still trouble you should stay away from."

"I've got Linda; you know that."

Kozlowski nodded skeptically. "You had her; I know that. Now I don't know what either of you have."

"She left because of the job, not because of me."

Kozlowski raised his hands. "Don't get me in the middle of this. I told you when I took this office, I don't want to have anything to do with whatever happens between the two of you. She was my partner on the force for five years. You'll never get me to take sides against her."

"Who's to say there are any sides to take? Last I knew, we were still together."

"When's the last time you talked to her?"

"She called last night," Finn admitted.

"Did you pick up the phone and actually talk to her?"

Finn shook his head. "I thought about it, though."

"You thought about it? Seriously? Sounds solid to me, then."

"We'll work it out."

"Good. Until you figure out what's going on with Flaherty, I'd still stay away from any office romances."

"Thanks for the advice, but I'm not the one I'm worried about with Lissa." Finn smiled at the detective maliciously.

Kozlowski laughed. "What is she, mid-twenties? I'm old enough to be her father."

"She's in her early thirties. You're only old enough to be her perverted uncle."

"Good to know. I'll keep that in mind."

"Besides, maybe what she's looking for is a father figure."

"If she was, I'm guessing she'd be searching for a good-looking banker who drives a big brand-new Mercedes, not some haggard old ex-cop who drives a ten-year-old Lincoln. I have no doubt I'm safe."

Finn shrugged. "You never know, do you?"

Chapter Six

THE HONORABLE JOHN B. CAVANAUGH, at seventy-eight, suffered from a bad back and swollen joints in his knees that made it difficult for him to sit for extended periods of time. His condition had made his already prickly disposition nearly lethal on the bench, and whatever patience he'd had as a younger man was long used up. His thin six-foot-four-inch frame had always been imposing, and the slight stoop in his shoulders accentuated the impression that he was continually looking down on the lawyers who appeared before him—an impression that was usually closer to reality than not.

At the moment he was directing his condescension toward Finn and Dobson as they sat at counsel table before him. It made Finn question whether his decision to take Salazar on as a client had been hasty.

"Gentlemen," Cavanaugh said slowly, looking back and forth between Finn and Dobson on the one hand and Assistant District Attorney Albert Jackson on the other. Finn knew Jackson well from various criminal matters he'd handled, and liked him. He stood nearly six feet tall but was pushing three hundred pounds. Finn had often wondered whether his parents had been aware of Cosby's cartoon when they'd chosen his name. Jackson bore the inevitable ribbing well, though, and he was one of the better attorneys in the DA's office.

Cavanaugh cleared his throat before continuing. "I've read the briefs, but I'm willing to hear argument. Mr. Finn, it's your motion; would you care to lead us into the abyss?"

"Thank you, Your Honor," Finn said, getting to his feet. "As you are aware, we are here today seeking an order requiring the district attorney's office to turn over skin and blood samples taken from underneath Officer Madeline Steele's fingernails on the evening she was attacked. We are confident that DNA testing of these samples will definitively show that our client was not the person who attacked Officer Steele."

"Really, Mr. Finn? You're confident?" Cavanaugh leaned forward in his chair. "On what is this confidence based? It is my understanding that the evidence at trial included positive identifications, both through the eyewitness testimony of the victim and through fingerprint comparisons. What is it that magically gives you this confidence?"

"Well, Your Honor, the fact that the DA's office is resisting this motion, for one thing. After all, if Mr. Salazar is actually guilty, the evidence in question should only prove his guilt. Why, then, should the DA's office oppose this motion so vehemently? In addition, Mr. Salazar has an alibi. At the time of the attack, Mr. Salazar, who was a medical doctor in his own country, was providing medical attention to a woman up the street from his residence. The witness who can confirm that alibi is now willing to come forward and testify. As a result, it is impossible that Mr. Salazar was the individual who attacked Officer Steele. The district attorney's office is in possession of evidence that could affirmatively establish the guilt or innocence of our client. In the interests of justice, it's hard to find a reason for this evidence to be withheld."

Cavanaugh considered this. "Mr. Jackson?"

Albert Jackson stood up. "Yes, Your Honor. What Mr. Finn fails to recognize is that Mr. Salazar has already been given a fair trial and a fair opportunity to demonstrate his innocence. Our refusal to open the door to additional evidence at this time is hardly reflective of any fear that the wrong man is in jail. Indeed, Mr. Salazar's guilt has already been definitively established by a jury of twelve. A central and necessary principle of our criminal justice system is the finality of a jury's decision. If we abandon our reliance on that principle, the system would become paralyzed and collapse."

Cavanaugh sat upright in his chair, his back pain evident. He looked down at Finn. "I have to say, Mr. Finn, that having read the papers, I'm inclined to agree with the prosecution. I see nothing out of the ordinary about this case, and if I were to allow your client a second bite at the apple, how could I deny that same opportunity to every defendant to come into my courtroom with a similar request?"

"First, Your Honor, this case isn't the same as every other case. There is a witness who is willing to come forward now and corroborate Mr. Salazar's alibi."

"Where was this witness fifteen years ago, when Mr. Salazar was on trial? I assume that the defendant was aware of the identity of his own alibi witness at that time, correct?"

"Yes, Your Honor, but at the time the witness was afraid to come forward. She was in the country illegally then, and she was afraid of being deported. Since the trial, she has earned her citizenship, and she is no longer afraid to testify."

"Mr. Finn," Cavanaugh said, shaking his head. "The same claim could probably be manufactured by any defendant currently behind bars. It still seems to me that I would be setting a precedent that would allow an opportunity for every person in jail who claims that DNA evidence could exonerate them."

"And what would be so bad about that?" Finn asked abruptly. He hadn't planned to join the confrontation on this level, but the words just came out of his mouth, and he could feel the judge's look harden at the challenge to his authority. Finn was tempted to back off, but he figured he had nothing to lose. "If innocent people are in jail, don't we have a responsibility to identify them? We're not asking the state to pay one dime for these tests—tests that were not even admissible in courts in Massachusetts at the time of Mr. Salazar's conviction. DNA testing has been used to identify hundreds of wrongly convicted—innocent—people in the past few years. I see no reason why the state would resist the opportunity to make sure that every person in its custody is actually guilty, particularly when it comes at no cost to itself."

"Mr. Jackson?" Cavanaugh invited.

"No cost to itself?" Jackson scoffed. "The district attorney's office must respond to each of these frivolous motions. This hearing alone is costing the state thousands of dollars in my time and yours, Your Honor."

"Mr. Jackson has a point," Cavanaugh said to Finn. "Besides, your client was convicted on the basis of eyewitness testimony and fingerprint evidence. How do you explain that?"

"First, Your Honor, as to the state's 'cost,' the only cost that Mr. Jackson and his bosses in the district attorney's office are really worried about is the cost of a civil lawsuit if it turns out that Mr. Salazar was wrongly convicted. As to the other evidence used to convict Mr. Salazar, eyewitness testimony has repeatedly been shown to be the least reliable evidence available to the prosecution. We're also asking for the fingerprint evidence to be released to us so we can reexamine that as well. But as you well know, fingerprint analysis is far from an exact science. DNA evidence, on the other hand, is ninety-nine percent conclusive."

"Your Honor!" Jackson protested. "They're now looking to try their entire case over?"

"The histrionics are unnecessary, Mr. Jackson," Cavanaugh quipped. "I can see what's going on here." He looked at Finn again. "You still haven't given me a reason to think that this fishing expedition of yours is worth anyone's time. I just don't see the justification."

"Your Honor, we have no record that the defense was told the DNA material was available at the time of trial. We found out only recently; that alone should justify this exercise."

Cavanaugh's eyes narrowed. "Are you suggesting that potentially exculpatory evidence was withheld by the prosecution, Mr. Finn? Because you realize what a serious charge that is."

"I do, Your Honor." Finn was going for broke. "Let me be clear, we are not alleging any misconduct at this time. But the DNA evidence comes from under the victim's fingernails. When Officer Steele was attacked, she fought back valiantly and apparently scratched her assailant quite badly. Blood and skin were collected from under her fingernails. That fact was never disclosed to the defense and could have constituted exculpatory evidence. Mr. Salazar could arguably be entitled to a new trial on that basis alone. We're not looking for that. We're looking only to have the DNA in the scrapings tested."

"It wasn't exculpatory, Your Honor," Jackson fired back. "When the district attorney discovered that this material had not been disclosed, it was tested. It matched Mr. Salazar's blood type."

"O positive, Your Honor," Finn argued. "The most common blood type there is. In any event, the DA's office didn't run any DNA testing at the time."

"This is outrageous," Jackson protested. "DNA evidence wasn't even admissible at the time of trial, as Mr. Finn has already indicated. And the evidence from the skin and blood from under Officer Steele's fingernails was never presented as part of the prosecution's case!"

"Exactly," Finn retorted. "Whoever attacked Officer Steele would have had visible scratches, and there was no mention of any such scratches on Mr. Salazar at the time he was arrested. Had the defense known about the skin and blood under Officer Steele's fingernails, that discrepancy could have been brought out by the defense at trial."

"Maybe the police never looked for scratches," Jackson offered.

It was a mistake. Jackson had created an opening that might give Finn a chance. Both Finn and Cavanaugh looked at him with their eyebrows raised. "Your Honor," Finn continued in a reasonable tone, "can you imagine anything more preposterous? One of their own officers is attacked and shot, and the police fail to use every bit of evidence that could bring her assailant to justice? If the investigation was indeed run that sloppily, that's reason to question the verdict right there. There are too many questions. All we're looking for are answers, and the DNA evidence in the prosecution's possession can provide those answers."

Cavanaugh was silent on the bench.

"Your Honor," Jackson began, but Cavanaugh held up a hand to cut him off.

"Be quiet, Mr. Jackson. Unless you feel you can provide an adequate justification for why the police never dealt with the scratches at trial." Jackson shut his mouth. Cavanaugh leaned back uncomfortably in his large black leather chair, looking first up at the high courtroom ceiling and then down at Finn. "Congratulations, Mr. Finn, you've piqued my curiosity. I'm going to give you your DNA sample."

"Your Honor!" Jackson objected.

"Simmer down, Mr. Jackson. I've got good news for you, too." He addressed Finn. "I'm concerned about the viability of this evidence. It may very well be too old or too spoiled to be of any value. I'm not willing to suggest that the Commonwealth is responsible for keeping all the evidence from all of its cases pristine indefinitely. As a result, while I'll allow you access to whatever there is, I am in no way saying that I will or will not order a new trial based solely on the results of DNA testing." He leaned over and looked closely at Finn. "How long will the DNA testing take?"

Finn had no idea. He looked over at Dobson.

"The testing itself takes a day or two, but there's a backlog in getting the tests run. Two weeks if it's rushed, Your Honor," Dobson said.

"Very well. Gentlemen, it appears that you have two weeks." The judge looked at his calendar. "I'm scheduling a hearing for Monday, December twenty-fourth. Christmas Eve. By then I expect that you'll have some reasonable answers for me. One of you will have quite a Christmas present." He looked at Finn again. "I want to make sure I'm being clear, though, Mr. Finn. DNA testing alone is not going to cut it in my courtroom. Until you offer me some explanation as to why your client's fingerprints were on Officer Steele's gun, and why the eyewitness testimony implicated Mr. Salazar, your client will stay in jail."

Chapter Seven

Finn and Dobson stood in the hallway outside the courtroom, waiting for the elevator. Neither would look at the other.

"At least we got the DNA evidence," Dobson said.

"Yeah," Finn said. "A Pyrrhic victory is better than none at all, I suppose."

"You never know. We've got two weeks to see what we can find."

Finn gave the younger lawyer an incredulous look. "You're kidding, right? Look, Dobson, you seem like a pretty good guy, and I'm sure you're excited to be out here 'fighting for justice' or whatever it is you think we're doing. But you really need to get a grip on the reality of our situation."

"Which is?"

"Which is that we just lost, and there's virtually no chance that Salazar's getting out of jail. Did you hear what Cavanaugh said?" Finn threw his thumb over his shoulder back toward the courtroom. "He said that even if the DNA evidence comes back and doesn't match Salazar, he's still not going to order a new trial. Unless we get Officer Steele to recant her testimony, and we come up with a reasonable theory as to why Salazar's fingerprints were on Steele's gun, your boy's gonna die behind bars. And guess what? Neither of those things is going to happen."

"So what? You just give up now?"

"Did you have a better plan?"

"You better believe it. We start our own investigation. We go over everything in that file, and we see what we come up with. We've got two weeks, and if we spend enough time on this, who knows what we'll come up with."

"I do, Mark. We'll come up with nothing. And in the meantime, my bills will pile up so high, I'll probably have to shut down my office. You see, I don't have a large law firm that's willing to pay me for a few weeks and write off my time to good intentions. I've got to work to eat, and that means for paying clients. Not to mention the fact that—and I don't say this lightly—he's probably guilty anyway."

Dobson looked thrown. "Who is?"

"Salazar." Finn could see that he'd wounded Dobson with the mere suggestion. "I'm sorry to be the one to break this to you, and believe me, there's a big part of me that would like to believe the guy, but the reality is he probably did it." Finn reached over and jammed his thumb repeatedly into the elevator button.

Dobson stared at Finn in disbelief. "Why did you even bother showing up today, then?" he asked. "Why get involved at all?"

Finn thought about that. The answer wasn't obvious to him. Finally, he shrugged. "I don't know. I had it tough growing up, and it would've been easy for me to end up behind bars. Maybe I'd like to think that if that had happened, someone would've listened to me. Maybe this guy's good enough at selling his story, so that I even bought into it a little." He looked down at his shoes, shaking his head. "Or maybe I just felt like spending a couple of days tilting at a windmill or two."

The elevator door opened at last, and the two of them stepped on. "You do what you want," Dobson said defiantly. "But I'm not letting this go. I can't."

"I admire your determination," Finn replied. "If not your judgment."

"Do me one favor?" Dobson asked. Finn looked at him, waiting. "Don't file your notice of withdrawal just yet. Give me a week, and if I can come up with something—anything—promise you'll take a look at it and make up your mind then."

Finn was tempted to say no: just put the matter behind him and move on. But Dobson was so desperate, and so passionate. It would have felt like kicking a puppy dog, and Finn didn't kick puppy dogs anymore. Besides, what would holding off on filing a withdrawal cost him? He reached out and pressed the button for the ground floor. "Fine," he said. "I'll give you a week."

"Thanks," Dobson said, and he looked relieved. Finn wished he shared the man's optimism.

The two of them faced forward as the doors started to creak closed. Just before they came fully together, a thick hand with grimy, stubby fingers forced its way into the breach, pulling the doors open again.

"Sorry," the owner of the hand grumbled, stepping onto the elevator with them. He was around Finn's height but much older, with a paunch that hung far over his belt. His hair, what there was of it, was silver-gray and cut close to the scalp, and his suit looked as though it had been purchased when the man weighed at least twenty pounds less. He held a file folder under one arm.

He forced his girth into the small space, standing closer than necessary, his head inclined toward Finn, making clear that he was giving him a good looking-over. It made Finn uncomfortable, and he was almost glad when the man spoke. "You Finn?" he asked.

"Yes," Finn replied. "I'm Scott Finn. Have we met?" He offered his hand.

The man looked at the hand but kept his own at his sides. "No, we haven't." He leaned in closer, squinting. "You sure you're Finn? I was expecting someone bigger."

"I can only imagine your disappointment. Is there something you want?"

The man kept staring. "Yeah, I'd have guessed you were bigger. I mean, for someone to take on the case of a man who shot a cop, I would've thought you'd have to be huge. I wouldn't have guessed a skinny guy like you would feel comfortable fucking with the cops on a case like that."

Finn felt his scalp tingle, as it often had in his youth out on the streets when a challenge had been issued. "And you are?"

"Macintyre. My friends call me Mac. You can call me Detective."

"Pleasure to meet you, Detective." Finn smiled without warmth. "Is there something I can do for you on this case?"

Macintyre continued to stare at Finn, his eyes small and dark. "No," he said. "I thought maybe there was something I could do for you. Maybe something that'd save you a whole lot of time and aggravation."

"By all means," Finn replied. "I'm generally in favor of saving time and aggravation."

"Stay away from this Salazar guy," Macintyre said. His voice was low and full of gravel. "It's not worth it."

"Thanks for the advice; it's helpful," Finn replied. "I'll take it into account."

Macintyre pushed his finger into Finn's sternum. "I'm serious. He's a bad guy." He reached under his arm and pulled out the file. "I shouldn't be showing you this, but we had our eye on this guy fifteen years ago. You ever heard of the street gang VDS?"

Finn shot a look at Dobson. "It rings a bell."

"Bunch of scum. Real nasty fuckers—they were the ones who raped that crippled girl in Porter Square a couple years ago. Your guy Salazar was one of the leaders here in Boston. We never got enough evidence to prosecute him, but he was at the center of everything. So not only did he shoot a cop, but he was responsible for a whole lot of other ugly shit as well." Macintyre opened the file. "Take a look. You can't keep it, but I wanted you to know who you're trying to get out."

Finn looked over the top of the file. He could see what appeared to be notes from a number of surveillance stakeouts. He looked over at Dobson. "Mark, meet Detective Macintyre. Macintyre, this is Mark Dobson. My involvement in this case is going to be minimal, Detective, if I'm going to be involved at all. The man you need to convince is right here." He pointed to Dobson and noticed the fear in his face.

Macintyre looked back and forth between the two lawyers. "Seriously?" he asked. "You're out?"

"I am," said Finn. "Though I'm not making it official for a week. Young Mark, here, will be leading the charge. If you really feel that Mr. Salazar is not deserving of another chance, Mr. Dobson is the man to talk to." The elevator doors opened onto the ground floor, and Finn patted Dobson on the shoulder. "So your boy Salazar wasn't just a doctor after all," he commented. "He was a leader in VDS. My view of your judgment keeps going up and up. Good luck." He shook his head as he started to walk away.

"Mr. Finn," Dobson called after him. Finn turned around. Dobson walked after him and away from Macintyre, so that the cop couldn't hear him. "You're wrong about Salazar. So is this detective. Give me a week, and I'll prove it to you."

Finn nodded. "I already gave you a week, and I'm a man of my word. Just don't expect too much from yourself. Hard as you try, you can't always fix the world."

Finn walked away. As he reached the door that led outside, he bundled his coat around him, giving one last look behind. Macintyre had approached Dobson, and the two of them were flipping intently through the file the detective had brought with him. Finn pushed the door open and stepped outside. Sometimes he wished he were still young enough to believe in miracles.

Chapter Eight

THAT EVENING TOM KOZLOWSKI walked a circuit around Boston Common. It was the closest he ever came to therapy. A light snow was falling, adding to several inches that had accumulated since Thanksgiving, washing away the last hints of autumn. He loved to wander Boston during the holiday season; when he was feeling down, it gave him some of his spirit back. He was desperately lacking in spirit at the moment.

Finn had told him earlier in the day that they were off the Salazar case. After hearing where Judge Cavanaugh had set the bar for them, Kozlowski could hardly question Finn's decision. If DNA evidence alone wouldn't be enough to spring the man, they both knew that the judge had no real intention of entertaining his release. Finn couldn't be expected to sink his own time and effort into the case with no chance of success, and as Finn had told Kozlowski, "I wouldn't ask you to write off your own time, either."

"Okay," Kozlowski had replied. "Your call."

It was a crutch he seemed to be leaning on too heavily recently. *Your call.* How had it come to that?

On the other hand, he should have felt relieved that Finn had made the decision for both of them. What good would it do to dredge up the past? It would only hurt a woman he'd cared about once; a woman he'd let down; a woman who'd already been through hell. He couldn't drag her back through that.

Yet in spite of it all, he was tempted to tell Finn what he knew. As Finn was explaining that he was dropping the case, Kozlowski had kept his mouth shut for fear that if he pried his lips apart, he'd start spilling the secret he'd kept for such a long time. Finally, when he had opened his mouth, all that came out was his new anthem: "Your call."

Walking down the path parallel to Beacon Street, he paused, looking down at the Frog Pond, frozen for weeks now. The trees were trimmed with white fairy lights, blending into the snowflakes illuminated by the streetlamps. He forced his thoughts to go quiet as he listened to the enchanted cries of the children skating on the brightly lit pond below. The squeals of excited delight warmed him, if only briefly.

His own youth had been as different from those of the children he was watching as anyone could imagine. He'd been born to first-generation immigrants, refugees from the Soviet-style repression that crushed the spirit of the Polish people in the 1950s and '60s. His parents had made it to Boston, though, where they'd carved out an uneasy survival for the family. In a city split tectonically between the Brahmins, the Irish, and the Italians, the Polish were often crushed in the fissures. His father had been a skilled steelworker in the old country, but no one would hire him for such a high-paying job in Boston. As a result, everyone in his family worked to make enough money to get by. Tom Kozlowski got his first job when he was six, helping clean down the fish stalls in North Market, where his mother sold scrod for pennies. "If he can walk, he can work," he remembered his father saying in broken English when the owner of the stall questioned whether it was right to hire out a boy so young.

When his father's heart gave out at forty-five—Koz was only seventeen—no one was sure the family would survive. The night they laid his father to rest, Koz, who'd never been devout, sat in the neighborhood Catholic church praying for guidance. The reply came in the form of a young parish priest whose brother was a sergeant in the Boston Police Department. The brother took pity on Kozlowski, and arranged for him to join the force on his eighteenth birthday. Since that day, though he'd never quite qualified as a true believer, Kozlowski had stayed generally loyal to the Church. After all, who was he to question an answered prayer?

And in the cosmic game of quid pro quo, his devotion to the BPD had more than compensated for his failings as a Catholic. For over twenty-five years, he'd been a crusader, dedicating his life to the force. To him, "To Protect and Serve" had been more than a catchy motto; it had been a calling. And whenever he'd been bothered by the sacrifice of his personal life, he'd sought out scenes like those below him at the Frog Pond. That his job provided a level of civic trust and security, allowing kids to enjoy a childhood he'd been denied, seemed enough to him. More than enough, usually. After all, you can't miss what you never had.

And yet tonight the relief felt illusory. The Salazar case ate at him. Finn was probably right; the man was probably guilty. That rationalization had certainly allowed Kozlowski to bury his guilt for a decade and a half, but now the dirt had been kicked off the shallow grave of his conscience, and it seemed that the rot was infecting his soul.

He took one more look at the children gliding in circles over the illuminated ice at the bottom of the hill, their laughter reaching up to him. He wondered in that moment what Rosita Salazar's laugh sounded like. He tried to push the thought out of his mind, but it fought its way back with irrepressible force. Against his will, he found himself wondering what it must have been like growing up without knowing her father; what it must have been like to wander through life blinded. And in the shadow of those brutal musings was the real question that he'd been avoiding for such a long time: Had he done the right thing?

The question haunted him as he stuffed his hands into his pockets and turned to walk away. It wasn't his fault, he consoled himself. After all, it hadn't been his call.

Chapter Nine

FINN DIDN'T GIVE the Salazar case another thought. After all, he'd convinced Judge Cavanaugh to order the release of the DNA evidence for testing—no small feat. That was what he'd been called in to do. It was hardly his fault that the judge had made clear that he didn't actually care what the DNA might reveal, and that he had no intention of releasing Salazar. And if Mark Dobson wanted to wallow in futility for a couple of weeks, that was his own call. Finn was a realist, and he had too many other things to pay attention to.

Finn was an exceptional trial lawyer, and he could work wonders in front of a jury, but he hated the business of law. The administrative contortions required to make sure that bills to clients got out the door and paid with some semblance of regularity; to ensure that vendors were satisfied enough to keep the lights on and the computers humming; and to see to it that he, Kozlowski, and Lissa had nominal health insurance were enough to stretch him beyond his capacity for minutiae. He had a part-time assistant who came in two days a week to help him with the process, but it was unquestionably the worst part of being on his own. At his old firm, he'd been responsible only for keeping track of his time; the firm had fully staffed departments devoted to making sure the mundane details were attended to. He hadn't realized what a benefit that had been.

As it was, dealing with administrative hassles took up much of his Thursday and Friday that week. He negotiated discounts for a couple of clients unhappy with their bills, made sure that no invoices were over thirty days past due, and spent two hours trying to get some expensive new software, designed to be more efficient, to work. By late Friday afternoon, he was worn out and could muster little motivation to embark on any new tasks. Instead, he offered to buy the first round at O'Doul's.

"Sounds good to me," Lissa replied when he made the offer. A beer clearly held more appeal to her than the research project she had been gnawing on throughout the day.

"Koz!" Finn called to the back office.

"What?" The reply was barked, and Finn was reminded of the dark mood the private detective had fallen into in recent days.

"We're going for beers. I thought you might want to join us, if you can manage a civil word or two."

Kozlowski walked out of his office and leaned against the door. His frown seemed indelible. "Only girls drink beer. Men drink booze."

"I'm a girl," Lissa said, looking at Kozlowski. The emphasis was evident to Finn, but it seemed to escape Kozlowski's attention.

"So's he, apparently." Kozlowski nodded toward Finn.

"Ooooh," Finn said. "I get it, I drink beer—so I'm a girl. Good one. You know, at least when I'm in a shitty mood, I can still be funny."

"Still?"

"See, that's better." Finn grabbed his coat. "Why don't you join us? I'll order you a Scotch, and Lissa and I will try not to give you cooties, okay?"

Kozlowski shook his head. "Can't right now. I've still got some work to do."

"You sure?" Lissa pushed. "We'll get you a scotch, and I'll try my hardest *to* give you cooties."

Kozlowski again failed to see through her transparency. "Later," he said. "Gimme an hour, and maybe I'll try to meet you guys over there." He walked back into his own office.

"Right." Lissa sighed. "Fuck." She looked at Finn. "Fuck," she said again. "You know? I mean . . . ?"

"I know," Finn said. "Fuck. Come with me. I'm still buying."

"Fuckin' right you're buying. I'm getting plastered." She shook her head in disbelief as she picked up her purse.

"Sounds good to me," Finn agreed. "I don't think I've ever seen you good and drunk. What's that like?"

She shrugged. "Not really that different. Although I've been told I swear a lot when I'm drunk."

"Compared to what?"

"Compared to normal, I guess."

Finn paused as he opened the door for her. "Seriously?" He looked at her, frightened.

"Fuckin' A."

"No, seriously?"

"Kozlowski was right," she scoffed. "You are a fuckin' girl." She walked past him and out into the darkness as he hurried after her.

East Boston was the Hub's afterthought. Nestled against Logan International Airport, it sat bleak and lonely across the harbor from downtown, Southie, Charlestown, and all the other sections of the city that polite society considered part of civilization. It was dominated by small blue-collar clapboard row houses set flush to the sidewalk. As with almost every area in Boston, a steady and varying stream of immigrants had flushed through the neighborhood over the years. It had started with the Irish and continued with the Italians and Germans, but had in recent years given way to a new wave of recent arrivals, many from Asia and South and Central America.

Mark Dobson sat in the front seat of his BMW 325 across the street from the Church of St. Jude, a few blocks from the water and a stone's throw from Logan. Its name, taken from the patron saint of lost causes, seemed prophetic as Dobson looked out at the boards that darkened its windows. Built in the early 1900s with contributions from the impoverished residents, it had once sat at the edge of tidal flats, looking out on the short cinder-block runways of the original airport sunk into the marshy expanse at the edge of the harbor.

Over the years, the flats had been reclaimed by landfill, and the airport had grown, attracting storage depots and industrial developments that crowded in on the little religious outpost. The church had survived for a century, supported by its parishioners, who contributed cash when they could afford it and sweat equity when they couldn't. In 2004, though, the Boston archdiocese, facing a cash crisis brought on by mismanagement and liability from lawsuits over pedophilia charges, announced that it would close the place down. It made sense from a business perspective. The tithing of the poor provided an insufficient economic justification for keeping the church open, and there were other parishes in East Boston that could absorb those who still frequented it. Angry residents staged sit-ins and filed lawsuits, but in the end, there was little they could do, and the doors were closed. Now it sat on a lonely parcel of land waiting to be sold; waiting to be swallowed up by the secular interests of economic development.

Dobson had no idea what he was doing here, exactly, but this was his only lead, and he refused to let Salazar down. After absorbing everything he could from Macintyre's file, Dobson had headed out to Billerica to demand some answers from his client. He'd gotten answers. Answers he hadn't expected. Answers he wasn't sure he believed. But he couldn't let it drop; he was in this until the end, even if meant he had to sit in his car on this deserted street, watching this deserted church, until he froze to death.

Oddly, the notion excited him. Having spent a few years holed up in the firm's law library doing legal research and writing briefs for mega-glomerates in securities and tax litigations, he felt good being out in the real world, doing real work for a real flesh-and-blood client.

He smiled as his teeth chattered, and he pulled his coat tighter around himself. Perhaps being a lawyer was what he was really meant to do with his life after all. *And besides,* he thought, *it's not like the cold will kill me.*

Finn was still on his first beer as Lissa put down her second. She drank like someone twice her size and seemed to hold it better. Finn considered being shocked but quickly realized there was little about her that would surprise him at this point.

"What the fuck?" she said, looking at him as she leaned forward on her stool against the bar. She raised her hand to order another.

"Sorry, I didn't realize we were racing," Finn replied, lifting his glass to polish off what beer remained. He nodded to the bartender and tipped his glass.

She shook her head. "I'm not talking about your drinking—although now that you mention it, you might want to hike your skirt up if you don't want the hem to drag in the mung. No, I'm just pissed at the Neanderthal you keep in the back office."

"Koz?"

"No, the other one, genius." She rolled her eyes as she wrapped her petite hand around a fresh beer and poured a third of it down her throat. Putting the glass down, she wiped the back of her hand across her mouth. It was a pretty mouth, Finn thought, no matter what kind of language came out of it. "I mean, shit, what the fuck do I have to do, throw myself at the guy?"

"You mean more than you already have?"

"Fuck you." She glared at Finn. Then she stood up and flattened her sweater and skirt against her body. "Look at me," she said. She raised her arms above her head to accentuate her athletic curves.

Finn shaded his eyes. "I think that would be a violation of all sorts of employment laws."

"Fuck you. I'm not gonna sue you. I've seen your receivables; it's not worth my fuckin' time. Just look at me," she ordered him. "Is there something hideous about me or anything?"

"Clearly not," Finn said, looking though the gaps of the hand he still held in front of his face.

She dropped her hands and put them on her waist, rolling her hips slightly as she struck a seductive Marilyn Monroe pose. She smiled and licked her lips seductively. "Can you honestly tell me there's a straight man this side of the South End who wouldn't kill to get close to this?"

Finn noticed several of the men at the bar shifting restlessly as they watched her. "No, I can't," he said. "I *can* tell you that a few of the guys at the bar look like they're ready to kill to get close to that, and I don't feel like being the one they pick on to prove it."

She straightened up and let her shoulders slump as she plopped back down on her bar stool. "So what the fuck is wrong with Tom Kozlowski that he doesn't want to take a shot at me?" She picked up her beer. Then, as a thought struck her, she leaned in and said in a confidential tone, "You don't think he's gay, do you?"

Finn snarfed a mouthful of his beer at the notion, drawing an annoyed look from the bartender. As Finn wiped his face with a napkin, he began to wonder whether he'd make it out of the bar without having someone take a swing at him. "Gay? Koz? No, he's definitely not gay."

"Well, then, what the fuck?"

Finn put his hand on her shoulder. "It's got nothing to do with how you look," he reassured her. "Trust me. It's just that Koz is a nineteenth-century man trying to cope with a twenty-first-century world. To say

78

that he's traditional doesn't even begin to do his condition justice. Honor and honesty and respect—and stoicism about them all—are at the core of the man. That's just who he is."

"I know," Lissa agreed. "That's what I like about him. He's solid. Other guys try to project an image of themselves, and then when you really get to know them, you realize too late that it's all a fucking mirage. You can wave your hand, and it passes right through the image of who you thought they were. With Tom, there's no posturing, no pretense."

"Please, can we call him Koz? Calling him Tom makes it seem like this conversation is actually happening."

"I'm just saying I think he is exactly who he seems to be."

"Only more so, I suspect," Finn said.

"Exactly. So what the fuck am I doing wrong?"

"You have to understand, things are pretty black and white in his world. I think he works more at the 'me boy, you girl' level. I'm just not sure he knows what to make of someone like you."

"What the hell does that mean? 'Someone like me'? That's a shitty thing to say."

"You know exactly what it means. You're an intelligent, independent, modern woman. I'm not sure you fit into any mold that his brain can deal with."

"Who said it was his brain I was interested in?"

"There. See, that's what I'm talking about. I'm not sure, for example, that the idea of a woman with a libido is something he's ready for."

She shook her head. "You're wrong. Women can sense these things. He's more than ready for it."

Finn shrugged. "Then, of course, there's your vocabulary."

"What the fuck are you talking about now?"

"Exactly."

She paused, and Finn could tell that she was playing her words back in her head. Then she picked up her beer and took a contemplative sip. "Fuck you. I don't think you're giving Koz enough credit," she said sullenly.

The voice came from behind them, over her shoulder. "That's been the problem my whole life. People don't give me enough credit."

They both turned to see Kozlowski as he sidled up between them. Finn noticed Lissa's face go white. "Koz," he said. "How long have you been standing there?"

"I just walked in. Why? How long have you been badmouthing me?"

Lissa's face instantly went from white to red, and Finn had trouble choking back a laugh in spite of the awkwardness. "Pretty much since we got here."

"Really? Anything important I should know about?"

"Naw. We were just speculating about whether or not you were gay," Finn said. Lissa kicked Finn hard in the shin, and he let out an involuntary yelp.

"Wishful thinking on your part, no doubt," Kozlowski grunted to Finn, though there was good humor in his tone for once, if you knew where to look for it.

"No doubt," Finn agreed.

"What do you want to drink?" Lissa offered, clearly desperate to change the subject.

"Scotch," Kozlowski replied.

"Any particular flavor?"

He looked at Finn. "This asshole buying?"

Finn nodded.

"Then whatever's most expensive."

Chapter Ten

THE THREE OF THEM drank at the bar for another hour before Finn decided it was time to call it an evening. He had to stop by the office to pick up some work before heading home, and he wasn't in for the long haul. He assumed he was the glue keeping the three of them together and that his departure would kill the gathering, but he was wrong.

"You want to stay for one more?" Lissa asked Kozlowski as Finn stood up. Finn viewed it as far too aggressive a move, and he cringed for her as he waited for the cavalcade of excuses to pour forth from the private detective: *I have to get home or my frozen dinner may spoil. The History Channel is replaying my favorite episode of* Weapons of the First World War. *It's my night to host the retired homicide detectives' book club.*

"Sure" was the response Kozlowski actually gave.

"Seriously?" Finn was unable to disguise his shock, and he could feel the sting of Lissa's stare.

"Problem?" Kozlowski asked.

"No." Finn felt like his tongue was too big for his mouth all of a sudden.

"Have a good weekend, then."

"Fine. You two, too. Also." Finn stood there like an idiot. Then, without another word, he turned and walked to the door.

He shook his head all the way back to his office. Was it possible that he'd been wrong about Kozlowski? The notion of the detective together with Lissa was too weird for his mind to grasp, but why? Kozlowski was older but not outrageously so. And in many ways, they might be good for each other. Something about it just seemed so odd. It couldn't actually work between the two of them, could it?

Finn was still wrestling with the notion as he approached the office. In New England, night falls early in December, and it was pitch-dark out even though it was just past six o'clock. As he took out his key and slid it into the lock, a shadow emerged from around the corner of the little building.

"You Finn?"

Finn looked up. The man was standing directly in front of a streetlamp, making it difficult to see anything other than his general shape. It seemed like a large shape, though. "I am."

"I need to talk to you."

"About what?"

"About a case. Not here, though. Inside."

Finn squinted, trying to get a better look at the man. He was tempted to tell him to come back on Monday during normal working hours, but he'd lost so much time on administrative matters over the previous two days that he felt guilty. A couple of years on his own had taught him that you had to pounce on any potential new business without hesitation. You never knew where the next meal was coming from, and hustle was 70 percent of surviving as a solo practitioner. "Okay," he said. "Come on in and we'll talk." He opened the door and stepped inside, holding it open behind him to let the man in.

"So, you need a lawyer?" Finn took off his coat and threw it over a hook on the wall.

"Not really," the man replied.

Finn turned to get a good look at him. The impression from the street had drastically underestimated his size. He'd seemed large, but he was in fact huge. He had to be at least six and a half feet tall, though neither thin nor gawky. He had massive shoulders from which hung long solid slabs of muscle ending in hands the size of baseball gloves. His neck, which rose from a giant cask of a torso, was as thick as a telephone pole and looked as solid. As he took off his hat, a shock of red hair stood on end, and his complexion was ghostly white. He looked young, early twenties at most, but he had the eyes of someone much older. "You look familiar," Finn said. "Have we met?"

"No," the young man said.

Finn shrugged. "Well, if you don't need a lawyer, I'm not sure how I can help you."

"Mr. Slocum sent me."

An alarm charge ran through Finn. This was not a good sign. "Why?" he asked.

"He said he's considered your offer to settle this divorce."

Finn stood in the center of the large central office space, only a few feet from the giant. The man had an odd resolve about him; he looked neither excited nor nervous.

"And?" Finn asked. "Does he have a response?"

The man nodded. Then he took two quick strides toward Finn—surprisingly graceful, almost balletlike strides for a man his size—and swung one of his massive arms, driving a sledgehammer fist into Finn's abdomen so hard that Finn thought he felt it push its way through his organs and connect with the front side of his spine.

Finn doubled over and fell to his knees as the giant took two steps back. For over a minute, Finn was unable to move or make a sound, and he seriously considered the possibility that he was going to die. He'd taken plenty of beatings in his youth, and dished out his fair share as well, but he was sure he'd never been hit this hard. He'd heard stories of guys taking a punch to the head that killed them, and he wondered whether it was possible to have the same result from a gut shot.

Gradually, he regained the ability to move, if only slightly, and his lungs expanded enough that he was at least making some noise as his jaw worked up and down in what he'd initially thought would be his silent death scream. Had his attention not been dedicated to weighing the odds of his survival, Finn probably would have been fascinated by his assailant's reaction. He was watching Finn with what looked like concern, and he seemed almost relieved when Finn started showing some signs of life again.

It was another minute or two before Finn could straighten himself and speak, still on his knees. "I'll take that as an indication that the offer's been rejected," he coughed out, wiping his mouth and looking for blood as he drew his hand away from his face.

"I don't want to do this," the young man said quietly.

"Good. That makes two of us," Finn said, placing one foot on the ground while still supporting his weight with his other knee.

"I'm serious."

Finn could tell he was. "So don't do it," he offered. It seemed simple enough.

"No choice. Mr. Slocum wants this resolved. He's willing to double what Mrs. Slocum would've gotten under their prenup. My instructions are to make sure that's acceptable to you. Tonight."

A light sweat had broken out on Finn's forehead, and he put his hand up to mop it off. "Four thousand a month?" He considered it.

"It's more than I make," the young man said. "And she don't have to do anything to earn it."

Finn shook his head. "She won't go for it."

"I'm sure you can convince her. If not, I can." The young man crossed his arms. "It's the way it's gotta be. You agree now, and I don't have to do anything more to you. Shit, I'll even take you to the bar on the corner, buy you a beer, so you know I'm not such a bad guy."

Finn nodded, leaning his weight forward onto an arm slung across his knee. "Help me up," he said, exhaling loudly.

The young man was visibly relieved. He uncrossed his arms and stepped forward, leaning down to pull Finn off the floor. As Finn came off his knee, he drove his head up, snapping it forward into the man's face as he was bent over, sending him stumbling back.

Finn was sure that would end the altercation. He'd been in enough fights to know that a solid head butt to the face was generally enough to put even the stubborn brawlers down. Sometimes there was some finishing work left to do—a quick kick between the legs to close the deal, or maybe a blow to the back of the head with a heavy object—but it was always a mere formality.

Finn got to his feet and moved in for the kill, watching and waiting for the man to go down to the floor in front of him and present an easy target. But something remarkable happened: The man didn't fall. He stumbled back a yard or so, his hands to his face, but he stayed on his feet. After a couple of seconds, he pulled his hands away, and all Finn could see was a trickle of blood running from his nose. Other than that, he looked unfazed. That was the moment Finn realized he was in trouble.

"That was a mistake," the man said simply.

"I'm getting that feeling," Finn replied.

"That was a really big mistake."

"Yes, I think we're agreed on that point."

He was unbelievably quick for such a huge man. His hand shot out, grabbing Finn by the throat. Another hand came up and attached itself to the front of Finn's shirt, lifting him up off the ground.

"Wait," Finn protested. "You haven't heard my counteroffer."

The young man tossed Finn over the desk and into the exposed brick wall. Finn landed hard and at an awkward angle, wrenching his knee. He had no opportunity to evaluate the damage, though, as his tormentor came around the corner of the desk and reached down to pick him up again. Finn felt like a character in some twisted fairy tale as he was lifted off the ground once more. All that was missing was a beanstalk.

The giant heaved him across the room and pinned him against a section of drywall. He held Finn with one hand while he pulled the other back and swung his enormous fist at Finn's face. It took all of Finn's strength to break free enough to duck his head slightly, so the blow glanced off his ear, the fist smashing into the drywall and blowing a hole through the plaster and paint.

As the young man pulled his hand out of the wall, Finn knew this was his last chance, and he swung his own fists twice at the man's stomach. It was like punching a sandbag; the man gave no indication that he'd even noticed Finn's efforts. He pulled Finn's head up again, holding him firmly under the chin this time, and Finn caught a glimpse of the gaping hole in the wall from the first blow. He shuddered as he understood the damage that was about to be inflicted on his face. He suddenly regretted that he'd skimped on his health plan.

The door to the street groaned open and slammed shut. "What the fuck?"

Finn had never been so happy to hear Tom Kozlowski's voice.

The young man didn't seem particularly concerned, but he was at least distracted enough to pause in his assault. That was something, Finn thought. "Get outta here, old-timer," he said to Kozlowski. "This isn't your business."

"I work with him," Kozlowski said. "So I think it is my business. Besides, I forgot my keys back there in my office, and you're blocking the door, so it's definitely my business."

The huge man flung Finn to the ground. "Fine," he said. He moved quickly toward the ex-cop, so quickly that Kozlowski didn't have time to pull out his gun. That was bad news, Finn thought. Koz was a rock, but he was probably seven inches shorter than this behemoth, and was giving away at least a hundred pounds and a quarter decade to boot. Finn had serious doubts that Kozlowski would last much longer than Finn had in a hand-to-hand battle with the young man.

Finn watched as the man pulled his arm back and swung at Kozlowski's head. Koz ducked it easily, then kicked out hard with his heel, connecting with the inside of the man's right knee. Finn heard an ugly popping sound as the man wobbled, roaring in pain. He fell to one knee in front of Kozlowski, looking up at him in anguish. Kozlowski didn't hesitate. With remarkable efficiency, his fist shot out and slammed into the man's Adam's apple. The man went silent, his eyes wide with terror and his hands flying to his throat as he toppled heavily to the floor. He lay there, flopping like a beached shark, helpless, as Kozlowski stood over him.

Finn got to his feet and walked over to Kozlowski. "Is he dead?"

Kozlowski shook his head. "Not yet."

"Will he be?"

"Don't know. Don't think so." Koz leaned over and tried to pull the man's hands away from his neck. "Let me see." The man pushed Kozlowski's hands away, still struggling in panic to breathe.

Kozlowski pulled out his gun and put it to the man's forehead. "I have to figure out whether you need an ambulance," he said. "Now move your hands or I'll shoot you." The man relented and took his hands away from his throat, and Kozlowski leaned in close to take a look. "Nope," he said, standing up. "Nothing's broken; the windpipe's just choked off temporarily." He spoke directly to the man on the ground. "Relax. Struggling makes it worse. You'll be able to breathe in a minute or two." Kozlowski kept his gun out and his eyes on the man lying on the ground, who was starting to get some air back into his lungs. "Unsatisfied client or angry husband?" he asked Finn.

Finn shook his head. "Messenger from Slocum."

Kozlowski nodded. "Ah. Playing hardball? I take it he thought your last offer was unreasonable?"

"Apparently."

"So? Should we call the police, or should I just shoot him? Send a message back?"

The man on the floor, who had regained enough breath to prop himself up on an elbow, choked out a plea. "No, please!"

Finn shook his head. "He's kidding." He looked at Kozlowski. "You're kidding, right?"

Kozlowski shrugged.

"Let's talk to him a little first," Finn suggested. "Then we'll figure out the best plan."

"Fine with me. It's your wall he put a hole in, not mine. I just rent." Koz looked down at the young man. "Can you get up and sit in a chair?" The man nodded. "Okay, you understand that if you do anything to make me even a little nervous, I'll shoot you, right?" The man nodded again. "Good. Get up. Slowly."

The man rose and sat in a chair against the wall.

"What's your name?" Finn asked, leaning against his desk.

"Charlie."

Finn shook his head. "Full name?"

Charlie hesitated. "Charlie O'Malley," he said after thinking it over.

Finn chuckled. "I thought you looked familiar. You're related to Michael O'Malley, aren't you?"

Charlie nodded.

"You remember Big Mick?" Finn asked Kozlowski. Kozlowski shook his head. "Big Mick O'Malley," Finn repeated. "He ran a crew out of Charlestown. Great guy. He saved my ass a dozen times back when I was a kid running with Tigh McCluen in the eighties." He looked at Charlie. "He your father?"

Charlie shook his head. "Uncle."

"How's he doing?"

"Dead."

Finn frowned. "Shit. How?"

"Cancer."

"Too bad. Beats a bullet in the head, I guess. And now you're following him into the family business? Doing a little muscle work?"

Charlie shook his head. "Like I told you, I don't want to be doing this. I don't have a choice."

"Why not?"

He folded his arms. "Three years ago, I was out riding with a friend. Not even a friend, really, just a guy I knew. He got into a hassle, and we ended up getting pulled over. He had half a kilo of smack in his bag in the back. I did two years for it."

"Why?"

"It was my car. The guy lied and said it wasn't his bag. Cops didn't know and didn't care. Long as someone went away, it was all the same to them. Now I'm out on parole, and Slocum's one of the few people who would sponsor a guy like me—give me a job—which is a condition of my parole. He sponsors a lot of ex-cons."

"Sounds like a prince," Kozlowski commented.

Charlie nodded. "A regular fuckin' Gandhi. But it all comes with a price. He tells me to do something, I gotta do it."

Finn scratched his head. "Who's your parole officer?"

"Hector Sanchez."

Finn looked over at Kozlowski. "Name mean anything to you?"

Kozlowski nodded. "I've dealt with him. Not a bad guy. Overworked, overstressed, but reasonable for the most part."

Finn considered his options. "You really looking to get out of the life, or are you just bullshitting me?"

"I swear. I don't want this."

"What do you want?"

Charlie looked embarrassed. Finn thought it was an odd expression for such an enormous man. "I want to be a musician."

"A musician?" Finn stifled a laugh.

"Sounds weird, right? I'm pretty good, though. I used to sing at the church, and my grandfather taught me some guitar when I was little."

"Bullshit. You were never little."

"When I was in the can, the only good thing was they let me keep a guitar, and I got to practice. I'm not lookin' to be a star or nothing. I'd just like to play at bars. I'd be good at that."

Finn was bewildered. He looked at Kozlowski, who shrugged back at him. Finally, Finn said, "All right, here's the deal. We'll put in a call to Sanchez. I'll also find you another job. You stay away from Slocum; don't go back to work."

"Why would you do all this?"

"Like I said, your uncle bailed me out of a lot of jams when I was young. Maybe this is my chance to pay some of those debts back. Besides, this shit doesn't really involve you; it involves me and Slocum. Give me a phone number, and I'll call you tomorrow."

Charlie looked back and forth between the two other men. "Seriously? That's it? I just walk out of here?"

"You could stay, I suppose, but it would seem weird," Finn said.

"Slocum's gonna be pissed. He'll send someone else after you."

Finn considered that. "Are there any other guys like you who are unhappy with what Slocum's making them do?"

Charlie shrugged. "A few, I guess."

"Introduce me to them. Then let me deal with Slocum, and just wait for my call."

Charlie stood up and walked to the door. "This is fucked up."

"You'll find that more and more as you get older," Finn said. "Enjoy it when it goes your way."

Chapter Eleven

SATURDAY EVENING LUCINDA GOMEZ lit the candles in the window of her first-floor parlor overlooking the desolate East Boston street where she lived. It was a ritual of hers, one she had been looking forward to for over a month. Every year she began decorating for the holidays on the second Saturday before Christmas, and the first symbolic step was to light the candles in the window. She would light them every evening between now and January 2. Three weeks of holiday celebration were enough, in her mind; she couldn't condone the overzealousness with which some strung their red and green the day after Halloween, commercializing the birth of the Savior. They probably weren't even real Christians, and she was sure Jesus would be appalled.

She sat back in her favorite chair overlooking the street and took a sip of her sherry. It warmed her throat. Evenings like this one were the last joy left for the seventy-eight-year-old widow. She had spent most of the day in church, and she felt sanctified. Should her time come tonight, as she often prayed it would, she would meet the Lord with the confidence of someone who, to her certain knowledge, had committed and confessed her final sins long ago.

The BMW was still there, she noted as she sat back comfortably. The young man inside was sipping yet another cup of coffee. He'd been there for several evenings, at least since Thursday night, when she first noticed him. He disappeared during the days but showed when the sun went down, which, at this time of year, wasn't much past four o'clock. She'd been tempted to call the police on the second evening, but after watching him, she decided that she really couldn't imagine a more clean-cut, respectable person to be sitting on her street.

In an odd way, he even made her feel safer. She'd taken to thinking of him as her guardian angel, and it gave her comfort that his attention was focused on St. Jude's across the street. Satan's house. That dark, menacing structure, which would remain deserted for weeks at a time and then see a flurry of unholy activity. She missed the days when the place was still a house of God. It had been her solace for over fifty years, and it had been taken away from her. The clandestine activities that seemed to go on there only confirmed her belief that the church's closing was the work of the devil, and she had complained numerous times to the police, but they seemed to take little notice. Perhaps, she thought, they were taking her seriously now. Perhaps the young man was a police officer, sent to investigate. She thought probably not, but it would be nice.

In any event, she was happy to have him as a buffer against whatever evil took place there. As she sipped her sherry again, she felt a rush of danger sweep over her. Not for her but for the man in the car. It was nothing more than a geriatric delusion, fed by loneliness and alcohol, and she consciously dismissed it. Yet it was more stubborn than most of her fantasies. She shook her head as she finished her drink and headed off to bed. She would keep him in her prayers that evening. It occurred to her that the man might very well need God's help more than he knew.

Mark Dobson yawned as he brought the coffee to his lips. He was jittery-tired from lack of sleep and too much caffeine, and he had to fight his body to stay awake. The novelty of investigative work had worn off by the third night, and doubts were starting to creep into his mind. Perhaps Finn had been right; perhaps Salazar really was guilty. Dobson pushed back against the notion. He needed Salazar to be innocent. He needed it more than anyone.

He yawned again and pulled a hair out of his forearm to revive himself. It was a trick he'd learned in law school: Pain stimulated the adrenal glands and gave you a little burst of energy to fight off sleep. It had gotten him through his exams. The only problem was that, like any chemical, adrenaline began to lose its potency with each dose, and the effects were shorter- and shorter-lived. He was at the point where the crashes were coming within five minutes of each yank. Not to mention that he was running out of hair on his arms.

His thoughts drifted back to law school, and he considered again the hardships of a well-planned life. The only son of an overachieving, hypermotivated couple clinging to second-tier wealth, he had been programmed from birth to succeed, and to define that success in the narrow terms of material wealth and recognition of the appropriate professional set. It wasn't until he was in college that he'd started questioning his parents' priorities—and his own. By then it was too late. Competition was too much a part of who he had become. He tried to refocus, even tried to sabotage his studies, but nothing worked. He graduated at the top of his class. After law school, he initially planned to work for some sort of public interest concern, a place where he would make little money but might have an impact on something that actually mattered to him. But then Howery, Black made him an offer, and no one turns down a firm like Howery, right?

Now he was at a crossroads, and part of him thought this was the last chance he would have to redefine himself. After three years of serving well-heeled, demanding clients, he had come to the realization that, while he got no thrill or even satisfaction from his job, he was good at it and it was safe, and in all likelihood, he could continue doing it for the next four decades. Then he'd started working on the Salazar case, and it was like falling in love. He'd been so thrilled that he viewed the case as a test. He'd vowed that if he was successful in clearing Salazar's name, he'd give notice at the firm and start his life over. If he failed, however . . . Well, at least there would be a gold watch and a retirement place in Florida for him.

He set his coffee down on the armrest between the two front seats, trying to pull a notebook out of his briefcase in the back. As he turned, he knocked the coffee, sending it crashing into the passenger seat, where the plastic top jarred open, spilling half the cup over the new leather. Dobson cursed his clumsiness and grabbed some napkins out of the door's side pocket, leaning over to blot up what he could.

When he picked up his head, he almost spilled the coffee again. Two vans had pulled up to the church across the street, and a man was out, unlocking the gate on the fence in front. After four days, Dobson had actually begun to think nothing would ever come of his surveillance. He sat as still as possible, afraid that any movement would chase away the mirage.

It took a moment, but he was finally satisfied that the vans were not apparitions. He watched as they pulled out of sight behind the church, around toward the rectory and the flat, ugly building that had once served as a church-run day-care center. A light went on inside the rectory, and then a blind was quickly drawn, and the building went dark again.

Dobson sat there for several minutes, wondering what to do next. From the information Salazar had given him, he had an idea what was happening inside the church, but knowing it and proving it were two different things. He hadn't thought through his next steps thoroughly, other than making sure he had his camera phone with him just in case. He'd just assumed something would come to him once he determined that his client wasn't lying to him. Now that the moment was upon him, he wished he'd put together a more coherent plan.

He was about to get out of the BMW when another vehicle approached the cluster of church buildings from the other direction. It was a boxy late-model American car, and it slowed near the entrance. A man got out of the driver's side and walked, with his back to Dobson, to push open the gate. He paused there for a moment before turning and giving Dobson a clear view of his face.

Dobson was so shocked that he dropped his camera phone before he could snap a picture. It couldn't be, could it?

He scrambled his hand around the car floor, searching for the camera, but by the time he had it again, the man was back in his car, pulling through the gate and around back in the direction the vans had disappeared.

Suddenly, it all made sense, and Dobson was out of his car, crossing the street, and scaling the fence.

———

Carlos Villegas stood in a darkened room on the second floor, looking out the rectory's front window. He had the look of a falcon, with a strong, prominent nose hanging from a sharp brow. His eyes probed the night.

He had the phone to his ear as he took a deep drag on his cigarette. "When do we move them out?" he asked.

"Two hours."

"And the money?"

"Ten apiece. One hundred thousand in all. It will be there."

"Only seven. Not ten."

"My people told me ten. Did you lose three?"

"Three of them were contract jobs," Carlos said. "That's the way they wanted it."

"Is that the way you want it?" It was the devil's voice coming over the line, dripping temptation.

"As I said, they were contract jobs. I honor my contracts."

Laughter on the other end. "Of course you do. No one has ever suggested otherwise. But you're out thirty on the exchange, that means."

"Seventy. Agreed." Carlos hung up the phone and took another drag from his cigarette. The other two men in the room remained silent. They knew better than to speak when Carlos was thinking. "Is everything ready?" he asked them.

"Sí, Padre," one of them replied.

Padre. How had he gotten so old? It seemed like only yesterday he'd been there at the start of it all, fighting for survival on the streets of East L.A., hemmed in by the Mexicans—the Chicanos—to the east, and by the blacks—the Crips—to the west. It had been a meat grinder, almost as bad as El Salvador at the height of the rebellion. The only way to survive had been to be crazier than everyone else. *Loco.* That had been his street name back then, and he'd earned it. Soon no one wanted to mess with his crew. It just wasn't worth the blood. And so they kept slashing out until they were no longer fighting for survival but for supremacy.

Now here he was, two decades later, the old man. Padre. A leader in one of the most feared criminal organizations in the world. They were more than one hundred thousand strong, stretching from El Salvador to Michigan—nothing was beyond their reach. And it was all at his disposal. A loyal battalion of mercenaries and unlimited cash flow. He was, he thought, like many of the great leaders in history. Rockefeller. Kennedy. Fidel. They had all laid their claim to power in the shadow of the law until they were powerful enough to become the law. He was following in their path.

Not that anyone would draw that connection by looking at him. He stood just under six feet tall and was just over 150 pounds of weathered steel cable. The veins stood out on his arms, his legs, his neck, giving life to the artwork that adorned his body. His markings. They covered every inch of skin from his toes to his bald scalp. Snakes and dragons and Aztec gods crawled over his body, as he felt them crawling through his soul. But the only one that mattered took up his entire chest: an elaborately styled rendering of his true identity. VDS. It was who he was. It was what he was.

He looked out across the front of the church and felt comforted. In an odd way, he had always considered himself a religious man. The Catholic Church was strong in El Salvador, and his mother had been devout, trying desperately to raise all her children to respect the Church and its teachings. In the end, it had been the radical priests who had caused her death, putting the peasants on the front lines of a war in which they had no say. When she was killed, he turned his anger against the Communists, joining with the death squads as a means of venting his anger, but for some reason, he could never quite bring himself to hate the Church—or at least not the part of it that had been such an important part of his mother.

Perhaps that was why he had chosen this place. Here, he felt closer to her than he had in decades. He would be sad to leave, but he had learned long ago the dangers of remaining in one location for too long. Another week and they would move on, but that week was crucial to him. The delivery due next Saturday would provide him more money than any ten had before. Then he and his men would slip away and find a new headquarters, as they had for fifteen years. He would miss this place, though.

He turned to face the others. "Two hours," he said. "We wait."

"Our friend is here," one of his underlings reported.

"Good. We have much to discuss with him." Carlos turned back to the window, his mind working through all the angles and all the plays. He'd always been good at figuring out the angles; that was what had kept him alive. As he clicked through complicated scenarios, his eye caught a shadow rolling across the cement at the front of the rectory. He reached out and tugged at the corner of the shade to give himself a better view. His eyes narrowed as he added another variable to what lay before him. "It seems we have more than one visitor tonight." He looked at the other two men in the room. "We should make our guests welcome."

Mark Dobson stood with his back to the exterior of the rectory. So far, so good, he thought. He rested there as his breathing returned to normal. Crossing the parking lot in the front of the church had been the only dicey part of his reconnaissance mission, and it appeared he'd cleared that hurdle. All he had to do now was get one picture. He waited another several minutes to see whether someone would burst forth from the rectory to grab him. He was ready to run, but it looked like that wasn't going to be necessary.

Slowly, silently, he began moving around toward the back of the building. Twice, as he passed first-floor windows, he popped his head up to determine whether he could see enough to take his picture and head back out to his car. Each window was blackened, and he was forced to continue.

When he reached the corner, he crouched down. The ground fell away in front of him, following the driveway toward a sunken two-car garage underneath the rectory—the driveway that the vans and the sedan had taken around toward the rear of the facility. It occurred to him that he was placing himself in significant danger. If what Salazar had told him was true, then these people had been protecting their business for decades. They wouldn't take kindly to any intrusion. Still, what would they do, really? Rough him up? For Dobson, perched on the edge of a whole new life, the risk seemed worth it.

He edged around the corner, concealing himself behind a barrel against the wall. From where he was, he could see the vans, their doors open at the back. Empty. But not entirely empty. Something remained of what had been in them in a putrid stench pouring from the interior.

Stench wouldn't show up in a picture: He needed more. He raised himself up on the balls of his feet, still crouched, ready to move.

That was when he saw her.

She couldn't have been over six years old, her dark hair hanging in clumps in front of her face, her clothes stained with dirt and grime. She was standing in the doorway next to the garage doors, peeking around the corner, watching him. She said nothing, and her eyes had the vacant look of stolen youth.

He put his finger to his lips, imploring her to be quiet. Taking his camera phone out of his pocket, he held it up to show her. She frowned in curiosity and poked her head a little more out of the doorway. He aimed the camera in her direction, focusing his attention on holding it steady. His hands were shaking as he pressed the button to take the picture. The camera flashed, and he held the digital display close to his face to make sure he had the image.

She was there, sure enough, and his heart pounded with satisfaction. He had the evidence he needed. With the picture and Salazar's story, they might actually have a chance.

As he knelt there, looking at the little girl in the picture—the little girl who might very well hold the key to his client's freedom—he noticed something odd. In the split second it had taken him to snap the picture, her expression had changed. It was no longer a look of muted curiosity but one of abject terror. Her eyes were wide, and her mouth was open, as though she was witnessing something too terrible for words.

As he looked more closely, he noticed something else that struck him as odd: Her eyes no longer seemed focused on the camera. Instead, she was gaping at something else. Something above the camera, off behind it—behind him. The revelation hit him so hard he almost fell over. He thought to turn around, but he never got the chance. He took one last look at the image on the tiny phone screen. Then everything went black.

Chapter Twelve

"It's your show, Mr. Finn," Dumonds said. "You called for this meeting."

Finn sat on one side of a large table in a respectfully ornate conference room in Dumonds's firm's offices. They were high above the city on the fortieth floor of a glass and steel monstrosity. Dumonds had demanded that any meeting take place in his offices, and Finn understood why. Dumonds wanted the benefit of the home court advantage. Many lawyers swore by it and fought tooth and nail to maintain the psychological advantage that came with waging skirmishes on their own home turf. It gave them a sense of control.

Finn was fine with that. Growing up an orphan, he'd never really had a home, and as a result, he never felt particularly intimidated by the home court advantage. Every game was an away game to him. But there was something satisfying about away games—if you beat someone in his own house, you owned him forever.

He was flanked by Kozlowski and Lissa. Across from him sat Dumonds and Slocum. Slocum seemed surprised by how healthy Finn presented, though unsurprised by the fact that Finn had sought a settlement conference. He had the smug look of a man who thought he couldn't be touched. Finn was about to touch him.

"Yes," Finn began. "I wanted to talk with you and your client about our settlement offer. We've reevaluated the situation, and we would like to amend our previous offer."

A broad grin broke across Slocum's face.

"We'll obviously listen to any offer that's reasonable," Dumonds commented, his voice oozing condescension.

"Of course you will," Finn agreed. He reached into his jacket pocket and pulled out an envelope. He placed it flat on the table, covering it with his palm. Then he pushed it across the table toward Slocum.

Slocum's smiled continued to grow as he reached for the envelope. Finn wondered whether it might swallow his entire face.

Slocum picked up the envelope and shot Dumonds a look that said, *See, I told you I could handle this, you useless fucking suit*. He held it up like a trophy and then tore it open.

Finn had trouble not laughing as he watched the man's face. The grin morphed, showing the transition from shock to confusion to anger, until it was the scowl of an angry troll who'd been trifled with. "What the fuck is this?" Slocum demanded, slapping the paper back down on the table.

"Our latest settlement offer," Finn replied. "Was I unclear?"

Dumonds, still left out of the loop, lunged for the paper, picking it up and reading it. "I don't understand," he said after a moment.

"I think your client does."

Dumonds flipped the paper around to show it to Finn, almost as though he suspected that Finn had accidentally given him the wrong sheet of paper. "Mr. Finn, your last offer of settlement was for eight million dollars. This appears to be an offer for eight million six hundred and fifty-two dollars."

"And thirty-two cents," Finn added.

Dumonds looked back at the paper. "Yes, I see. And thirty-two cents." He looked up, bewildered. "Can you give me an explanation, please?"

"Sure. I had a contractor over yesterday. Six hundred and fifty-two dollars and thirty-two cents is how much it's going to cost to fix the mess in my office."

"Pardon me?" Dumonds said.

"You slimy little shit," Slocum said. "You think I can't reach you?"

"Of course you can reach me," Finn replied. "I've even got an ad in the Yellow Pages. What you can't do is intimidate me."

"Oh, no? Where is that slut of a client of yours?"

"Careful whom you call a slut, Mr. Slocum, I have a full report of your encounter with Ms. Prudet in Las Vegas. I'm not sure that's a character battle you want to take on," Finn said. Slocum turned crimson with rage. "I thought it best if my client wasn't here for today's meeting, so we can discuss some issues more openly."

Dumonds looked back and forth between Finn and his client. "Would someone please explain what's going on here?"

Finn looked at Slocum. "Do you want to? Or would you prefer it if I did the honors?" Slocum sat silently, stewing in his rage. "Very well," Finn said. "Last Friday I received a visit from one of Mr. Slocum's employees. Charles O'Malley. He came to deliver Mr. Slocum's response to our previous settlement offer."

Dumonds's face went white. He looked at his client. "Sal, you didn't. Not after we talked—"

"Shut up, Marty," Slocum snapped.

"See, that's what I don't get," Finn said, looking at Slocum. "You pay your lawyer, what, six hundred dollars an hour for his advice? And then you don't take it?" He shook his head. "This time it's going to cost you."

"Bullshit," Slocum said, a shadow of his former grin returning. Now the grin wasn't about victory; it was about revenge. "Fine. So you took care of O'Malley. You think that gets you something? That gets you shit. I'll send someone else. And you'll never prove I had anything to do with this in the first place. O'Malley will never back you up."

"Actually, I think he will," Finn said. He picked up his briefcase and put it on the table, opening it so that the top flipped up toward Slocum, blocking his view of its contents. Finn reached in and pulled out a five-page document. He looked it over and then handed it to Slocum. "This is an affidavit signed by Charles O'Malley, detailing the 'work' he's done for you since you sponsored his parole. Paragraphs seven through fifteen deal directly with his instructions from you with respect to his visit to my offices last Friday."

"I'll fucking kill him," Slocum growled.

"My client is speaking metaphorically," Dumonds was quick to add. Slocum just glared.

"You won't have to deal with Mr. O'Malley anymore, I assure you," Finn continued. "My investigator, Mr. Kozlowski—I think you've met him before—is a retired police detective, and he's arranged to find Mr. O'Malley a new job."

"I'll still fucking kill him."

"Still metaphorically." Dumonds seemed to be trying to keep up on the treadmill of his client's unraveling life. He was failing.

Finn said to Slocum, "I understand your feelings." He reached into his briefcase again and pulled out two more documents. "These are also affidavits. One is signed by Mr. Kozlowski, and the other is signed by me. In all respects, they corroborate the substance of Mr. O'Malley's affidavit with respect to the events of last Friday."

Slocum briefly looked them over, then threw them back across the table at Finn. "You think this scares me? The three of you? I deal with bigger problems than this every fucking day. You just signed your own death warrant."

"May I have a moment with my client?" Dumonds pleaded. "Sal?"

"Shut the fuck up."

Finn went on. "You know, it occurred to me that this might not be enough to convince you, so I had Mr. Kozlowski spend some time this weekend talking to Mr. O'Malley—poking into your affairs, so to speak. It turns out you do wonderful work with the parole board. According to our count, your various companies employ twenty-seven individuals currently trying to straighten out their lives after various periods of incarceration. Very admirable. We contacted them all."

Slocum's face went white.

Finn continued. "Many of them—most, in fact—refused to speak with us. Six, though, were very cooperative." He went back to his briefcase and took out four more documents. "These are the affidavits of Jerome Jefferson, Randall Hess, Timothy Monroe, and Salvatore Gonzales. While they are, of course, grateful for your help in meeting certain conditions of their parole, they are unsatisfied with many of the work assignments you have given them. They detail those assignments in the affidavits—activities ranging from extortion and gambling offenses to vandalism and assault. These gentlemen feel that they might be more productive in a different work atmosphere, and Mr. Kozlowski has already arranged with the parole board for new jobs." Finn passed the affidavits over to Slocum, who was no longer capable of speaking.

Finn went into his briefcase one last time. "I also have affidavits from two of the other individuals we spoke to. They are perfectly happy to continue working at their current positions. However, they are no longer willing to undertake illegal activities—activities that they have also detailed in their affidavits—at your direction." He took these affidavits and slipped them into a manila envelope, sealing it and putting it back in his briefcase. "I will not reveal the identities of these last two individuals. Understand, though, that if you force any of the ex-convicts currently working for you to engage in illegal conduct, you may be dealing with one of these individuals, and he will report you."

There was silence in the room. "I don't understand," Dumonds said cautiously. "You are not going to report this to the police?"

Finn looked shocked. "Of course not."

Dumonds and Slocum exchanged confused looks.

"Have I not made myself clear?" Finn asked. "I represent each of these individuals. I am their lawyer. They have retained me to resolve their employment issues, as well as to represent them in dealing with the parole board. The information in these affidavits discloses illegal conduct engaged in by my clients, albeit under duress, that I have learned about in connection with my representation of them. As I'm sure you've explained to your client on numerous occasions, Mr. Dumonds, that means this information is covered under the attorney-client privilege. I am not at liberty to disclose the nature of what I've learned to the authorities without their permission."

"So what happens now?" Slocum asked.

"Now copies of all of these affidavits have been placed in a safe-deposit box, which is controlled by an attorney I have retained. If anything happens to me, or to Mr. Kozlowski, or to any of the others who have sworn out affidavits, that attorney has been instructed to deliver the entire package to the police. Oh, and by the way, I've also included an affidavit from Ms. Prudet detailing the nature of your encounter with her in Las Vegas. There's nothing against the law about the activities described in that, unless we're talking about the laws of nature, but it makes for some fascinating reading."

Slocum thought about this for several minutes. Finn continued to stare across the table at him. "And what happens to me?" Slocum asked at last.

"You, Mr. Slocum, now have the opportunity to clean up your business practices in the future. I suggest you make the most of it." Finn closed his briefcase, stood up, and walked to the door. Kozlowski and Lissa followed his lead.

"That's it?" Slocum was incredulous.

Finn turned around and looked at Slocum again. "No, that's not it," he said. "You also settle this divorce case for eight million six hundred and fifty-two dollars and thirty-two cents. Today."

"That was just about the funniest thing I've ever seen," Lissa choked through her laughter. They were back at Finn's office. Three sandwiches and a couple of bags of chips were spread out on the long table against the wall. It was time to celebrate. "I mean, holy shit, did you see his face?"

Finn beamed. "I did."

"God, for a second there, I thought he wasn't going to go for it. I really thought he was going to throw all that shit back in your face. What would you have done then?"

Finn shook his head. "He couldn't. He had no choice. He might have been able to deal with a couple of us, but there's just no way he could have taken out the number of people who were involved without it getting too messy. Besides, he's getting off cheap. We've been able to account for over twenty-two million in his assets, and if we'd started a full investigation, I'm sure we would have found a lot more. Most of it hidden and unreported. Even coughing up eight million, he's still got plenty to keep himself going. Ultimately, we gave him no choice."

Kozlowski cleared his throat. "That's always the key to extortion, isn't it," he said. It wasn't a question; it was an observation.

Finn looked at him. "Is that how you look at this? Extortion? We went around and around on this for days. This was the only way. We didn't have enough to go to the police with anyway, not without the cooperation of the parolees. And they weren't about to cooperate if it meant copping to the stuff they'd done for Slocum. That would've put them right back in jail. I wasn't going to sit around waiting for Slocum to take another shot at me, was I?"

Kozlowski nodded. "It was the right thing to do," he agreed. "But it's extortion all the same. I'm just calling it what it is."

Finn shook his head and turned to Lissa. "You believe Mr. Sunshine over here? We have the best day in the short history of this little firm, and all he can do is bitch. We got seven clients out from under Slocum; we put a serious dent in his ability to keep up with his illegal activities; we took away a major risk to my own personal safety, and, oh yeah, we settled a case for one of our clients for over eight million dollars, and he still can't be happy."

"Sorry," Kozlowski grunted. "Like I said, it was the right thing to do. It's just that sometimes breaking the rules, even for the right reasons, can go bad quickly."

"Hey, I broke no rules. I might have bent them slightly."

"Like a Slinky."

"I'm not listening to this."

Kozlowski picked up the morning's paper and flapped it open, effectively putting a barrier between him and Finn. Finn didn't mind. Nothing could spoil the moment for him.

"How much do you make off this?" Lissa asked.

"A third."

"Of eight million?"

Finn nodded.

Lissa let out a slow whistle. "Holy shit. That's . . ." She thought for a moment. "That's over two and a half million."

Finn nodded again. "Of course, about a million of that will go into taxes, and then I've got to pay off some overhead, and pay you and Koz, but it'll be enough to keep the place running for a little while."

"I'd hope so," Lissa said. "Shit, you might even be able to hire a full-time associate this summer." She waggled her eyebrows.

Finn wagged his finger back at her. "Concentrate on graduating and passing the bar. You do that, and we'll see where we are in August."

"Thank God," she replied. "The prospect of looking for a real job was scaring the shit out of me."

Finn smiled at her as he leaned back in his chair, taking a bite of his sandwich. These were the moments that lawyers lived for. The thrill of victory. The money was nice, and the sense of security it would provide—at least in the short term—couldn't be underestimated, but that was all administrative bullshit to Finn. To him, as to most good lawyers, law was a contact sport, and the thrill of besting an opponent was a large part of what motivated him. He would never play in the Super Bowl or the World Series; this was the closest he'd ever come, and the feeling couldn't be bought for any amount of money.

He scanned his cramped office space with satisfaction. There was no mahogany. There was no artwork. There was no deep-pile carpeting or solid hardwood flooring. All he had were a few steel-gray filing cabinets, two functional desks, a secondhand computer, and some basic office supplies. And yet he was making a go of it. He was the classic underdog, and there was nothing more satisfying than winning as the underdog.

He looked over at Kozlowski, still hiding behind his newspaper, and chuckled to himself. The man was a class-A pain in the ass, there was no doubt about it. But he was also the best at what he did, no doubt about that, either. In any battle, in any case, Finn would take Kozlowski and Lissa over an army of overeducated, underexperienced, high-priced lawyers. They were his secret weapon.

He smiled again, musing over his quirky friend behind the newsprint. Ah well. Even Kozlowski's demeanor wouldn't dampen his mood. He was determined to enjoy this moment, and nothing was going to stop him.

And yet something did. It wasn't Kozlowski's moralizing, it was something that caught Finn's eye on the front page of the morning newspaper Koz was using as a shield. It was a headline. Not quite large enough to be considered a banner, but still at the top right in bold twenty-four-point font. It screamed at him from across the room, and Finn was swept away by a wave of nausea as he leaped from his chair. He crossed the office in three strides and snatched the paper from Koz's hands.

"What the fuck?" Kozlowski protested. "I told you, it was the right thing—" But Finn wasn't paying attention, and Kozlowski went silent when he saw Finn's expression.

"What is it?" Lissa asked, the strain on Finn's face reflected in her voice.

Finn had skimmed the first paragraph. It was all he needed, and now he couldn't breathe. He slumped into a chair next to the table, the paper falling faceup so the others could see the headline.

BOSTON ATTORNEY MURDERED, it read.

PART II

Chapter Thirteen

THERE'S A REASON newspaper articles are called stories. That's what they are most of the time. Stories. A reporter is nothing more than a storyteller when it comes right down to it. He has a limited number of facts to work with, and from those facts he must weave a tale that will hold the reader. Some of the facts the reporter has are accurate; some are not. But either way, the facts are not the story. The story lies in the inferences, the color, the spin. These are what reporters are paid for, and their job—their sacred oath—is to make the news pop. It has to sing. It has to thrill. Without all that, it isn't really news to anyone.

Finn could tell from the very first line of the article that the reporter in question was one of the better storytellers in the business. *Mark Dobson, a prominent Boston attorney, was found brutally murdered yesterday.* It was clean, it was to the point, and it was accurate in the strictest factual sense. And yet the article was already spinning. Already dragging the reader in.

For example, the phrase *prominent Boston attorney* was intended to give the story a boost of gravitas. *This isn't just a regular person we're talking about,* the article implied, *or even a simple attorney, but a* prominent *attorney.* Already the story was more important. Never mind that Dobson had been a midlevel associate—a position that carried with it slightly less clout than that of the guy who filled the vending machines at a place like Howery, Black. Finn had been a midlevel at Howery five years ago, and he still hadn't reached prominence on any relative scale that mattered.

The phrase *brutally murdered* was another tip. Finn had been on the streets long enough to know that every murder was brutal. Some might be more gruesome. More sensational. More twisted. But brutality was the defining characteristic of every murder, no matter what the means or method. Had the reporter gotten any real details from the cops about the specific nature of the murder, they would have been in the article. But the article merely indicated that Dobson had died from stab wounds, so *brutally* was as far as the reporter's color commentary could credibly go.

"Shit," Finn mumbled to himself, sitting in the chair in front of the newspaper. The three of them were crowded around it, each reading the report for the third time, still unable to formulate a coherent response.

Kozlowski sat down across from Finn. The frown that had been plastered on his face for a week was deeper than ever, and the crease on his forehead seemed permanently carved into an expression of concern. "Shit is right."

"You're not thinking this had anything to do with the Salazar case you were working on last week, are you?" Lissa asked.

Finn looked at Kozlowski. Neither of them answered.

"The paper makes it sound like it was a random attack," Lissa pointed out. "There's nothing here to suggest it has anything to do with Salazar."

"The paper makes it clear that they know next to nothing," Finn corrected her. "If they had any real information, or even any suspicions, they'd be in there. The cops are giving them nothing."

"Maybe the cops have nothing to give," Kozlowski suggested.

"Maybe," Finn said.

They sat in silence for several minutes, each thinking about a dead attorney none of them had met until a week before. Bright, engaging, and a little too overeager, he hadn't been one of them. He'd never been close to them. And yet here they were, stunned into silence by his death.

"What do you want to do?" Kozlowski asked finally.

Finn stood up and walked over to his desk. He looked down at all the pointless mail accumulated on top of his in-box. "I don't know," he said.

"You don't have to do anything," Lissa said. "It's not your fucking problem, after all. You never really wanted the Salazar case anyway. You have no obligation to anybody."

"That's not true, exactly. I have to do something."

"Why?"

Finn held up a court order that had been delivered the day before. It officially notified the DA's office and the Boston Police Department of their instructions to transfer the fifteen-year-old skin and blood samples from underneath Madeline Steele's fingernails to the laboratory Dobson had given to Finn. "I never filed a notice of my withdrawal with the court," Finn said, gesturing with the notice he'd been sent by the court. "Now that Dobson's dead, I'm the only lawyer on record. The judge wouldn't let me out even if I asked."

"You can't drop the case?" Lissa asked. "How can that be?"

"It's against state court rules. Once I've made an appearance, I can't withdraw unless there's another lawyer on the case to take over for me. Now that Dobson's dead, I'm Salazar's only attorney."

Finn sat heavily. All thoughts of celebration were gone. Kozlowski just looked at him. "What do you want to do?" he repeated.

"I don't know," Finn replied. "I just don't know."

Finn stood out in back of the little brownstone that housed his office, under a crooked overhang that protected the rear entrance. The forecasters had called for sun throughout the day, but they'd missed on the fifty-fifty odds that characterized New England meteorology. A freezing rain spat down on Charlestown, dribbling off the overhang and pooling in the uneven gravel behind the building. Finn looked at the glowing ember of his cigarette, trying to organize his thoughts.

The back door slammed open as Kozlowski stepped out. "Figured you'd be out here."

"Good guess."

"Haven't seen you smoke in a while."

Finn took a long drag and let the smoke drift out of his mouth and nose. "Somebody told me it wasn't good for you." He ashed in the gravel. "I was going to have one to celebrate the Slocum settlement."

"It's a good settlement," Kozlowski said. "It's a good deal for everyone involved. I wasn't trying to question it in there."

"I know."

The two of them stood there, not talking, letting the freezing rain splatter unevenly around them. It looked as though it might turn to snow, but it was just barely too warm to commit.

Finally, Kozlowski stuck his hands in his pockets, pulling his jacket tight. "Seems to me you've got three choices," he said.

Finn looked at him. "Which are?"

"First, you could go to Judge Cavanaugh and ask for permission to drop the case. Tell him you're unwilling to go forward based on what's happened."

Finn shook his head. "Even if I was ready to declare myself a coward, like I said in there, he'd never let me out at this point. I stood there last week and argued that Salazar was innocent, and that the judge should order the release of the DNA to prove it. He's not going to let me abandon the client at this point."

"Agreed. So you're down to two options."

"Right. I'm still listening."

"You could do nothing. Show up in court in a week and do a half-assed job arguing for Salazar. Keep your head down in the meantime and let him get sent back to jail to rot."

"Not exactly the honorable option, is it?"

"No, it's not."

"So what's that leave?"

Kozlowski looked hard at Finn. "Get involved," he said. "Find out what happened. Figure out whether Salazar's really innocent. Figure out who really killed Dobson. Do your job, and stop being such a pansy about it."

Finn took a last drag of his cigarette and threw the butt in a puddle. "You ever consider social work, Koz? With your sensitivity, you'd be a natural."

"I just call it like I see it."

Now it was Finn's turn to stuff his hands in his pockets. "All right, sensei. So what are we supposed to do next?"

"Next we go to the cops. We see what kind of information they're willing to give up. Maybe even trade some of our own."

"And then?"

"Then you go see your client."

Chapter Fourteen

The clean glass shell of the BPD's headquarters in Roxbury stood out like a diamond in mud. It was bordered by fresh, clean sidewalks with wide approaches and trim green grass. Two blocks to the south, though, the neighborhood sagged quickly into despair. The theory had been a good one: Put the police department in the middle of one of the city's most dangerous areas, and it would likely yield deterrence as a dividend. There had even been an understanding that some of the parcels of land nearby would be developed as well.

Except that a theory was all that it had been, and reality beats theory every time. What the overeducated criminologists had failed to take into account was a dearth of options for the residents. It was all well and good to assume that a more visible police presence would reduce the frequency with which people committeed crime, but that assumed the availability of an alternative, or at least the perception of one. If the criminals had perceived the option of moving to another area or pursuing legitimate work instead of committing crime, the theory might have panned out. As it was, those options seemed like little more than illusions to the people in question, and both the cops and the criminals realized quickly that little was going to change. As a result, putting police headquarters in the area had done nothing more than shine a flashlight in the fog. Eventually, the notion of redevelopment on a larger scale had been abandoned.

Finn brought Kozlowski along with him—it never hurt to have an ex-cop with you when you wanted to get some cooperation from the police. They left Lissa at the office. She was in charge of digging into the Salazar case: coordinating with the DNA lab, contacting Dobson's secretary to have all of his files forwarded, getting a line on fingerprint experts, and clearing the administrative hurdles to get them all the information they would need. There was a mountain of work to climb, and the sooner they laced up their hiking boots, the sooner they'd reach the top.

Finn and Kozlowski walked into the building and up to the reception desk in the lobby. A young female officer looked over the desk at them with a bored expression. "Can I help you?"

"I hope so," Finn said. He always felt that the first strategy in dealing with any bureaucracy was to be polite. Most people behind government desks had a far greater ability, if not actual authority, to solve problems than they let on. "We're here to see the detective in charge of investigating the murder of Mark Dobson."

She frowned. "What is your connection to the investigation? Do you have any information that might help?"

Finn said, "I don't know. Probably not, but I was working with Mr. Dobson. The newspaper reports didn't have much information, but depending on where the investigation is headed, it's possible that we may be able to help."

"Do you have a card?"

Finn produced one, and she inspected it. Then she rummaged through a stack of forms until she found one in triplicate and made a few notes on it. She stapled Finn's card to the sheets and handed them back to him. "If you fill these out with a brief statement of any information you have and then give them back to me, someone will call you to follow up." After a pause, she added, "If they think it's necessary."

Kozlowski stepped up to the counter, taking out his wallet and flipping it open. Behind clear plastic in the top interior fold was a card with a picture of Kozlowski and the official seal of the commonwealth of Massachusetts, identifying him as a retired detective. "Officer," he said, "we wouldn't have come down if we didn't think we could at least be of some help. Is there any chance that you could see whether the detective in charge is available? It might save both us and the detective squad some valuable time."

She looked at the identification, taking note of Kozlowski's name, and gave a shrug that indicated it was no skin off her nose one way or another. She picked up the phone behind her and turned so that they couldn't hear what she was saying. After another minute, she hung up and turned back to them. "He'll be down shortly, if you'd like to wait," she said.

"Thank you," Finn replied. "That would be fine."

———

Kozlowski had a bad feeling about this. His stomach was churning, and he felt light-headed. It was probable that Dobson's murder had nothing to do with the lawyer's involvement with Salazar; the paper gave no details, so it could just as easily have been a random killing. People were murdered all the time. There didn't need to be a reason. There was a better than even chance it was nothing but bad luck and timing. Kozlowski didn't like those odds.

It was strange being back at headquarters. It had been over a year since he'd been drummed off the force. He'd taken a bullet in the knee in the line of duty, and the brass had pushed him into retirement. He was past his twenty, a full pensioner with disability to boot, and yet he'd wanted to keep doing his job. It was the job he'd been born to do. It was a job he was good at. But he was a pain in the ass to his superiors, and they'd used his injury to push him out.

It wasn't nearly as bad as he'd thought it would be, though. Finn kept him fairly busy, and there were a number of other law firms that recognized his competence, which led to some additional jobs from time to time. It was a second salary, what with his pension. Still, he missed being a cop, and he'd consciously avoided coming down to headquarters since he'd become a civilian. He still kept in touch with his friends on the force, and he used them to get information other investigators generally couldn't. But he hadn't been back in person. It felt strange, like being in your own house as a guest after you've sold it. Everything's pretty much the same, but now you have to ask permission to take a crap.

Kozlowski was over at the honor wall—the space reserved for the pictures of the men and women who'd given their lives in the line of duty. He'd never understood why it was called the honor wall. When he'd been a cop, he'd bled with every police officer who went down in the line. Respected their sacrifice. Contributed to the college funds for their kids. But honored their deaths? No. There was no honor in death, as far as he was concerned. The job was to catch the bad guys. The job was to kill them, if necessary, before they killed you or anyone else. You couldn't do that when you were dead, could you?

"Mr. Finn."

Kozlowski heard the voice and recognized it before he turned around.

"Detective Macintyre, right?" he heard Finn reply from a few feet away. "You're in charge of the Dobson investigation?"

"I am."

Kozlowski turned. "Mac," he said. He kept his voice even. No trace of friendship. No animosity, either.

"Kozlowski," Mac said. "You in for a visit?" His voice was even as well. He clearly hadn't grasped that Kozlowski and Finn were together.

Kozlowski nodded. "I guess so. You know we were working with Dobson on a case."

Macintyre said, "Salazar. I tried to warn him off the case. Looks like it didn't work. I had no idea you were involved too."

"You think this was related to what he was doing for Salazar?" Finn asked.

Macintyre looked around as though worried that someone might be listening. "Let's go somewhere we can talk," he said, ushering them toward a door. "We can use one of the interrogation rooms."

Finn fell into step next to the detective. Kozlowski followed. He knew the way. He'd never been in an interrogation room as anything but a cop. He wasn't looking forward to the experience, but it made sense, and he didn't have much of a choice.

Macintyre looked back at Kozlowski. "How's retirement?" he asked.

Kozlowski thought he heard a note of derision. He shrugged. "Could be worse."

"You were in, what? Twenty-three, twenty-four years?"

"Twenty-seven."

Macintyre shook his head. "Can't imagine being a civilian after all that time. Gotta suck, huh? Like having your balls cut off?"

Kozlowski considered his answer. "I don't know, Mac; I've never had my balls cut off. What's that like?"

Macintyre looked behind him again, this time with an exaggerated smile. Kozlowski had never seen anything more unnatural. The man's great hog jowls were pushed up to the sides of his face to make way for a display of dark, crooked teeth. "Good one. We need more guys like you still in the department. It's like no one has a sense of humor anymore. Shit, you can get written up these days for the slightest little comment. If the sensitivity squad even heard that 'no balls' comment, they'd probably have me up on sexism charges. It sucks."

"Tragic," Kozlowski deadpanned.

Finn cast a look over his shoulder now, but Kozlowski waved him off. Like it or not, this was no longer his territory. It was Macintyre's house now; he was just a visitor.

———◆———

"I'm glad you came in, Mr. Finn. You were on our list of people to talk to, so you saved me a trip," Macintyre said.

They were settled in an interrogation room on the second floor of the building. It was like thousands of other interrogation rooms in police stations around the country, only newer and cleaner. There was a sturdy, nondescript table in the center of the room, with four chairs pulled up around it. The walls were white and unadorned. On one wall was a large picture-sized mirror, the two-way kind. Finn was familiar with the setup.

"What can you tell me about Vincente Salazar's role in Mr. Dobson's murder?"

The question surprised Finn. That was probably the goal. There are several well-developed approaches to examining a potential witness. One is to draw information out slowly, to start the interrogation as a discussion, friendly and nonthreatening, and pull out bits and pieces of information like so many lengths of string from a poorly knit sweater. Sometimes the person being interrogated doesn't know what is happening until he's naked. Another method is to attack the witness head-on—ask the brutal questions right off the bat to put the person off balance. Off balance is a bad place for anyone to be when answering questions from the police.

Finn took a deep breath before answering. "I should probably make a few things clear, Detective," he started. He kept his voice genial but firm. "I represent Mr. Salazar, for good or for bad. I would like to be of whatever assistance I can be without violating my ethical obligations to my client. All that said, I have no reason to believe that Mr. Salazar had anything to do with Mr. Dobson's murder."

"That's bullshit, Counselor, and we both know it." Macintyre smiled for the second time that afternoon. Finn didn't like it when the man smiled. "If you have no reason to believe that Salazar has anything to do with this, then why are you here?"

It was a good question, and Finn didn't have a good answer. "As I said, I met with Dobson a number of times last week. Now he's dead. If there's any way I can help without compromising myself as an attorney, I want to do it." Macintyre looked at him. He was silent. He was waiting for Finn to give him more; sweating him out. It was another good technique. Finn continued. "You seem certain that Dobson's murder had something to do with Salazar. Maybe if you tell me why Salazar would have his own attorney killed, I'll have a better idea of what information might be useful."

Macintyre leaned back in his chair, considering it. "It was the way he was killed," he said.

Finn looked back at the detective. It was his turn to be silent; his turn to get more information. It worked.

Macintyre got up and walked out of the room, closing the door behind him. Finn looked at Kozlowski, who shrugged. A minute later, Macintyre returned carrying two manila folders. He laid one on the table in front of him, looked at Finn for a long moment, then pushed it over toward him.

Finn looked down at the folder and flipped it open. The image on top shocked him, almost made him puke. He wrenched his gaze away and looked at the floor. "Shit," he said quietly, holding his hand to his mouth, willing the nausea down.

Kozlowski leaned over and took a long look. He let a low whistle escape his lips.

Finn took a deep breath, like a diver getting ready to go under the surface. Then he pulled his head up and looked at the picture again.

It was Dobson, that was pretty clear, but only from the circumstances. The body in the picture was unrecognizable. It had been hacked to pieces. The head was barely hanging on to the body, and at least one arm was missing. The torso had been sliced and diced like nothing Finn had ever seen before. Several ribs, slashed and broken, jutted up from a mess of red-gray flesh, and Finn couldn't even tell whether it was the back of the body or the front he was looking at.

"Hell of a thing, isn't it?" Macintyre said. The words were sympathetic, but it seemed as though he was enjoying the difficulty with which Finn was flipping through the pictures. They were taken from different angles, but they showed the same pile of mutilated corpse.

"I don't understand," Finn said, his voice little more than a whisper. "Why?"

"Because that's what they do," Macintyre replied.

"Who?"

"VDS." Macintyre leaned back in his chair again, sucking the air through his teeth as though trying to free a piece of food from his last meal. "There was a similar incident a couple of years ago north of D.C. The gang's pretty strong down there, too. The feds had a line on an informant, and it looked like they were going to get enough to bring them down—the top guys, at least. Then the informant disappeared, along with his FBI handler. They were found a couple of days later in a tidal basin in Maryland. Same condition as Dobson. Worse, maybe, because the fish had had a couple of days to go at 'em." Macintyre leaned forward and picked up the top picture. "See these long gashes? The way the force of it not only cut through the skin and muscle but went clear through the ribs?"

Finn looked, but only for a moment before he had to turn away. Out of the corner of his eye, he saw Macintyre smirk.

"And here," the detective continued. "In this one, the blade split open the man's face. Three or four swipes there, tops, and yet most of the bone and skin's gone."

Finn didn't bother looking. "So what?"

"Machete," Kozlowski answered for Macintyre.

The detective gave a look like Kozlowski had spoiled his party.

"That's right. Machete." He glared at Kozlowski. "I keep forgetting, you used to be a cop."

"Yeah, well, you got a lot on your mind, I'm sure," Kozlowski replied.

The staring match continued until Macintyre broke it off and turned back to Finn. "You see, the machete is VDS's weapon of choice, particularly for something like this. They'll use guns when they're running drugs or conducting everyday business, but when they're taking someone out specifically, to make a point, they like to use a machete."

"Why?" Finn croaked out.

Macintyre shrugged. "It's some sort of macho South American thing. Scares people. Maybe it's tradition. Maybe they're just sick, psychotic bastards. Who the fuck knows? What we do know is that your boy Dobson, here, was targeted by them."

Finn took a deep breath, still trying to recover from the shock of the photographs. He had to think. None of this was making any sense. "Fine," he said at last. "Let's assume you're right. Let's assume that Dobson was killed by this gang. How does that tie it all to Salazar?"

"Like I tried to tell you the other day—like I tried to convince Dobson the other day—Salazar's one of them. Maybe very high up. We know he was the doctor they used whenever they got shot or stabbed when he was on the outside. Plus, he had the connections in El Salvador when he was there. That's why he fled."

"How do you know that?" Finn asked.

Macintyre pulled out the second folder and opened it, holding up a set of pictures showing Salazar in deep conversation with several heavily tattooed men. "Look at the markings," he said. "VDS, all the way. There's no doubt he's tied in. We never could have made a case based solely on these, but there's no question who he was with."

Finn looked closely at the pictures and thought about it. "That it?"

Macintyre laughed like he knew he was being hustled, but he played along. "*That it?*" he mimicked Finn. He laughed again. "No, that's not it, but it would be enough. This Dobson guy kept very careful track of his hours. Entered them into his firm computer every day, even remotely from his home when he needed to. Turns out, over the last week, the Salazar case was all he was working on. Looks like day and night—up to eighteen, nineteen hours a day a couple of times. Right up to the time he got killed."

Finn thought about that. Then he shook his head. "It doesn't make sense. What's your theory? Dobson was trying to get Salazar out of prison. If Salazar is VDS, why would they kill him? Why would Salazar order a hit?"

"Oh, I'm not saying for sure that Salazar ordered the hit. Maybe some of his homies did it because they don't want him out. Maybe they don't want him reasserting himself on the outside. Or maybe Dobson learned something Salazar and his boys didn't want him to know. Maybe he found out the truth and they had to waste him. Who knows? All I'm sure of is that Salazar is mixed up in this somehow." Macintyre leaned forward. "Now, Mr. Finn, I'd like some answers from you."

Finn shook his head.

"No?"

Finn shook his head again.

Macintyre folded his arms. "Seems like there's been a lot of information flowing here, but it's all been in one direction. Seems like that's not right."

"I've got to talk to my client," Finn replied. "I'm sorry."

Macintyre scratched his ear. "Funny, that's what Dobson said, too. I laid out Salazar's connections to VDS, and he said he was sorry, too." He picked up the photographs and waved them in Finn's face. "How sorry do you think he is now? You want some friendly advice? Stay away from this. Tell me everything you know, and then get as far away from Salazar as you can. He's bad news." He waved the pictures of Dobson's mutilated remains at Finn again. "How much more proof than this do you need?"

Finn shook his head a third time.

"So that's the way it's gonna be?" There was a thin, evil smile on Macintyre's lips. Finn still didn't like it when the man smiled.

"That's the way it has to be," Finn replied.

Chapter Fifteen

IT WAS NEARLY THREE O'CLOCK when Finn pulled his car out of the lot at police headquarters, Kozlowski sardined in next to him. Finn had enough time to get up to Billerica to talk to Salazar. This time, however, he would talk to him alone. Regular visiting hours would be over, and Finn would have access to Salazar only in his role as the man's attorney. Kozlowski would not be permitted in. As a result, they decided that it made sense to drop the private detective back at the office so he could help Lissa get the investigation under way.

"Thoughts?" Finn asked as they pulled out onto Melnea Cass Boulevard.

"Plenty," Kozlowski replied.

Finn spun the wheel to avoid a pothole larger than his tiny car. "I'd love to hear some," he prodded. Kozlowski was the best at what he did, but Finn sometimes found it aggravating how tight-lipped he was.

"You didn't tell me Macintyre talked to you last week."

"Yes, I did," Finn said. "I said, as I was leaving the courthouse, some cop came up to tell us to keep Salazar in jail."

"*Some cop,*" Kozlowski repeated. "Not the same thing as Macintyre."

Finn looked across at Kozlowski. "Does it matter?"

Kozlowski looked out the passenger window. "It might."

129

"You know him, I take it."

Kozlowski nodded. "We worked together a few times way back, twenty years, maybe more. Been a long time since we had close contact to speak of, but we were in the same station house for a while."

"Good guy?"

"Only if you prefer assholes."

Finn considered this. "I do hang out with you quite a bit."

"Funny."

"You think it's a coincidence that he was assigned to the Dobson case?" It seemed like a remarkable coincidence to Finn, and it had him concerned for some unidentifiable reason.

Kozlowski sighed. "Officially, cases are assigned randomly—unless there's some known connection to an ongoing investigation. In reality, if a senior detective has an interest in a particular case, it ain't hard to mess with the system."

"So where does that leave us?"

"In limbo, I guess. Everything he says about Salazar could be true. He could turn out to be one bad fucker. That happens, you need to try like hell to get off this case, 'cause it's gonna end badly one way or another. On the other hand, from what I know about Mac, I can't take his word as gospel. He's got some tarnish on the badge, you know what I mean?"

"You think he's dirty?"

Kozlowski tilted his head. "Don't know. But I'm not sure he's entirely clean. The last time I worked with him, he bent the rules. Not badly. Not nearly as badly as I'd seen others do, but I tried not to get assigned with him again. Once you start bending some of the rules, it gets a hell of a lot easier to bend some others. I didn't want to be there if he asked me to back him up."

Finn focused on the road as he pulled out onto Storrow Drive, headed east toward Charlestown. It was just past three o'clock, and the sun was already settling along the horizon behind them, on the other side of the Charles River. The snow had let up, and it had turned into one of those wonderfully crisp, cold days of early winter, with the sky so clear that the sunlight off the fresh snow covering the city was difficult to look at. The MG was churning hard to kick out enough heat to warm the little convertible, but Finn could still see his breath, and he wasn't sure whether the frost on the windshield was on the inside or the outside. He shivered as he drove, thinking about his upcoming encounter with Salazar. It felt like he was getting himself into a mess, and he was tempted to take Macintyre's advice—cut and run, and leave it all to be cleaned up by someone else. After all, Lissa was right: He hadn't wanted the case in first place.

Except that he had. Dobson was a smart enough lawyer to know which of Finn's buttons to push to get him involved. Dobson had been a believer. In law school, the professors had talked about the law in terms of justice. Perched high in their ivory towers, they had preached the gospel of the law as a tool for social good, for correcting the world's inequities. Most of the other students, fresh from their boarding schools and four-year-college campuses, had bought into it. Not Finn. Finn had spent his life in the real world, and he knew that justice was an illusion. The victory over Slocum had been sweet and satisfying, but it hadn't been justice. The real world was too gray for justice to play much of a role.

And yet, as he'd sat in law school classes, snickering internally at the naïveté of those preachers, there was a part of him that wanted to believe it. Like a kid reading a comic book, he wanted to live in a world of right and wrong, where victory didn't mean winning only for himself but for some greater principle as well. It was to that part of him that Dobson had appealed. It was that part of him that was murmuring in the back of his head right now, whispering that this was his chance—maybe his only chance—to find a little justice. If not for Vincente Salazar, at least for Mark Dobson.

He guided his car off Storrow, down Monsignor O'Brien Highway, around three corners, and skidded to a stop in front of the office. Kozlowski opened the passenger door and hauled himself out. He leaned over and looked at Finn. "Good luck," he said.

"Any last words of advice?"

Kozlowski frowned. "Be careful" was all he could muster. Then he closed the door.

Finn pulled out and pointed his car northwest, toward Billerica. The sun had fallen below the horizon, and only a pale, thin glow was visible in the distance. It felt as though the temperature had already fallen another ten degrees.

It felt to Finn like it was about to get even colder.

Chapter Sixteen

FINN PACED BACK and forth in the interview room at Billerica, his footsteps a full cadence behind his heartbeat. He tried to work through what he would say to Salazar—what he would ask him—but it was useless. His thoughts were coming too quickly and defied structure.

He heard explosions of steel on steel from deep within the prison, as doors were slammed open and closed, the sounds coming steadily closer, until the door to the interview room swung open and Salazar, bound at the wrists and ankles, was escorted into the room by two heavyset guards. He stood by the doorway, a look of surprise on his face at seeing Finn. Then he shuffle-stepped over toward the plastic chair set in front of the table in the center of the room.

The guards watched their shackled prisoner sit, then gave the lawyer a quick glance. "Fifteen minutes," one of them said. They turned and walked out, slamming the door behind them, leaving Finn alone with Salazar.

The two of them stared at each other. Neither moved. Finn stood several feet behind the table where Salazar sat, one hand partially raised, as if he'd been cryogenically frozen in midspeech. Salazar's head was tilted slightly as he regarded Finn with a mixture of curiosity and suspicion. Finn wondered who would be the first to break the silence.

"Mr. Finn," Salazar said at last. "I was under the impression that you were no longer interested in my case. I was told you no longer found it easy enough for you. Have you changed your mind?"

It took a moment for Finn to respond. "Maybe," he said. He still didn't move.

Salazar placed his cuffed hands on the table. "Mr. Dobson said you'd given up hope. He said you were out."

"When did you talk to him?"

"Mark?"

"Dobson. Yes."

Salazar frowned. "The days sometimes run into each other here. What is today? Monday?"

"Yes."

Salazar went through a mental calculation. "It must have been last Friday, then."

"You haven't talked to him since?"

"No."

Finn gave a skeptical look.

"You can ask him if you don't believe me, Mr. Finn," Salazar replied.

"No, I can't," Finn said. "That's why I'm here."

Salazar looked at Finn, tilting his head farther in confusion. "I don't understand."

"He's dead." Finn watched Salazar's reaction closely, scrutinizing his facial expression. It revealed nothing. Salazar stared straight at Finn, his eyes never twitching, his face granite. He didn't flinch, though Finn thought he sensed the man's breathing quicken.

"How?" was all he said.

"Butchered," Finn replied. After a pause, he added, "With a machete."

Again Salazar showed no reaction, no emotion. He sat still, and Finn had no indication of what was going on in the man's head. Finally, he nodded, then stood. "Thank you for coming," he said to Finn. He walked to the door. "Guard!" he shouted.

"What are you doing?" Finn asked.

"Going back to my cell."

Finn had no idea what to say. "That's it?" he demanded. "'Thank you for coming, I'm going back to my cell'? That's all you have to say to me?"

"What more would you like me to say?"

"I want a goddamned explanation!"

The door opened from the outside, and one of the guards stood there, looking at the convict and his lawyer.

"I'm not through with my client!" Finn yelled.

The guard looked both annoyed and amused as he turned his attention to Salazar, raising an eyebrow.

After a moment, Salazar nodded at the guard, who stepped back out and closed the door behind him. "I thought you were no longer interested in my case, Mr. Finn. I thought you'd resigned."

"Yeah, me, too. Only I never filled out the paperwork, so we're stuck with each other, at least for now."

Salazar mulled that over. "I appreciate your dedication, Mr. Finn. But please, for both of our sakes, go back to your office and fill out the paperwork."

"Why? I may be willing to help, and there's no one standing in line behind me. Without me, you die here in jail. You really think it's smart to dismiss me so quickly?"

"You sound like Mark Dobson now," Salazar said. "Look what happened to him. I can't take that responsibility." He shook his head. "I've already survived a lifetime in here. I can certainly do a few more. There's nothing I have left for them to take. Thank you again for coming, but you can't help me."

"Thanks, but I like to make those kinds of decisions myself," Finn replied. "You don't need to worry about me. I can take care of myself."

Salazar gave a thin, pained smile. "That's what Mr. Dobson said also."

Finn folded his arms. "You know who killed him, don't you? You know who killed Dobson."

Salazar took a deep, reluctant breath and nodded. "Yes, Mr. Finn, I know who killed him."

"Tell me," Finn demanded. "I only knew him briefly, but he had balls and brains enough to drag me into this shit. That means something to me. I want to know who killed him."

Salazar stared through Finn, his shoulders slumped. He looked like a man in agony. "Very well," he said. "It was me."

Finn looked back at Salazar, not comprehending. "What?"

"That's right, Mr. Finn. I killed Mark Dobson."

———◊———

Kozlowski stood in the doorway to Finn's main office. Lissa Krantz was sitting at her small desk, pecking furiously at her keyboard as she stared at her computer screen. She was engrossed in her task, and she didn't notice him enter the room. He watched her, lost in his own thoughts.

Finn had just been messing with his head, he was sure. There was no chance that someone like Lissa would have any interest in someone like him. It wouldn't make any sense. And yet . . .

He wasn't sure he'd ever looked closely at her before. He knew she was attractive—and young. That was probably why he'd never taken a good look. For him, she was like an expensive car: He knew a Maserati was a fine-looking automobile, but he also knew he'd never drive one, so he'd never bothered to examine one close up.

Now here he was, standing in the doorway of the office, admiring this attractive young woman, appreciating her looks for the first time. Strangely, he felt self-conscious. He shook himself in annoyance. Fuck Finn.

He cleared his throat as he stepped fully into the room. Lissa turned and looked at him briefly, then went back to her work. "What's going on, Koz?" she asked in a bored tone.

"Nothing," he replied. All of a sudden he was noticing everything that came out of his mouth, and it sounded dull-witted to him. He cursed himself. "Do we have a fingerprint expert yet?" Perhaps if he turned the conversation toward the Salazar investigation, he would feel more comfortable.

"I've got some calls out," she said. "There's a guy named Jim Brannagh who's been doing some freelancing since he left the fingerprint lab and started teaching at B.U. He looks promising. And Finn gave me Kelley LeBlanc's name, so I've got a message in to her. She's younger, but she spent fifteen years doing this stuff for the cops."

"They both worked for the BPD, right?" he asked.

"Yeah," she replied. "We need someone with some decent credibility, and anyone local who's any good came out of the goddamned department."

"We've gotta go outside Boston for this," Kozlowski commented, trying to sound authoritative. "There's too much of a conflict if we stay here. We probably won't get the full scoop if we use someone local with ties to the fingerprint unit."

"Thin blue line?" Lissa asked.

Kozlowski nodded.

"Still?"

"Grim, isn't it? But it's still there. Cops protect each other, especially cops they know, or cops in the same department."

"But these people are retired."

"Doesn't matter. Once a cop, always a cop."

She turned to look at him. "Where does that leave you?"

Kozlowski felt himself squirm under her scrutiny. "What do you mean?"

"You were a cop. Would you protect other cops?"

He shifted his stance uncomfortably. "Depends, I guess."

"On what?"

He shrugged. "On the situation. On the cop."

"What happened to that black-and-white view of morality you were talking to Finn about earlier? Is that just for other people?"

"No, it's not. But it's a little different for cops. It's like being in the military. You're out there in a war zone, and people are trying to kill you. The only ones you know have your back are the other cops you work with. You start messing with that trust, and the world becomes a very dangerous place very quickly. That's drilled into you, and it's tough to get out."

"So? Is it out of you yet?"

He tried a smile. "I think so, but I'm a little bit of an oddity."

She turned back to the computer. "No fucking argument here," she mumbled.

"What?"

"Nothing."

Neither of them said anything and the silence weighed on Kozlowski in a manner it never had before. "Anyway," he said, "I've got some thoughts on who we might use if we go outside Boston on the fingerprint issue."

"I'm all ears."

"I've got a list back in my office. I'll get it." He turned and started back through the door, paused, started into his office again, and then stepped back out once again. He looked over at her. "I've got a couple things I have to finish up, and it's starting to get late. If you want, we could grab a drink in a little while. Maybe talk about it over dinner."

She looked at him again.

"I mean, only if you want. You may have other things going on, and we can always get to it tomorrow. But if you want . . ." He heard his voice trail off. He felt intimidated. It was a bizarre experience for him.

Her expression betrayed her surprise. "Sure," she said. "What the fuck, right?"

"Good. An hour or so?"

"Sounds good."

"I'll come get you."

"From the other room?"

"Right. From the other room. I'll pop my head in."

"Good. I'll see you then."

"Okay." He turned and walked back to his office. It was only four paces, but it felt like a journey. Once safely in his own space, he rested against the wall. He felt exhausted and confused, and yet he couldn't ever remember feeling quite so alive.

"I killed him," Salazar repeated. They were seated at the table in the attorney visiting room, and the convict's head was in his hands, his elbows resting on the chipped-wood surface. "I might as well have swung the machete myself."

"What happened?"

"I wanted out so badly. Too badly. I wanted to sit with my daughter without guards watching me every time I gave her a hug. I wanted to sit on the back porch of my brother's house—I've seen it in pictures and in my dreams—and talk quietly with him about medicine. I try to keep up with many of the new procedures and treatments, but it's not the same reading about in journals as it is living with it." He ripped his hands through his long hair. "I wanted it all so badly, I was willing to put Dobson's life in danger. He was the only person outside of my family who has ever believed in me—in my innocence—and I got him killed."

Finn watched Salazar, trying to determine whether he was acting. "I was at the police department earlier today," he said. "They blame you."

Salazar looked up at him. "Well, that's the first time I've ever agreed with the police," he said. "I suppose there's a first for everything."

"No," Finn said. "They don't think you got him killed; they think you *had* him killed."

Salazar rubbed his eyes in disbelief. "Why?"

Finn leaned back. "They say you are a member of VDS. A leader, in fact."

"That's a load of *mierda*. Bullshit. Did they give you any proof?"

"They had pictures," Finn said.

"Of?"

"You with VDS gang members. You looked like you were conferencing pretty seriously about something."

"No," Salazar said. "It's not true."

"I saw the pictures."

"Of course you did. And I'm sure they had pictures of me with VDS. I treated them. I was the closest thing to a real doctor to everyone in the neighborhood. That included VDS gang members. I treated them when they got sick. When they got shot. When they got pregnant. It wouldn't be very hard to have pictures of me with them."

"You treated these scum?" Finn's tone was indignant.

"I treat everyone," Salazar said, matching Finn's outrage. "I told you that. I treated both sides in El Salvador. I treat the criminals in this godforsaken place—no matter what their crimes. And yes, I treated the 'scum' in VDS. It is my place to heal, not to judge."

"But these people—"

"Exactly, Mr. Finn. *People*. These are people. I'd treat the police officers who blinded my daughter if they were injured." Salazar rattled the chains around his wrists as he wrung his hands. "But think about it: Even if what the police say is true, even if I was a member of VDS, why would I have my own lawyer killed? He was trying to get me out of this place. What possible motive would I have to get him killed?"

"I asked the police that," Finn admitted.

"And did they have any kind of answer?"

"Not one that made any sense to me."

"Because it could make no sense," Salazar said. "I will blame myself for Dobson's death for the rest of my life, but not because I wanted it. Only because I let him put himself in danger. In fact, I led him into danger. Of that, I am truly responsible."

"How did you lead him into danger?"

"I told him too much."

"What did you tell him?" Finn asked.

Salazar smiled bitterly. "God might forgive my mistake once, Mr. Finn. I'm not sure I'll be welcome in heaven if I greet Saint Peter with your blood mixed with Dobson's on my hands."

"I can help you, though," Finn protested. "If you tell me what I need to know."

Salazar shook his head. "It's too dangerous."

Finn gave it some thought. Then he leaned forward in his chair and stared intently at Salazar. "Fine, don't tell me," he said. "But am I safe in assuming that whatever you told him had something to do with VDS?"

Salazar considered the question before answering. "Yes," he said at last.

"And it has something to do with why you're in here?"

Salazar hesitated. "I think so. I don't know for sure. I only have what I've pieced together in here over the past fifteen years. It's bits and scraps of rumors and gossip, but it all fits."

The two men looked at each other, measuring. "You were framed, right?" Finn asked. "This wasn't just a mistake. It wasn't just bad luck. Someone did this to you on purpose."

Salazar's expression hardened. "There's no such thing as a mistake. Not like this, and not in my case."

Finn closed his eyes and thought. "It couldn't have happened without someone on the inside," he said, as much to himself as to Salazar. "Cops."

"It couldn't have happened without cops," Salazar agreed.

"Do you have any thoughts about who it might have been? Any names you can give me?"

"No," Salazar said. He looked closely at Finn. "But you have some, don't you?"

"One. But it's only a suspicion."

"Maybe it's better that you not tell me until you're sure."

"That was my thought." Finn stood up and walked to the door. "Guard!" he called.

Salazar looked at him. "What are you going to do?"

Finn turned. "I'm your lawyer," he said. "I'm going to do my job."

"I can't be responsible for putting more people in danger."

"You're not responsible for anything," Finn replied. "You didn't tell me whatever it was that got Dobson killed, did you? I'm not going to focus on his murder right now. I'm going to prove that you didn't attack Madeline Steele. I'm not going after VDS, am I?"

"What about the police? You're going after them?"

Finn smiled. "I've dealt with cops before."

The door opened. "You done now?" the guard asked.

Finn turned and looked at him. "No. I'm just getting started, actually." He stepped past the guard and headed out toward the prison's exit.

Chapter Seventeen

TOM KOZLOWSKI STOOD bent over the sink in the men's room at the Ritz-Carlton, splashing cold water on his face. He let the streams drip from his nose and chin before he stood and regarded his reflection in the mirror.

What the hell was he doing here? What was he thinking? That was what the image staring back at him was asking. Who was he trying to fool?

Lissa Krantz was the answer. He was trying to fool Lissa Krantz, and what was most disturbing was that it seemed to be working.

The words had come out of his mouth so casually, as if he uttered them all the time. He'd walked out of his office to see whether she was ready to go grab a bite and talk about fingerprint experts in the Salazar case. She was, and he'd grabbed his coat. But before he could get to the door, she'd asked the question: one that, against all logic, he somehow hadn't expected. "Where do you want to go?"

He'd been startled. He never would have admitted out loud that he'd panicked, but deep down he knew that was what had happened. They always went to O'Doul's, around the corner from the office. Who would have thought there was any other option? He answered without thought or hesitation. "How about the Ritz?"

As much as the answer had surprised him, he knew where it came from. The old Ritz-Carlton was on the corner of Arlington and Boylston, right next to the Public Garden. It had been renamed the Taj recently, but to true Bostonians it would always be the Ritz. It was one of those special places that existed for other people, not for him. He'd passed by it often on his circuit of the Common in search of inner peace. He'd stood by the window and seen the revelry during the holiday season, but he'd always been on the outside looking in. If there was ever a chance for him to dip his toe into that world, even for just a moment, it was now, with this woman.

And now here he was. She'd raised an eyebrow at his suggestion. "Holy fuck," she'd said. "I mean, that'd be nice."

Climbing into his boxy Crown Victoria, they'd left her BMW behind and cruised across the Charles River. They'd circled around Beacon Hill and the Common and found a parking spot on Commonwealth. Walking through the door to the dining room, Kozlowski had felt surreal, as though he'd been put in someone else's body—someone else's life.

The food was delicious, he was sure, but he hardly tasted a thing. He was so focused on her. The conversation had started out stilted and uncomfortable, but he'd brought some notes on various fingerprint experts, and once the ice was broken, they moved the conversation from the professional to the casual to the personal. It was intoxicating. He was still convinced that she was just being nice to him and that there was no chance of progressing past dinner, but it was still one of the best evenings he could ever remember.

After dinner, he'd forked over half a month's income, and they'd headed down to the bar. It was a legendary spot, with deep carpeting and luxuriously upholstered seats looking out onto Arlington's wide thoroughfare and across the street to the Public Garden. Bostonians hurried by the window in a Dickensian swirl, dodging the snowflakes with their packages of early holiday cheer, and Kozlowski began to understand for the first time why some people worked so hard for a taste of the good life.

He took a soft towel from the bathroom attendant and wiped his face, then dug through his pockets for a dollar to drop in the tip jar. Tipping another man just because he'd taken a leak was too weird for him to think much about, but other than that, it had been a truly memorable night.

At the door, he paused and sucked in a lungful of reality. *Just don't do anything stupid now,* he told himself. A single clumsy, unwanted advance from him could turn one of the best experiences of his life into one of the worst. Better, he thought, to be satisfied later with what the evening had been than to regret what it hadn't.

He blew out his breath, opened the door, and stepped back into the lobby of the hotel.

———

Lissa sat in the bar, waiting for Kozlowski to return. She leaned back and let the soft chair swallow her. It was set perpendicular to the picture window, allowing her equally advantageous views of the street outside and the scene in the bar. It was the interior view that fascinated her most. Confident creatures in impeccable dress moved in and out of the bar, pulling apart, then jelling like quicksilver in intimate groupings, bubbling on carefree waves, as though no ugliness could reach inside the place.

She picked up her drink—a thimbleful of Grans-Fassian that had cost forty dollars—and took a sip. It was good, she had to admit. She'd have felt guilty for ordering it had Kozlowski not insisted, and had he not ordered an even more expensive taste of vintage port. He had surprised her throughout the evening. She was used to this type of place; it was the kind of spot many of her wealthy, more boring dates took her, but she had gotten a look at Finn's office finances once, and she knew what Kozlowski made. In an odd way, the fact that he couldn't afford the evening was one of the things that made it special.

She saw him re-enter the bar, and she stifled a laugh at how out of place he looked. All the other men there were cleaned and pressed and seemed so polished they glowed. Physically, the majority of them fit into two basic categories: the fat and the effete. Here and there an ostentatious bulge of gym-fed muscle stood out, but it was painfully fake. There was nothing fake about Kozlowski's physique, and she found charm in the brown wool blazer she thought might be back in style in a few years if it held together that long. He might have been handsome in the heavy-browed style of 1940s Hollywood if not for the thick scar that split the right side of his face from the corner of his eye to the bottom of his ear. Even that, though, she felt gave him character and sex appeal.

In all, she was certain he was the most attractive man in the place.

He moved through the crowd, bumping several self-absorbed men out of the way, drawing disgruntled looks. But even those who were clearly annoyed kept their mouths shut after a brief evaluation.

At last he made it to their table and settled into his chair across from her. He picked up his own drink and took a sip. "Sorry about that."

"About what?"

He shrugged. "Leaving you?"

"To go to the bathroom?" She laughed. "What were the options?"

"I know, I just—"

"I didn't seem to wilt," she assured him.

"No chance of that, I guess," he conceded. "You seem like a survivor."

"I guess. I've certainly survived worse than being abandoned in the Ritz. Anyway, what is it they say, whatever doesn't kill you makes you stronger?" She raised her glass. "So here's to getting stronger."

He raised his own glass and touched it to hers. "To getting stronger."

They both sipped their drinks, looking at each other across the table. She leaned back in her chair again and surveyed the room once more. "So, tell me something, Koz," she began.

"What?"

"Do you come here often?"

He turned in his chair to take a look around the bar himself as he considered the question. "I suppose that depends on how you define 'often,'" he replied.

"How about ever?"

He looked back at her. "Oh. Okay, if you define it like that, then no, I don't come here often. You?"

"A few times," she admitted. "But I'm not sure I've ever enjoyed it as much as I have tonight. One more question?"

"Okay."

"Does anyone ever call you anything other than Koz?"

"Sure. I'm usually called much worse."

"You know what I mean."

He looked down at his hands. "I had a sister once. When I was a kid. She was a couple years older than me. She called me Tom."

"Not anymore?"

"She died."

"Oh, shit. I'm sorry." Lissa wanted to bite off her tongue. "I'm really sorry. I didn't know."

"Don't worry about it. It was a long time ago. Car accident. She was sixteen. She was just crossing the street, and some guy came around a corner too fast. They say she didn't suffer."

"Oh. I feel like an asshole now."

"Don't."

"They ever catch the guy?"

"Yeah, but it wasn't much of a catch. He stopped. Young guy—early thirties—driving home to three kids and a wife. Maybe he'd had a drink or two after work. Not enough to make a difference, and this was

147

before people looked too closely at the drinking-and-driving thing. He walked."

Lissa shook her head. "I don't know if I could've lived with him walking. I mean, I've never had any brothers or sisters—or any decent family to speak of—but if I did, and I cared about them, I don't know what I would have done."

"It was an accident," Kozlowski disagreed. "Sometimes these days we forget that accidents do happen. Besides, the guy did a pretty good job of punishing himself. He was a wreck over it—lost his job, got divorced. I lost track of him years ago, but it wasn't pretty. I wonder about him every once in a while. I hope he didn't eat a gun; it wasn't really his fault."

She considered this. "You're not exactly normal, are you?"

He smiled at her. "What tipped you off?"

She looked at him without answering. Then she tossed back the last of her drink. "Pay the bill, okay?"

He looked disappointed as he glanced at his watch. "I suppose you're right. We should probably both be getting home. I had a good time, though. Thanks."

"Too bad I'm not sleepy. I live a few blocks from here; I was kinda hoping you'd come up for a quick nightcap. Seems like the least I can do after you picked up the tab." She watched him go white. It amused her.

"You sure?" he asked.

She folded her arms in mock indignation. "That's the first time anyone's ever questioned my sincerity following an invitation to my apartment."

"No, no, no," he stammered. "I'm not questioning. It's just that . . . Are you sure?"

"Koz, do me a favor, okay? Pay the bill and shut the fuck up." She stood up and took his hand as he tossed a handful of cash on the table, more than enough to cover the bill. Then the two of them walked hand in hand out into the street.

———— ◆ ————

Vincente Salazar sat in his cell after lights-out. His mind was racing. There were too many variables in play, and he felt powerless sitting in the dark with no way of evaluating the risks as they unfolded. He needed a way to stay informed so the mistakes with Dobson wouldn't be repeated.

He glanced at his watch. Ten thirty. He looked up just as the guard passed by his cell. Consistency was one of the few comforts of the prison environment. Schedules were set, and schedules were kept. Like the trains in Nazi Germany: no variation, no exception. There were occasional outbursts of mayhem—fights, murders, rapes—but they happened relatively infrequently, and they were dealt with as internal matters, for the most part, with swift and brutal punishment meted out by the prison administration: no trials, no appeals. Beyond those circumstances, though, life was regimented. For eighteen hours a day, they were in lockdown. If you could survive the other six, doing time was mainly an exercise in keeping your sanity in the face of mind-numbing boredom. Salazar was strong enough to deal with the boredom.

He looked at his watch again. Ten thirty-five. He heard the guard's footsteps as he passed the cell again, heading back to his station. It would be two more hours before another guard would patrol the area.

Salazar reached under his mattress and pulled out a small bundle wrapped in a T-shirt. He untied the shirt and pulled out a disposable cell phone. Cellular technology had become a staple of prison contraband, ranking with heroin and sex as marquee items in the currency of the underground jailhouse economy. He seldom used his phone, but he kept it for emergencies. This qualified.

Dialing, he still wasn't sure what should be done.

"Hello?" the voice came from the other end of the line.

"It's Vincente," he said.

"Vincente! How are you? Is everything okay?"

"Fine. I have to talk quickly. The other lawyer—Finn—he's going to stay on the case."

"Even after Dobson was killed?"

"Yes."

"Brave man. Stupid, but brave."

"Yes," Salazar agreed. "We need to watch him."

"By 'we,' I assume you mean me."

"Given the circumstances—"

"It will be difficult."

"I know," Salazar conceded. "But we must. There are too many risks. I want you to take care of it yourself."

It took a moment for the voice to answer. "I will."

"Thank you." Salazar hung up the phone. He wouldn't sleep that night; there were still too many things that could go wrong—too much that was out of his control. Now, at least, he would have eyes on the outside.

———⋄———

Kozlowski had a good notion that Lissa Krantz had some money. She exhibited subtle telltale signs. Her clothes were always the latest styles; she drove an expensive car; her nails and hair were always perfectly kept. That kind of maintenance took cash, and Finn wasn't paying her enough to keep her in that kind of lifestyle, so she had to have some other money elsewhere.

Nothing had prepared him for her apartment, though, and once he saw it, he realized that he'd vastly underestimated her financial resources. It took up the entire top floor of one of the grand town houses on Beacon Street overlooking the Charles River—prime real estate in one of the world's most expensive cities. There were two bedrooms and an office that was overrun with boxes and papers and mess. The rest of the place was immaculate, and he guessed that someone other than Lissa came in to keep it that way. It was expensively decorated, and a wide carved staircase swept up from the center of the living room to a sizable roof house opening onto a private deck that had to be over a thousand square feet. That was where they were, out on the roof in the freezing cold, when he poured the expensive bottle of Chablis she'd given him to open.

He put the bottle down on the snow-covered Italian wrought-iron table and tipped his glass to her. She returned the gesture. Neither of them drank.

He walked around the perimeter of the deck, the icy crust of the snow crunching beneath his feet. It was a spectacular panoramic view. To the north, he could look out over the esplanade, across the river to the Cambridge shore. To the south, he could look down past the Public Garden to the Common. To the west, an endless string of similarly privileged roof decks stretched out toward the Fens.

He returned to her and leaned against the wall of the roof house. "Nice spot," he commented.

"Thanks."

"You'll warn me if a helicopter is about to land, right?"

"You'd hear it coming." She walked over to him, standing close enough to start his heart racing.

"Seriously, what's a place like this go for? Three million? More?"

"Does it matter?" She moved even closer, placing her wineglass on top of a planter that hung off the house. She took his glass from him, putting it down next to hers.

"It's gotta matter to someone, otherwise places like this wouldn't exist." He was back on his heels, leaning his head farther and farther away, the closer she came. He looked over her shoulder, avoiding eye contact.

She moved her head to the side, into his line of vision, and he ducked back the other way. She bobbed and weaved with him to force him to look at her. "What the fuck is it?" she asked. "Is it the apartment?"

"There's no way around the fact that we're used to different things," he said.

"I could sell it."

"No doubt. And make a killing, I'm sure."

"What do you want me to say? My father was a very wealthy man before he died. That's most of what I know about him, for all he was around to deal with me before he died. My mother and I don't speak. I'm not this goddamned apartment, and this goddamned apartment isn't me. You think I wouldn't trade this to have grown up differently?"

"It's not the apartment," he said, still avoiding her eyes.

"What is it, then?" she asked, leaning in even farther. Her voice was quiet now, raspy and breathless. "Is it me?"

He shrugged, avoiding her touch.

"What is it?"

He looked at her finally. "You could do better."

She continued moving in. "I've done worse." She kissed him on the cheek, and he sucked in a chest full of frozen air.

"You may kill me, you know that?"

She smiled. "Maybe." She was up on her toes, and her lips slid across his cheek toward his mouth. Her hands were on his chest. "I don't think so, though." She kissed him. His defenses were crumbling, but he still couldn't bring himself to kiss her back. Maybe he was afraid of hurting her, he thought. In his heart, he knew that wasn't it.

Gradually, his muscles relaxed as she continued to kiss him. Whatever fight had been in his body ebbed away, and he drew her in closer to him. Her legs straddled his knee, and he could feel her moving against him. He broke away from her kiss with one final effort and looked deep into her eyes. Then he smiled. "You will kill me," he assured her.

"I'll take my chances," she replied, looking back at him. It was the most erotic look he'd ever seen, full of longing, and desire, and need. She leaned in close and kissed his cheek again. Then she whispered into his ear, "Besides, whatever doesn't kill you only makes you stronger."

Mac walked from the kitchen to the living room in his little house in Quincy off Wollaston Beach. Most of the lights were off; his path was illuminated by the blue flickering of the television. It was tuned to a recording of the Celtics pregame from earlier that evening. He was wearing a dirty T-shirt and his boxer shorts and was carrying a pizza box heavy with a meat lover's special from the local Italian joint on the strip. He hadn't bothered to pull the shades; fuck his neighbors. If they wanted to look in, they could see what they could see. What did he care?

Sad to say, this was now his idea of a perfect evening: a pizza, his recliner, and his beloved Celts. To be sure, the team was a shadow of its former greatness. Back in the day, it had been a team of champions that an old-timer like Mac could be proud of. Bird, McHale, Ainge. In a league overrun with ghetto blasters, the Celtics had proved that a bunch of old white guys could still dominate by playing the game the way it was meant to be played—as a team. They didn't need flash to win. Show up, do your work, get the job done. To Mac, that was what the Celtics had been about. And the epic battles between the Celtics were about more than Boston versus L.A., more even than east versus west. They were about old versus new; work time versus showtime; white versus black. And the Celtics won more often than not. Those were the days, he thought with a pang of longing.

Now the Celtics were just another team. For Mac's money, the decline had started when they put their future in the hands of a coke addict who took his signing bonus right out onto the street and blew his heart open in an overdose. Served them right, really. You get away from your roots, and God will smack you in the head, remind you who's boss. No big surprise there—that's the way Mac saw it. He still loved the team, but it wasn't the same. It would never be the same.

And so it was with a sense of resignation that he plopped himself down with the pizza balanced on what little lap remained in the ongoing battle with his bulging midriff. The tip-off had just taken place, and he'd just taken his first bite, when the phone rang.

"Fuck," he said out loud. He reached over, mouth full, and grabbed the receiver. "Yeah?" he grunted.

"Salazar still has a lawyer," the voice said.

"No shit," Mac replied. "He's entitled. It's in the Constitution."

"He can't get out of prison. You know that."

"No judge is gonna let him out. Certainly not Cavanaugh. Not with what he did. Not with the shit they've got."

"That's not good enough."

"Fuck you." Mac couldn't help himself, but he knew taking the offensive was probably a bad strategy.

"If that's the way you want it . . ." The voice trailed off.

"This isn't what we bargained for. None of it. Not the shit you're doing. And sure as hell not what you're asking me to do."

"If you believe this is merely a request, that may be part of the problem. I must not be making myself clear. If you need a reminder, that can be arranged."

Mac considered his response carefully. "I don't need a reminder. Let me work on it."

"Fine. Work on it. But remember, we're on a very tight time line."

"I know."

"Things have gone too far for hesitation."

"All right. I know. I'll contact you soon."

"Do that. You don't want me to have to contact you." The line went dead.

Mac threw the phone on the floor. He looked down at his pizza, but he'd lost his appetite. He looked up at the television. The game was only minutes old, and the Celtics were already down by eight—to the Grizzlies, no less.

"Fuck," he said out loud again. The world had changed when he wasn't looking. And it wasn't for the better.

Chapter Eighteen

FINN WOKE EARLY the next morning. Truth be told, he hadn't really slept at all. He'd just lain in bed, replaying every conversation he'd had with Mark Dobson over and over in his head. Every rational impulse told him that he bore no responsibility for the young man's death, but for some reason, he couldn't let go of his guilt.

By four thirty he was up and moving, in and out of the shower for a quick rinse, scarfing down a piece of dry toast, and out the door by five. It was still pitch-black when he unlocked the door to his office.

He sat down at his desk and pulled out a yellow legal pad and stared at it. His goal was to organize his thoughts on the Salazar case. In his head, the questions and issues were free-flowing, swirling out of control, like bits of paper in a city wind. They would do him little good in that form, and his hope was that by reducing them to writing he might impose some order on them, which might allow him to proceed in some sort of logical manner.

As always, he started with the assumption—the required belief— that his client was telling him the truth, and that Salazar was, therefore, innocent. Finn pulled the pad toward him and began scribbling across the page. Then he paused and looked at what he'd written.

Madeline Steele identified the wrong man.

He thought about it. Below that, he wrote a simple but important question.

Why?

After another pause, he started on a fresh line.

How did Salazar's print get on Steele's gun?

Underneath that:

Framed?

He sat back in his chair and picked up the pad, examining what he'd written. It was a start, but that was all. There were so many other pieces to this, pieces that didn't seem to fit, no matter how hard he tried to force them. Slapping the pad back onto the desk, he began scribbling furiously, channeling any notion that popped into his head down onto the paper without thought or analysis.

Who had a motive to kill Steele?
Who had a motive to kill Dobson?
Who had a motive to frame Salazar?
Is Salazar a member of VDS?
Are there cops involved?
Macintyre?
What did Salazar tell Dobson?
What was it like growing up blind and fatherless?
Would Salazar have been deported?

Finn wrote out all the questions in a stream. When the questions ran dry, he stared at the piece of paper for a long time. It was a good list of questions; a hard list of questions. Somewhere in there were the right questions, and the right answers would free his client and, to some degree, himself.

He drew a bold line under the questions and wrote in large capital letters: TASK LIST. He underlined that and then wrote out a list.

Question Madeline Steele
Hire fingerprint expert/evaluate fingerprint match
Interview Salazar family
Interview trial witnesses
Research VDS
Contact DNA testing lab

He tore off the sheet of paper, put away the legal pad, and put his new lists in the center of his empty desk. Now, at least, they had a plan to follow. Well, perhaps not so much a plan as a list of random activities, but Finn's general view was that one of the most important aspects of preparing a case was to keep your feet moving at all times. Even if you weren't sure exactly where the goal line was, without motion, you'd never advance the ball, and mere intellectualism would never accomplish that. Advancing the ball took legwork.

He stood up and looked at his watch. Six thirty. He'd been at the office for well over an hour, and it was still dark out. At least the donut shop around the corner would be open. That was one of the things he loved about New England: There was a donut shop on every block. He had no idea what it was about the circular puffs of dough that so tantalized people in the region, but he was as much a victim as anyone, so who was he to complain? He also needed coffee to really start the day, and while there was a machine in the office, only Lissa could make it function. Served him right for going top-of-the-line. It had more buttons and switches than any car he'd ever driven. No matter. He'd head around the corner and pick up some coffee and a dozen mixed donuts. Both Kozlowski and Lissa generally arrived early, so the breakfast and the coffee would still be fresh when they arrived.

Finn put on his coat and wrapped a scarf around his neck. He already felt better than he had the night before. Things were moving, at least, and with only a week to find some answers, motion was desperately needed. As he stepped out onto the sidewalk, he felt as though he had a sense of purpose for the first time since he'd read the headline about Dobson's murder.

Kozlowski lay on his back on Lissa Krantz's bed. A sheet was pulled over his hips, leaving his legs and torso bare. Covering himself was an unconscious nod to etiquette that was probably unnecessary, given their activities over the preceding six hours. Still, when Lissa had gotten up and walked into the bathroom, he'd felt a little odd lying alone in all his splendor.

He rubbed his wide chest as he reflected on what had happened between the two of them. In many ways, it seemed odd. They had nothing in common. Nothing. They came from different backgrounds, different economic situations, different cultural and religious upbringings. And then there was the age difference. Fifteen years was probably not considered drastic by most people in today's world, but Kozlowski didn't consider himself part of "most people." To him, fifteen years seemed like an eternity. It felt like a gulf potentially too wide to bridge. It felt like cradle robbing.

And then there was the other thing—the sex. Would she really be satisfied with someone older? It hadn't seemed as though it had bothered her the night before. If anything, she'd seemed very pleased with . . . everything. And yet he had no real basis from which to judge. His experience with her was such an anomaly in his life that he had no frame of reference to determine whether he was evaluating her reactions accurately. He'd had only a few "lady friends" in his lifetime, and they had been nothing like Lissa. They'd been demure and proper: good marriage material, as his mother used to say in heavily accented English. When he'd been intimate with them, it had been perfectly pleasant, but there had been little communication, no experimentation, and never an encore.

His evening with Lissa had been a different experience entirely. They hadn't slept. Ever. They had crawled over each other nonstop throughout the evening, doing things to each other he'd only read about. While they were together, it hadn't occurred to him to worry about his performance—about whether or not she was being satisfied. He'd been too busy trying to keep up.

Not that it had seemed difficult. He'd simply done what seemed natural, following his body's impulses and reacting instinctively to her movements, matching the rhythm of her body and the intensity of the expressions of ecstasy on her face. If those expressions were any indication, then he'd performed acceptably for her. And yet there was no way he could be sure. He'd heard about women faking pleasure to make their partners feel better about themselves. Lissa's reactions had seemed genuine, but how could he know?

He stretched his arms over his head and let go of his doubts. Doubts wouldn't help him, and there was nothing he could do about it now. It wasn't in his nature to dig too far down emotionally, anyway. In personal relationships, he'd always found it easier to accept people at face value unless they gave him reason to question. Lissa Krantz had done nothing to raise his suspicions, so he thought it better to enjoy the memories of the evening for what they were.

———

Lissa looked at her reflection in the bathroom mirror. "Holy shit," she whispered to herself. Then she laughed, putting a hand over her mouth to muffle the sound. "Holy fucking shit."

She ran her hands over her body, tracing some of the infinite paths Tom Kozlowski had blazed during the night, closing her eyes as she relived the experience in her mind. She ran her fingertips over her hips and around the curves of the small of her back, then up her sides and over her breasts, feeling her nipples stiffen at her touch, as they had at his.

From her breasts, one hand crawled down her abdomen, making her stomach flutter in anticipation as it wandered farther down. When she touched herself between her legs, she paused as the electricity flared up her spine. She let her hand linger there, as his had, touching herself lightly, with a curiosity that mimicked his as she teased herself, swallowing a moan as her entire body shuddered.

She took her hand away and leaned forward on the sink. She shouldn't be doing this; she could tell that she'd be walking gingerly for a day or two as it was. It had been worth it, though. She laughed quietly again at her reflection. She probably had more sexual experience than any three friends of hers combined, but this had been completely different. Her evening had been a total immersion in pleasure and abandon. As much as her body ached from it, it still wanted more.

She opened the door and stepped out of the bathroom, walking over to sit on the side of the bed. He was lying there, eyes closed, hands behind his head. She touched his thigh, and his eyes opened. She wondered what he was thinking, whether he was having any regrets. It wouldn't be unusual, she knew from experience.

"Tired?" she asked.

"No," he said. "I probably will be later, but not now."

"Me, neither." She leaned over and kissed his cheek, then immediately regretted it. "I had fun."

"Me, too."

She looked away from him. "We probably shouldn't tell Finn. It'd only freak the shit out of him."

"Okay."

"Besides, it's not like this has to be some big fucking deal." She'd given the same assurance to dozens of men in the past. This time it rang hollow to her.

He frowned. "If you say so."

"I mean, it's just a night, right? It's not like we're dating or anything."

"Okay." They were quiet for a moment. He reached out and stroked the inside of her leg. It was all she could do to keep herself from collapsing into him. "You dumping me already?" he asked.

A hint of relief nudged her. "No," she said quickly. "I just didn't want . . . No. I don't want you to feel trapped, is all."

He continued touching her, his hand sliding up her leg. "I'll let you know if that becomes a problem."

She smiled and slid her own hand up his thigh, underneath the narrow slip of sheet covering his hips. He was hard, and her smile widened as she ran the tips of her fingers lightly up and down over him. Then she pulled aside the sheet and climbed up on her knees, straddling him without letting their bodies touch.

The look in his eyes as he watched her body made her melt. He reached up and ran his hands over her legs, up her body, and over her breasts. His hands were thick and strong but gentle, and her body moved involuntarily against his touch.

Suddenly, he stopped. His face went serious. "I want you to know, I didn't expect this," he said. "When I asked you out, I wasn't expecting this. I'm not sure I'd even thought to hope for it."

She smiled again as she lowered herself onto him. Leaning forward, she whispered in his ear, "This was exactly what I had hoped for."

Chapter Nineteen

By NINE THIRTY Finn was annoyed as he sat alone in his office. He was anxious to get moving on the Salazar case, but he needed Kozlowski to reach out to Madeline Steele and set up a meeting for that morning. He needed Lissa to coordinate with Dobson's office and get the files transferred so they could begin their substantive analysis. Neither of them had arrived.

He supposed he had no technical right to take umbrage with Kozlowski; notwithstanding appearances, Koz wasn't his employee. True, most of the work he did was for Finn, but he was still an independent contractor, free to take on whatever jobs came his way. And the reality was that he was a good enough private detective that he'd be able to keep busy with or without Finn. Still, they had such a well-established routine that Finn felt let down, particularly because Kozlowski knew the time pressure they were under with the Salazar case.

As for Lissa, he had every right to be perturbed with her. She was an employee; an intern from law school, to be sure, but she still had to take orders and show up on time. With her brain and skill, she'd be able to get a job after graduation at lots of firms that would pay more than he could, but she still needed him to review her work to graduate. More than that, he'd come to depend on her, and she knew it.

He'd used the morning as efficiently as he could, contacting Billy Smith, a fingerprint expert in the D.C. area whom he'd worked with on another case involving an unfortunate paternity dispute. Smith was former FBI, and recognized as one of the leading experts in fingerprint work, so he had the added bonus of being unimpeachable. If Billy gave them a good report, they'd be home free. Finn had other experts he could go to if they needed to fudge the analysis, but he wanted at least to start with the best.

He was turning the case over in his head, trying to figure out what else he could accomplish on his own, when the door banged open and Lissa hurried in. "Fuck," she said as her momentum carried her to the coat rack and she hung up her winter gear.

"Good morning to you, too," Finn grumbled, looking at his watch. "Yep, still morning. Barely."

"I know. I said 'fuck.'"

"Is that some sort of euphemism for 'I'm sorry'?"

She thought about it. "Pretty much, yeah."

The door slammed open again, and Kozlowski walked in. "Morning." He nodded at Finn.

"Don't you mean 'fuck'?"

"What?" Kozlowski looked confused. He looked back and forth between Finn and Lissa. "Problem?"

Lissa shrugged.

"Are you two serious? We've got a dead lawyer and an innocent client rotting in jail with a week for us to figure out how we're going to get him out, and you want to know if there's a problem with both of you showing up at nine thirty?"

"He's innocent now?" Lissa asked.

"He's a client now. That makes him innocent," Finn said.

"He was a client last week, too," Kozlowski pointed out.

"He was only technically a client last week. Dobson was representing him then. Now he's all ours, and he's innocent. Get used to it."

Kozlowski held his hands up. "No argument here. So what do you want us to do about it?"

"You and I need to talk to Madeline Steele," Finn replied. "I want to see how sure she is about her ID of Salazar fifteen years later. I figure you know her, so she'll be more willing to talk to me if you're there."

Kozlowski leaned against the wall where Charlie O'Malley had punched through the plaster. He looked at his feet. "It's possible," he said. "But remember, I haven't talked to her in years. I don't know that I'll get you much more mileage."

"Yeah, but you were friends, right?"

"'Were' being the operative word. Like I said, it's been years."

"And you were *just* friends, right?" Finn pushed.

"Right," Kozlowski replied without hesitation. Finn saw Lissa flinch, but he thought nothing of it.

"So at least you know her. And you were a cop. That gives you a hell of a lot more credibility than I have. If she gets a call from Salazar's lawyer out of the blue, I won't get through the door. You can at least set up the meeting, maybe smooth things over when we're there. Don't even tell her what it's about; just tell her you need to talk to her."

"I'm not sure that's the best idea," Kozlowski said.

Finn challenged him. "Well, it's the only idea I've got. If you have something better, by all means, I'm listening."

Kozlowski was silent.

"Okay, then. Set it up for this morning."

"What can I do?" Lissa asked.

"Call Dobson's secretary again and get copies of all his files sent over today. Immediately. It may take a little finessing; she's probably pretty freaked out. But you've got to make her understand that we're on the clock with this, so we need whatever she's got as quickly as possible."

"I'll try," Lissa replied. "You're probably right—she's probably pretty fucked up—so it may not be that easy. Shit, how often is a lawyer murdered at a place like Howery, Black?"

"More often than you might think," Kozlowski deadpanned.

She looked at him, then turned back to Finn. "That's right, a woman was killed a couple years ago, right? I'd forgotten. That must've been when you were there."

Finn nodded.

"Did you know her?"

Finn nodded again.

"Well aren't you the fuckin' lucky charm?"

"Thanks, that's helpful."

"Sorry."

"I also need you to coordinate with our fingerprint expert," Finn continued.

"Right. Koz and I talked about that a little last night. I've got a list of candidates we could use."

Finn shook his head. "No need. That's what I was doing during my solitude this morning. I've got Billy Smith from D.C. lined up."

"He's good," Kozlowski commented. "On the top of my list."

"Glad you approve," Finn said. He turned back to Lissa. "As soon as we get the files, make sure the fingerprint records get down to him."

"Will do, boss."

"Good."

"Everything else all right?" Kozlowski asked.

"Fine. We've got a week to prove this guy's innocent and figure out who killed Mark Dobson. What could possibly be wrong?"

Kozlowski sat in his back office, staring at the phone. He'd dreaded this moment, and now it was here.

He picked up the receiver and dialed the number in front of him. She answered on the second ring.

"Victims' Services. Can I help you?"

"I'd like to speak to Madeline Steele," he said. He knew it was her on the line already, but he wanted to make sure. Or maybe he was just stalling.

"This is Sergeant Steele."

"Maddy, it's Koz." He could feel the phone line ice over. "How are you?"

"Koz," she said. She sounded stunned.

"How are you?" he repeated.

"Compared to what? Compared to when? Compared to yesterday? Compared to last year? Compared to fifteen years ago, the last time you bothered to ask?"

"I'm sorry, Maddy."

"Bullshit." She went quiet, and Kozlowski had no idea what to say. "What do you want?" she asked at last.

"I need to talk to you."

"So talk."

"In person."

"About what?"

"I'd rather not do this over the phone," he said. "Do you have any time this morning? We could come in."

"*We?*"

"A guy I work with. A lawyer."

"That's right, you're in private practice now. Private dick." Kozlowski could tell that the pun was intentional. "Injured in the line of duty, right?"

"Shot in the knee. I'm fine."

"Must be. At least you're still walking. Count your blessings." He didn't take the bait. "What does this lawyer want to talk about?"

"Like I said, I'd rather not discuss it over the phone. Can we come in this morning?"

"Just like that, huh? A decade and a half without a word. A decade and a half of the silent treatment, and you just call up and want to walk into my office to chat?"

"It's important, Maddy."

"I needed you."

"I know. I'm sorry. It's important."

He waited as she thought about it. "Eleven thirty," she said after a moment. Then she hung up.

Kozlowski held the receiver out from his face, looking at it. Then he set it down on the cradle and took a deep breath. The call had actually gone better than he'd expected. He wouldn't have been surprised if she'd hung up at the beginning of the conversation. It was, he supposed, a good sign. It would get worse, though. In person, it would get much worse when the shock wore off. And when she learned what they wanted to discuss . . . "worse" didn't begin to describe how it would get.

Finn had one call to make before they went to talk to Madeline Steele. Tony Horowitz was the head technician at Identech, the DNA testing lab where Dobson had sent the scrapings from under Steele's fingernails. Finn had worked with Horowitz on other cases and figured it was worth checking in. He had to go through two secretaries and wait on hold for several minutes before he got the man on the line.

"Tony, it's Scott Finn here."

"Finn. Good to hear from you. How's business?"

"Pretty good these days, actually."

"That's good to hear. Things busy enough that you have some more stuff for us to do here? You know we can always use the work, and we'd be happy to lend a hand on anything you've got."

"That's why I'm calling. You're already working on one of my cases— you just may not know it."

"Really? Which one?"

"It's a criminal matter for a client named Salazar. The lawyer who gave it to you was named Mark Dobson. Fifteen-year-old DNA samples. Sounding familiar?"

Finn could hear the man suck in air. "Shit, you're working on that now? I had no idea. Shit."

"Problem?" Finn asked.

"Just that we took that case out of the queue yesterday. I was having the samples bagged back up."

"Why?"

"Didn't you hear? Dobson was killed this weekend. Without him around, I had no idea how we were going to get paid. We don't work for free here, y'know."

"I understand," Finn said. "But do me a favor and put it back online, okay? I'll take care of the payment."

"If you say so, but we've lost some time, and now I've got some projects that have taken priority. I'll see what I can do, though."

"Tony, do more than that, okay? This guy's innocent. I know it, and I've got a hearing in a week, so I need the results by the end of next weekend."

"That's not going to be easy, Finn."

"I know it. But I'm asking you to do it. When I tell you this guy is innocent, I mean he is innocent. I really need your help on this."

Finn heard the sigh on the other end of the line. "I'll have to work it up myself," Horowitz said. "It's gonna involve working next weekend, and that's gonna run into overtime. Are you prepared for that?"

"As long as I get the results by Sunday," Finn said.

"Fine," Horowitz replied. "But you're gonna owe me for this."

Chapter Twenty

FINN AND KOZLOWSKI arrived for their meeting with Madeline Steele at Police Headquarters fifteen minutes early and were asked to wait in the lobby. Finn felt as though every cop who passed him could read his suspicions. It was his imagination; it had to be. No one knew why he was there, and Finn hadn't shared his thoughts about possible police misconduct even with Kozlowski. After all, Koz was a cop, too. As much as he bitched about the way the department had treated him, Finn had heard him say dozens of times, "Once a cop, always a cop."

Finn was wrestling with whether to tell Koz about his theories when he heard a woman's voice behind him.

"Koz. It's been a long time." Finn detected a hint of anger. He turned and looked at Madeline Steele and was surprised at what he saw. He was expecting a beaten shadow of a woman. Instead, he beheld a formidable woman with eyes that matched her last name. She sat tall in a short-backed wheelchair, the wheels of which were angled in at the top to provide a wider base and greater stability. It was the kind of wheelchair Finn associated with serious para-athletes, and it fit her appearance perfectly. She was in her mid-thirties, with a long, thin torso and broad-cut shoulders. She wore a sheer silk blouse that clung to her arms, showing off taut, sculpted muscles. Her long brown hair was neatly combed but not styled, and she wore no makeup at all that Finn could tell.

"Maddy. It's good to see you," Kozlowski said. "You look good."

"Thanks. You look old."

"I guess looks don't lie."

She didn't reply.

"This is Scott Finn." Kozlowski waved his hand at Finn. "He's the lawyer I work with. The one I told you about."

Finn stepped forward and offered his hand. "It's nice to meet you," he said.

She looked at his hand suspiciously. "Likewise." She reached out and shook his hand, squeezing hard enough to make Finn wince. She looked back at Kozlowski. "Fifteen years. This must be pretty important. What do you want to talk about?"

"Is there someplace we could talk privately?" Kozlowski asked.

"Sure." She spun her chair and was off at a sprinter's pace across the lobby and toward a long hallway on the first floor. The two men had to move into a near-jog just to keep up.

"You're pretty fast in that thing," Finn said, trying to break the ice. As it came out, he knew it sounded wrong.

She looked back over her shoulder at him, then said to Kozlowski, "Where'd you get this guy?"

Kozlowski didn't answer.

She slid around a corner, almost steamrolling a young officer who scurried out of the way without a word, as though it was a common occurrence. After another fifteen yards, Steele skidded to a stop in front of a door marked VICTIMS' SERVICES COORDINATOR. To the side of the door was a silver nameplate. SERGEANT MADELINE STEELE. "This is it," she said, pushing open the door and heading in.

Finn was impressed. Municipal offices were not generally noted for their size or their decor, but entering Steele's office from the hallway felt like slipping into the inner sanctum of a trusted family doctor. A large

Oriental rug covered the floor, and a midsize polished wood desk stood in the center of the room. Two comfortable chairs stood in front of the desk, and a couch was pushed against the far wall. There was no chair behind the desk, which confused Finn until she wheeled herself around to the other side and he realized that she didn't need one.

"Nice office," Kozlowski commented.

"Yeah. Thanks. What do you want?"

"I mean it," Kozlowski said. "It's very nice."

She leaned forward on the desk. "Fine. You want to talk about the office? It was specially designed for me. It's so big because I need the space to move around. They had to knock down a wall between two offices to create a space this big. Hell, for that matter, they created this entire position for me. Victims' Services used to be farmed out to private companies. But they needed a place to put me when I wouldn't go away. It was kind of a big thank-you for getting myself shot. Don't get me wrong, I make the most of it for myself and the department. I understand a little about what most victims are going through, and I can talk to them. I can get them to talk to me. We've made dozens of busts based on what I've gotten people to confide in me about—busts that never would have been made without me. So, yeah, it's a nice big office, but I earn my keep. We done with the bullshit now?"

"I wasn't suggesting—" Koz started.

"I know you weren't. What do you want?"

Kozlowski turned to Finn. "It's your show."

Finn sat in one of the chairs in front of the desk. Kozlowski remained standing, looking ready to move quickly out the door. "This may be a little awkward," Finn began. He cleared his throat. "I represent Vincente Salazar."

A look of total shock and revulsion spread over Steele's face, and Finn could tell the meeting was not going to go well. But she seemed too stunned to interrupt him, so he figured he might as well push his way through it.

"We think he might not be responsible for what happened to you. DNA tests are being run now, and we believe those tests are going to prove Mr. Salazar was not the man who attacked you." He let that sink in.

The appalled look still hung on her face, but Finn had to give her credit for keeping her composure. She was impressive. "And?" she asked.

"And because of how old the DNA samples are, and because they could have degraded or been contaminated, even if the tests come back and show it wasn't Mr. Salazar, the judge still may not let him go free unless we can offer some explanation for the other evidence in the case. Like your testimony. So I wanted to ask you how sure you were about your identification of Mr. Salazar."

"My ID?"

"Yes. Can you tell me exactly what you remember?"

"You're kidding, right?" She looked at Kozlowski. "He's kidding, right?"

Finn shifted in his seat. "I'm not. An innocent man may be rotting in jail. I'd like you to think back as clearly as you can. Are you positive Vincente Salazar was the man who attacked you? Is there any chance you could have been mistaken?"

She looked as though she hadn't heard Finn. She was still staring at Kozlowski. His eyes met hers evenly. "You're behind this, aren't you. You motherfucker."

"No."

"Bullshit. It's not enough that you— Now you walk back into my life fifteen years later and throw this shit in my face? You asshole. You absolute sadomasochistic asshole."

"It's important," Kozlowski replied. "I told you."

"His fingerprints were on the gun!"

"Ms. Steele, I'm not asking about the fingerprints," Finn said. "I'm asking about what you remember."

She turned to look back at Finn. "You want to know what I remember, you slimy son of a bitch? I remember your client attacking me. I remember him trying to rape me. I remember him shooting me. I remember lying in the gutter, waiting to die. But you know what I remember most? Do you? Mostly, I remember what it was like to walk. I remember what it was like having legs instead of this fucking chair. I remember what it was like being able to take a crap without hauling myself onto the toilet with my arms and shoulders. I remember all that very well. Do you understand that?"

"I do," Finn said. "But—"

She cut him off. "No. No buts. No fucking buts. I've told you what I remember. Now I want you to remember something." She practically spat in his face. "I want you to remember that if you ever come near me again, I swear to God I will put you in a chair just like this one for the rest of your fucking life. Then we'll talk about what it is that both of us really remember. Now get the fuck out of my office." She looked at Kozlowski. "Both of you."

———◦———

"That could have gone better," Finn said as he pulled out of the police parking lot at Schroeder Plaza.

"I warned you," Kozlowski said. "What did you expect? We're asking for her help in freeing the man who shot her and put her in that chair for the rest of her life."

"Except that he didn't do it."

"Fine. Let's assume that's right. It still doesn't change the fact that she believes he did. Did you really expect her to pour some nuts in a fucking bowl, make us some tea, and ask us to sit down for a goddamned heart-to-heart?"

"No. But I also didn't expect her to have so much animosity toward you even before we told her why we were there. I thought you were friends, but no, we start with two strikes against us."

"I told you. We *were* friends. We hadn't talked in years."

"Fine. But there are lots of people I haven't talked to in years who I was friends with, and I wouldn't expect them to rip my throat out if I got in touch with them. I mean, hell, you were more of a liability in there than anything else. What the fuck happened between the two of you?"

Kozlowski stared out the car window. "She went through a rough time after she was shot. I wasn't there for her the way I should have been."

"I thought you were just friends."

"We were just friends. I wasn't there for her as a friend." Kozlowski sighed. "Maybe I was wrong. Maybe we were more than friends, but not in the way you mean. There was never any funny business between us, but I was her mentor. I was the one she came to with problems. I knew her father and her brothers; they were cops, too. She had it tough, trying to live up to them. I was the person she talked to most. The person she trusted most. Maybe that did make us more than friends."

Finn looked over at Kozlowski. "So, if you were that close, why weren't you there for her when she got shot?"

The large man shifted uncomfortably in the tiny car, and the cuff of his jacket sleeve caught on the door handle. "Fuck," he said as he tried to free himself. "Motherfucker." He swung his arm hard, and the handle popped off the door and landed in his lap. He looked at it, held it up to examine it, then handed it to Finn. "You may need this later."

"Jesus Christ, Koz," Finn yelled. "What the fuck has gotten into you?"

"It's your car, asshole. Maybe if you drove something big enough for a normal-sized person to sit in, shit like this wouldn't happen." Kozlowski watched as Finn guided the little car around the remnants of the Big Dig and into the Callahan Tunnel, heading toward Logan Airport. "Where are we going?"

"East Boston."

"No shit. Why?"

"While you were AWOL this morning, I did some checking around. Salazar's brother, Miguel, spends his afternoons twice a week at a free clinic over here. I want to talk to him."

"Free clinic?" Kozlowski scoffed. "I thought he was some big-shot doctor."

"He is," Finn said. "He's a surgeon at Mass General. Probably one of the top positions in the country."

"So what the fuck is he doing wasting his time in a free clinic?"

"How should I know? What does it matter? You have other plans for the day?"

"No."

"Good." Finn put the door handle on the dashboard. "You gonna tell me what the hell happened between you and Steele? Why you weren't there for her 'as a friend' when she got shot?"

Kozlowski continued staring out the window as they emerged from the tunnel and East Boston rolled past them. "No," he said. "That's between me and her."

His tone made it clear to Finn that the discussion was over from Kozlowski's point of view. "Fine. Perfect. You'll tell me if there's anything else important that you intend to keep to yourself, right?"

Kozlowski turned his head to look at Finn. There was anger in his expression, but Finn didn't care. He had enough of his own to compete. "I'll let you know," Kozlowski said.

Chapter Twenty-one

THE FREE CLINIC was located on the flat of East Boston, near the airport, in one of the poorest sections of town. It made sense, Finn supposed, but it was hard to figure why someone doing as well as Miguel Salazar would choose to spend any significant amount of time in the area. It appeared that he shared at least some of his brother's genuine dedication to his profession.

Finn pulled his car up alongside a nondescript, dingy clapboard building that matched the address he'd been given. The street was deserted, and there was nothing to identify the structure as a medical facility.

"You sure this is the right place?" Kozlowski asked.

"I'm not sure of anything anymore," Finn replied, opening his door and climbing out. He was at the door to the building before he realized that Kozlowski wasn't with him. He looked back at the car and saw Koz sitting there, staring back at Finn. Finn walked back to the car. "You joining me?" he asked through the window.

Kozlowski glared at him. "I can't get out."

It took a moment for Finn to clue in: There was no handle on the door anymore. He opened the door from the outside. "Serves you right," he said. "Maybe I should just leave you here. You haven't pissed off anyone in here that I don't know about, have you?"

"Not yet," Kozlowski grumbled.

They walked over to the door; it was little more than a sheet of plywood on hinges, covered with chipped white paint. There was no sign of life. Finn looked at Kozlowski and shrugged, then pulled the door open.

It was like stepping from the surface of the moon to the streets of Calcutta. As soon as the door opened, a profusion of parents talking, children screaming, and people coughing and moaning assaulted them. All eyes turned to the door, and a protest went up at the blast of cold air that flooded the room.

They walked in, careful not to step on the fingers or toes of the small children who littered the grubby floor, playing or lying down in exhaustion. There had to be more than fifty people crammed into the tiny room. From the Spanish that was being spoken and the light brown complexions of those gathered, Finn guessed that most there were from South or Central America. He saw a few Asian faces as well, and thought he heard a smattering of Italian and Russian being whispered in the corners. Most of the adults in the room glanced nervously at Finn and Kozlowski.

A door at the far end of the room opened, and a young woman in a white doctor's coat poked her head out. "Martinez!" she called. Then, after a pause, again: "Martinez!"

Finn saw a woman sitting against the wall get to her feet, then stoop to gather up two small children. She headed toward the far door and gave a shy "*Hola*" to the woman standing there.

"*Hola*," the woman replied with a smile that betrayed exactly how tired she was. She let the woman pass through the door before she looked around the room. Finn could almost see her mind calculating the length of the rest of her day based on how full the room was.

Then her eyes came to rest on Finn and Kozlowski, and her expression changed instantly from fatigue to anger.

"No!" she yelled, stepping over patients as she came toward them. "No!" she yelled again. "We paid! We put that check in the mail last week! We'll get a restraining order if it's really necessary; this kind of intimidation is despicable! Out! Out right now!"

"Sorry?" Finn said defensively.

"You will be if you don't leave," the woman confirmed. She was short and stocky, and judging from the way she was moving, Finn suspected that she knew how to handle herself in the event of a physical confrontation. "Out! Now!"

"We're looking for Miguel Salazar," Finn said. "Is he here?"

The woman stopped in her advance, clearly caught off guard. "Are you from the landlord?" she asked.

"No," Finn replied. He looked at Kozlowski. "You from the landlord?"

"Not last time I checked."

"We're not from the landlord," Finn concluded, addressing the woman again.

"We've been having trouble with the landlord," the woman said. "He's an asshole, and he's looking to evict us. He thinks he can make more than we're paying."

"Right," Finn said. "Sounds like a bastard. We're not with him."

She looked relieved, but some suspicion still hung in her expression. "What do you want to see Miguel about?"

"I'm his brother's lawyer," Finn said. "This is one of my colleagues, Tom Kozlowski. We're here to talk to him about his brother's case."

A smile dawned on her face. "Vincente? You're Vincente's lawyer?"

Finn was confused. "You know Vincente?"

She shook her head. "No. Although I sometimes feel like I do. Miguel talks so much about him, I feel like there isn't much I don't know about the man. He's an inspiration, and he's largely responsible for all this." She waved her hand around the grimy waiting room. Finn looked at the dense glass and chicken-wire windows set too high and plaster hanging off the walls and wondered whether she was trying to be ironic. He thought not.

"Is Miguel here?" Finn asked again.

"Yes," she said. "Of course. I'm sorry to be rude. I'm Dr. Jandreau, but you can call me Jill. He's in with a patient, but he'll be done in a few minutes, and I'm sure he'll want to talk to you. We're all keeping our fingers crossed for his brother. It must be awful to be trapped in prison for a crime you didn't commit."

"But you don't know Vincente, I thought," Finn said.

"No, that's right. But I know Miguel. That's enough." She nodded, as though that explained it all. "One of our doctors called in sick this morning, so there's an empty examination room in the back. You can wait for him there, and he'll be with you once he's done with his patient."

⸻

Mac sat at his desk at headquarters at One Schroeder Plaza, sweating in spite of the fact that the building was ten degrees below comfortable. He felt like everything was coming apart, and that made him physically ill. Early that morning he'd been unable to choke down any breakfast, and when he'd tried to drink some coffee, the resulting wave of nausea had him doubled over.

He was sure that the people around him had noticed the change in his demeanor. What had once felt like confidence now echoed as defensiveness and anger. He no longer had the energy to dress himself properly, and looking down, he noticed a pasta stain on his shirt.

He picked up the phone and dialed the number.

"Yes," the voice on the other end of the line answered.

"It's me." Mac kept his voice low, lest anyone try to eavesdrop. He knew he should use a pay phone, but he was too weary to make such an effort.

"I was beginning to think I was going to have to contact you. I'm relieved it hasn't come to that."

"Yeah. Whatever. I think I've figured a way out of this."

"Good. You will take care of the lawyer, then?"

"No," Mac said. "That wouldn't solve the problem; it would only buy some time. Salazar could always find a new lawyer. Besides, two lawyers killed on the same case within a week? It'd raise some eyebrows."

"I'm not concerned with eyebrows," the voice said. "What is your solution?"

"Salazar."

There was silence on the line. "Are you sure it can be done?"

"Happens all the time. Easier on the inside than in the real world."

"Yes, but Salazar spends much of his time in the infirmary. He is difficult to get to."

Mac grunted. "It's prison. You can get to anybody."

"It cannot be traced back to us. You cannot use any of my people."

"Understood," Mac said. "It's already been arranged."

"When?"

"Tomorrow."

Again there was no reply. Then: "What about the lawyer?"

"What about him? We deal with Salazar, and the lawyer's reason to follow the trail disappears."

"I'm not so sure."

"Look," Mac said, hating the pitiful tone of his voice. "You told me to take care of this. That's what I've done. You don't like the way I handle things, then don't call me again."

Mac could hear the contemplative breathing through the phone. "Fine. We'll try your way first. If it doesn't work, though . . ."

"It will work." Mac hung up the phone. He could feel the perspiration damp and cold under his arms and at his shirt collar. He tried to stand, but the nausea took him off his feet, and he closed his eyes as he crumpled into his chair.

"You okay, Mac?" Detective Koontz called from the far side of the room.

"Fine," he choked out. *Like she cares? Answer the fucking phones, then go home and make your fucking husband some goddamned dinner. Don't sit there in my fucking squad room and ask me if I'm okay like you belong and I'm the one who's out of place.*

He opened his eyes and looked at her. She was regarding him with an expression of concern. "You sure?" she asked.

On the other hand, she wasn't a half-bad piece of ass for a cop. No tits, but you couldn't have everything, could you. He forced a smile. "I was out for some drinks last night. Might have overdone it, you know?"

"Been there," she said. "I've got a kiwi Powerade in the fridge. It's great for a hangover. Replaces the electrolytes. You're welcome to it."

His head spun. "Sure. Sounds good."

She got up and went out toward the kitchen to get him the drink.

Kiwi Powerade. Electrolytes. What the fuck had the world come to? Whatever happened to black coffee and Alka-Seltzer? One thing was painfully clear: The world had changed around him as he'd been sitting still, and it might very well be too late for him to catch up.

Jimmy Alvarez stood quietly, watching as the Padre closed his cell phone.

"Our friend says that it will be taken care of," Carlos said. "On the inside."

Jimmy said nothing. He had survived with Carlos against all odds because he knew when to keep his mouth shut. He was Mexican—and only half Mexican at that. Ten years ago that would have precluded his participation in VDS. True, good soldiers of other nationalities had been recruited in the past decade, but it was still an organization that beat with the heart of El Salvador.

But Jimmy had been instrumental in establishing the cross-border penetration that allowed the organization to carry on many of its most profitable activities. He'd grown up in El Cenizo, just across the border from Rio Bravo, Texas, a town made famous by the 1959 movie starring John Wayne and Dean Martin. His father was American; his mother wasn't. As a result, he knew everyone along both sides of the border. Without him and the information he provided, VDS would be at a loss. That was why Carlos kept him alive.

At the same time, the Padre kept him close, and Jimmy knew that his loyalties were always being deliberately tested. Because he was a Mexican. Because he was an outsider. Jimmy thought he had made the big time when Carlos first recruited him, and he swaggered around his hometown for a month. Now he knew it had been an illusion, and he would give anything to be out. Carlos, he realized, was a stone-cold killer, and Jimmy was nothing more than a hustler at heart. He'd never committed any greater violence than slapping around a few hookers to make himself feel tough, and he had the feeling that Carlos was beginning to sense his weakness. That put him in a very precarious position.

"What do you think, Jimmy?" Carlos asked him.

The others in the room looked at him. The Padre seldom asked for advice. It made Jimmy wary, and he considered the question carefully before answering.

"If he wants to fix the problem himself, there's no point in not letting him."

"But . . ." Carlos said.

Jimmy went on. "But we need to have a backup plan in place. Next weekend is too important. If Macintyre can clean up his own mess, then so be it. If not, we have to clean it up ourselves."

"What of our detective friend? What would you do with him?"

"From what you have told me, he was useful in the past, but he has also created unnecessary risk. If he fails in his attempt to resolve this matter, he must be dealt with."

"And if he succeeds?"

Jimmy thought about this, but only briefly. "He still should go. He's old and sloppy."

Carlos laughed without humor. "Is age such a handicap, my young friend?"

The others in the room laughed as well, but Jimmy pressed his point. "Not if age makes you stronger." He looked carefully at Carlos. "Do you think age has brought wisdom to Detective Macintyre?"

The laughter ceased. Everyone turned back to Carlos.

"No," the older man said. "Our friend is certainly not wise."

"I didn't think so. And given his weakness, he's no longer useful, either. We have others in better positions to help us. He is nothing more than a liability."

Carlos considered this. "Agreed," he said at last. "After Saturday, we will make sure to eliminate that liability." He turned and faced the window. "I also agree with your view as to the more immediate issue. We must have a contingency plan in place. I would like you to handle that."

"Of course, Padre. I'll take care of it."

"Personally," Carlos emphasized.

Jimmy's heart skipped a beat. It was another test, he knew, and there was no way to evade the challenge. "Personally," Jimmy agreed. He hoped no one heard the tremble in his voice.

Carlos walked over and placed a hand on Jimmy's shoulder. "I am glad you are with us," he said. "Otherwise I would wonder how you might judge my own age." He looked at the younger man, his eyes narrowing as though they might peer through Jimmy's eyes to read his thoughts. Jimmy kept his gaze even and unblinking, looking directly back into Carlos's dark pupils.

After a moment Carlos broke into a grin, and he gave a sharp laugh. "Indeed," he said, turning to the others in the room. "I will be always sure to have my wisdom grow faster than my years with this one around. I would never want to be viewed as a liability myself."

Jimmy smiled back as the dark laughter filled the room. He was well aware, though, when it was best to keep his thoughts to himself.

The examining room was no cleaner than the waiting area. If anything, it was more depressing. There were no windows, and the examining table was a rickety piece that looked like it had seen its best days around the time Ted Williams was still playing for the Sox. There was a chair in the corner and a rolling doctor's stool that floated on rusty springs in the center of the room, but neither Finn nor Kozlowski chose to sit. It seemed wiser to avoid contact with anything in the room. Through the thin walls, they could hear a deep chest cough that sounded like a child's last dying gasps.

Kozlowski's head throbbed. The meeting with Maddy had gone no worse than he'd expected, but that hadn't made it any easier. He'd warned Finn, but that fact, too, provided little consolation. He could tell that Finn wanted to talk, to thrash things out, but Kozlowski avoided any movement or speech that would indicate a willingness to engage. To some degree, that was just his way; he wasn't much of a conversationalist.

They waited silently in the examining room for ten minutes before the door opened and a young man in a white coat walked in. There was little question that he was Vincente Salazar's brother. He was a little taller and thinner, but he carried himself with the same quiet confidence, and he had the same distinctive widow's peak and dark skin coloring. He regarded both of them for a moment and then held his hand out to Finn. "Mr. Finn, I'm guessing," he said.

"Yes," Finn replied, shaking his hand. "Dr. Salazar."

"My brother talked to me about you. Thank you for helping him."

"Don't thank me yet. I haven't accomplished anything."

"You've given us hope. You've given him hope. That's more than you may understand." He looked at Kozlowski and held his hand out again. "And you must be the skeptical Mr. Kozlowski," he said. "My brother described you as well."

Kozlowski remembered his demeanor with the man's older brother and wondered whether he was supposed to feel guilty. "I may have given the wrong impression to your brother," he conceded. "I'm suspicious of convicts by nature." It was as far toward an apology as he was willing to go.

"No explanation is necessary, Detective. It's understandable. My brother said you were honest. It is a trait he admires greatly."

Kozlowski nodded. There was no question that there was something compelling about the brothers. They both looked you straight in the eyes, and there was a leadership quality that emanated from them. For the first time, Kozlowski found himself believing in Vincente Salazar's innocence.

"Interesting place you have here," Finn said, interrupting Kozlowski's thoughts.

Miguel looked around the room as though seeing it for the first time. "It's humble, I admit," he said. "But you'd be surprised how many lives a place like this saves."

"Must be a significant difference from your usual practice," Kozlowski said.

"It is. It's far more fulfilling." He sat down on the rolling stool. "Tell me, Mr. Finn, what can I do for you?"

Finn leaned against the wall. "We wanted to talk to you about your brother. Assuming he's innocent—"

"He is innocent."

"Right. Which means that someone must have set him up. I've asked your brother whether he was aware of anyone who would want to frame him, but he couldn't think of anyone. We figured we should talk to you and see if you could suggest any possibilities. Sometimes it's harder to answer questions about your own enemies honestly. I thought you might be able to give us a more unvarnished view."

Miguel twisted on the stool, thinking. "No one," he said. "I can't think of anyone who might have wanted to do anything to hurt my brother."

"No one?" Finn asked. "We all have enemies."

"We're not all like my brother."

"I didn't mean to suggest anything bad about your brother, and I understand how you may feel," Finn said. "He's a very impressive guy in person. But no enemies?"

Miguel shook his head. "You say he's impressive as though you really know him. You don't. You have met him, what, two or three times over the past week? This is after he spent fifteen years in hell? After he was forced to leave his home in El Salvador only to come here and have this happen to him? He has had everything taken from him, and still, all he thinks about is other people. He has never thought of himself. Believe me, Mr. Finn, 'impressive' doesn't even begin to describe my brother."

Finn said, "Fair enough. You're right, I don't know your brother all that well. But I still have only a few days to come up with a reasonable theory to explain why all the evidence in this case points to the fact that your brother shot Madeline Steele. And that theory has to be good enough to sell to the judge, otherwise, regardless of what the DNA tests say, your brother will stay in jail for the rest of his life. So any help you can give me in developing that theory would be great."

Miguel looked embarrassed. "I'm sorry, Mr. Finn. I know you are only trying to help, and I shouldn't get so emotional. The fact that, of all the people in the world to get caught up in something like this, it is my brother is enough to make me lose my grip on my temper."

"It's understandable," Finn said. "Anything you can tell us would be helpful."

Miguel took another moment to think. "I suppose there could have been people he tried to help who might have thought he didn't do enough. It seems hard to believe, but it's possible."

"People like who?"

"Immigrants. Other illegals. Back then there were no free clinics in the area. Going to the hospital risked detection and possibly deportation. My brother was the only medical help many in the community could get. He charged people only what they could afford, which was often nothing or next to it, and he treated everyone who came to him. Some of them . . . there was nothing he could do. Even at Mass General, with the best facilities and technology in the world, there are times when there is nothing doctors can do. My brother was without an office, without supplies, without any support whatsoever. It is safe to say that there were times when he could do nothing to help his patients. Perhaps some of them blamed him for not doing more."

Finn considered this. "He treated everyone who came to him, right?"

Miguel nodded. "To the best of his ability, yes."

"Including those in VDS." It was a statement, not a question, and Kozlowski paid close attention to Miguel's reaction.

Miguel hesitated. "Why do you ask?"

"They're clearly dangerous," Finn pointed out. "If one of them got angry with your brother, they might very well seek revenge."

Miguel scoffed. "You're right, Mr. Finn, they would. They would have had him killed. They wouldn't take the time with the subtleties of framing Vincente. But yes, you are right, I'm sure he treated members of VDS if they needed medical attention. That is what doctors do."

"Was he a member of VDS?" Kozlowski asked.

"No." Miguel's answer was emphatic, and Kozlowski could read nothing beyond indignation from his expression.

Finn let the answer sit, and Kozlowski thought that Salazar might augment his answer. He didn't.

"Okay," Finn said. He turned to Kozlowski. "Can you think of anything else that might be helpful?"

Kozlowski shook his head.

"Then I guess we're done for now."

Miguel said, "I'll walk you out."

They left the examining room and walked down the hall. Miguel opened the door to the waiting area. All eyes turned to look at the three of them, then quickly found the floor. Kozlowski got the distinct impression that he and Finn were not welcome in this place.

"*Está bien*," Miguel said to the patients waiting. More quietly to Finn and Kozlowski, he explained, "They think you are the police. Most of our patients, as I'm sure you've already guessed, are illegal. If it wasn't for this place, they would never seek medical treatment. There are just too many dangers for them, particularly now that the government is cracking down."

"How many patients come to this place a week?" Kozlowski asked.

"Nearly a thousand," Miguel replied.

"That many?" Finn sounded shocked.

"Yes. Without us . . ." Miguel's voice trailed off. He picked his way through the crowded room, nodding and smiling reassuringly to those who dared to look toward them. "In a way, this place is a monument to my brother," he said.

"How so?" Finn asked.

"I saw what happened to my sister-in-law. How she died. It could have been prevented, but they were too scared to go to a hospital. When she died, a part of my brother died, and if it wasn't for her death, my family never would have come to the attention of the INS. None of this would have happened. When I started as an intern at Mass General years ago, I lobbied for the supplies and funding to set this clinic up. I didn't want what happened to my brother to happen to anyone else."

They were at the door. "Your brother seems very proud of you," Finn commented.

"I wish he could see it. I wish he could be a part of it." Miguel reached out to shake their hands. "Please let me know what else I can do," he said. "There is nothing I wouldn't do to help my brother."

Chapter Twenty-two

JOEY GALLOWAY RAN his nightstick along the bars of each cell as he walked the forty-yard stretch. "Morning call, scumbags!" he yelled as he walked. "Stand at attention!"

He loved the rat-a-tat the nightstick made. It echoed with power and control. The only sound that pleased him more was the dull thud it made on those occasions when it smashed the knuckles of any prisoner stupid enough to grasp the bars of his cell as he passed. Most of them were savvy enough to avoid being hit, but every once in a while he got a newbie—a fish—unfamiliar with his brutal streak. He made sure they spent the week eating one-handed.

Galloway hated the convicts. Some of the other guards felt an odd kind of kinship with their charges, not unlike the Stockholm syndrome that sometimes develops between captors and their hostages. Galloway referred to those misguided coworkers as "the fairy patrol." He would never fall into that trap; he took any opportunity that presented itself to torture those he'd been hired to watch over. It was the only way he knew to keep the separation between them clean.

He threw his shoulders back as he came to the end of the line. "Block Three, open!" he called out.

A buzzer sounded, and the steel doors rang out with a squeal as they slid open. "On the line, assholes!" he yelled.

In unison, the orange-clad men stepped out of their holes, putting their toes on the painted line that ran down the cell block.

"Okay, faggots! Chow time! You know the drill. Keep your shit wired tight and your hands to yourselves. Don't piss me off, and I may let you live through this miserable fucking day!"

He turned and walked through the large metal gate at the end of the corridor, listening to the footsteps of the prisoners in line behind him. He smiled inwardly. Another day, another chance to fuck someone up.

Henry Womak had been incarcerated for most of his life, and there was no question that he was doomed to spend the rest of his days behind bars. He'd grown up in Dorchester, the son of an angry, unemployed dockworker. "Fuckin' niggers stole my job," his father used to say between beers in the morning. "Fuckin' niggers stole my life."

When busing came to his neighborhood in the late 1970s, Henry was seven. He was young enough that the first time he attacked a black boy with a baseball bat, he'd only been suspended. A six-month stint in a reformatory had followed the second attack two years later, and that was probably only because he'd shattered all of his second victim's teeth against a brick wall. The boy had spent three weeks in the hospital. By the time Henry was eighteen, murder seemed more like career advancement than a crime, but it was the horrific nature of the murder that guaranteed him a lifelong stay in Billerica.

He'd seen the man as he was walking along the docks in South Boston, at a moment when the storm was already gathering force in his troubled mind. The man was black and wore the faded, beaten jacket of a dockworker. He was just getting off work and heading to his truck for the drive home to his family. It was a nice truck: a Ford F-250. Not new, but not old, either.

Whatever sanity that still struggled within Henry deserted him for good that evening. *Fuckin' nigger like that with a new truck while my father sits at home sucking on a bottle and coughing up a lung?* Henry couldn't live with it.

The man never saw Henry coming. Not that he could have protected himself if he had. Henry was crazed and wouldn't have been denied his revenge without a bullet in the head.

The first time he'd swung the pipe as hard as he could. It slammed into the man's stomach. The next three swings went to his head. There was some unintended mercy to that. The coroner said that the man had likely been unconscious when Henry stripped him of the short handheld grappling hook used by dockworkers and swung it at the man's face. It caught him under the chin and drove itself though the flesh underneath the tongue, the point slipping out of his mouth and catching securely on the jaw.

Henry claimed he didn't remember attaching the handle of the hook to the chain that ran off the back of the man's truck. Or starting the engine. Or driving the thirty yards it took for the man's jawbone to come loose and separate from his face. It hadn't mattered, though. Memory be damned, he wasn't sorry, and he wouldn't say so. Not even his family felt any sympathy when he went away for good. They were too tired and scared to feel much of anything for him anymore.

And so it was with nothing but adrenaline-fueled anticipation that Henry approached Samuel Jefferson on Wednesday morning on the chow line. They were heading toward each other, and Henry slipped the shiv out of his pocket. It was made from a steel rod stolen from the metal shop, and had been shaped carefully into a six-inch knife. It was not nearly as effective for killing a man as a glass blade would be. Glass could be broken off into a man and left to continue wreaking havoc after an attacker fled. But steel would work well enough for today's purposes. Jefferson had given it to him the night before. Along with fifty dollars.

As they approached each other, Jefferson gave a nod.

Henry raised the shiv and drove it into the large black man's belly.

A soldier. That was how Samuel Jefferson regarded himself, and a soldier doesn't question orders. It made sense. The brotherhood had agreed to the plan and he had been paid well to execute it. He was a huge man with a prodigious gut. A smaller man might be at real risk.

He saw the blow coming and raised his arm instinctively to block it, relaxed as the redneck asshole's hand passed through his halfhearted defense, and then felt the steel slip through the stretched skin of his belly, splitting him open.

Jefferson roared in pain, thrashing out as he went down, cuffing Womak hard on the ear. It felt good, and he could see the pain etched on the other man's face. *Serves him right*, Jefferson thought. Orders or not, he had to send a message to anyone in the prison who might sense weakness on Jefferson's part. Weakness was the only real sin behind bars. Everything else could be forgiven, but weakness was a disease that killed, and anyone seen carrying it was quickly culled from the ranks.

He even thought to get in another blow but saw the guards rushing in. He'd made his point. Better now to cover his wound and let the screws sort the shit out. This part of the job was done.

Joey Galloway was only a few paces behind Womak, watching him carefully. He saw the shiv come out as they approached Jefferson, and he quickened his pace. Not too much, just enough to control the situation before it got out of hand. He loved it when the cons went for each other, particularly when he was there to wade in and got the opportunity to take someone out as a result.

Suddenly, Womak's arm shot out and caught Jefferson in the gut. As the huge black man went down, he caught Womak's head with a stunning blow that made Galloway smile. Got to hand it to the man, he was a bear.

Sadly, that was as far as he could let the issue go. There were too many members of the fairy patrol nearby who would intervene, and they could interfere with the plan.

He took three long strides toward the two men. Jefferson was on the ground, and Womak, though off balance, was standing over him, looking ready to take another swing with his homemade knife.

Galloway focused on Womak. He raised his nightstick high and swung at the arm that held the shiv aloft. The contact was solid, and Womak's arm went limp, the blade skittering across the floor.

"You broke my arm!" Womak screamed. He fell to the ground, his arm hanging lifeless from his shoulder. He felt his bicep with his good hand. "You broke my goddamned arm!" he yelled again.

"Tragic," Galloway replied. He walked to the other side of Womak as the convict squatted on the floor, and he swung his nightstick with brutal force at Womak's other arm.

Womak let out another scream, this one reverberating off the walls like the sickening cry of a dying animal. "No! Please!" he yelled. He was lying on the floor, looking at both of his arms as they dangled like sausage strings. "I can't move my fucking arms!" he screamed.

Just then the prison alarm sounded. "Lockdown!" one of the other guards yelled, and a unit of specially armed riot guards appeared, padded down like heavily armed umpires ready for a rumble. They weren't needed, of course. The moment had come and gone, and the prisoners were filing back to their cells, far more sated with the violence than they ever would have been with the runny egg gruel that passed for breakfast.

"We're gonna need two gurneys here," Galloway said to one of the umpires. The man nodded and spoke into a radio.

Galloway crouched between the two men. A stream of blood ran from Jefferson's stomach, pooling in a sticky smear beneath him. Womak looked helplessly at his useless arms, gasping for air. Galloway looked back and forth between them. "Well, gentlemen, it looks like you're headed to the infirmary. Enjoy the spa time, my little faggots, because I guarantee that your next stop will be in the fucking hole. And you will stay in the hole until you've forgotten your own names, I shit you not."

Vincente Salazar was alone in the infirmary when the riot horns sounded. He sighed as he went to one of the medical cabinets to prepare a crash cart for every contingency he could. Looking at the clock, he felt a light sweat break out on his forehead. It was only eight o'clock, and Dr. Roland was no doubt just beginning the second set of his weekly squash game. Every Wednesday Salazar reported early to the infirmary to take care of patients while the real doctor enjoyed a brief respite from the pressures of the job. It was unusual, but all the medical staff felt confident with Salazar on duty. If necessary, Salazar would have the guards page Roland, who could be there in fifteen minutes. Salazar could generally hold down the fort until then.

The door to the infirmary buzzed and then slammed open. Two men were wheeled in on gurneys, one pushed by a member of the riot patrol, the other pushed by Officer Galloway. Salazar was familiar enough with Galloway to recognize his cruel brand of psychopathology. He was as dangerous as any of the inmates.

Salazar was at the sink, washing his hands. He picked up a towel and headed over to the two patients. "What happened?" he asked no one in particular.

Galloway responded. "This guy," he said, pointing to the white man lying on the stretcher he was pushing, "stabbed that guy."

Salazar looked back and forth between the two men. The stab wound on the large black man was evident and would require immediate attention. He looked stable, though. The other man appeared to be in greater pain.

"What happened to him?" Salazar asked, pointing to Womak.

"He needed to be subdued," Galloway replied. "He had a knife. I broke his arms."

"Both of them?"

Galloway stared at Salazar without answering, daring Salazar to challenge his authority. Salazar was too smart to make such a mistake.

"Right. Wheel him into bay two," Salazar said, pointing to a medical treatment area on one side of the room. "I'll get the bleeding from the stab wound under control, then take a look at him." He wheeled the stabbing victim over to a medical bay on the other side of the room. Pulling out some scissors, he cut off the man's shirt. He pulled an overhead light toward the patient and focused it on the wound, snapping on some gloves as he took swabs to wipe away the blood. He was concentrating on his patient when he heard a commotion over in the other bay.

"Fuck! No! Get away!" the other patient was screaming.

Salazar hurried over and looked behind the curtain. "What's happening here?" he demanded.

"I'm handcuffing him to the bed," Galloway replied.

"Fuck you! It hurts!" the prisoner pleaded.

Salazar's gloved hands were covered in Jefferson's blood, so he leaned in to take a cursory look at the man's arms. There were deep purple welts along the upper arms, where he'd been hit. It didn't look as though the bones were misaligned, but based on the amount of pain, it was likely that the humeri were fractured. "Just cuff his ankles," Salazar said.

"Fuck that," Galloway said.

"Officer." Salazar tried to make his voice sound reasonable. "Where do you think he's going to go?"

Galloway looked angry at first. Then he gave Salazar a demented smile. "Fine," he said. "You want him, you got him." He put some ankle chains on the patient and attached them to the bottom of the stretcher. Then he looked at the other guard, who was hanging back by the door to the infirmary. "C'mon, Dan. Let's grab a cup of coffee." To Salazar, he said, "You're on your own, asshole."

The two men left the infirmary, and Salazar heard the door lock behind them. He was glad to have Galloway out of the room; there was no telling what mischief the man could cause with the patients. Salazar looked at the injured man lying on the gurney. "I have to stop the bleeding on the man you stabbed," he said. "Then I'll be back to take a good look at your arms."

Womak nodded. "Thanks."

Salazar returned to his first patient and continued cleaning out the wound. He pressed his fingers on the man's abdomen and pulled the wound apart. "This is going to hurt a little," he said. "I'd give you some painkillers, but they don't give me the keys to the good stuff."

Jefferson grunted through the pain, gritting his teeth. Salazar leaned in for a closer look, his fingers probing through the flesh as the over-head light shimmered off the brilliant red seeping out of the large man. "It's deep," Salazar said. "But it doesn't look like it penetrated deep enough to get near the internal organs." He pulled his hands away, and Jefferson relaxed a little. "They'll probably run some tests on you and do some more probing when the real doctor gets back, but you're going to be fine."

Jefferson smiled up at him. "Thanks, Doc. Guess I am lucky, huh?"

Salazar snapped off the sterile gloves covered in blood and tossed them in the biohazard container. He patted Jefferson on the shoulder. "Now I have to look at the other guy."

He turned to head back to the other medical bay but stopped short.

The other patient was standing directly in front of him. He had an excited smile on his face and a length of aluminum piping he'd pulled off the gurney in his hand. The gurney itself was still chained to his ankle and dragging behind him. "Hiya, Doc. That won't be necessary. I'm feeling much better now." He raised his hand up, and the metal slashed down through the air, connecting with Salazar's head.

"So, what now, boss?"

Lissa Krantz was in a good mood, in spite of the fact that the investigation into the Salazar case seemed to be going so poorly. Kozlowski had spent the night again, and this time they'd even managed a few hours of sleep . . . after.

She loved his simplicity. His honesty. His sincerity. She loved the way he made her feel protected. She also loved his body, and by all indications, that adoration was mutual. The age difference didn't bother her at all; she never even thought about it. Truth be told, she'd always felt as though she had wear and tear beyond her years; the wild days of her youth had put miles on her that didn't show but were felt deep in her soul.

"I need you to meet with the alibi witness when you get a chance," Finn responded. "What's her name?"

"Maria Sanchez?"

"Right. She lives in West Roxbury. According to her story, at the time Steele was being attacked, Salazar was at her house, helping to deliver her baby. She says she was too afraid to come forward before because she was in the country illegally. She ended up marrying an American, so she doesn't have that problem anymore. Of course, her testifying about things that happened fifteen years ago is going to be subject to all sorts of challenge, but we still need to get it down in an affidavit for her to sign. That way we can put that issue to rest."

"I'll do that today."

"Good." Finn scanned his schedule. "I have a conference call with Billy Smith later this morning. He got all the fingerprint material yesterday, so I'm hopeful he'll be able to give us a preliminary analysis today."

She looked across the room at him. There were dark circles under his eyes. "When was the last time you slept?"

"Sleep's overrated."

"When was the last time you spoke to Wonder Woman down in D.C.?"

He glared at her. "Minding your own goddamned business is not overrated."

"All I'm saying is that you're worrying me. You're putting every bit of your heart into this case, and I'm having trouble figuring out why. You're losing your perspective, and that's a dangerous thing to let happen. Assuming Salazar is innocent—"

"He is innocent."

"Right. Assuming that, what happened to him is really shitty, but it's not your fault."

"How about Dobson? I guess that's not my fault, either."

"You're goddamned right it's not." Lissa looked hard at him. "Dobson was a big boy. He made his own decisions, same as me and you. You can beat yourself up over his murder all you want, but it didn't have a fucking thing to do with you. You need to get a grip. This Salazar guy is your client, not your family."

"My clients are my family."

"That's fucking pathetic, boss."

"I'm sorry, have we not met?" He extended his hand. "Scott Finn, Esquire. I make my living in pathos."

She shook her head. "You can make your money anywhere you want. It doesn't mean you have to live there."

"You'll make a really mediocre lawyer with that attitude."

"That's bullshit, and you know it."

He withdrew his hand and turned away from her for a moment. When he looked back at her, she could see his determination. "Vincente Salazar is my client. He's innocent, and it wasn't his choice to spend the past fifteen years of his life in prison. I'm not going to let him die in there."

———

Salazar saw the aluminum rod flash in Womak's hand as it swung toward him. There wasn't time to deflect the blow, but he managed to duck and absorb much of the impact. The metal caught him on the side of his head, and he felt the skin split, unleashing a torrent of blood, but the force wasn't great enough to separate him from consciousness.

He stumbled back, falling into Jefferson, who grunted in pain. Salazar looked up and saw Womak advancing on him, baring his yellowed teeth in a sickening display of ecstasy. For a moment Salazar thought the man was trying to finish off Jefferson and viewed Salazar as a mere hurdle, but as he came closer, Womak's attention never wavered.

"Time's up, you fucking spic," Womak spat as he swung again.

Salazar dodged the second blow entirely, the aluminum clanging off the restraining bars on Jefferson's stretcher. The swing, combined with the awkwardness of dragging around his own bed, left Womak exposed, and Salazar saw his chance. He went to swing his arm with all his might, aiming for Womak's neck, but something was wrong. His arm wouldn't move. He looked behind him and saw that Jefferson had grabbed his shirtsleeve and was holding on.

"Don't think so, motherfucker," Jefferson cackled. Then to Womak, he said, "Finish this, you stupid fuckin' redneck!"

With his arm held stationary, Salazar was trapped. He looked up again and saw that Womak had regained his balance and was going in for the kill.

Salazar reacted without thought. He whipped his free elbow around behind him. His aim was perfect: He caught Jefferson's stomach square on the open stab wound. The large man screamed, letting go of Salazar's arm and doubling over.

Womak was still coming. Salazar kicked out as hard as he could, connecting with the gurney attached to the convict's ankles. The wheels slid backward, pulling Womak's feet out from under him. He went down hard, face-first on the tiling.

Salazar felt Jefferson grabbing for him and gave him another quick elbow to the gut. Then he turned to see Womak struggling to get to his feet. He had one hand on the gurney and was pulling himself up, his elbow balanced on his knee.

Salazar lifted his foot and brought it down hard on the killer's forearm with his entire weight. He caught it at its weakest point—directly in the center of the span running from the man's elbow on his knee to his wrist on the gurney—and split both bones of the arm in two. As his foot continued on its floor-bound trajectory, the splintered ends of the bones tore through the man's skin and rattled together as they hit the ground.

Womak's scream was ear-shattering but brief as shock overtook him and he collapsed on the floor.

Salazar's heart was pounding, and the adrenaline was coursing through his veins as he brought his booted foot up again, hovering over the unconscious man's head.

"What the hell is going on here?" someone yelled.

Salazar looked up and saw the riot guard in the doorway. Behind him stood Galloway.

"Yeah, what is this?" Galloway managed.

Salazar put his foot back on the floor and leaned over Womak's gurney. He felt nauseated. "They attacked me," he choked out.

"What?" the riot guard said. "How?"

"His arms weren't broken," Salazar replied. The spit in his throat had gone dry, and he gagged.

The riot guard walked over and looked down at the mess on the floor. "Well, looks like his arm is broken now."

Salazar looked down also. Then he looked at Galloway. The man seemed to be searching for words. "I thought you said you broke his arms."

Galloway looked at him, his hand going to his nightstick. "I thought I did. You're the fucking doctor, right? You should have checked."

"You said you broke his arms."

"Fuck you, convict."

Salazar pulled himself together. Then he bent over and grasped Womak under the arms. "Give me a hand," he said.

"What are you going to do?" the riot guard asked.

"If I don't get his arm taken care of quickly, he could lose it. Then I've got to check this man's belly wound. It's going to be another couple of minutes before Dr. Roland gets here."

"They tried to kill you," the riot guard said. "You really care what happens to them?"

"I'm a doctor," Salazar said. "It's my job. Now give me a hand."

Chapter Twenty-three

"Sorry, Finn. I wish I had some better news for you."

Finn held the phone to his ear and struggled against the impulse to smash the receiver into the desktop. "How sure are you, Smitty? I mean, it's not like this is entirely an exact science, right?"

"It's science enough for me to know for sure that the two prints match. In some cases, it can be a close call, but not here. I found nineteen clear points of similarity."

Finn hung his head but fought back against the odds. "Okay, so nineteen points. That's not an exact match, right?"

"There's no such thing as an exact match," Smith replied. "When you take prints from two different places or at two different times, there are always going to be small differences, even when it's the same finger. Depending on how much pressure is applied to the finger when it touches the surface, the nature and qualities of the surface itself, the angle of the finger, whether or not it's a partial print, and so on. There are a million different variables, so even the same finger never leaves the exact same print twice. That's why we look for points of similarity—distinctive swirls or ridges that match up—to compare prints. You get enough points of similarity, and you know you've got a match."

"How many are enough?" Finn was sounding desperate, and he

knew it. He'd been counting on Smitty to come back with a result that would let him cast doubt on the testimony of the fingerprint expert who'd helped put Salazar away.

"It depends."

"On what?"

"On the degree of similarity, on whether or not there are different levels of similarity that can be seen on a clear print, and on how all the factors add up in the judgment of the fingerprint technician."

"You mean there's no magic number?" Finn had trouble accepting that notion.

"It depends on the state. Some states require six points of similarity. Some eight. Some ten. Other states leave it up to the discretion of the examiner. In some states, matches have been admitted based on as few as three similarities depending on all the factors taken together."

"How about Massachusetts? Is there a rule here?"

"You guys are a discretionary state."

"Great." Finn was disgusted. "So all we need here is some cop on the stand who says, 'Yeah, taking everything into account, I think it's a match'?"

"More or less, yeah. Shit happens, y'know? These guys are professionals." Smith sounded defensive, and Finn quickly realized that he wasn't doing himself any favors by antagonizing his own expert.

"Okay, but all we've really got here is the opinion of one guy on the stand. That's something, at least."

Smith laughed derisively. "That might be something in another case. It's nothing here."

"Why?"

"Because. You'll never find another credible expert who's going to disagree with the fact that these two particular prints match. We're talking about nineteen points. There's no place in the world where that's not considered a conclusive match. You're never going to find anyone to say different—for any fee."

Finn considered his next question carefully. "Not even you?"

"Sorry, my friend," Smith said. "I value my reputation more than any single fee, no matter how high. Hell, you don't even pay as well as some of the bigger firms I work with. If I didn't like you in the first place, I probably wouldn't take your calls anymore."

Finn blew out a long breath. "This guy's innocent, Smitty," he said. "Innocent. You know what that means?"

"Sure. It means he got fucked somehow—if you're right. He's not the first, and he sure as hell won't be the last. It's a simple matter of odds. There are more than two million people in prison in this country. You lock up two million people, and you're gonna get it wrong a few times."

"And you can live with that?" Finn demanded.

"Hell yes. And I'm sure as shit not going to get myself locked up in there with them by getting myself caught up in a perjury count. I don't care how much I like you."

"I know," Finn said. "You're right." He thought for a long moment. "Is there any way we can attack the match? Anything you can give me?"

"If I was up there, I could buy you a beer. I'm not, though, so . . ."

"Nothing? No suggestions?"

Smith considered the question. "Okay. Let's assume you're right and this guy really is innocent. That would mean someone fucked up the evidence, either accidentally or otherwise. So the logical question is: Who could have done that?"

"Cops," Finn answered without a thought.

"Makes the most sense," Smith agreed. "Cops have the best opportunity to frame someone. But why Salazar?"

"I don't know," Finn admitted. "But then I don't really care why. I just want my guy out. Salazar was sent up for shooting a cop. Maybe they just wanted to make sure that someone did the time."

"Could be," Smitty said halfheartedly. "It's never good for the boys in blue if a cop gets shot and everyone thinks someone got away with it. Sometimes it's better for the cops if they arrest someone—anyone—rather than let it go officially unsolved."

"So," Finn pushed the thought along, "let's assume for the moment that the cops did this deliberately. How would they go about it? And more importantly, how do we prove it?"

"Interesting question," Smith said. "The easiest way would be to lie on the stand. Claim that two prints matched when they didn't. That didn't happen here. Like I told you, these prints definitely match."

"Okay," Finn conceded. "So how else could they do it?"

"They could lie about whose prints they were comparing."

"I don't understand."

"I mean, they've got the set of prints from the gun, a set of prints from Salazar, and a set of prints from the real perp. They switch the names on the prints belonging to Salazar and the perp. Then they're telling the truth that the prints match, but they're lying about whose prints they are."

"Could they do that and get away with it?"

"Why not?"

"I don't know. Wouldn't someone notice that the prints weren't Salazar's?"

"How? It's not like anyone recognizes their fingerprints by sight. I could flash anyone's prints up on a screen and tell you they're yours, and you'd have no way of knowing. Hell, the reality is that a jury will usually believe any so-called fingerprint expert no matter what the prints look like."

"It's just a little disturbing that it could be that easy to frame someone and get away with it." Finn forced himself to get beyond his disbelief. "Okay, let's assume that's what happened here. How do we prove it?"

"That's easy," Smith said. "Just send me a fresh set of Salazar's prints—ones you know for a fact are actually his. If they don't match up with the two sets I've got here, then bingo: We know someone pulled a switch."

It would be difficult, but Finn would find a way to get it done quickly. "Okay. Now let's assume that's not what happened. Are there any other ways someone could have done this to set Salazar up?"

"Sure," Smith said. "They could've planted Salazar's prints on the gun."

"How would they do that?"

"They just get something with a clear print from your boy—a glass or something that holds the finger's acids well—cover the print with tape so the adhesive picks up the print, pull the tape off, and put it on the gun. The tape transfers the oils that make up the fingerprint to the new surface—in this case, the gun. Take off the tape, and you've got yourself some fake evidence good enough to send someone away nine times out of ten."

"Can it be detected?"

"Depends on how well it was done. Sometimes you can leave some of the adhesive on the gun as well. It doesn't prove that the print was planted, but unless there's some other logical explanation, it certainly raises doubt."

"Doubt's all I'm looking for."

"Don't get your hopes up too high, Finn. After fifteen years, the likelihood that you'd find something is pretty slim. It's worth a try, but I wouldn't bank on it. Can you get ahold of the gun?"

"I don't know. Salazar's defense had a right to examine it when he was tried, but now that he's been convicted, I get only what the district attorney or the court gives me. They won't give it up without a fight."

"I sure wouldn't," Smith said.

"I'll try to figure something out. Can you think of any other way someone could have messed with the evidence?"

"Not offhand, but I'll give it some thought."

"Would you?" Finn asked. "I'd really appreciate it."

"No, you'll really pay for it. You may work for free for this guy. I don't."

"Fair enough. Send me your bill, and I'll take care of it."

"I like the sound of that," Smith said. "And send me a fresh set of Salazar's prints when you get a chance. I'll compare them with the prints I've got down here."

"Will do. And, Smitty?"

"Yeah?"

"Thanks."

Finn spent much of the rest of the morning on the Internet, learning more about the process of fingerprint identification. It was helpful to have Smitty guiding him through through the morass, but there was no substitute for independent research. Besides, Smitty relied on the perception of fingerprint analysis as a firm science for his livelihood, and Finn had some reason to question his objectivity on the subject. The expert's description of the subjective nature of the process had surprised Finn, and he was anxious to learn more.

What he discovered shocked him. He'd always assumed that fingerprint analysis was an objective science: Either the prints matched or they didn't. But in reality, whether two sets of prints matched was often more a matter of opinion than fact, and there were numerous recent examples of misidentifications. In 2004 an Oregon man had been arrested based on a match of his fingerprints with those of prints found on items tied to the terrorist bombing of a Madrid train that had killed dozens of people. Two FBI fingerprint experts had confirmed that the prints were a clear match, and the man had spent six weeks in prison as they investigated him to shore up their case. Ultimately, it was determined that the prints, while similar, did not match, and the man was released. The clear error had led several courts to examine whether fingerprint matches were based on sufficiently reliable science to be admitted as evidence in prosecutions. While no court had yet barred the practice, the confidence in the science had been shaken.

Finn was lost in his research when the phone rang. He let Lissa answer it.

"Law offices of Scott Finn," he heard her say. "He is, can I tell him who's calling?" There was a pause. Then she looked across the room at him. "It's your client," she said.

"What client?"

"Salazar. Who the fuck do you think?"

"On the phone?"

"No, under my desk. Of course on the phone. Pick up."

He pushed the button on his extension and picked up the receiver. "Vincente?"

"Mr. Finn, I'm sorry to disturb you."

"No problem. I just wasn't expecting your call." Finn looked at his watch. Eleven thirty. "Aren't you in lockdown? I thought lunch wasn't until noon."

"I'm in the infirmary," Salazar replied.

"Right. I forgot you work there."

"Normally, yes. At the moment, though, I'm technically a patient. I was calling to warn you: You're in danger."

The man's tone made Finn's toes go cold. He wasn't hysterical or melodramatic; his voice was calm and even. "What happened?" Finn asked.

"I was attacked," Salazar answered. "They tried to kill me."

"Who?"

"Whoever's behind this."

"Wait," Finn said. "Start from the beginning."

Salazar explained what had happened that morning in the infirmary, highlighting some of the more graphic and disturbing aspects to drive home the seriousness of the situation.

"Are you all right?" Finn asked once Salazar had finished.

"I have a cut on my head," he replied. "The doctors here have closed the wound, and other than that, I am fine. For now."

"Can they get to you again?" Finn asked.

"Hard to say. The doctors will keep me here in the infirmary for as long as they can, for 'observation.' That can't last forever, though. The prison officials won't let it; they will get suspicious. Besides, if this morning is any indication, I am not completely safe even in here. Once I'm back in the general population, I will have to be particularly careful."

"What can I do?" Finn asked.

"Nothing," Salazar said. Then, after a moment: "Get me out of this place. That's all you can do."

"I'm working on it."

"I know." The man's voice was raspy and distant, and Finn could tell he was exhausted. "I have papers in my cell," he said. "Notes, a diary, things like that. If anything happens to me, I want you to make sure my daughter gets them."

"Nothing's going to happen to you."

"Of course. I know they are coming now, and that gives me somewhat of an advantage. I will be expecting them. I will be waiting for them. But if . . ."

"I'll make sure she gets them."

"The first thing they do when a prisoner is killed in here is clean out his cell. They need to make space for more bodies. They throw everything out, so you'll have to act fast and make it clear that you know the papers are there. They are the only thing I have that I can leave to Rosita. Promise me you'll save them for her."

"I promise," Finn said. "We're going to get you out."

"You seem confident," Salazar said. He sounded anything but. "Is there any word on the DNA tests yet?"

"None," Finn admitted.

"And the fingerprint and eyewitness identifications?"

Finn wasn't sure what to say. "We're still chasing down some leads," he lied. "I'm going to send someone up there today to take your fingerprints again, okay?"

"Why?"

"It's just a hunch, but do it."

"I will."

"We're going to get you out," Finn said again, but there was less conviction in his voice this time.

"Thank you," Salazar said.

Finn struggled for something else to say. "Is there anything else I can do?" he asked.

"Yes," Salazar replied. "You can be very careful. Whoever is behind this has already killed Mark Dobson. Now they have tried to have me killed. They will not hesitate to come after anyone who is helping me. You are in danger."

"I can take care of myself."

"I hope so," Salazar said. "I truly hope so."

Chapter Twenty-four

"You sure this is the way you want to handle this?"

Finn glared at Kozlowski as they drove the short distance from Charlestown to downtown Boston. "I'm sure," he said. "Full-frontal assault. Try to shake them and see what falls out of the trees."

Kozlowski grunted. "Cops usually don't shake. Not without some serious pushing, anyway. And it doesn't feel like we've got a hell of a lot to push with."

"You want me to pull over and you can get out?"

"That'd be a good way to get you killed. Send you into a police station by yourself to start throwing accusations around. You think we got a chilly reception from Maddy Steele? She was the fuckin' welcome wagon compared to the reaction you're likely to get here."

"We don't have any options. They tried to kill him."

"Who tried to kill him?"

"I guess that's the sixty-four-thousand-dollar question, isn't it?"

"And you act like you've got the answer all worked out. Maybe it's not the real question. Maybe the real question is why even our own fingerprint expert says Salazar's prints are on the gun. You seem unwilling to consider the possibility that the man actually did what he got himself convicted of."

Finn shook his head. "After my talk with Smitty, I did some research on my own. He said there were no real consistent standards for fingerprint identification. Turns out that was the understatement of the year. In England, examiners are required to find at least sixteen points of similarity to declare a match between two sets of prints. Here in the States, some identifications are made with as little as six. Plus, there's no official standard for what constitutes enough 'similarity' to have a point match. The so-called experts aren't required to pass any tests to prove they know what they're doing, and lots of them have never even had any formal training other than being on the job for six months. Seems like it's far more opinion than science."

Kozlowski shrugged. "Let's assume that's all true. So what?"

"So what?"

"Yeah, so what?"

Finn sat in silence, clenching and unclenching his jaw. "Do you realize that there have never been any studies done to determine exactly how accurate fingerprint identification is? No studies. No tests. Nothing that even remotely qualifies as science. Anytime anyone has suggested that might be a good idea, the law enforcement community bands together to fight it tooth and nail. You know why?"

"Maybe because it would waste a bunch of taxpayer money to test a method of identification that has proved reliable for over a hundred years?" Kozlowski suggested.

"No. Because they know any studies testing the accuracy of fingerprint evidence might just show that it's bad science. And then what would you do with all the people who've been convicted based on it?"

"Again, even assuming everything you say is true—and I'm guessing at least half of it is nothing more than bleeding-heart-liberal bullshit—so what? Smitty said he had a nineteen-point match on these particular prints. And he's on our side. So even if there are times when people screw up or stretch their identifications, this isn't one of those times."

"We'll see," Finn grumbled.

"Shit, you've got a fingerprint match positively confirmed by our own expert, as well as an eyewitness identification, and you still can't bring yourself to allow for the possibility that the man's guilty. That's fucked up."

"Great. You're going to throw the eyewitness identification at me now? They actually *have* done studies on the accuracy of eyewitness testimony. Do you know what they found? They found that people get it wrong much of the time. Even with a good, solid look at someone, people who 'positively' identify someone in a lineup are often wrong. Does it matter? No. You put a victim on the stand, or an eyewitness, and have him point at the defendant during a trial and say, 'That's him; that's the man,' and a jury buys it every single time."

"I hear you, but what's the alternative? You take away fingerprint analysis and eyewitness testimony, and how are you going to prosecute anybody? How are you going to prevent or punish crime at all?"

"Have you ever heard the expression that it's better to let ten guilty men go free than put one innocent man in jail? That's one of the fundamental principles our system was based on. That's why we require guilt beyond a reasonable doubt."

"Fine," Kozlowski agreed. "Let ten guilty men go free to protect one innocent man. How about one hundred? Is it better that a hundred guilty bastards go free than one innocent man goes to jail? How about a thousand? Or ten thousand? How many killers and rapists and child molesters are you willing to let out on the streets to protect that one innocent man?"

"You're taking it to its illogical extreme."

"No, you are. You want to wipe away the basic tools that allow us to be reasonably sure that we've got the right guy."

Finn pulled into the parking lot across the street from the station house for Division B-2, where the latent fingerprint unit was located. He whipped the car into a spot and turned off the engine. "I don't know," he said, unbuckling his seat belt. "What I do know is that someone tried to kill our client this morning. I know that the last lawyer who represented him was hacked to pieces. That says to me that something is very fucked up here, and it all comes back to the fingerprint evidence. I need to know that you're on board with what we're doing here."

"I am. But you also need to know that things aren't always the way they seem."

Finn opened the door, and a blast of cold air filled the little car. "Trust me," he said. "No one knows that better than I do."

———

Lissa Krantz stood on the front porch of the small, neatly kept Cape where Juanita Sobol—formerly Sanchez—lived in West Roxbury. By all indications, it was a solid middle-class neighborhood where working families piled into minivans and cooked out on their barbecues during the summer.

Lissa rang the doorbell, checking her watch as she waited quietly. She should have called first, just to make sure Mrs. Sobol was there. She was going to be annoyed with herself if she'd wasted the trip. She was sure the woman was home, though—Dobson's notes indicated that she was a stay-at-home mother, and the telltale three-year-old Grand Caravan was sitting in the driveway. Dobson's notes also indicated that fifteen years earlier, when Sobol was still Sanchez, she was an illegal immigrant living a few blocks from the apartment Vincente Salazar had shared with his family. She was giving birth at the time Madeline Steele was shot, and according to what she had told Dobson, Salazar was there helping with the delivery. At the time of Vincente's trial, she had been unwilling to come forward because of her fear that she would be deported, but now that she was married to a U.S. citizen, she had agreed to tell her story.

This was what Dobson had indicated in his notes, but it was now Lissa's job to lock in the woman's story and get her to sign an affidavit. Lissa looked at her watch again and rang the doorbell a second time. At last the door was unlocked from within and pulled open a crack. Lissa could see a sliver of a woman in her late thirties with straight black hair and nervous eyes.

"Yes?" the woman said. She had a heavy accent.

"Hi. My name is Lissa Krantz, and I'm looking for Juanita Sobol."

Lissa's friendly tone did nothing to chase the nervousness from the woman's eyes. "I am Juanita," she said.

"Great. I work with the attorney who represents Vincente Salazar, and I just wanted to go over your statement with you—get it all down on paper and have you sign it. Can I come in?"

"There's been a mistake," Juanita blurted out.

"A mistake?"

"Yes. I am sorry, I can't help you."

Lissa was stunned. "I don't understand. How has there been a mistake?"

"There just has. I was wrong."

"About what?"

"I don't know whether I was with Mr. Salazar. I can't help you."

Lissa took out a copy of the affidavit she had drafted from Dobson's notes. "But you spoke with Mark Dobson. Didn't you tell him that Vincente Salazar was with you at the time the police officer was shot?" She waved the draft affidavit in front of the woman.

"I'm sorry," Juanita said as she started to close the door, but Lissa stuck her foot in the way.

"They can't deport you anymore," Lissa said. "You're an American citizen."

Juanita shook her head. "I can't be sure it was the same night," she protested.

Lissa crossed her arms in front of her chest. "What's your son's birthday?"

"What?"

"I'm sure you know your son's birthday, right? And Vincente Salazar was there to deliver your son? All we have to do is match up the dates."

The woman's look went from nervous to scared. "Leave, please," she said.

"No."

"I will call the police."

"Why won't you talk to me?"

"I have a family. I have a husband. I have children."

Lissa took a step back and looked at the woman carefully. "Did someone threaten you? Did someone tell you to change your story?"

"I have a family," Juanita repeated.

"I know. Including a son that Vincente Salazar delivered."

She shook her head. "I am sorry, as I said. But I will call the police if you don't leave."

She closed the door, and Lissa was left standing on the front steps of the neat little Cape. "Fuck," she said. She slapped the door once. "Vincente Salazar has a family, too, you know!" she yelled.

She waited another minute to see whether that fact might move Juanita Sobol to change her mind, but the door remained closed. At last she picked up her bag and walked back to her car.

<hr>

B-2 was an old cement structure built in the 1950s, with all the postmodern utilitarian warmth of the period's architecture. As cold as the December winds were, Finn didn't really feel the chill that morning until he stood outside the police station.

"Charming," he commented.

"Yeah," Kozlowski replied. "It's worse on the inside."

They walked into the station house, and Kozlowski headed straight for the front desk. The man behind the desk was a roly-poly specimen in his fifties with huge jowls and a double chin that looked like it was competing for goiter status. "Koz," the man greeted him genially. "They didn't let your sorry ass back on the force, did they?"

"No such luck for you, Sarge," Kozlowski replied. "They figure they got to give the bad guys a fighting chance, I guess."

"Good to see you. How's everything going?" The man held out a flabby hand, and Kozlowski shook it.

"Good. How's everything here?"

The sergeant shrugged. "You know, same shit, different decade. It never really changes; we just keep fighting the tide. What brings you down?"

Kozlowski nodded toward Finn. "This is Finn, a guy I work with. We need to talk to Eddie Fornier, down in the fingerprint unit."

The desk sergeant's face darkened. "'Bout what?"

"Nothing serious," Kozlowski replied. "Just an old case. We need some details."

The frown hung in on the man's face. "Okay," he said skeptically. He looked over the roster behind the desk. "He's downstairs. Checked in an hour ago or so."

Kozlowski looked at his watch. "It's almost noon. They pulling night shifts down there these days?"

The sergeant shook his head. "That's just Fornier. Always has been." Finn had the distinct impression that the man would have said much more had he been alone with Kozlowski. Finn made a mental note to have Kozlowski follow up with him later to get the whole story. "You know where the unit is, right?" he asked.

"Yeah," Kozlowski replied. He shook the sergeant's hand again and turned to head through a door toward the back of the lobby.

Finn followed Kozlowski down the hallway to a steel door, saying nothing. As Kozlowski pulled the door open, Finn was assaulted by a wave of warm, humid, putrid air.

"What the fuck is that stench?" he asked.

"Mold, for the most part. That and car exhaust. The motor pool is attached to the fingerprint lab, and they have to keep the door open to get any circulation."

They walked down the concrete steps, along another corridor, to a dark door with white stenciling that read LATENT FINGERPRINT UNIT, chipping at the edges. Kozlowski pulled the door open, and the two of them stepped inside.

It took a moment for Finn's eyes to adjust. The jaundiced fluorescent lights pulsated, giving the small room a strangely cinematic quality that made it difficult to focus. There were no windows, and the aging ventilation system delivered a steady stream of mildewed air that choked his nostrils. Finn wondered what manner of sins an officer had to commit to be sentenced to this dungeon.

A young woman was sitting at a desk near the door, hunched over a stack of greasy, inky fingerprint reports, moving a magnifying glass back and forth from sheet to sheet with passionless assembly-line efficiency. She looked up at her visitors. "Can I help you?" she asked. She was dressed in a gray pantsuit, her jacket slung over the back of the chair to reveal a white cotton dress shirt that flickered yellow under the fluorescents.

"We're looking for Fornier," Kozlowski said in a neutral tone.

"In the back," she replied. She turned back to her task.

She reminded Finn of an automaton from some Orwellian nightmare. "Thanks," he said. She didn't acknowledge him.

The room was partitioned into four separate areas by large gray dividers. Finn noticed that the fabric was stained and fraying and falling off in numerous spots. As they moved back, deeper into the space, Finn saw a half-eaten meatball sandwich sitting deserted on a desk. Two flies jousted above it.

They passed into the back area and found a diminutive man in his late forties sitting with his feet up on his desk, staring at the ceiling with a vacant expression. A can of Coca-Cola was wedged into his crotch.

"Fornier?" Kozlowski asked him.

It took a moment for the man to react, and Finn wondered briefly whether he was dead. Then he spoke. "Who wants to know?"

"Officer Fornier, we have a few questions to ask you about a case you worked on awhile back," Finn said.

Fornier pulled his legs off the desk, and the shift in his balance pulled his body forward, snapping his head upright. He closed his eyes and pinched the bridge of his nose between a thumb and forefinger, then rubbed his eyeballs as though attempting to focus. "Why?" he asked.

Kozlowski opened his wallet and displayed the card identifying him as a former police detective. "It's just routine," he said. He sounded like he was still a cop.

Fornier crossed his arms. "Fine. Ask away."

"Do you remember the Vincente Salazar case?" Finn asked.

Fornier's posture stiffened. "No."

"Your testimony put him away," Finn said.

"My testimony has put away a lot of scumbags," Fornier retorted. "I can't be expected to remember every one of them." His eyes were lined in red, and what little was left of the whites shone a sickly yellow-gray, but he seemed determined to hold his own.

"We have reason to believe the testimony you gave in this particular case was wrong," Finn said, instilling his tone with confidence. "Are you going to talk to us, or are we going to have to get a subpoena and do this under oath?"

"Who the fuck are you?"

"I'm Mr. Salazar's lawyer, and I can assure you that we're going to have this conversation one way or another."

Fornier's resolve seemed to slacken. "It was a long time ago," he said. "What the fuck do you want to know?"

Finn glared at him. "I thought you said you didn't remember the case. Now you know it was a long time ago?"

"Fuck you. He shot a cop. I do maybe twenty cases a week, but I remember the ones who shoot cops."

"So, you want to tell us about the prints?" There was a threat in Finn's tone, though he had nothing to back it up with.

Fornier studied Finn closely, sizing him up. Finally, he said, "Fuck you. You've got shit. I can see it in your eyes. I did my job."

"What I've got," Finn said, "are the results of a DNA test that show Salazar didn't do it. He's innocent. You talk to us, and maybe you can get out ahead of this thing before it ruins your career."

Fornier sneered. "Bullshit. If you had DNA tests that backed you up, you wouldn't be wasting your time here. Besides, even if you did have test results, you think I give a shit? Check the prints yourself. They match, so you can get the fuck out of my face. Besides, the cop he shot identified him, right?"

"Are you saying you were told about the ID before you ran the prints?" Finn pushed.

"What I'm saying is that I'm done talking to you." Fornier stood up and started walking around his desk to get out. Kozlowski took two quick strides and stood in front of him, trapping him behind the desk. The size differential between the two men was comical, but Fornier wasn't backing off.

"Careful, big boy," he said. "You're in a police station now, and the word 'retired' is printed in big bright letters across that fucking ID you showed me. You want a world full of trouble, you just keep standing there."

Kozlowski leaned in close to the man, meeting him eye to eye. Then he closed his eyes and gave a sniff. "I smell fear," he said, opening his eyes again.

Fornier shoved the bigger man in the chest. Kozlowski didn't move, and Fornier managed only to push himself back farther behind the desk. "Motherfucker," Fornier said. "You got any issues, you take them upstairs. Like I said, I'm done talking. Now back off and let me out, or I swear I'll call the desk sergeant and he'll have a SWAT team down here in a matter of seconds."

Kozlowski stepped back, and Fornier squeezed between him and the wall.

"This isn't done," Finn said. "Expect a subpoena and a lot more questions."

"Fuck you." Fornier walked past him toward the door at the front of the room. "You got shit, and you know it. Your boy is where he belongs, and that's where he's gonna stay."

———⊕———

Back out on the street, Finn and Kozlowski headed toward the parking lot. The day had grayed while they were in the windowless basement, and their moods were a fine match for the weather.

"Nice bluff," Kozlowski said. "Let me know the next time you want to get up a game of poker. I could use the cash."

"You're one to talk. 'I smell fear'? Did you really just say that?"

"He knew what I was getting at."

"What, are you part dog now?"

Kozlowski stopped. "You didn't smell it?"

"What? Fear?"

"No, courage," Kozlowski said. "Straight out of the bottle."

Finn raised his eyebrows. "Booze? You serious?"

"No question about it. That's why I leaned in close to him. It was oozing out of his pores, so that takes care of last night. But it was also on his breath, so he had this morning covered as well. He's been soaking in it for a long time, from what I could tell. And I can tell you this for sure: That wasn't just Coke in the can between his legs. That was what you might call an Irish soda pop."

"That's an offensive slur," Finn said, defending his ancestors. "Fornier's French. You really gotta go after my people?"

"Fine, it was the champagne of soft drinks, then. No matter what you call it, he was already hip-deep and sinking fast."

As the two of them kept moving toward the car, they heard someone calling from behind them. "Kozlowski! Koz! Wait up!"

They turned and saw a fit man in his fifties running toward them from the police station.

"He looks familiar," Finn said.

"He used to be my boss," Kozlowski said. "Captain Weidel. You probably dealt with him at some point during the Natalie Caldwell murder investigation—most likely when we thought you were our best suspect."

"Great," Finn said. "This day just keeps getting better."

Weidel reached them quickly. In spite of the fact that he'd been moving at a full sprint, he wasn't even breathing hard. "Kozlowski, we gotta talk," he said.

"How's it going, Cap?" Kozlowski said. "Long time. You remember Scott Finn, I'm guessing?"

The man looked Finn up and down; it took a moment for the recognition to show on his face. "We had you made for the Little Jack deal a few years ago, right?" he said. He didn't offer his hand. Or an apology. Instead, he looked back at Kozlowski. "I see you're hanging out with only the most respectable people these days, huh, Koz?"

"Hey, I was cleared," Finn protested.

Weidel ignored him. "Word's out in the department, Koz. You're trying to buy a walk for the piece of shit who shot Maddy Steele. Is it true?"

"No," Kozlowski said. "I'm not trying to buy anything. We're just trying to figure out whether the guy who went away was the same guy who pulled the trigger. If he is, then he stays in jail, and I'll do whatever it takes to make sure he stays put. If not . . ."

"You know what this kind of shit does to those of us on the front line, right?" Weidel was pointing a finger angrily at Kozlowski.

Kozlowski frowned. "I never really thought of you as a front line kind of guy, Cap. You were really always more in the rear with the gear, from what I remember."

Weidel crossed his arms. "Fine, Koz. You can play the comedian, but there are people you used to work with who go out there on the streets every day and put their asses on the line. Then a bunch of liberal candy-asses come along and try to free some asshole who put one of our own in a chair for life. How do you think that looks to us?"

"Excuse me, Captain," Finn said. "I really think of myself as more of a libertarian candy-ass. Just an FYI."

Weidel ignored him. "It's wrong, Koz. It's just plain wrong, and you know it."

"There's a lot wrong with this case," Kozlowski said. "I know that much for sure."

The police captain stared at him. "You and I never really got along all that well when you were on the force. And I'm not going to stand here and lie to your face and tell you I miss you, or that I was sorry when you left the department—"

"When you forced me out of the department," Kozlowski corrected him.

"Like I said, you were a pain in the ass, and I never liked you. But I at least had respect for your dedication to the job and to your fellow officers. I never would have thought you were capable of this kind of betrayal."

"That's quite an indictment coming from someone who knows as much about betrayal as you."

The man looked away, and when he turned back, there was real hatred in his eyes. "Being a PI can be pretty tough work. You've had it a little easier than others because of your connections on the force. It's given you access a lot of PIs don't ever get. That's over as of now, you know? Don't bother calling anyone here anymore. I can guarantee that no one's going to return your calls. And if I was in your shoes, I'd take great care to make sure I was doing everything by the book. You step even close to the line, and I promise everyone in this department will land on you with both feet. You get that?"

Kozlowski just stared back at the man. Then Weidel turned and headed back toward the station house.

Finn and Kozlowski walked on to the car in silence. When they got there, they looked at each other across the soft top.

"A libertarian?" Kozlowski asked. "Seriously?"

Finn shrugged. "More or less."

"What's that mean, exactly?"

Finn thought about it as he unlocked the doors. "It's basically a conservative who likes sex and drugs."

Kozlowski shook his head. "Huh," he grunted as he slid awkwardly into the car. "I wouldn't have guessed."

Chapter Twenty-five

"How'd everything else go with the investigation today?" Lissa asked.

Kozlowski was lying on a mountain of pillows piled on Lissa Krantz's living room floor. A fire roared in the hearth, and the bay windows gave them a panoramic view of the Charles River and the Esplanade. He'd never believed that anyone really lived life like this. Throughout his life as a cop, the only time he ever came into contact with people who had this kind of money was in the course of an investigation. Invariably, the crime—whether murder or rape or domestic violence—seemed to have its origins in wealth, and he'd been left with the impression that money was, first and foremost, corrosive and corrupting. And yet none of that was in evidence here. Here in this beautiful apartment, with this beautiful woman, everything seemed perfect.

"You were in the office," he answered. "You heard the conversation."

"You call that a conversation? The two of you didn't say more than ten words to each other all afternoon. It was like working in a fucking library." Lissa was lying with her head on his chest. She rolled over onto her elbow to look at him. "Do I look like a goddamned librarian?"

She was naked, and the firelight danced over her smooth dark skin.

He looked at her for a long time before answering, taking in every inch of her. "I don't know," he said. "I haven't been to the library in a while. If you do, I need to get a library card."

"Well, all I know is that I didn't sign up to work in silence. So what the fuck happened today?"

"You mean after someone tried to kill Finn's client, we found out that his fingerprints are really on the gun that shot Maddy Steele, and we lost our alibi witness?"

"Right. After that."

He teased his fingertips across her collarbone. "Nothing."

She lay back down on his chest as he continued touching her. "Nothing?"

"Nothing."

"How the fuck could nothing happen?"

He laughed. "You kidding? That's ninety-nine percent of investigative work. Sitting around, waiting, and watching while nothing happens."

"How does that work in a case like this, when you have only a week before you need to be back in front of a judge with actual answers?"

"Not very well. But all you can do, ultimately, is work the case, be patient, and try to keep your sanity."

"I'm not sure Finn is managing all that well with the last part." As the fire crackled, she wondered what he was thinking, but she knew better than to ask. He wasn't the type of man who enjoyed being probed. "I'm worried about him," she said at last.

"Finn?"

"Yeah, Finn."

"Why?"

"He's so crazed over this fucking case. It's like he's letting everything ride on it, and it's not healthy. He's gonna get hurt."

"Maybe," Kozlowski said after considering it. "He's a fighter, though. Tougher than you think. He'll be fine in the end."

"I don't know. He's really far gone. If this comes out badly, you'll have to be there for him. He needs you, you know?"

"I'm with him. He knows that."

"I'm not talking about just being there for him on the case," she said. "I mean you need to be there for him if the whole thing collapses. You need to tell him that you care about him."

Kozlowski gave a great, hard laugh. "Guys don't say things like that to each other."

"You don't?"

"No."

"Why not?"

"Because we're guys."

"So?"

"We just don't. If I want another guy to know how I feel, I'll buy him a drink."

She was baffled. "A drink says you care?"

"If it's a good drink, yeah."

"Men are fucked up."

"And this is news?"

She rolled over so that she was draped across his chest, and slid a leg over his thighs. She looked at him, and he looked back at her, meeting her eyes without hesitation or avoidance. She ran her hand over his shoulder and up his neck, tracing the outline of his face the way a blind person might. She touched the long scar that ran down the length of his face, and felt him tense ever so slightly. She was tempted, but she didn't ask. He would tell her if he wanted to.

She smiled at him and pinched one of his nipples playfully. "So if a drink means you care, how come you didn't buy me one tonight?"

He slid a hand around her hips and swept her on top of him. "I know a better way to show you how I feel about you," he said, returning her smile.

Finn sat at his desk, staring at the two lists he'd written out two days earlier. Each of the tasks he'd put on his second list had been checked off, yet none of the questions on the first list had been answered. A stack of Redwell folders was piled on one side of the desktop. They contained every slip of paper he had on the Salazar case. He'd been through them all. Three times. He'd spent hours on the Internet, researching fingerprint procedure and evidence; researching DNA procedure and evidence; researching the perils and shortcomings of eyewitness testimony. Nothing seemed to help. Nothing seemed to fit.

He leaned back in his chair and stared at the phone. He probably shouldn't, but he needed to talk to someone. He picked up the receiver and dialed Linda Flaherty's office in Washington. He hung up before the phone rang, though, and put his head in his hands. "Bad idea," he said to himself.

It was at moments like this that he felt her absence most acutely. He'd had friends in the past—good friends, even—but he'd never had anyone in his life with whom he could share his thoughts as freely as he'd been able to with her. Trust wasn't an instinct that came naturally to him, but she had fought through his defenses. As far as he could remember, it had been the first time he had ever let anyone get that close.

It was inevitable, he supposed. They had met when she was a police detective, and she and Kozlowski—her partner—were investigating the murder of one of Finn's coworkers at his old law firm. Finn had been their primary suspect at one point, and though most of the evidence pointed to him, she had refused to believe he was guilty. In return, Finn had saved her life, and the bond between them had been sealed so tightly, he thought it would never be broken.

As he thought back, it seemed that he had no distinct memories from their first month together. They had gotten lost in the newness of their passion, and all he could recall was a blur of excitement and happiness. She'd moved in after that first month, and they'd fallen into a pattern of hectic contentment. Finn had been busy setting up his own practice, and she'd been heading up the Massachusetts Department of Homeland Security. They'd seen each other less and less often, but Finn had still felt the bond, so when she told him she was taking a new job in the federal government, it had hit him like a lead pipe to the stomach.

"How can I turn it down?" she had asked him. "It's the opportunity of a lifetime."

"I thought we were the opportunity of a lifetime" was all he'd been able to say.

"I thought so, too," she'd replied.

The day she'd left, he didn't even drive her to the airport. The taxi arrived, and she kissed him. Then she left without either of them saying a word. Perhaps that was why he still thought there was a chance for them. She hadn't ended it, after all; she hadn't been able to. Instead, she had left in silence, and that was enough to give him hope. Besides, he couldn't imagine that he could ever feel the way he did if they weren't meant to be together. He needed her, and he was convinced that she needed him just as much, even if she couldn't admit it to herself.

He picked up the phone and hit redial.

"Department of Homeland Security, Deputy Secretary Flaherty's office, how can I help you?" The voice was pleasant and crisp, even at nine thirty in the evening. He could almost hear the starch in the young woman's collar.

"Linda Flaherty, please," Finn said. He knew that few people had Linda's direct dial at work, and as a consequence, every call that came over this particular line was taken seriously.

"May I tell her who's calling?" He thought he heard a touch of the Southern accent that had probably been beaten out of the assistant.

"Scott Finn," he replied. The pause on the other end of the line was just long enough to be noticed, and Finn wondered how much of her personal life Linda shared with her assistants.

"Just a moment, please."

Finn sat on hold, listening to a techno-synthesized version of "Stairway to Heaven" that seemed to suggest that, if there were a God, He had a serious vendetta against Led Zepplin. Just as the computer-generated flute picked up some momentum on what had once been a kick-ass guitar solo, the woman came back on the line. "She'll just be a minute."

"Thanks," Finn said, but the woman was already gone. He was back on hold, trapped in the land where decent music goes to die. The Zepplin cover was ending, and it bled troublingly into a candy-coated, upbeat instrumental version of "Welcome to the Jungle." There was no percussion in the arrangement, and Axl Rose's reedy screams had been replaced by two dueling violins. It was, Finn thought, a sign that some-one in Musicland had at least a trace of irony and humor. Mercifully, the torture was short-lived.

"So, you decided to call," Linda Flaherty said when she picked up. "Only two weeks; I suppose I should feel flattered."

Finn had hoped that the sound of her voice might soothe him, but all he heard was anger and sarcasm. He deserved it, he supposed, but it made him question whether his decision to call had been wise.

"I should have called earlier," he admitted. "I'm sorry, I just . . . couldn't."

"What do you want now?" She was even angrier than he had ex-pected.

"Nothing. Just to talk."

"So talk."

He had no idea what to say. "How's everything going with you?"

"Great," she replied.

"How's the job? Is it everything you'd hoped it would be?"

"Oh, sure. Let's see, our country's popularity around the world is at an all-time low; my boss is in the middle of a second term that's turned so ugly, he couldn't get a bill through Congress to save Christmas; and every radical Islamist in the world is trying to buy his way into heaven by blowing up Americans. To top it off, this morning the guy who's second in charge of domestic intelligence was caught by the local cops soliciting sex from a fourteen-year-old in an online chat room. Other than that, the job's an absolute breeze."

"You could always come back to Boston," Finn said, and then regretted it immediately.

"You just won't give it up, will you?"

"I'm sorry, I shouldn't have said that."

"I'm doing something important here, hard as the job is. In fact, if it wasn't important, it wouldn't be hard."

"I know."

"Do you?"

Finn said nothing, and the two of them remained locked in a silent standoff.

"So, what's the case?" she asked at last.

"What case?"

"Don't bother bullshitting me, Finn. I know you better than that. Something's eating at you, and it's not the mess we've made of our relationship."

"At least you called it a relationship. That's something."

She sighed. "What's the case?"

Finn scratched his head. "I'm trying to get a guy out of prison."

"Aren't you always?"

"This is different. This guy is innocent."

"Of what?"

Finn wondered how she meant the question. "Of shooting a cop fifteen years ago." He could almost feel her shaking her head over the line.

"Cops don't like it when you shoot one of their own."

"Good, 'cause my guy didn't do it."

"Did he shoot anyone I knew at the BPD?"

"I don't know. Did you know Madeline Steele?"

"Holy shit, Finn," she said. "Maddy Steele? You're crazy, getting mixed up in something like that."

"Probably. You knew her?"

"Not before the shooting; that was before my time. But I dealt with her a few times afterward, when she was running Victims' Services. She was a good woman."

"She may still be. I couldn't tell. She was too pissed off when I talked to her for me to judge."

"Can you blame her? You're trying to free the man who ruined her life."

"He didn't do it."

"How do you know?"

"I've gotten to know the guy. He didn't do it." It sounded pathetic even to Finn.

"And you've always been such a stellar judge of character."

He moved off in another direction. "He has an alibi now."

"Now? He has an alibi *now*? Do you know how that sounds?"

"And the DNA test is going to come back and show that he didn't do it."

"For your sake, I hope so."

"People tried to kill him in prison this morning."

"Finn, people try to kill each other in prison every day. If getting into a prison beef was a sign of innocence, there'd be no need for jails at all."

"And his last lawyer was murdered." It was a bomb Finn hadn't planned on dropping, but as he sat there, he realized that Dobson's murder was what had really sold him on Salazar's innocence. He needed Linda to understand.

The impact of the news had clearly taken a toll on Flaherty. She was quiet for a moment. "You mean his lawyer fifteen years ago?" There was concern in her voice.

"No," Finn admitted. "This past weekend."

"Jesus Christ, Finn!" He couldn't tell whether she was angry or scared, but in either case it felt good to hear the emotion in her voice. "What the hell are you doing? Why would you take on a case like this?"

"Technically, I had already taken it on before the other guy was killed. I was planning on withdrawing, but then he was murdered. What was I supposed to do?"

She paused before replying, obviously taking it all in. That was how she worked, Finn knew. It was what had made her such a good cop. It was what had made her such a great choice to help run the Department of Homeland Security. She gathered as many facts as she could before coming to final conclusions. "How was he killed?" she asked.

"You don't want to know," he said.

"Finn . . ."

"Fine. He was killed with a machete. There's a gang up here—"

"VDS."

"You've heard of them?" He was genuinely surprised. "The cops thought my guy was involved with them, but it seems pretty clear that they're trying to keep him in prison, so it doesn't make sense that he was a member. I'm still trying to figure all this out."

"Drop the case, Finn." It sounded like she was giving him an order, and it made him bristle.

"What?"

"Now. Drop the case now. File the withdrawal papers in the morning."

"I don't understand."

She groaned. "Sometimes you don't need to understand. Sometimes you just need to listen to people and take their advice. These are very bad people you're dealing with."

Finn laughed. "I've dealt with bad people before, remember?"

"Not people like this. Trust me."

The tone of her voice chilled him. But it also made him curious. "How do you know so much about them?"

"Let's just say they're on our radar screen."

"Why? What for?"

"I can't talk about it. You know that. Just please stay away from anything having anything to do with VDS, okay?"

He thought about it. "I'm not resigning this case. I can't."

She sighed heavily. "No, I suppose you can't." He wondered whether she meant that as criticism. "Can you at least be careful?"

"Don't worry about me; careful is my middle name. A strong sense of self-preservation has always been one of my few redeeming qualities. If I see trouble coming, I'll be the first one out the door."

"I know better than to believe that."

"Can we talk about something else?"

"I don't know," she said. "Do we have anything else to talk about?" In spite of the challenge in her tone, there was a softness, and Finn smiled at the thought of how she must look at the moment: leaning back in her chair, the gray fitted suit he'd bought for her clinging to her body at the end of the hard day, her blouse collar undone. She always looked best at the end of a hard day.

"I hope so," he replied. "I certainly hope so."

———

Vincente Salazar watched the guard pass by the door outside the infirmary. He had much more freedom as a patient than he did in his cell. That was a small blessing, at least.

He slipped his cell phone out of his sock and dialed the number.

"Hello?"

"Are you watching the lawyer?"

"When I can."

"Not good enough. You heard about today?"

"Yes. Are you sure you're all right?"

"For now, but it makes your job with Mr. Finn all the more important."

"I understand."

"Do you?"

"Yes."

"Good." Salazar closed the phone and slid it back into his sock. He folded his arms over his chest and watched the door. Sleep was a luxury he could no longer afford.

Chapter Twenty-six

Thursday, December 20, 2007

Mac shuffled into work at a little past ten thirty. In close to thirty years on the job, he couldn't remember ever having been late to work. It was a point of honor and pride for him: Only slackers show up late for work. He was no slacker. At least he hadn't been . . . before.

He caught a few looks from his coworkers as he passed their desks on the way to his. He knew why; he looked like shit. The clothes he had on had been worn at least three times since they'd last seen the inside of a washing machine, much less a dry cleaner. He hadn't shaved in a couple of days, and the thick gray stubble had grown like uneven weeds on his face. His hair, which he'd kept high and tight with weekly trips to the barber for his entire time on the force, hadn't been cut in weeks, and as it had grown, it had revealed in starker contrast than ever before the extent of his expanding baldness.

Worst of all, he smelled. Bad. Bad enough that he could smell himself, and he knew that if he was ripe enough to self-offend, people around him must be fighting back their gag reflexes.

Still, there was little he could do at this point. The downward spiral had picked up too much speed, and it seemed all he could do now was watch the world spin wildly out of control around him on his descent. He'd hoped, briefly, that he might be able to climb out of the hole he'd dug for himself, but when he'd heard that Salazar had survived the events of yesterday morning, he realized he was in too deep to be saved.

All he could do was avoid the concerned and disturbed stares of his colleagues as he passed them in the squad room. *Fuck them all, anyway*, he thought. They'd never really cared about him in the first place. He'd been on top for such a long time, and all of them had just been waiting for him to stumble. Now their prayers had been answered, but he wasn't about to give them the satisfaction of acknowledging their pity.

He got to his desk, having survived his walk of shame, and looked down at the stack of case files and unanswered phone messages piled high. He pushed the messages around, looking to see whether it was there. He knew it would be, but he had to make sure.

It was the third one from the top: no name, just a number. It was a number he knew well; a number he'd grown to dread. He sat down and placed the call.

"Hello?" Carlos's voice was familiar and yet somehow different.

"It's Mac."

"I've been calling."

"I've been busy." Mac tried to infuse his voice with steel, but it sounded more like tinfoil.

"Our problem has not been solved."

"Yeah, I know. I'll take another run at it shortly." In reality, Mac wasn't sure he had the juice to even organize another attempt on Salazar's life. It didn't matter; they would never take him up on his offer. This was all for show.

"We've decided to handle this ourselves."

"The lawyer?"

"That's no longer your concern, is it?"

"Right." Mac swallowed the air in his lungs.

"Cheer up, *amigo*. All is not lost, and our problem can still be solved." The voice was understanding.

"I tried," Mac said. Could he get more pathetic?

"We know. We should talk early next week. We have another security issue in one of our operations. It may be the sort of thing you would be useful in taking care of."

"Sure," Mac said, grasping at the thin reed. "Sure. That sounds good. No problem."

"We have worked together for a long time."

"We have."

"Get some rest, and don't worry about this other matter."

"Okay, I will. Thanks." The line went dead.

It was the tone of Carlos's voice that was the tell. He'd been friendly. He'd been kind. He'd been reassuring. That was how Mac knew he was a dead man. They wouldn't wait until next week, either. They might be lying in wait for him already, down in the parking lot, or standing silently in a closet at his home. Ready to jump from any dark corner. They were waiting with their long blades aching to slide into his soft, round belly, underneath his rib cage, taking his breath away and silencing him quickly, but allowing him to survive for a few minutes as they put the blade to further, terrifying use. He thought about the pictures of Mark Dobson and felt dizzy.

"Mac? You okay?" It was Koontz. He tried to smile, but it was pointless. "You look really awful," she said.

Mac opened his mouth to respond, but he couldn't speak. His jaw floated up and down, his bubbly lips wagging, but no sound came out. He tried to force the air out of his lungs without success. Suddenly, he felt the panic fully take hold, and before he knew what was happening, he vomited onto his desk.

Jimmy Alvarez had watched the lawyer, Scott Finn, for a day and a half. It wasn't enough time. Not really. Not to do it right. He'd been told that endlessly by the ruthless men he'd hired in the past to take care of messes such as this—you had to plan carefully and make sure you knew your target's patterns so you could pick a place with no crowds around. Someplace where escape was guaranteed.

He'd been told that on the other side of the border, in Mexico, it was easy. Murder and kidnapping were practically part of the economy, and even the police could be convinced to turn a blind eye if the payment was large enough. Here in the States, it was different. Here you couldn't count on people looking the other way. Here you needed to pick the right spot.

Not that he had any firsthand knowledge of such things. He was a businessman. At least that was how he thought of himself; he had never needed to take a life personally. The thought of it made him sweat. Killing carried with it a permanence and a threat of divine retribution that he was still unable to fully comprehend.

And so he waited, telling himself that the delay was all about the logistics. That was a rationalization, he knew. The reality was that he wasn't sure whether he could go through with it. He had little choice though. Carlos was not a patient man, and if the job was not done and done quickly, Alvarez would be dealt with severely, no matter how valuable he was to VDS's operations.

And so he sat outside Scott Finn's offices. Waiting and watching and building up his courage.

———

Lissa Krantz stared at Finn from across the office. She had never seen him so down before. There seemed little for them to do at this point. Their own fingerprint expert had come back with a damning report, and getting Steele to change her story had been a nonstarter. The trip to the fingerprint unit had been an interesting look into the laxity with which the BPD approached fingerprint evidence, but without more, it seemed a dead end. There was little left to follow up on, so the three of them had spent the morning inventing tasks for themselves. Finn was doing additional online research on DNA testing. Lissa was checking over the legal research she'd done earlier, which she already knew to be complete and accurate. Kozlowski had disappeared into his office as soon as he'd arrived and hadn't so much as poked his head out.

Just thinking about Kozlowski brought a secret smile to her lips. They made an odd pair, there was no question of that. And yet everything seemed so natural with him, so easy and comfortable. He was everything she had expected and more. Quiet, funny, strong, taciturn, and above all else, trustworthy. He was a rock, and she was falling in love.

She shook her head in wonder, then turned her attention back to Finn. "Whatcha doin' over there, boss?"

He didn't look up. "Going over the research on DNA testing."

"Again?"

"Yes, again." The frustration was evident in his voice.

"Just fuckin' asking."

"Ask all you want; the answer's the same. I'm going to keep going over and over every aspect of this case until I find whatever it is that we're missing here."

She stood up and walked over to him, standing in front of his desk. He kept his head buried in his work.

"We're going to lunch," she said.

He grunted. "Fine. Have a good time."

"Not me and Koz, me and you."

He looked up at her finally. "I need to keep working. So do you, for that matter."

"You need to take a break, and so do I."

"Our client is in jail."

"Hey, no shit, thanks for the update. You think I don't know that our client is in fuckin' jail? You think all three of us in this office aren't doing everything we can to get him out? But here's a fuckin' news flash for you: Salazar's gonna be in jail tomorrow, too. And the next day and the next day. Chances are, he's gonna be in jail for the rest of his fuckin' life, no matter what you do. You, on the other hand, are not in jail. And you're not gonna be in jail tomorrow or the next day. You'll probably never be in jail for the rest of your sad, sorry life—a life, by the way, that may be cut short by one of your angry employees if you don't stop being such a moody shit. Now get up off your bony little ass, get your coat and hat, and join me for some fuckin' lunch, okay?"

He stared at her. "I don't have a hat."

"You really want to fuck with me? I'll give you two seconds."

Finn stood up, walked over, and pulled his coat off the hook near the hole Charlie O'Malley had punched through the wall. Putting his coat on, he went to the door and opened it. "You coming?" he asked. "I want to get back quickly; I've got a lot of work to do."

She put on her own coat and walked past him. "You're pushing your fuckin' luck with me, you know that, right?"

———※———

Deep down, Finn was relieved to get out of the office. The hopelessness of the Salazar case had seeped into his blood like sepsis, paralyzing him. All he could do was keep covering the same ground over and over again, and that was getting him nowhere. As guilty as he felt unchaining himself from the case even for a moment, it was nice to clear his head.

They walked over to O'Doul's and took a booth in the back corner, and by the time the waitress set his plate of scrod on the table in front of him, enough of the stress had fled his shoulders that he could roll his neck normally for the first time in days.

"So?" Lissa asked as he dug into his fish. She picked at her Cobb salad.

"So what?" he replied with his mouth full.

"So what the fuck is going on with you?"

"Nothing." He could feel his shoulders tightening again, just slightly.

"Bullshit, nothing. There's something going on with you and this case, and I don't understand it. You've had a dozen criminal cases since I started here, and some of those were guys who, near as I could tell, you actually were friends with at some point in your life. Some of those guys went to jail, and you didn't seem to give a shit. I mean, you clearly hated losing, but it wasn't like you took it personally. Now this guy you don't know, who has already been in jail for fifteen years, shows up and turns you into a basket case. What the fuck is that?"

He pushed the brussels sprouts that had been served with the fish to the side of the plate. "I can't explain it, so I'm not even going to try."

She kept looking at him, clearly waiting for him to say more. She would make a good lawyer once she passed the bar, but he'd been playing the game a little too long to be drawn out by her silence. She finally gave up.

"So what's the deal with your personal life?" she asked, changing focus.

"Not sure what you mean," he lied.

"Oh, sure you do. You still seeing this woman down in D.C.? You seeing anyone else? What's going on with that whole part of your life?"

"Are you hitting on me again?" He chased the last piece of fish around the obstacle course of brussels sprouts.

"Fuck you."

"Sounds like a yes to me."

"That's definitely not a yes. Has it ever occurred to you that maybe you wouldn't be so caught up in this case if you had something—any-thing—else in your life? A good woman has been known to do wonders for a man's attitude. A bad woman can do even more. You should think about it."

"Don't go getting maternal on me or anything, okay? It doesn't suit you."

"Fuck you," she said. "I can be just as maternal as the next woman. Eat your fuckin' vegetables. See?"

He tipped his hand back and forth in a skeptical gesture. "Needs a little work, to be honest."

"Fine. You can make fun of me all you want, but I can spot a guy who's in desperate need of getting laid from a mile away."

"Ah, yes. The true sign of a solid maternal instinct."

"Like you'd know, asshole."

He gave a conceding look. "Fair enough. My experience with mothers is at least one shy of most people. Growing up in orphanages and foster care might have skewed my point of view."

"Is that why you keep fucking up this thing with what's-her-name in our nation's capital?"

"I'd like to think I haven't actually fucked it up. Hope springs eternal."

"Sounds like the mantra of a truly lonely man."

"Touché, but in this case, there isn't a whole lot I could do. She left. She got a job offer she couldn't turn down, and now we live four hundred miles apart. That seems like an easier concept to grasp than some Freudian psychobabble bullshit about my never having had a mother, don't you think?"

"Not really. Seems to me you could have gone with her."

Finn frowned. "What do you mean? My life is here."

"What life?"

"That's just mean."

"I'm not trying to be mean, I'm trying to be serious. You've got no family. Near as I can tell, other than Koz, you've got no friends. All you've got is your job."

"I like my job."

"Finn, it's a fucking job. And to be honest, lots of times it's a really shitty job. Plus, you could actually do it in D.C. My understanding is they use lawyers down there, too. So what the fuck is your problem?"

His head was beginning to hurt, and his shoulders were back up around his ears. "Can we talk about something else?"

"No, we can't. I'm really worried about you. How much have you slept in the past four days?"

"I told you before, sleep is overrated," he replied.

She rolled her eyes.

"Look," he tried again, "one way or another, this Salazar thing is going to be over in less than a week. All I've got to do is make it until then, and things will go back to normal, right?"

"Will they?"

"They will," he assured her. "But for the next five days, this case is all I'm thinking about. I have to give it everything I've got, even if it comes close to killing me."

She nodded grimly. "If you say so. Do you have any idea where to go with the case from here?"

He considered the question. Their conversation was the longest he'd gone without thinking about the substance of the case since Dobson had been killed. Now, as he came back to it, his perspective seemed to have shifted slightly, as though he were looking at it from a new angle. Something seemed misaligned. "I don't know," he said slowly. "Something bothers me about the night Steele was attacked."

"What?"

"I don't know. I can't put my finger on it."

"That's it? That's all you've got? Something bothers you about a night when a woman was shot and sexually assaulted? That's the key to the case?" Lissa sounded disappointed in him.

"It's something. It's more than I had an hour ago."

"What are you going to do with it?"

He looked at her. She had a lot of spirit. If it weren't for the way he felt about Linda Flaherty, maybe . . . But that wasn't the way he was built. Still, something about her energy gave him life, at least for the moment. He felt better than he had in days, and he figured he might as well take advantage of the mood. "I have to go out to where she was attacked," he said. "Out to Roxbury."

"Why?" she asked.

He threw twenty dollars on the table to cover lunch. "Honestly?" he said. "I don't really know."

Chapter Twenty-seven

THE SNOW WAS FALLING again as Finn pulled his car to the curb at the corner of Columbus and Lenox in Roxbury. The sun was down, and his headlights sparked the snowflakes like fireflies. The dusting lent the area a quiet evening glow.

He stepped out of his car and looked around. He was in the no-man's-land of urban renewal. Across the street, a large warehouse was undergoing radical reconstruction, and a giant sign on the fence surrounding the building heralded the anticipated lofts as models of modern convenience and city living. Three brownstones on the block had been gutted and were being refitted with new trim and shining new brick facades. On the corner, a local dive had been knocked down to make way for a high-end corporate coffee shop. But interspersed between the harbingers of the neighborhood transformation were the distinctive signs of urban decay that had held the area in its grasp for decades. Sooted tenements with darkened windows and paint peeling from the doors still dominated, and the bodega across the way still advertised discount bourbon rather than expensive chardonnay.

The alley where Officer Steele had been attacked was halfway up the block, and after taking the neighborhood in, Finn set off through the snow.

He wasn't sure what he was doing out here. There was nothing specific he could put his finger on, no theory or solid view of what he was looking for. Something just seemed out of place about the reports from that night fifteen years earlier. He walked slowly and had the uneasy feeling of being watched, but looking around, he couldn't see a soul. The residents seemed to have pulled up their ladders and retreated into the safety of their homes.

As Finn neared the alley, he nearly stepped on a homeless man whose legs, covered by a swath of dirty canvas, protruded from a shadowy doorway.

"What the motherfuck!" the man shouted, sitting up and taking an aggressive posture. "Fuck you think you are?" His eyes shone white from the dark outline of his face, fierce and combative.

"Sorry."

"Sorry costs a dollar," the man shot back.

Finn reached into his pocket and pulled out a bill. He crumpled it into a ball to give it heft and keep the wind from taking it. Then he dropped it in the man's lap.

The man laughed. "Damn straight, motherfucker. You *are* sorry."

Finn walked on another twenty yards to the mouth of the alleyway. What had brought him here? Why was this place, this random spot of violence, so important?

He stepped into the alley, just a short ways at first. Even covered in a pristine layer of new snow, it reeked like sewer water in a landfill, and his nose, which was already running from the cold, began to sting.

He walked in a little farther. He could see nothing remarkable about the place. Like so many of the alleys in the aging city, this one was paved in uneven granite bricks and bordered by a high curb on both sides. Above him, fire escapes dangled like the fraying inner seams of a cheap suit, twisting and turning haphazardly, rusted through in places. Finn wondered idly whether, faced with the choice, the inhabitants might take their chances against the flames rather than risk a trip down the iron deathtraps.

Farther down the passage he heard a cat rustle in a garbage can. At least he thought it was a cat, but when the creature emerged into the sliver of light from the street Finn got a good look at it. While it was large enough to be feline, Finn couldn't remember ever seeing a cat with such a fleshy tail and a pointed snout.

He looked around again, searching for something—but what? By his reading of the testimony at Salazar's trial, he was standing on the exact spot where Steele had been found, the blood drenching the bricks, her life running out of her almost too fast to stop. It was a tragic scene, to be sure, but he could find no meaning to it now that he was here, no enlightenment. By all accounts, the place had little connection to Salazar, who lived over ten blocks away, and even less to Steele, who lived in South Boston, over five miles from the spot.

Then it hit him all at once, and he broke into a sweat in spite of the cold. He balled his hand into a fist and put it to his forehead as the thoughts flashed through his brain like a migraine. He'd read through the trial transcripts so many times, he could play them all back at will. Now he ran through them in his head, trying to remember whether the question had ever been addressed.

Certainly Steele's testimony on the attack had been vivid. She'd been walking down Columbus, passing the mouth of the alley, when she'd been hit on the head and dragged to this spot. She'd been half conscious, coming back to full reality only when the machete was held to her throat. Even on paper, her testimony had been riveting, and Finn knew from experience that Salazar never stood a chance once she took the stand.

But the power of the testimony had distracted everyone, including Finn, and left one basic question unanswered: What was she doing here? Why, when she was officially off duty, was she wandering around one of the most dangerous neighborhoods in the city, miles away from her home? As scruffy as the area seemed to Finn this evening, it had been far worse fifteen years earlier. It had been the kind of area even cops hesitated to visit alone without a good reason.

There was only one possible answer, and Finn felt like a fool for having overlooked it before: She was conducting some sort of independent investigation; something she was keeping off the official record for some reason.

"She was on the job that night," Finn said quietly to himself as he opened his eyes deep in the intestines of the alley. So the question he had to answer now was: What was it she was out here investigating?

He smiled a little to himself, gratified that his own inquiry had some footing, slippery though it might be, against which he might move forward. His relief, though, was short-lived. He heard something move behind him, too large this time to be a cat of any size, and he realized he wasn't alone in the alley.

At that moment, he was grabbed from behind and thrown into the brick wall that edged the alley. He was hit in the face with something hard and heavy and cold, which disoriented him. It took him a minute to regain his bearings, and when he did, he realized that a large blade was being held to his throat.

His eyes followed the blade down toward the hand that held it, then back up the arm to the shoulder, moving slowly until he found himself looking into the eyes of his assailant.

"Mr. Finn," the man said. "Talk quickly or die."

———————

"Where did he go?"

There was something about the tone of Kozlowski's question that made Lissa uneasy. "Roxbury," she replied.

"By himself? Where in Roxbury?"

Lissa frowned. "How the fuck should I know? We had lunch, we came back here, and he poked around in his files for a little while; then he said he was heading out to go check on something."

"But you didn't ask where?" Kozlowski seemed concerned. She'd never seen him like this. It set off alarm bells in her head.

"Like I said, he was going to Roxbury, but no, I didn't ask for an address."

"And you just let him go?"

"What the fuck does that mean?" she replied. "He's my goddamned boss. I'm supposed to chain him to the desk?"

Now it was Kozlowski's turn to frown. "No. But I don't like him heading out on his own. Not the way this case has been heading. Dobson gets murdered, Salazar gets attacked in prison, and now we seem to have the entire BPD down on our asses. Finn likes to think he can take care of himself, but he can't. He takes too many risks, and it's gonna get him killed. Until this thing is over, I should be with him when he does something stupid."

"Yeah, well, maybe if you stuck your head out of your office every once in a while, you'd be able to keep better track of him." Lissa could see that the point had wounded Kozlowski, and she was sorry she'd said it. She softened her voice. "How can you be sure he's doing something stupid?"

"It's Finn. It's what he does."

She considered this. "Fair point." She tried to remain calm. "I'm sure he's fine," she said, as much to comfort herself as Kozlowski.

"Maybe," Kozlowski said. "Was he coming back to the office?"

"I don't know. I assumed so. He left at around four, and I wasn't thinking he'd be gone for longer than an hour or so." She looked at the clock. It was approaching six. "I'm sure he's fine," she said again.

Kozlowski looked out the window. Warren Street was dimly lit by the old-fashioned gaslights on the corners, but other than that, the darkness of the evening was total. A heavy layer of storm clouds blotted out whatever moon and stars might have added illumination.

She watched him there, staring out onto the quintessential New England winter scene. If still waters ran deep, he was a bottomless fjord. Even his eyes refused to blink as he stood motionless with his thoughts. "Is there something bad out there for him in Roxbury?" she asked.

He turned to her. "I don't know," he replied, and the concern in his voice drove her to the edge of panic. "But given everything that's happened in the past few days, I can tell you there's nothing good out there for him."

Lissa stood next to him, staring with him out at the street. Then she reached into his jacket pocket and pulled out his cell phone and handed it to him. She could barely keep her voice from breaking. "Call him," she said.

"I said talk quickly, Mr. Finn."

Finn stared at the man in front of him, who had light skin and dark hair and was in his early twenties. He spoke with an accent as he held the blade of the machete to Finn's throat. In spite of the fact that with the flick of his wrist, he could end Finn's life, there was something oddly nervous about his demeanor. Finn had grown up around psychopaths—men and boys who could bludgeon another human being to death one moment and chow down on a rare burger smothered in grilled onions and ketchup the next. This man didn't have the right look in his eyes for a killer.

"Talk about what?" Finn leaned back to try to get some separation from the blade, but the young man stayed with him.

"Don't fuck with me. What did he tell you? We need to know."

"What did who tell me?"

The man pushed the machete blade harder into the skin over Finn's Adam's apple. "I told you not to fuck with me."

Finn spoke carefully, so that the motion wouldn't sever his jugular.

"Trust me, under the circumstances, the last thing I want to do is fuck with you. I don't know what you're talking about."

"Salazar. What did he tell you?"

"About what?"

The pressure on the blade increased again, and Finn thought it was all over but the embalming. He felt a trickle of blood running down the front of his neck and onto his shirt. It was a nice shirt, too. Probably the one he would have liked to be buried in.

"Tell me or die," the young man said.

"Okay, okay," Finn protested. His mind echoed with a thousand lies, but picking among them was the hardest thing he'd ever done. It occurred to him that the truth might be better, at least to start with. He could wade into the deception as necessary. "He said he didn't do it."

"Do what?"

"The attack. He said he didn't attack Steele. It was someone else."

The man frowned. "What else did he tell you?"

"I don't understand," Finn stalled.

The man stared at him closely, the frustration showing on his face. It looked as if he was trying to figure out whether Finn was telling the truth. Then his expression changed. It was as though he had crossed over a line and come to an irreversible decision. Finn had the distinct impression that he was about to die. There was still some hesitation remaining in the man's eyes, but there was something else, too. Something stronger. Fear. The man increased the pressure on the blade and began to slide it across Finn's throat.

"Wait," Finn choked out. "There was something else."

The man paused. "What?"

"It's . . ." But all the lies were gone, and Finn could think of nothing to say. Looking into the man's eyes, he knew his bluff would fail.

"Goodbye, Mr. Finn."

Finn closed his eyes.

"What the fuck are you doing in my alley?"

Finn sensed his assailant turning toward the street, toward the angry shout. Finn opened his eyes and looked over, thankful, at least, for the brief reprieve.

It was the homeless man Finn had almost stepped on. He was standing in the shadow of the alley's entranceway.

"I said, what the fuck are you doing in my alley?" he shouted again.

"Get out of here, old man," the man with the machete said. "Now."

"Fuck you," the homeless man replied, and there was no fear in his voice. "Fuck you, I say. This is my alley, an' you wanna use it, you gotta pay me a dollar, at least!" He weaved as he walked forward, until he saw the long blade. Then he smiled. "An' if you're gonna kill him here, it'll be five dollars. Cops'll shut this place down for a week." He nodded as though running through the calculation in his head. "Yep. Five dollars, at least."

A nervous smile appeared on the face of Finn's assailant. "Fine, old man. Let me do my business, and you'll get your money." He turned back to Finn.

Just then Finn's cell phone rang. Its tone was sharp and loud, and it made both of them jump.

Finn looked up. The interruptions had shaken the young man, and the hesitation was crowding onto his face again. "I don't suppose you'd let me answer that, would you?" Finn asked him.

The man was beyond speaking, but he shook his head as he screwed his courage together. Finn thought there was a chance he wouldn't go through with it, but it was too great a chance to take. He slid a foot back and positioned his fist carefully, preparing to swing up and out. It was a desperate maneuver, as likely as not to drive the machete up into the soft palate where his neck met his chin. It would do serious damage, Finn knew, but he thought he might survive. For a while, at least. It was likely that the man would get a clean second swing at him, and that would end the matter, but he was short on options, and this seemed the best one he had. He readied himself for the blow and was about to take his chance when he heard another shout from near the alley's entrance.

"Let him go!"

The voice came from over near where the old man had been standing. The old man's gravelly, plaintive growl had been replaced by a young, strong, authoritative shout. Finn looked over. The homeless man was gone, and standing in his place was a slim, dark figure holding a gun. It was pointed straight at the head of the man with the machete, and there was no waver in the muzzle. In the shadows, Finn couldn't make out the face of his savior.

"Let him go," the man with the gun said again, with even more conviction this time. He raised the pistol, and Finn heard the hammer cock.

The blade of the machete was still against Finn's throat, but there was less pressure on it; the man who had been about to slice through Finn's neck a moment earlier now had his attention focused on the entrance of the alleyway. The man with the gun was probably forty feet away, and it was a nearly impossible shot from that range for anyone other than an expert marksman, particularly with Finn so close to the machete. Still, all it would take was one lucky shot . . .

Finn looked back at his assailant and could read in his face that he, too, was weighing the odds against the man with the gun. With each passing second, the pressure of the blade against Finn's throat relented ever so slightly. When Finn felt the connection break entirely, he acted without hesitation, pulling his body back and swinging his fist up into the man's arm in one fluid motion.

The man was taken by surprise, and his arm launched skyward, the blade hissing by Finn's ear, just missing the side of his face. Finn ducked back against the alley wall, and a shot rang out, but the man with the machete held his ground. With the decision made for him, he, too, acted quickly, swinging the blade hard and fast toward Finn's head.

Finn put his arm up to fend off the blow. It came at him at an awkward angle, but the blade was still sharp enough to slice through the meat of his forearm. Finn screamed in agony.

As another shot echoed through the alley, Finn dove to the ground. The machete came at him again, wildly, missing him and connecting with the bricks behind the spot where Finn had stood only a second before.

Looking up, Finn saw the man with the gun running toward them, taking aim from closer range. Finn's assailant took one more swing, missing his rib cage by a matter of inches, and then he was gone. Running deeper into the alley, he fled into the darkness. The man with the gun, who was almost on top of Finn now, took aim and fired off three quick shots. Finn heard a scream from deep within the cavernous passage and looked up to see the fleeing man, who was little more than a shadow, stumble and fall into the wall, then get to his feet and continue into the darkness as the man with the gun ran after him.

Left alone, Finn glanced down. The snow covering the brick alley underneath him was stained maroon-black, as was a swath of his suit pants underneath the spot where his injured arm dangled. He pulled off his overcoat and jacket to assess the damage.

"Fuck," he whispered to himself as he beheld the mess. The flesh was hacked through, and a solid chunk flapped loosely in the cold. With his right hand, he reached up and loosened his tie, slipping it over his head and then pulling it over the wreckage of his left arm to the elbow. He put one end of the tie in his mouth and used his free hand to tighten the tourniquet.

When he was done, he looked up to see the man with the gun hurrying back toward him. Finn thought to run but decided that if the man wanted him dead, he wouldn't have risked his life to save him. He still couldn't see the man's face clearly, though he had the feeling that he knew him. As the man approached, Finn finally recognized him: It was Miguel Salazar. Finn had no idea what to say.

Miguel bent down in front of him, and it became clear that the doctor in him was taking over. He pulled Finn's arm toward him to take a look at it as Finn began to shiver. "Where did you learn to tie a tourniquet?" Miguel asked.

"I used to get into knife fights when I was younger," Finn said.

"Seriously?"

"Seriously. Not something I'm proud of, necessarily, but the life experience can come in handy at times."

Miguel didn't respond but continued his examination. "He caught you in the middle of the muscle, and it doesn't look severed. The bones aren't broken, which is a blessing. We need to get you to a hospital, though, where I can take a good look at it." He noticed Finn shivering and took off his coat. "You may be going into shock."

"I'm not going into shock, it's just cold."

"Better to be safe than sorry." Miguel put his coat over Finn, then piled Finn's suit jacket and overcoat on top of that. He pulled out a cell phone. "I'm calling an ambulance here. Don't move, okay?"

Finn started to sit up. "I'm not going to lie here in an alley waiting for an ambulance, Doc. I'll be fine."

"No, you won't." Miguel was calm but firm. "Stay here; it'll only take me a minute to call 911."

Just then there was the faint whine of sirens in the distance. "Looks like someone beat you to it," Finn said.

Miguel listened intently until he was sure that the emergency signals were coming closer. "Looks like you lucked out."

"Bit of an understatement. Where did you come from?"

Miguel gave a distracted but reassuring smile. "My brother. He made me promise to keep an eye on you."

Finn stared off into space. "I'll have to thank him," he said. His hearing seemed to be fading. His voice sounded distant to him.

"Stay with me, Mr. Finn. You're losing blood, but you're going to be fine as long as you stay with me. If anything happens to you, I'll have to answer to Vincente. I'd hate to disappoint him."

"Fair enough." Finn refocused his eyes. They were directed down into the alley, and he nodded in that direction. "Where'd he go?"

Miguel looked back over his shoulder. "It splits down around the corner and opens onto two different streets. He got away."

"You hit him, I think," Finn said, slurring a little. "He screamed, and I saw him stumble."

"I think so, but it must have been superficial. It didn't slow him down at all."

The sirens turned rapidly from a distant drone to an overpowering scream as two police cars pulled up at the mouth of the alley. The blue and red lights flickered off the wet bricks and sparkled against the tiny flakes that still drifted from the sky. The scene reminded Finn of the carnival he used to visit every summer in Revere: wild and exhilarating and enthralling but somehow also dangerous and strangely perverted.

"They're gonna have a lot of questions," Finn said, nodding at the squad cars.

"Good thing you've got a lot of answers," Miguel said.

"I don't know that they're gonna like the answers I've got. It's not like your brother's very popular with the police. And it seems I've become public enemy number one since I started working on his case."

Miguel smiled again. "You know one of the things I love about this country? Even the corrupt pretend to be fair and impartial when they have to be. In El Salvador, the police would just stand around and let you bleed to death." He looked up at the officers as they exited their cars and started into the alley. "They may not like you, but they'll help you. At least for the moment. Worry about tomorrow when the sun comes up. For the time being, let's just get you through the night."

Finn fought to keep his eyes open. Against every rational impulse, he felt reassured. As he looked up, the similarities between Miguel

Salazar and his brother struck Finn again. Only age and circumstance seemed to separate the two siblings. They were probably fewer than ten years apart in age, but it seemed like twenty. Maybe more. Prison ages a man beyond his years, Finn reflected. Scenes from his own misspent youth flashed through his head briefly, and he suddenly realized how lucky he was.

He leaned up on his elbow and dug his hand into his pocket, pulling out his cell phone. He didn't need to check who had called him; he knew already. He'd known the moment the phone rang, startling the man who'd tried to kill him, probably saving his life. He pressed two buttons to dial.

"Who are you calling?" Salazar asked.

Finn gave him a thin, weary smile as he held the phone to his ear. Through chattering teeth, he said simply, "My friends."

Chapter Twenty-eight

FINN SAT ON THE BED in the emergency room at Massachusetts General Hospital, watching with interest as Miguel Salazar dressed the wound on his arm. He was intrigued by his client's brother, this young man who had shattered the odds and crawled from poverty to become a respected physician. The first time he'd met the younger Salazar, he'd been impressed but not overwhelmed. It had been clear that the staff at the free clinic in East Boston revered him, but that had meant little to Finn. Those who worked there were crusaders, and crusaders always craved a messiah.

But over the course of the past few hours, Finn had seen Miguel in action, and it was clear that he was built from more than convenient platitudes. When the police had arrived on the scene in the alley, Miguel had taken control, delivering orders as though he were in charge. The police had sought to question Finn at length, but Miguel had intervened, asserting his medical authority, and demanded that Finn be given immediate medical attention at the hospital. The officers had objected, but Miguel told them that if they interfered with Finn's medical treatment, he would ensure they would face disciplinary charges and be held personally liable for the detrimental effects of any delay. That had ended the debate, which was fine with Finn; one of the cops on the scene had already made clear that he was aware of Finn's connection to the case involving Madeline Steele and his attempts to get her attacker released. Finn could tell already that the police were lacking zeal in their determination to find his assailant.

When they loaded Finn into the ambulance, Miguel had climbed in behind him. "Mass General," he ordered.

"City Hospital's closer," the driver objected.

"Mass General," Miguel had repeated in a tone that defied argument. The driver shook his head but pulled out onto the street in the direction of Beacon Hill, where Mass General was located. Miguel leaned over and whispered to Finn, "It will be easier for me to make sure you get the proper attention at my hospital."

Through it all, Miguel had never needed to raise his voice. He'd spoken clearly, calmly, and with an authority that came from someplace deep within him where diplomas had no influence.

"Thank you," Finn said as Miguel wrapped a tight sterile bandage around his arm and taped it down securely.

"No need." Miguel waved off Finn's gratitude. "You are helping my brother, and by doing so, you've placed yourself in danger. It is my family that owes you."

"How did you know I would be in Roxbury?"

Miguel said, "I didn't. I was following you. I requested time off from work here at the hospital, and I've been following you as much as possible for the past few days."

Finn whistled. "Pretty crappy way to spend your vacation time."

"It's not an issue, Mr. Finn. I haven't taken a day off in three years. I thought the chief surgeon was going to have a coronary when I put in the request. I'm pretty sure he thinks I'm dying."

Finn wasn't sure how to ask the next question. "And the gun?"

Miguel looked up from applying the tape to Finn's arm. "The gun?"

"The gun," Finn replied. "The one you used to save me. It didn't look like standard hospital issue."

Miguel shrugged. "I work in a free clinic in a very rough neighborhood, and I'm often carrying drugs."

"Drugs?"

"Prescription drugs, Mr. Finn. They are very much in demand on the streets these days. We've had doctors assaulted a number of times for them. A year ago I got a permit to carry some protection."

"What would Hippocrates say?" Finn asked.

Miguel gave an embarrassed smile. "I don't think he intended the physician's oath to bar doctors from practicing reasonable self-defense. Besides, I have a family to think about. If something were to happen to me, I'm not sure what my mother and niece would do. They've been through enough already."

"I'm not in a position to complain at the moment. In fact, I'm sorry the police took it from you."

"It makes sense," Salazar said with an air of resignation. "It appears that I shot a man this evening. They have to carry out their investigation."

Finn scoffed. "Don't count on it. They already know who I am. Once they discover that you're Vincente's brother, I'm guessing the investigation will last all of around five minutes."

"I'm surprised you're so bitter," Salazar said.

"I'm surprised you're not," Finn replied.

The doctor held up Finn's arm, admiring his own handiwork. "You have to be careful with this for several weeks," he said. "It took more than sixty stitches to pull the tissue back together. You were very fortunate that the muscles weren't severed; that would have required surgery. Still, it will be very painful for a while, particularly once the local wears off. I'll prescribe some painkillers."

Finn stood up. "Thanks, Doc. That'll save me a trip to my local dealer." He winked at Miguel. Then he took a step toward the door, wobbled, and caught himself on the bed. Miguel took his arm and guided him back so that he was sitting again.

"You're not going anywhere yet, Mr. Finn," he said. "You lost a lot of blood. We're going to set you up with some fluids and an IV antibiotic drip to make sure there's no infection. You'll be here for a few more hours." He looked at the clock on the wall. "Given how late it is already, I'm going to admit you. It will be easier that way."

"No can do," Finn replied. "I've got an important case I'm working on, as you well know. I can't lose the time."

"You can't help my brother if you collapse. Your friends are outside; I'll send them in. But you are going to have to stay here through the night."

Finn wanted to argue, but all at once he felt too tired to think. He sat back on the bed. There was something to be said for getting a little rest, he supposed. Then he could start out fresh in the morning—the first thing he needed to find out was what Steele had been investigating in Roxbury on the night she was shot.

Finn looked at Miguel, who was making some notes on Finn's medical chart, looking at his watch, and then writing some more. It was starting to sink in that, were it not for this young doctor, Finn would in all likelihood be dead.

Miguel hung the clipboard with Finn's medical charts on the wall. "I'll be back," he assured his patient.

As the younger man walked to the door, Finn called out to him. "Hey, Doc?"

Miguel turned around.

"Thanks. Seriously."

Miguel shook his head. "Thank my brother when you see him."

———

Jimmy Alvarez sat against a brick wall in the shadows of the main temple of the Church of Christ, Scientist on Huntington Avenue. The

Mother Church, as it was known in Boston, was a palatial domed structure on several acres, fronted by an endless reflecting pool. The church was built in 1894 to celebrate the philosophy of Mary Baker Eddy, who stressed the connection between the mind, the spirit, and the body. Central to the tenets of the religion was the belief in the ability of people to heal themselves through faith and prayer. Jimmy felt his shoulder and was doubtful that faith alone would mend the gunshot wound that throbbed excruciatingly.

The pool was dry for the winter, but the storm had picked up, and it was already half filled with powdery white snow. As Jimmy looked out on it, he longed for the warm winters of his Mexican border town and wondered how it was that he had found his way to this godforsaken urban tundra.

He pulled off his jacket, shivering as he looked down at his shoulder. The wound was still oozing, though the flow had eased, at least. He craned his neck to get a better view and saw clearly both the entry and exit wounds, which made him feel better. He could be reasonably sure that the bullet had not lodged within the flesh, and as he probed the wound with his fingers, it seemed the bullet had passed cleanly through the muscle without damaging any of the bones or joints. That was fortunate. While the pain was excruciating, he still had the full use of his arm—for now.

He couldn't go to a hospital, he knew. A gunshot wound would raise all sorts of questions, and he didn't have any good answers. Nor could he seek help from his associates in VDS. He had failed miserably in his assignment, and until he had corrected the mistake, he was a liability to them. He had seen how the Padre dealt with liabilities. His options were limited.

He picked up a handful of snow and spread it on the wound, hoping to stem the bleeding even further, fighting off the scream that the agony tried to force from his lungs. But the cold seemed to deaden the pain, and he relaxed a little, with his back to the bricks.

He thought through his predicament carefully. He was tempted to ditch town altogether—pack it in and head back south. It wouldn't work, though. The only home he'd ever known was two thousand miles away, and even if he made it back, Carlos's people would find him there. It might buy him a few weeks, but no more, and the terror of what they would do when they did catch up with him was too grotesque to consider.

On the other hand, setting things right in Boston would be no easy task. The lawyer would be on guard, and it would be difficult to get to him. More important, even if he had another chance, Jimmy recognized now that he didn't have the mental strength to kill. He'd known that it would be difficult, but he'd thought he'd be able to do it. He'd ordered people beaten before, and while he'd never been directly involved in a killing, it was commonplace enough in his hometown for him to believe he would be able to cross the line without any significant problem.

He'd been wrong. Having people roughed up was one thing. That was business, and the lack of permanence in a beating allowed Jimmy to settle into a comfortable rationalization that still permitted him to sleep. As he'd held the blade to the lawyer's throat, Jimmy had realized that the gulf between ordering a beating and slitting someone's throat was too wide and deep for him to cross. Irrespective of the potential retribution from Carlos and his henchmen, he knew that he could never look someone in the eyes as he ended a life.

He had only one option. He'd studied Finn's patterns enough to identify his weaknesses, and he thought in his heart that perhaps the man didn't need to die. Perhaps there was another way.

Jimmy pulled his jacket back over his shoulder and stood up, battling a light head. He had work to do before he could rest. Taking a deep breath, he steadied himself, working through exactly what must be done. It wouldn't be easy, but it was possible, he told himself.

He looked out one last time upon the reflecting pool, pale blue in the streetlights and covered in drifts. As he pulled his jacket tight around his shoulders and headed out toward the Back Bay, he wondered why anyone would choose to live in a place so cold.

"What the fuck were you thinking?"

Kozlowski stood against the whitewashed wall of the hospital room, shaking his head. He felt like a father scolding his teenager, but he couldn't help himself. Lissa sat in an uncomfortable-looking, semi-recliner by the side of Finn's bed. Salazar had left the room to check in with the hospital staff.

"I was thinking I might learn something that could help us," Finn replied. "I think maybe I did."

"I think you almost helped yourself into the fucking morgue."

"You're not listening to me."

Kozlowski shook his head. "No, you're not listening to me. The pictures of Mark Dobson weren't enough to clue you in? Whoever we're dealing with is playing for keeps. Not the way Slocum plays for keeps, sending some Irish pituitary case to try to scare you. These people will cut your heart out and feed it to you. Literally. You get that now? You're a target, and until this goddamned case is in the rearview mirror, you don't go out on any part of this investigation without me, you understand?"

Finn sat up straight, almost tearing the IV out of his good arm. "I pay you, not the other way around. I can take care of myself." The line feeding antibiotics and fluids into his system caught on his neck, and he struggled to free himself.

"You're an arrogant idiot," Kozlowski said, his face flushing. "You can't even defend yourself against your fucking saline solution, but you want to take on these psychopaths on your own?"

"Fuck you."

"No, fuck you."

"No, fuck both of you," Lissa cut in. "Jesus motherfucking Christ, what is it about testosterone that turns men into kindergarteners?" She looked back and forth between them and then mimicked in baby talk, "'Fuck you.' 'No, fuck you.' 'You're an asshole.' 'No, you are.' You guys going to get into the whole 'I'm rubber and you're glue' discussion next?" She turned to Kozlowski. "You can't just bully people into following your orders, even if you know you're right." Then she looked at Finn. "And you are, in fact, an idiot if you don't realize that you're in real danger because of this case. Shit, look around you, Finn. This is a hospital you're in, not the fucking Four Seasons. From what Salazar's little brother said, you're lucky to still have your fucking arm. No, wait, check that. If he hadn't been keeping an eye on you, you wouldn't be worried about your arm, you'd be fucking dead. You're lucky you still have your head, forget about the arm. If you don't take Koz up on his offer to watch your back through the rest of this, you're dumber than you look. And trust me, after tonight, that's hard to fucking believe."

Kozlowski fought to suppress a smile. Lissa was a phenomenon. She was smart, and direct, and there wasn't an ounce of bullshit anywhere in her. She was entirely different from any person he'd ever known. He looked over at Finn and saw that her speech had had an impact. Finn was looking down at his arm with guilt and concession in his eyes. "Sorry," he mumbled.

"Me, too," Kozlowski offered.

Lissa looked back and forth between them again. "Good," she said. For a moment her stare kept its intensity, as if to dare either of them to reopen the debate. Then she let out a breath and seemed to relax. "My work is done here, then." She stood up. "I'm going home to get some goddamned sleep." She looked at Kozlowski. "I take it you're staying here, after all your bitching about keeping an eye on him?"

Kozlowski looked at Finn. "It makes sense."

"Fine," Finn agreed, not meeting Kozlowski's eyes.

"*Fine?*" Lissa's voice was sharp and accusing.

Finn's eyes drilled through the floor. "I mean *thank you*."

"Very nice," she praised him. "Was that so fucking hard? See, all you assholes needed was the softness of a woman's touch." She leaned forward and kissed Finn on the forehead. "I'll see you at the office in the morning."

"Thanks."

"I need to talk to you for just a second," she said to Kozlowski as she passed him on the way out the door. He followed her out and she walked a short distance down the hallway and around the corner before she stopped, still facing away from him.

"What is it?" he asked.

She spun and, in one fluid motion, put her arms around his neck, pulling his head down and kissing him. It was a fierce, passionate kiss, her fingers running through the hair on the back of his head, her tongue slipping into his mouth, probing, her body pressed against his. He was aware of people staring as they passed by the pair locked in public intimacy, and at first he felt self-conscious. After a moment, though, the rest of the world faded away, and the thought of their public display aroused him. There was little question that she could feel his body respond.

She laughed through the kiss and pulled away from him. "My, my," she said. "What a nice reaction. I'm flattered." She pulled his head down again and kissed him gently on the lips. "Right now you have other things to concentrate on." She nodded in the direction of Finn's room. "You need to keep an eye on him."

"I'd rather keep my eyes on you," he admitted. Sexual innuendo was new to him, and he felt clumsy with it, like trying on someone else's shoes, but he kind of liked it.

She smiled at him. "When all this is over, I'll be sure to treat you to a little show. For now you need to stay sharp."

He looked at his watch. It was one o'clock in the morning. "You go get some sleep. I'll make sure he survives the night."

"Okay," she said. "Just make sure you're both being careful. I don't want anyone taking a shot at him and hitting you by mistake."

"Couldn't happen. Bullets bounce off me."

"Right," she said. "Just don't start believing your own bullshit."

"Good advice."

She kissed him once more, then turned and walked down the hallway to the elevator. He watched her, admiring the slight sway to her hips and the way her arms brushed her sides as they swung confidently with every stride.

He laughed softly to himself as the elevator door closed. It had actually happened, he realized. It had taken nearly half a century, but for the first time in his life, he was in love. He wiped his mouth discreetly and realized he could still taste her.

It had been worth the wait.

Chapter Twenty-nine

Lissa had left her car at the office, and she should have taken a taxi home from the hospital. The snowstorm had intensified, and while it still wouldn't qualify as a blizzard in the minds of most New Englanders, it was falling hard enough to blur her vision; even in the spots where the city workers were making the effort to keep up with the snowfall, there were several inches of accumulation. A cab would have been the best way to get to the Back Bay. But when she walked out of the main entrance of the hospital, she could see several people already huddled in a line at the empty cabstand. On a snowy night, that would mean at least an hour's wait. Looking up at the sky, she judged that the storm was likely to let up soon, and in any case, her apartment was under a half mile away. Even in the snow, it shouldn't take more than fifteen minutes to walk, and there was a reasonable chance that she might be able to hail down a cab on Charles Street at the foot of Beacon Hill. So she bundled her scarf around her throat and headed out without a second thought.

She loved to walk the city, in part because the application of the word "city" always seemed ambitious to her. She had been raised in Manhattan, and as a consequence, she viewed Boston as more of a small town than a city. More than once, she had walked the entirety of

Boston in a day, while she was quite sure she could live an entire life-time in New York and never experience every part of it. That was the attraction of the Hub for her, though—its intimacy.

She rounded the angular corner at the traffic circle where Cambridge and Charles streets met in a brackish transition from modern urban redevelopment to ageless brownstone tradition. The snow had piled up even higher than she had anticipated while she had been at the hospital, and she struggled slightly to pull her feet from a couple of knee-high drifts. At least it was cold out; the ground cover was light and fluffy in spite of its depth. A few people moved about on the brick sidewalks, hurrying home from dinner or a late evening's work, or heading out for a night of cozy drinks at one of the local pubs, but they moved like ghosts in the night, their footsteps and voices swallowed in the snow-fall.

Her own feet crunched softly in the uneven snow, losing traction on every third or fourth step. But she was accustomed to the necessary duck walk of moving about in the winter, and like most Bostonians, she kept her dress shoes tucked into her oversize purse, opting for clumsy tractor-soled hiking boots as outdoor wear. Nonetheless, she had to concentrate so hard on keeping her balance that twice she nearly col-lided with other pedestrians coming the opposite way, appearing out of the storm and taking her by surprise.

When her eyes were not on the snowy, uneven sidewalks, they darted about in search of a taxi, but what few she saw were already engaged by souls luckier than she. Had she known how hard it was snowing, she would have waited it out at the cabstand at Mass General, she thought, but there was nothing to do for it now. She put her head down to gut out the second half of the walk.

She was halfway down Charles Street toward Beacon before she caught a sense that she was in danger. The feeling grew quickly from no particular seed she could identify, but she had an overpowering cer-tainty that was impossible to ignore. She looked around her and saw no one. Still, the fear grew—a fear that most women who have lived in a large city would have recognized. It was the fear and vulnerability of being alone on a quiet street, and the terror that, were an attack to come, no one would hear the screams.

Lissa shook her head, trying to rattle the premonition loose; after all, she was in one of the safest areas of the city. However, no section of town was entirely free from danger. She tried laughing at herself. "C'mon, Lissa," she said under her breath. "You're being a fucking pussy. Since when have you been afraid of anything?" The nervous sound of her own voice failed to reassure her. Even if it had, the relief would have been short-lived.

He was standing in a doorway, smoking a cigarette. She didn't notice him until she was even with him on the sidewalk, close enough for him to reach out and touch her. His sudden appearance startled her, and she gave a light shriek. She spun to face him, and her left foot slid in the snow, throwing her off balance. In trying to keep from falling, she caught her right foot on an uneven brick concealed under the buckets of white. Without anything on which to brace herself, she went down hard on her knees.

The man reached down and grabbed her elbow.

"Get the fuck away from me!" she yelled, pulling herself to her feet and grabbing her bag, readying herself to run.

"I am only trying to help," the man said. He had a slight accent she couldn't place, and his smile made the ice that caked her knees seem warm by comparison. "Your knee is bleeding."

She looked down and saw it was true, but that seemed the least of her concerns. Looking back up at him, she started to back away slowly.

"Please," he said, moving forward. "I have a car. I can help you."

She turned and headed up the block, away from him, without saying a word. Turning back briefly at one point, she could see that he was following her, calling out to her, though his words were lost in the storm.

The fear pounded in her ears as she thought quickly. Hurrying as fast as the footing would allow, she turned right on Chestnut Street and ducked into an intimate bistro. The place was empty except for a bartender, who was busy cashing out his register.

"Sorry, ma'am, we're closed," he said to her, hardly looking up. His voice was polite but firm.

"Please," she said, "there's a man following me."

His eyebrows raised with real interest. "A stalker?" he asked.

She looked at him closely. He was tall and heavy, but the kind of heavy that hinted at solid, indestructible muscle underneath a comfortable layer of padding. He looked like he might be more at home bouncing at one of the rowdy college bars in the Fens instead of tending bar in a swank restaurant on Beacon Hill. She thought perhaps he was encouraged by the prospect of delivering a beating in her defense, and she was more than happy to encourage the notion.

"I think so," she said honestly, though she realized the man on the street hadn't actually done her any harm. She quickly dismissed any notion of guilt in favor of self-preservation and hardened her response. "Yes."

The bartender patted the bar in front of one of the stools, inviting her to sit. "He comes in here, and he'll be sorry," he said. Then he extended his hand. "I'm Ian."

"Lissa," she replied, shaking his hand and taking a seat, turning her body to the side so she could see the door.

"Can I get you anything to drink while you wait this out?" he offered. His eyes, too, were on the door.

"You look like you just closed out."

"On the house." He gave her a warm, nonthreatening smile. "You look like a wine drinker."

"Scotch."

He seemed impressed. "Okay, then. I'll pour us both a glass of the good stuff, and if no one shows by the time we're done, I'll call you a cab. How's that sound?"

She smiled back at him. "Deal."

When Kozlowski came back into the room, Finn could sense that the armistice was uneasy, as it often is with friends after an argument. They would get past it quickly, he knew. The trick was to return to normalcy as quickly as possible, no matter how strained it seemed.

"How does the arm feel?" Kozlowski asked. He, too, was trying. That made it easier.

"Hurts like a bitch," Finn replied. "And that's with half a bottle of Percocet in my system."

"I'd take a bullet over a blade any day when it comes to pain. Most people don't realize that knives tend to be more deadly than guns."

"I wouldn't know," Finn said. "I've never been shot. I'll have to wait for that merit badge."

"What were you doing out there, anyway? What were you thinking you'd learn?"

"I wanted to see where Steele was attacked. I needed to. Something about it didn't fit, and I couldn't figure it out by staring at words on a police report or on a trial transcript. I had to be out there myself."

"Did you figure it out?"

"I think so."

"And?"

"I think she was on the job that night. I remember what that neighborhood used to be like. There's no way she was just hanging out up there off duty. She had to be working a case."

Kozlowski appeared to consider this but said nothing.

Finn pressed on. "She lived in Southie, and I can't find anything to tie her personally to that area of Roxbury. That leaves only the possibility that she was out there for work. But there's nothing in the record about what she was working on. Neither the prosecution nor the defense even bothered to ask her. I find that very weird."

DAVID HOSP

"Does it matter?"

Finn was appalled by Kozlowski's disinterest. "*Does it matter?* Of course it matters. It may be the thing that matters most, for all we know. If we can figure out what she was working on, maybe we can figure out who else might have had a motive for trying to kill her. Don't you see? It could be the key to this entire case."

Kozlowski looked as though he were chewing on his cud. "Maybe," he said. "Then again, maybe not. Seems like it's all speculation."

"Of course it's all speculation," Finn agreed, getting frustrated. "Every investigation starts with speculation. Mix in a few hunches and a bottle of luck, and sometimes you actually figure out what the fuck is going on. What the hell is wrong with you?"

Kozlowski shrugged. "I guess it's our best lead at the moment."

"Damned right it is. So?"

"So what?"

"What do you think she was working on at the time? What do you think brought her out to Roxbury that night?"

"How would I know?" Kozlowski asked.

"I don't know," Finn said. "You were friends with her. You two worked out of the same station house. I thought she might have told you."

Kozlowski shook his head. "I know she was on that illegal immigration task force with the INS joint effort. Other than that . . ." He held up his hands to show they were empty.

"Nothing else?" Finn asked.

"Nothing else."

Finn thought. "Okay. Then we'll have to go straight to the source. We have to talk to Steele again."

Kozlowski laughed. "She'll shoot you if you go near her again. I'm not even kidding."

"Then I'll get that merit badge. Besides, if a bullet hurts less than this"—Finn held up his arm—"then I'll be fine."

"She's not going to talk to us," Kozlowski said.

"She's going to have to," Finn replied, and his voice was firm. "I don't care how many times she tries to shoot me. I'm going to find out what she was doing on the street that night."

———◆———

The taxi dropped Lissa off in front of her apartment. She gave the driver a seven-dollar tip on a three-dollar fare and asked him to wait until she was inside before pulling away. He nodded wearily, and his cab was still there when she closed the door behind her, safe within the lobby of the brownstone apartment building.

She had stayed at the restaurant on Chestnut Street for a little over half an hour, looking nervously out the front door the entire time. Twice she thought she'd caught sight of the man who had accosted her. Well . . . not accosted her, but frightened her. She'd sipped two Scotches with Ian, the protective bartender. As the time passed, he seemed to lose interest in her pursuer and gain a more direct interest in her. He even offered to give her a ride home himself, an offer that she was tempted to accept, but she thought better of it and politely asked him to call her a taxi. He seemed disappointed, though not offended, and she left him a twenty-dollar tip for the drinks. By the time she left the bar, she was almost convinced that the man on the street had just been overly solicitous and had not intended any harm. All he had done was offer her a hand up off the sidewalk and a ride home. All the same, she was relieved to be home.

She walked to the elevator and pressed the button. From the familiar humming of the gears, she judged that the ancient elevator car was several floors up and headed in the wrong direction. It was an old building, and the lift moved with the speed of a constipated tortoise; it could be several minutes before the car returned to the ground floor. Her apartment took up the entire sixth floor, and the walk up was no minor aerobic commitment, but she was in good shape, and she figured the exercise wouldn't kill her.

As she trudged up the stairs, she thought about what had happened to Finn that evening. She'd been skeptical about Salazar's innocence from the beginning. Hell, "skeptical" hadn't even begun to describe her attitude; she'd genuinely thought Finn was crazy to pursue the case. But the attack on her boss had shaken her more than she cared to admit. For the first time, her mind was open to the possibility that Salazar was actually rotting in prison for a crime he hadn't committed, and the notion made her sick. She tried to imagine what it must be like to sit in an eight-by-ten cage while your family and friends went on with their lives. You would be, for all practical purposes, dead; suffocating in a tiny steel coffin, looking out on a world that couldn't help but forget your existence. She couldn't fathom it.

She rounded the stairwell on the fifth floor, and the door to one of the apartments below hers cracked open, a single eyeball staring at her through the slit. It was an eyeball that had viewed Lissa with disdain since the day she had moved into her apartment.

"Good evening, Mrs. Snowden," Lissa said without trying to hide her annoyance.

The door opened a little more, until the chain lock caught. "More like morning, by my clock," the woman said. Her gray hair was locked into some sort of complicated sleeping apparatus designed to allow her to wake to a perfect, if somewhat less than stylish, coif.

Lissa looked at her watch. "Goodness, you're right, Mrs. Snowden. It's after midnight. I can already feel myself turning back into a pumpkin. If you see a glass slipper on the stairway, make sure it gets back to me, okay?" She walked past her neighbor's doorway and around toward the last flight of stairs up to her apartment. She was in no mood to deal with her nosy neighbor.

Mrs. Snowden sneered at her. "Will you be having company again tonight?"

Lissa turned and glared at the older woman. "That's really none of your fucking business, Mrs. Snowden, now, is it?"

Mrs. Snowden looked as though she'd been slapped, but she held her ground. "It most certainly is, young lady. Every time you bring one of your male acquaintances into the building to do . . . whatever it is you do . . . you put everyone in the building at risk. Who knows who these men are—clearly not you."

"You want to know what I'm doing up there with them, Mrs. Snowden? Fucking them. All of them. Every man in Boston, okay?"

Mrs. Snowden gasped.

"That's right. Sometimes ten or twenty of them at a time—there are so many to get through, you know? You should try it sometime; it might even loosen up that hair of yours."

Mrs. Snowden shook her head. "Harlot."

"Good night to you, too, Mrs. Snowden. I'm going to try to get a good night's sleep, so if you could keep your vibrator on low, it would be helpful."

Lissa heard the door slam shut as she started up the stairway to her apartment.

———————

Kozlowski could see that Finn was nodding off. He was putting up a valiant battle, almost as though the prospect of slipping into slumber and allowing the dreams to come frightened him.

"Seriously," Finn slurred, "next time I'll let you know where I'm going." It was apropos of nothing; they hadn't said a word to each other in twenty minutes. Kozlowski figured the painkillers were taking over. He just nodded. "Remind me in the morning," Finn continued, "that we have to talk to Steele again. There's something there. We just have to find out what it is."

Kozlowski said nothing.

"We're going to win this one." Finn's eyelids were sliding down, with only a thin line of his eyes visible. Then they closed altogether. "I swear we're gonna get this guy off," he mumbled, barely audible.

Kozlowski got up and walked out of the room. He went down to the cafeteria to get a cup of coffee, his mind churning. It was time to come clean, he knew, and that knowledge felt like dawn on the day of reckoning. He had no idea how bad it would be, but he was running out of options. He thought about Lissa and wondered how she would react. The thought of losing her, or even losing any little part of her respect, was as real as the blade that had been held to Finn's throat earlier in the evening. It was paralyzing. Still, he could see no other way.

He walked back up to Finn's room, and as he turned the corner into the doorway, he nearly collided with a young orderly coming out of the room. Kozlowski struggled to keep his coffee from sloshing out onto the floor.

"Excuse me, *señor*," the orderly said.

Kozlowski looked at him. He was probably in his early twenties, with black hair and a dark complexion. He looked nervous, and Kozlowski was sure he hadn't seen the man on duty in the ward before.

"That's okay," Kozlowski said, staying between the man and the door. He looked over at Finn, who was lying perfectly still on the bed.

The orderly tried to step around him, heading out of the room. Kozlowski put his arm out to stop him. "Hold it," he said.

"What is it, *señor*?" the orderly asked.

"Stay right here." Kozlowski took two quick strides over to Finn's bedside. He put a hand on his chest and leaned down to try and listen for his heart.

"Please, *señor*, what is wrong?" There was real fear in the orderly's voice now.

Kozlowski couldn't tell for sure whether Finn was breathing. His ear was down close to Finn's mouth, and a sense of panic was starting to rise in his own chest. He turned his head to look at Finn's face, their noses only inches apart.

Suddenly, Finn's eyes snapped open.

"Shit!" Kozlowski grunted in shock, jumping back from Finn.

Finn frowned sleepily. "What the fuck?" he asked. "Are you trying to make out with me or something?"

Kozlowski looked from Finn to the orderly. Then a doctor appeared at the door.

"Is there a problem, Juan?" he asked the orderly.

The man shrugged, looking relieved to have the doctor there to take control of the strange situation.

The doctor looked at Kozlowski, the question still showing on his face. "Sir?" he said, redirecting the inquiry.

Kozlowski looked at all three of the other men in the room, feeling foolish. "Everything's fine," he said. "I must be jumpy, that's all."

Finn turned his face back into the pillow and closed his eyes again. "Relax, Koz," he said. "The danger's over for tonight, at least. Get some sleep."

The doctor nodded to the orderly, and the two of them left. Kozlowski shook his head and sat down in the faux-Naugahyde recliner at the foot of Finn's bed. He was being absurd. And yet he couldn't seem to dismiss a profound feeling of danger.

He scratched his chin and sat there, trying to shake the feeling. It took several minutes, but gradually, he, too, became weary, and he closed his eyes. After a few more minutes, he fell into a fitful, tortured sleep.

———⊙———

Lissa was still fuming at Mrs. Snowden as she closed the door to her apartment. She walked through the place to the kitchen, feeling the need for a little wine to calm her nerves after the evening she'd had. A half glass of chardonnay would take the edge off the two Scotches she'd had at the bar with Ian the horny bartender, and might even allow her to get a decent night's sleep.

She went to the cupboard and took out a wineglass. As she turned toward the refrigerator, she noticed a light on in the pantry, projecting an uneven trapezoid of light on the floor.

That's strange, she thought.

She walked over and pushed the pantry door open, leaning her head in. It was a small closet, four feet deep and six feet wide, and there was no place inside for anyone to hide. Still, she lingered with her head in the space, looking closely into all the corners. She reached her hand up to the light switch, letting it hang there as she tried to remember how she could have left the light on. Then she flipped the switch, and the room went dark.

She carried the wineglass back to the refrigerator and put it down on the Corian countertop, then grabbed the handle to the fridge door. She was looking forward to her wine, but the feel of the handle gave her a start. It was wet and sticky-slick, and she pulled her hand away quickly, holding it up to her face. Even in the semilight, she could make out the dark red stain of blood on her palm.

"I needed some water."

The voice came from behind her, and as she turned, she knocked over the wineglass. It tumbled across the counter and crashed to the floor, but she hardly noticed. There, standing before her, was a young man with jet-black hair. In his right hand, he held a bottle of spring water; she recognized it as the brand she kept stocked in her refrigerator. He lifted the bottle and took a sip. She looked down and saw that a machete dangled from his left hand, blood still drying on the blade. Following his arm up back to his face, she saw that he was bleeding from his shoulder.

"I hope you don't mind," he said.

She tried to speak but found no air in her lungs. She just stood there, an expression of fear and incomprehension on her face.

"About the water," he said, shaking the bottle in front of his face. "I hope you don't mind that I helped myself."

It took another moment for the reality of her predicament to set in. "What do you want?" she asked finally.

He laughed, and it seemed as though the sound got caught in his throat. "To live," he said. "Your boss has put my ability to do that in some doubt. When the people I work with find out that he's still alive, they will be very disappointed." He put down the bottle and transferred the machete to his good hand. "They are not the sort of people you want to disappoint."

She looked closely at him and saw that he was pale, with a thin, shiny layer of sweat covering his face and neck. "What do you want with me?" she asked.

He took a step closer to her. "I need you to take a message to Mr. Finn."

She tried to move away from him, but she was already up against the counter, and there was no place for her to go. "What's the message?" She could barely breathe.

"In good time," he said. He put the blade to her chest, slicing off one of the buttons on her blouse. "First we should get to know each other better." The tip of the machete gently traced its way up through the cleft of her breasts, over her collar bone, and came to rest under her chin. He put some additional pressure on it, lifting her head so she was looking him in the eyes. "Perhaps," he said, "we can even be friends."

He turned the blade, and the sharp edge grazed her throat. She closed her eyes as she felt the tears running down her cheeks.

Chapter Thirty

Friday, December 21, 2007

Finn awoke feeling better than he had in weeks. His arm ached heavily, but it was his first decent night's sleep in a long time, and the first time his mind had felt clear since he'd gotten involved in Vincente Salazar's case.

Miguel had slept in one of the doctors' bunk rooms and examined Finn first thing in the morning, declaring him fit enough to leave the hospital and discharging him by eight o'clock. Kozlowski, who had slept sitting up in the chair in the hospital room, accompanied Finn to pick up his car in Roxbury, where it took twenty minutes to dig the vehicle out from under the snow that had been plowed over it during the evening's storm. Then the two of them set out for the office.

It was just past nine o'clock when they walked up the steps to the brownstone off Warren Street in Charlestown. Finn was surprised to find the door still locked; Lissa was usually in and working by eight. He unlocked the office, and Kozlowski followed him in. As Finn flipped through his mail, the detective briefly disappeared into the back office, then reappeared and sat on a chair against the wall, looking at Finn.

"What now?" Kozlowski asked.

"Gotta go back to Steele, right?" Finn said. "Find out what she was working on out there in Roxbury when she got attacked."

Kozlowski rubbed his chin. "You think that has something to do with all this?"

"I don't know. Right now it's the only thing that makes sense."

"Maybe. Still, even if you're right, you're talking about an investigation from over fifteen years ago. The chances we'd be able to pick up any trail—assuming Steele would tell us what she was working on—are almost nonexistent."

Finn frowned back at Kozlowski. "I know you're skeptical by nature, Koz, but what the fuck?"

"No fuck. Just seems like a serious long shot, that's all."

"Fine. You see any closer targets, just call 'em out. Besides, I've got a good feeling about this case today, and I'd appreciate it if you wouldn't piss all over my mood, okay?"

"That's not your mood, it's the painkillers."

"Yeah, well, whatever it is, it's giving me a good outlook on shit, and I'd appreciate it if you wouldn't bring me down." The phone on Finn's desk rang, and he picked it up. "Finn here."

"Finn, it's Smitty."

Finn recognized the voice of his fingerprint expert. "Hey, Smitty. You got more bad news for me?"

"Actually, no. Just the opposite. This call might make your day. Hell, it may even make your whole year."

Finn felt his adrenaline start pumping, and he tried to keep his optimism in check. "Don't go messin' with my head just to break my heart, Smitty," he said. "Tell me you've got something good. Did you get the new prints we took from Salazar?"

"I did, but they just confirmed that the prints used to identify him as the shooter were really his prints."

"My year's not getting any better yet," Finn whined.

"Give it a minute. I started thinking about what you asked me—how would someone go about screwing with the fingerprint process if they wanted to frame someone? I ended up going through Salazar's whole file with a magnifying glass, looking for anything unusual."

"Tell me you found something."

"I think I did. There were two prints that the police said were on the gun. One was used preliminarily to get the warrant to go after Salazar and make the arrest. The other one was the one they used at trial."

"That's weird, isn't it?" Finn asked. "Why not use both prints for the warrant and the trial?"

"Yeah, I thought that was weird, too, so I started looking a little harder at those two prints. The first one—the one they used to get the warrant—was a full print, complete in pretty much every detail." Smitty paused as though he'd said something important.

"So?" Finn pressed him.

"So full prints are pretty hard to come by in the real world. Usually, when we pick something up or touch it, we're not being careful to make a full fingerprint. Our hands move around, and only part of the finger touches the gun or the glass or whatever. You end up with partial prints, smudged and incomplete, almost all the time. The only time we really get a good, full print is when we book someone and roll a full set carefully on the booking sheet. Even then it can take a couple of tries to get a good set of prints. And yet here was this perfect print they picked up off a gun lying in an alleyway in the rain after a struggle, and it's got this perfect crystal-clear print. It didn't make any sense."

"They got lucky. So what? How does this help?"

"It was weird enough that I kept digging through Salazar's files. Turns out, when his wife died in the hospital, he was arrested by the INS. They let him go, but they did process him, and they took his prints."

"Standard procedure, I'm guessing," Finn said slowly, wondering where the conversation was headed.

"Absolutely. So I compared the print they used to get the warrant to the one that was taken when the INS busted him."

"And?"

"They're a perfect match."

"That's bad, right?" Finn was confused.

"No, it's great. When I say they're a perfect match, I mean they're identical. I mean you can put one over the other, and there is no difference whatsoever. I told you before, no two prints are ever identical, even if they are from the same finger on the same person. The only way that happens is if you make a photocopy of the same print—and that's what I think happened here."

"I'm not sure I follow you," Finn said. This sounded good for his client, but he needed to understand it better if he was going to try to explain it the judge.

"The gun probably came into the lab without any usable prints. They knew they wanted to nail your boy because they thought he did it, and so they go to the computer, make a copy of the print already in his file, slap it into a report, and say they found it on the gun. That'd be plenty for a warrant. Then they arrest the guy, and they get a new print off a glass—a partial this time, something that's going to look normal at trial in case the defense comes up with a fingerprint expert with half a brain—and they plant that on the gun. It's the only thing that makes sense."

Finn took a deep breath. "Smitty, would you be willing to put all that in an affidavit?"

"You still gonna pay my bills?"

"With a nice Christmas bonus."

"I'll have it to you by noon."

"You're the best."

"Did I make your year?"

"There's still a week left in the year, and I've gotta see the affidavit, but you're in the running."

Finn hung up the phone and looked at Kozlowski. The older man was leaning back in his chair, his eyes on Finn, narrowed in curiosity. "Good news, I take it?" he asked.

"You bet your ass." Finn smiled. "That was Smitty."

"I gathered."

"He says that the first print they claimed was on the gun—the one they used to get the warrant for Salazar's arrest—was a copy of an old booking print they had for him. That means the second print was probably planted after they arrested him." Finn tried to keep the "I told you so" tone out of his voice. He knew it was a pointless effort.

"Could it have been an oversight? Maybe they just put the wrong print in the file?" Kozlowski looked oddly shaken. Finn knew how much he hated to be wrong, particularly in a debate with Finn, but the depth of his anguish in this case was unusual. Finn began to wonder whether Kozlowski really wanted their client to turn out to be guilty.

"You've got to be shitting me," Finn said, rising out of his chair. "Skepticism is one thing, but this is really bullshit, Koz. The man is innocent. What the fuck is going on with you?"

The phone rang.

Kozlowski shook his head but said nothing.

"Salazar is innocent," Finn said again. "And with or without your help, I'm talking to Steele this morning to find out what's going on."

The phone rang a second time.

Finn continued to stare at Kozlowski. He was angry now, and he wanted to make that clear. He wanted to make it clear that he wasn't backing down. "Are you with me, or are you going to bail?"

The phone rang a third time.

"Answer the phone," Kozlowski said.

Finn glared at the ex-cop for another brief moment. "You sure you want me to? The way this case is going, this is probably more good news. If it's the president with a pardon for our client, are you going to object?" He picked up the handset. "Finn here," he barked, redirecting his anger. He listened to the voice on the other end of the line, feeling the blood drain from his face. "N-no . . ." he stammered once, but the voice kept going. Finally, when it was over, he said, "We'll be right there."

He hung up the phone, looking at Kozlowski and seeing the question already on the older man's brow. "What is it?" Kozlowski asked.

Finn shook his head, almost unable to talk. "It's Lissa," he said. "She's at the hospital."

There was a pause as the two men looked at each other, seeing nothing but their own worst nightmares mirrored in the other's eyes. Then they were both moving toward the door at full speed.

PART III

Chapter Thirty-one

THEY SPOKE FIVE WORDS between them on the drive back to Mass General. In places, the roads were still covered with fresh-packed snow from the prior evening's storm, and Finn's tiny MG skidded and skittered around corners on the edge of control as he pushed the car well beyond speeds that could be considered safe given the conditions. As they passed the Museum of Science, Kozlowski, who hadn't been able even to look at Finn since they got in the car, asked, "How bad?"

Finn gripped the wheel tightly as the car slid into a turn. "They didn't say." There seemed no point in further conversation.

They parked illegally on a side street near the hospital to avoid the hassle of the parking garage, and ran to the emergency room. It had been under three hours since Finn had been discharged.

Kozlowski was first through the hospital doors and moving fast. He reached the ER intake desk at a gallop and spat out, "Lissa Krantz. Where is she?"

A young nurse sitting at a computer station behind the desk stood just as Finn caught up. She had real sympathy in her eyes. "She came in an hour ago," she said. "She's not talking much; just told us to call Tom and Finn at work. Are you them?"

Kozlowski nodded.

"How is she?" Finn asked.

The nurse's eyes went to the floor. "We think—" she began, but then she stopped as a doctor appeared from behind her. "You should talk to Dr. Cregany."

Hearing his name, the doctor looked up. "Can I help you?" he asked.

"Yes," Finn said. "We're friends of Lissa Krantz's. She was brought in this morning."

"What happened?" Kozlowski asked, his voice rough.

The doctor looked to the nurse for confirmation.

"Bay four," she said, identifying Lissa by location.

"Yes, right," he said. "Ugly scene. A neighbor found her this morning and called 911. One of those awful things that you think happens only to other people until it happens to you. You're friends, you say?"

"Yeah," Finn confirmed.

"Good. She'll need friends now."

"Please, Doctor, can you tell us how she is?"

He looked startled by the question. "In the grand scheme of things, she's fine, actually. At least she will be. She was beaten pretty badly; cut in a few places, too. But there's no permanent damage. It's mainly cosmetic." He said it in the cold, matter-of-fact tone that only those doctors who deal with the worst medical traumas have perfected.

"How badly?" Kozlowski asked.

"Hmm?" Dr. Cregany had been distracted by another patient's chart.

"How badly was she beaten?" Kozlowski's voice was louder now.

The doctor put the chart down on the counter. He shrugged. "We've called in a plastic surgeon. She'll be fine. Law student, she said, right? So she'll be making her living with her brains, not her looks, anyway."

Something in Kozlowski snapped, and he grabbed the doctor, slamming him up against a wall. Cregany tried to squirm away, but Kozlowski held firm to the lapels of the doctor's coat.

"Hey!" Cregany whimpered. "Let go of me!"

Kozlowski held a fist to the doctor's face, then drew it back, cocking his arm.

"Let go of him, Koz," Finn said in an even tone. "It's not worth it."

Kozlowski let his arm relax but brought his hand around, pointing a finger in the doctor's face. "I ever hear you talk about one of your patients that way again," he said, "and I'll make sure you're sharing a bed in the emergency room with them. And if I even suspect that Lissa Krantz isn't getting the finest medical care this hospital—and you in particular—can provide, I'll kill you. That's a promise."

Finn put a hand on Kozlowski's shoulder. "Easy, Koz."

Kozlowski let go of the doctor, who slid down the wall to the side. "I'm calling the cops," he said. Kozlowski just stared at him, and it was enough to drive any hint of a threat from the doctor. He stood up and slunk away.

"He's an arrogant asshole," said a woman's voice from behind them. Kozlowski turned around and looked down at one of the smallest people he'd ever seen. She couldn't have been over four and a half feet tall. She looked to be in her late forties, with short gray hair and a rough, practical manner that nonetheless seemed to make room for compassion. "He won't do anything," she said reassuringly. "It would involve admitting that someone actually pushed him around. I'm Maggie." She extended her hand, and the two men shook it in turn; her grip was startlingly strong for a woman her size. "I was Lissa's intake nurse. I've been with her for the last hour or so. She's had a rough go, but the doctor was essentially right: She will be okay."

"What happened?" Finn asked.

"Not entirely clear," Nurse Maggie said. "She hasn't told us very much. She was beaten pretty badly, that much is clear. She's got a couple of cracked ribs, a broken arm, a broken nose, lots of cuts and contusions—mainly on her face. It looks like whoever did this broke into her apartment. Could have been a burglary gone wrong, I suppose, but the police say nothing was taken. We're guessing more likely she knows who the guy was—maybe an ex-boyfriend or a stalker. Otherwise, she'd be telling us more than she is. Until she does decide to talk, I suspect it'll remain a mystery to us."

"Can we see her?" Kozlowski tried to keep his voice from breaking. He had no idea whether he was successful.

She looked at him. "You're Tom," she said.

Kozlowski could feel Finn looking at him, and he avoided eye contact. "Yes."

Maggie nodded. "She told me a little about you." Then she looked at Finn. "And you're her boss? The lawyer?"

"I am."

"She's been asking for both of you. That's about the only talking she's done. Said she wouldn't speak to anyone but you two." She looked them over with an evaluating gaze, as though trying to judge whether her patient's trust in them was justified. "You can go in and see her," she said at last. "She's in the last room on the right."

Kozlowski and Finn started heading down the hallway. "Hey!" Maggie called after them.

They stopped, and she walked toward them, looking around. "There's something you should probably know," she said in a confidential tone. She looked them both in the eyes to make sure they were paying attention. "We think she was raped."

Kozlowski felt a pain like a flaming dagger through his chest. He thought he might collapse.

"What do you mean, 'we think'? What does that mean?" Finn asked.

"We can't be entirely sure. We ran a rape kit, and we didn't come up with any semen or fluids, but he could have used a condom. And there are other indications."

"Like?" Finn asked.

"Bruising," she said. "In the vaginal area. And when her neighbor found her, she was naked, curled up in a ball."

"What does Lissa say?" This time it was Kozlowski who asked the question.

"Like I said, she's not talking. The bruising could have come from consensual sex, but she would have had to be very sexually active in the very recent past."

Kozlowski could feel himself turn crimson as he listened to the efficient, effective, plainspoken nurse describe Lissa's anatomy. He felt numb. He had no idea how to react.

"I just thought you should know," Nurse Maggie said. "She's going to need a lot of support, any way you look at it. She'll get through it—she's strong, that's easy to see—but she's still gonna need help. You need to know that."

Kozlowski looked at her, desperate for any additional advice she might have. She just shook her head slightly. He took a deep breath and straightened his shoulders. "Thanks, Maggie," he said. Then he and Finn turned and walked down the hallway toward the room where Lissa was.

———

When they walked into her room, she was lying on her back, her face turned toward the door, her eyes closed. Finn barely recognized her. Her bottom lip had been split down the center and was held together loosely by thick, ugly temporary stitches. Her nose was bent to one side at an awkward angle, and the rest of her face was battered and swollen. Sticking out from under her hospital gown were heavy bandages on her arms, mottled with crimson. He could hardly believe that this was the same woman who had walked into his office every morning for the past eight months.

Then she opened her eyes and returned. The eyes seldom lie, and though hers showed fatigue and fear, there were sparks of anger and defiance as well, fierce and unrelenting. Finn knew those eyes were still hers.

She saw the two men and turned her head away, staring at the ceiling. "Quite a sight, huh?" she said. A tear ran down her cheek.

"I've seen worse," Finn lied. Kozlowski was by the side of the bed, and Finn went to stand next to him.

"Yeah," she said. "In the fucking morgue."

"Nah," Finn reassured her. "They'll have you fixed up in time to go dancing on New Year's Eve." He looked down at the side of the bed and noticed that Kozlowski was holding her hand. He still hadn't said anything.

"The nose doesn't matter much. It wasn't mine to begin with, you know?"

Finn shook his head. "I didn't."

"It was a birthday present when I was seventeen. I never liked my real nose. I had great lips, though." She winced in pain as she spoke.

"What happened?" Finn asked.

She swallowed hard twice. "He said he wanted me to give you a message. He said that Salazar stays in jail. Otherwise he'll come back."

Finn didn't think at all about it. "Done. I'm off the case." Then he turned and paced away from the bed, letting the decision sink in. "Shit, I didn't want to take the case in the first place." He tried to shoot his voice through with conviction, but even he didn't believe it.

"If you're off the case," Lissa said, "then you'd better start looking for a new associate."

He turned and looked back at her. "You sure? These people aren't fucking around."

She looked hard at him, and he could see that the anger and defiance had grown. The fear seemed gone. "Neither are we, right? Not anymore."

"Right," he agreed.

"Good," she said. "'Cause I'm not gonna waste my fucking time working for some goddamned pussy who lets himself get bullied."

"Okay." Finn leaned against the wall, taking in the scene in front of him: Lissa, lying in her bed, broken but not beaten; Kozlowski, standing over her, silent and brooding, holding her hand.

"Finn?" Lissa said.

"Yeah?"

"I need a minute with Koz, okay?"

For a moment Finn was confused. "Sure," he said. Then, as he opened the door, an absurd thought crossed his mind, one that had tickled him before and been dismissed. He looked back at them and saw them as they truly were, for the first time—both of them searching for the same thing, now more than ever. "I'll be outside," he said.

As he walked out, he knew they hadn't heard him.

"Are you okay?" Lissa asked Kozlowski.

He wasn't, and the fact that she was asking him the question—and not the other way around—only drove his shame and guilt deeper. His jaw clenched hard.

"It's my fault," he said. "I should have known you were in danger. I should have seen this coming. I should have stayed with you."

"Don't be stupid."

He said nothing, and the two of them sat in silence for a little while. He couldn't bring himself to look her in the eyes, and his rage continued to grow.

"Koz?"

"Yeah?"

"Nothing."

He wanted to talk to her. Really talk to her. He wanted to hold her, but for some reason he wasn't sure how to anymore; not in this kind of situation. He wished to God he were better at this. He wished it were easier for him to reach out. Suddenly, the stoicism that had been his shield throughout his life seemed pathetic. "What is it?" he asked.

"I want you to do something for me."

"Anything."

She pushed her head back into the pillow and closed her eyes. "I want you to get this guy. I want you to get the people he works for." She opened her eyes and looked at him. "Do you understand?"

He nodded. "Yeah, I understand."

"The police won't give a shit, even if they catch him. Even if they make him talk. I won't be safe unless they're all gone."

"Yeah," he said. He realized for the first time that he was holding her hand. He couldn't remember when that had happened. Had he grabbed her hand the moment he'd walked into the room, or more recently? Whenever, he'd done it without thought and without fear. He gave it a gentle squeeze, and he could feel her grip tighten in his, as though she were holding on for dear life. Then she pulled it away.

"Go," she said. "You have shit you need to get done."

He looked down at his empty hand. He'd been alone his entire life, but he'd never felt lonely. Not really. Not until now. "Yeah," he said. He tried to force a smile and failed. "I'll come by later?"

"I'm not going anywhere. I think I'd like that."

He searched desperately for something to say, something useful or comforting, but it was hopeless. He walked to the door. As he put his hand on the doorknob, she said, "Koz?"

He looked back at her. "Yeah?"

"You didn't ask me."

"What?"

"What happened. You didn't ask me what happened to me. You didn't ask me whether he . . ." Her words faded off. "It seemed like that was all the doctors cared about. Did he or didn't he. I could even see the question in Finn's eyes. But not yours. You didn't ask. You weren't even curious. Why not?"

He thought about it. Then he walked back to the side of her bed and sat on the side of the mattress. "I'm not good at this," he said. "I never had any practice. If you ever want to tell me anything—if you ever want to talk about anything—I'll always listen. I may not have any answers for you, and I may not be able to fix everything, but I can listen. I'm never going to ask you any questions about it because I don't care. I don't care because nothing that happened to you—nothing that could happen to you—could ever change the way I feel about you. Do you understand?" Her eyes had watered over, and she wiped them with the back of her hand. He had to get out of the room or he was going to lose it.

"I think so," she said. She took his hand and brought it to her chest. "Thank you."

He nodded.

"Now, you go out and get this fucker, okay?"

Finn waited outside the room for Kozlowski. When he came out, he was moving with purpose. He blew right by Finn without pausing.

"Koz! Hold on!" Finn shouted, breaking into a jog to keep up. Kozlowski kept moving and said nothing. "Koz! Wait!" Finn caught him from behind and put a hand on his shoulder to slow his pace. Kozlowski spun around on him, the violence bubbling visibly to the surface. "Shit, just wait a second, okay?" Finn moved back out of Kozlowski's reach.

"What?" Kozlowski demanded. His face was twisted with rage.

Finn looked back toward Lissa's room, then met Kozlowski's eyes. "How long?" he asked.

The question took Kozlowski by surprise, and Finn could see that he'd guessed right. After a moment's internal struggle, Kozlowski relented. "A week. A little less, maybe."

Finn blew out a long breath, considering the implications. "That's good," he said at last. "It's good for both of you."

"Yeah." Kozlowski was looking through him. "Just fucking great."

"I'm guessing this isn't sitting very well with you right now."

"Good fucking guess, Carnac."

Finn scratched his head. "So? What are you thinking of doing about it?"

"I'm going to bring these fuckers down. Every last one of them. You got a problem with that?"

Finn considered the question. "No," he said. "Not really. You got a plan?"

Kozlowski shook his head.

"Good. Plans are overrated, anyway."

Kozlowski continued to stare at him.

"Fine," Finn said. "I'm in."

Kozlowski nodded, then started moving toward the hospital exit, more slowly this time.

"I guess all those bright lines of yours are pretty much out the window, huh?" Finn asked.

"My lines are still bright," Kozlowski said. "These people just stepped over them."

It was ten o'clock before Jimmy made it back to East Boston. He'd walked the entire way, too nervous to take a cab or a bus in his condition. The bleeding from his shoulder had slowed to an intermittent ooze, but he had lost a significant amount of blood. He needed medical attention, and he wouldn't get it without Carlos's help.

He walked around to the back of the rectory and slipped into the basement through the open door next to the garage. Raul, one of Carlos's confidants, was there, waiting for him. "We saw you coming up the street, I hope no one else did," Raul said. "You should be far more careful, particularly this close to a delivery." Something about the man's posture put Jimmy on edge, but he assumed it was just his exhaustion feeding his natural paranoia.

"I need a doctor," Jimmy said. He nodded toward his shoulder and realized with concern that he could no longer move his arm. "I got shot."

"Carlos is upstairs in his church." Raul turned and headed up the stairs. "You coming?"

"I need a doctor," Jimmy repeated. Something inside told him to run, but he was so tired, and he didn't know where else to go.

"Carlos is upstairs," Raul repeated. He never broke stride, and after a moment Jimmy followed him up.

The church was connected to the rectory by a short covered walkway, and the two of them slipped across quietly, careful to remain out of sight from any passersby. Carlos was in the church, kneeling in front of the altar—nothing more than a raised dais since the archdiocese had stripped it of anything of value. Raul motioned for Jimmy to sit in the front pew, then walked back out the door, headed toward the rectory. Jimmy sat for several minutes. He thought he might pass out, and he even considered interrupting Carlos's meditations, but he understood what a remarkably bad idea that would be. At last Carlos lifted his head, made the sign of the cross, and stood.

He turned and looked at Jimmy. There was no question that he had been aware of Jimmy's presence. "You have returned," he said.

"I got shot. I need a doctor," Jimmy said.

"You may need more than that," Carlos said icily. "I understand that the lawyer is still alive."

Panic ripped through Jimmy's chest, and in his weakened condition, the flood of adrenaline made him shake violently. "He is," Jimmy said. "He got away, but he's no longer a problem."

"No longer a problem? He is still alive, but he is no longer a problem? That is impressive. Most impressive. Particularly since I made clear to you that the lawyer would remain a problem as long as he was still alive. Are you telling me that I was wrong?"

Jimmy knew that he had to pick his way very carefully through the minefield of Carlos's questioning. If Jimmy said Carlos had been wrong, it would constitute a direct challenge. If he said Carlos had been right, it would constitute an admission that he had failed. Like everything with the Padre, this was a test, and no matter how tired he was, Jimmy had to stay sharp in order to pass. "I found another way," he said.

"Another way?" Carlos considered this. "How creative of you. What was this 'other way'?"

"I sent him a message. Using one of his employees—a woman."

"You sent him a message?"

"A very clear message. We won't have any more problems with the lawyer."

"You know this? You know exactly how the lawyer will react to this message?"

"I think so, yes." Jimmy wanted to rest. His head throbbed, and his arm was completely numb.

"You think?"

"I know."

"Which is it?"

Jimmy said nothing.

"In business, as in war, there is nothing more dangerous than uncertainty. You were sent to resolve this situation once and for all."

"I believe I did." Jimmy knew the conversation was getting away from him. He was failing. It occurred to him again to run, but he knew it was useless. He no longer had the strength.

Carlos walked over and sat down in the pew next to Jimmy. "I had high hopes for you. You know that?"

"Yes, Padre," Jimmy said. He realized he was crying. "I'm sorry."

"Very high hopes for you. You are not Salvadoran, but I thought you were strong. In some ways, I saw more of myself in you than I have in anyone else. In some ways, I thought of you as a son. I had a son once, did you know that?"

Jimmy shook his head, the tears wagging as they flowed down his cheeks.

"He's gone now, but you reminded me of him."

"Padre, I'm so sor—"

Carlos patted Jimmy's knee, cutting him off. "Not to worry. We are all in God's hands in the end." He looked up at the stained-glass window rising up from behind the altar. The morning light was streaming through it, casting a multicolored glow over Carlos's heavily tattooed face. The effect was kaleidoscopic, and Jimmy felt dizzy as he looked at the older man.

"Were you raised in the Church, Jimmy?"

"No. My mother was . . . She wasn't religious. My father was American."

Carlos nodded in understanding. "Do you know the story of Abraham?"

Jimmy shook his head.

"Abraham was God's chosen. He was God's favorite. He was the man God loved above all others. But God still knew Abraham needed to be tested. He needed to prove his trust and devotion to God. So God sent Abraham up into the mountains. He told him to bring his oldest son." Carlos stood and took Jimmy by the hand, leading him up to the altar. "God had Abraham build a great altar. Then He told Abraham to have his son lie down on the altar." Carlos gently pushed Jimmy down onto his knees. "And then God told Abraham to take his blade and kill his own son as a sign of his obedience to God."

Carlos reached behind him and picked up a machete that was leaning against the wall. He brought it up over his head. "Abraham raised his sword, ready to kill his own flesh and blood in the name of God. God, seeing that Abraham was worthy of His trust, took mercy on him. And as Abraham began to swing his sword, the hand of God came down and stopped the blade, sparing his son."

Jimmy was on his knees, looking up through his tears at Carlos as the light streamed in from the stained-glass window. He looked divine to Jimmy.

"So you see, Jimmy, there is really only one question for the two of us here today."

"What?" Jimmy sobbed.

Carlos stared evenly at Jimmy. "Whether God will have mercy on us." With that, he swung the machete in a swift, even arch toward Jimmy's head. Jimmy saw it coming and flinched backward a half foot in an effort to avoid the blade. His reaction saved him, but not by much. The machete sank cleanly into the meat of his left arm, just below the gunshot wound. It cut through the muscle and severed the bone, and Jimmy's arm fell onto the altar in front of him.

"No!" Jimmy screamed. He reached out with his remaining hand and grabbed his disembodied arm. All rational thought deserted him. "No!" he screamed again, and tried to make his way off the altar and toward the church door. His entire mental process was reduced to a single word: *Run!*

Unfortunately for him, the altar was now slick with the blood pouring from the stump below his shoulder. His balance was gone, and he slipped and went back down on his knees, dropping his severed arm and letting it slide across the floor.

Carlos stalked him from behind. He came up alongside Jimmy, stretched out at his feet. He held the machete in both hands, like a baseball bat. Jimmy looked up at him.

"Please! No!" Jimmy begged.

Carlos took a step and swung the machete in a low, strong uppercut, catching Jimmy below the rib cage, splitting open his belly. Jimmy looked down and saw ribbons of intestines spilling out of him onto the floor. The stench was awful. He tried to crawl, but the top and bottom halves of his body were no longer able to function together with any semblance of coordination, and he was able to do little more than squirm on the floor in a pool of his own innards.

Carlos looked down at him. "I'm sorry, Jimmy," he said. "God has no more mercy left." He brought the machete up again, and Jimmy watched helplessly as the blade swung hard toward his neck. There was nothing he could do, and the blow caught him cleanly in the throat, severing his head from his shoulders.

Perhaps God had some mercy left after all; Jimmy no longer felt a thing.

Chapter Thirty-two

Outside the hospital, Finn climbed into his car and started the engine. It had taken a few moments for them to find the tiny MG, as the plows had pushed piles of snow up against the convertible in uneven clumps.

"Where to first?" Finn asked. "Talk to Macintyre? He's got to be at the heart of this, right?"

"Probably," Kozlowski agreed. "But he's not going to be easy to shake; he's been around for too long, and he knows how the game is played. He's not going to show us his cards unless we can put a bigger pot on the table in front of him. Right now we have nothing to bet with."

"Fornier, then? He's a sleazy weasel. A little bit of pressure, and I bet he'll topple over."

"Maybe," Kozlowski said. "But he's our second visit. There's someone else we need to talk to first."

"Who?" Finn was pulling out of the parking space, craning his neck around the mountains of snow to avoid being sideswiped by oncoming traffic.

"Madeline Steele," Kozlowski said.

"Steele? I thought you said she wouldn't talk. You thought she'd shoot me instead."

"She may still shoot you. But I can get her to talk."

Finn cast a sideways glance at the private detective, who was inscrutable. "You wanna tell me what she's going to say before we get there?"

Kozlowski shook his head. "Better that you hear it from her."

———

Finn and Kozlowski headed to police headquarters in Roxbury to talk to Steele, but they were told that she was taking a few days off for the holidays. From there, they headed out to the South Boston neighborhood where Steele had grown up and where she still lived.

The small clapboard house where she rented an apartment was easy to spot from the street. The residences in Southie were packed tightly together and sat flush to the sidewalks, leaving little room for pedestrians. The dearth of space was even more acute in front of Steele's house, as a long iron-railed cement ramp sidled its way up to the front door.

Kozlowski rang the doorbell, and they waited patiently on the front steps.

Two minutes later, the door swung open, and Madeline Steele looked up at them from her wheelchair. She looked far less intimidating than she had at police headquarters. She was dressed in a pink sweatshirt and leggings that showed the atrophy in her lower extremities. In this setting, she seemed to Finn more like a helpless little girl than a formidable police officer.

"What the fuck do you want?" she shot at them. *So much for the helpless little girl.* Finn thought he detected something underneath her demeanor, though. It felt a little like fear.

"We want to talk to you about Vincente Salazar," Finn said.

"I told you, I'm through talking," Steele replied, going to slam the door.

Finn stuck out his foot to keep the door from closing. It was made from heavy oak and built to withstand whatever the city could throw at it. For a moment Finn thought he'd lost his foot. He jumped back, howling in pain. "Shit! That hurt!"

"Good," Steele said, reaching out to close the door again. "Next time keep out of the way."

"Please," Finn said. "We need to know what you were investigating on the night you were shot."

"Nothing," she said. "Stay the fuck away from me." She pulled the door back to gain some additional momentum and then swung it at them even harder.

Kozlowski stepped into the doorway, leading with his shoulder. In spite of the force with which she had pushed the door, when it collided with Kozlowski's body, the door took the worst of the encounter, bouncing back with a heavy shake and a pained rattle. Kozlowski looked as though he hadn't even felt it. He held her eyes with his, and the fear that Finn had sensed from Steele seemed to grow.

"Like the man said, Maddy, we've gotta talk to you. Turns out the fingerprints were faked; we've got the proof. You lied on the stand; you and I already knew that. An innocent man went to jail, and now other people are getting hurt. Bad."

As he spoke, the fear on Steele's face morphed into anguish. "No," she said quietly. "He did it. I know it. They told me so, and I can see his face still." The words came out as a whisper, with little force and no conviction. Then she dissolved into sobs.

Kozlowski let her cry for a moment. Then he pushed the door open wider, leaned down, and said softly, "It's time for us to get clean, Maddy."

———

Madeline Steele felt defeated. Worse than that, she felt betrayed. Worst of all, she felt responsible. "He told me Salazar was the one. He said they had the prints. He said there wasn't any doubt."

"Macintyre?" Kozlowski asked. "He told you they had a match on the prints?"

She nodded. "It was Mac. He was the one who was coordinating with the latent print unit. He was bagging most of the evidence."

"What did he say, exactly?" Finn asked.

"He came to my hospital room," she said. "In the first days—I don't even know when, exactly—I wasn't conscious most of the time, and when I was, I was so hopped up on the painkillers that I wasn't really coherent. He told me they had the guy, said it was a lock on the fingerprints, but that the DA was still going to want more. He said the DA wanted eyewitness testimony. Then he pulled a booking picture of Salazar out of his coat and told me to take a good look. He told me to memorize his face. He told me to remember that this was the face of the man who had done this to me."

"But you weren't sure? You're not sure now?" Finn pressed.

She looked at him, and then her gaze drifted out the window, out toward the street. "I don't know," she said. "For fifteen years his has been the face in my dreams. When I wake up sobbing at night, his is the face that I still see in my head."

"But . . ." Kozlowski said. It was directed at Steele with force and purpose, and shook her.

"But I never saw the man's face when I was attacked," she said. It was a struggle to get the words out, and once she had done it, they lay there in the room like a dead animal, grotesque and compelling.

"But you testified—" Finn started.

She cut him off. "They told me they had the guy. They said there was no question. It all made sense—I was trying to have him deported. I couldn't risk letting him walk, could I?"

Finn looked over at Kozlowski. "You knew." Kozlowski nodded, and Finn's head fell into his hands. "You knew the entire time."

Kozlowski said nothing.

"He only knew after the trial was over," Steele interjected. "I told him months later, and he told me I had to come forward. But what was I supposed to do at that point? Let them release the guy who had taken so much from me? Go through the trial all over again? I couldn't."

"It wasn't him!" Finn yelled. "It wasn't him, and you both let him go to jail anyway!"

"I had no way of knowing that," Steele said defensively. But even to her, it sounded weak. "I didn't know what was going to happen to me. Put yourself in my shoes—that was what I told Koz back then. He threatened to tell people, but I told him that I'd just say he was lying, and he would lose every friend he ever had on the force. We were never friends again." She felt sick. "I'm sorry, Koz."

The radiator in the corner of the room gave a squeal, punctuating a terrible silence.

"What were you working on?" Finn asked abruptly.

She looked at Kozlowski.

"You knew that, too?" the lawyer demanded of the former cop.

"Only a little," Kozlowski replied. "Not the details."

Finn turned back to Steele. "Well?"

"I was working on a joint task force with the INS, rounding up illegal aliens. In the course of that work, I kept running up against a new street gang that was just making headway in the Boston area."

"Let me guess: VDS, right?" Finn said.

She nodded. "I had never even heard of them at the time, but I kept hearing whispers that they were the ones bringing in many of the illegals from South and Central America. Word was they had a whole slave trade going."

"Slaves?"

"Yeah, slaves. They'd offer to bring people across the border, then charge them more than they could afford. When they couldn't pay, the gang would offer to get them work, but when the people got here, they were handed over to shady operations that didn't pay them enough to work off their debt. They ended up literally as slaves; VDS took an up-front payment from the employers, plus an ongoing revenue stream from the interest on the debt. It was a neat little racket."

"What happened to the investigation after you were shot?" Finn asked.

"It died. I was laid up for over seven months, and when I finally made it back into the game, the operation was shut down. They had been running it out of a bodega in Roxbury, but the place had closed up shop, and there were no leads. Plus, I was in no shape to chase them down at that point."

"And you never put two and two together and figured out that they were the ones responsible for you being shot?"

"What was there to put together? As far as I knew, the guy who shot me was in jail, and from what I knew about him, he didn't have any real connections to VDS. What was I supposed to think?"

The three of them sat there for several minutes, saying nothing. Then Finn stood up and walked to the door. He turned to her. "I want you to put all of this into an affidavit. We'll pick it up later this afternoon."

"I don't know whether I can do that," she replied.

"Bullshit," Finn said. "You'll do it."

"I could lose my job."

"An innocent man has been rotting in prison because of you. Your job security is the last thing I'm concerned about at this point. You'll do it voluntarily, or I'll see that formal charges are brought. You won't just lose your job, you could go to jail for perjury."

She felt like her world was collapsing, but she nodded. "I'll do it."

Kozlowski stood up and joined the lawyer at the front door. He looked back at her, and she found it difficult to look him in the eyes. "Looks like I fucked up, Koz. I should have listened to you."

"We all fucked up," Kozlowski said. "Now it's time for all of us to set it right."

Finn was already in his car with the motor running when Kozlowski squeezed himself into the passenger seat. He stepped on the gas and peeled out into the street.

"Three weeks," Finn said, his voice slicing through the cold. "Three fucking weeks we've been working this case. Three weeks since Dobson first came to us—ten days since he was chopped into fucking pieces. During all that time, it never occurred to you to mention to me that you knew the guy was innocent?"

"I didn't know he was innocent. I thought he was guilty. I just knew Maddy didn't get a good look at him. I still thought the fingerprint evidence was solid."

"You should have told me. We're partners on this. More than that, I'm your boss." Kozlowski gave Finn an ironic look. "Fine," Finn eased back, "but we are at least partners; you can't hold shit like this back from a partner."

"I couldn't tell you."

"Why not?"

"I gave her my word. I can't break my word."

Finn sighed. "You know, these fucking rules of yours are for shit. You act like they're all based on some black-and-white inviolable principles, but they're not. It's all a bunch of bullshit."

"I do the best I can," Kozlowski said.

"The world is gray, Koz. You gotta learn to live with that."

"Maybe," Kozlowski said. "Like I said, I just do the best I can."

"Right," Finn said. He pulled over to the side of the road.

"What are you doing?" Kozlowski asked.

"I just realized I have no fucking clue where we're going now. Do you want to take a run at Macintyre? See what we can get out of him?"

Kozlowski shook his head. "We still don't really have much on him. Even if he did step out of line with Steele, he'll just claim that he thought he was doing the right thing. Unless we can tie him to the faked prints, he'll bob and weave, and we'll get nothing. We need more to really rattle him."

"Fornier?" Finn asked. "He's the one who signed the fingerprint report."

"Fornier," Kozlowski confirmed. "But not yet. We've got to take him on outside the station house. He feels too safe there. We've got to make it clear to him that he's not safe; not on this. We get him scared, and we'll get the whole story—I can just about guarantee that."

"Great. So how do we make sure he doesn't feel safe?"

Kozlowski shrugged. "There's really only one way to do that."

"That's what I thought," Finn said, pulling out onto the street again. "Looks like those lines of yours are getting grayer by the second."

Chapter Thirty-three

AT EIGHT O'CLOCK that evening, Eddie Fornier sat on a bar stool in a pub on Columbus Avenue, just off Massachusetts. There were only two other patrons in the hole-in-the-wall tavern, and they were at the other end of the heavy, scarred wooden bar, minding their own business. The bartender was a tall, solid-looking man in his late forties who wore a crew cut, a goatee, and faded black tattoos on his forearms that Fornier recognized as of the prison variety. He was just attentive enough to keep Fornier's glass full without being nosy. The place had the decrepit feel of hell's waiting room, with its darkened windows, yellow lights, and torn upholstery. In short, it was exactly the type of place where Fornier felt most at home.

There had been a time in his life when he'd preferred the noise and action of the cop bars nearer the station house. Back then he'd enjoyed the camaraderie of the force and loved to trade stories over an endless stream of drinks with the others of the rank and file as they blew off steam. He'd even enjoyed watching as the younger, bigger cops—most of them chunks of angry muscle marinated in steroids—drew women to them like cripples to faith healers. It always amazed him how some women fell for cops without condition or demand, ignoring the violence visible on their faces and the wedding rings on their hands. It must be something about the power they exuded, he supposed—the invincibility of *being* the law rather than living under it.

The women had never been drawn to Fornier, of course. Everyone had always joked that with his narrow shoulders and thin frame, he was barely big enough to hang a badge on. He'd always felt like an outsider, drinking to capture a hint of the confidence those around him seemed to feel.

Those days were over. Now drinking was an end in itself. Sometimes it felt like the only end. It was all he cared about, and having people around him when he drank was nothing more than a distraction.

He pulled out his wallet and looked inside. Two crumpled tens and a five stared out at him with sad resignation. He did a slow calculation in his head; he'd been at the bar for five Scotches—he no longer counted time in minutes, but in drinks. They'd all been well drinks, the bargain brands, and two of them had been poured during happy hour. He'd have enough to cover the tab, though the barkeep would hardly be thrilled with the tip. *What the fuck*, Fornier thought. The man was clearly an ex-con, and he'd never given Fornier a free pour anyway.

Fornier counted out the money and left it on the bar, focused on getting home. It was around ten blocks for him, and he was trying to convert the distance into time to determine how long it would be before he could pour himself a glass of the discount vodka he had in his apartment. If he hurried, it wouldn't be long.

He took ten steps toward Washington Street, keeping his head down to pick his way around the pockets of snow and slush that quickly soaked through his shoes. His head was still down when the first punch took him in his stomach, just below the rib cage, driving the air from his lungs.

———※———

Finn and Kozlowski watched from the street as Fornier exited the bar. They had been trailing him since he'd left the station house after his shift, and they'd been trying to keep warm inside Finn's car for over two hours.

Kozlowski waited until Fornier was even with a narrow passageway between buildings to strike, and then approached him from the side, swinging his fist hard and low into the man's stomach. Fornier crumpled on impact, and Kozlowski pushed him into the little alley, out of sight from the street. Finn followed.

"Tell us about the Salazar case," Finn said as Kozlowski held the diminutive cop against a brick wall.

Fornier was still doubled over, but he managed to look up, and he recognized his attackers. His face showed both fear and anger. "Fuck you!" he spat out, still coughing.

Finn looked at Kozlowski. "Looks like he still needs encouragement."

Kozlowski punched Fornier in the stomach again, harder this time. Fornier's eyes bulged, and his tongue, swollen and bluish, wagged from his mouth. Kozlowski stepped back and hit him in the jaw, knocking him to the ground.

Fornier lay in an icy puddle up against the wall, spitting blood. "I'm a cop!" he yelled, a note of panic ringing in his voice. "You can't do this to a cop!"

Finn squatted in front of him so they were almost at the same level. "You're a cop who shit on his badge," he said. "You lost the right to claim any special status. Because of you, an innocent man has been sitting on his ass in prison for fifteen years."

"I don't know what you're talking about," Fornier whined. The lie was plain in his eyes, though. Kozlowski took a quick step toward him and kicked him hard in the side, drawing a fresh yelp.

Finn said, "Let me explain your situation to you, Fornier. Not only did you send an innocent man to jail, but you let the guilty guys go free. Now, whoever they are, they're hurting other innocent people. One of the people they hurt is a good friend of ours, and they hurt her bad. To make things worse for you, she's Koz's girlfriend. I've never seen him this pissed off. You understand? Right now all I want to hear from you are the details of how the Salazar case went down. We know you pulled an old print from a prior arrest to make the initial ID. We know that means the second print was planted."

Fornier looked between Finn and Kozlowski, his eyes wide.

"That's right; we know. And we've got an expert who's going to testify. You're done. We just need for you to tell us who put you up to it."

It looked as though Fornier might crack right at that moment. Then he looked at Finn and spat out another mouthful of blood. "Fuck you," he said again. Finn stood up and nodded at Kozlowski.

Kozlowski leaned down and pulled Fornier off the ground, and the man began screaming in terror. Kozlowski grabbed him by the back of the neck and threw him face-first into a hard-packed snow drift that had been plowed into a seven-foot pile along the wall. Fornier's face sank into the snow and ice, muffling his screams as Kozlowski pushed his head deeper and deeper into the pile. As the snow cut off his air, Fornier began to thrash about, trying to slap at Kozlowski to free himself, but it was pointless. He began to lose what little strength he had.

Kozlowski pulled him out of the snow, holding him up by his neck, facing him toward Finn. The man looked like a drowned alley cat. His nostrils were clogged with snow and ice, and he spat and coughed as he tried to catch his breath. A deep three-inch cut on his forehead—probably from the sharp ice of the snow pile—bled down into his eyes.

"You're a fucking mess, Fornier. You really want to keep going with this?" Finn asked.

The man continued to cough and sputter without answering. Finn gave Kozlowski another nod. "Back in again, then," he said as Kozlowski pushed Fornier back toward the snow drift.

"No! Please!" Fornier screamed just before his head was plunged into the snow.

"See," Finn said. "I knew you could talk. Next time try not to hesitate so long, and maybe you won't have to go back in there." He waited nearly thirty seconds, then tapped Kozlowski on the shoulder.

Fornier was fully beaten when he emerged this time. His face was turning blue, and a trickle of thin, watery vomit ran down his chin. "Mac!" he coughed out, collapsing to his knees with a painful thud. "It was Macintyre, okay! He told me to do it."

"What did he tell you to do?" Finn asked. "Exactly."

"He told me to pull the print from Salazar's record. He told me to plant a new one once Salazar was in custody."

"Why?"

"I don't know," Fornier whined.

"You wanna go back in the snow?" Kozlowski asked, yanking him up by his collar and pushing him toward the drift again.

"No! I swear!" Fornier was yelling, fighting desperately to avoid another round of asphyxiation. "He told me Steele had ID'd the guy! He said if I didn't do it, the guy might walk! He said they were sure, they just needed the evidence!"

"And you don't know why they chose Salazar? You didn't know what was going on behind all this? C'mon," Kozlowski said.

Kozlowski still had hold of the man's collar and was practically dangling him over the snow. From the terror in Fornier's voice, Finn would have thought he was being held over a tank full of sharks. "I swear to God! I swear on my mother!"

"Would you swear on your booze?" Kozlowski asked.

Fornier paused, but only for a moment. "Yeah," he said. "On my booze. May I never take another drink. Mac told me the guy was right for it. He said she knew it was him. I had no reason to doubt it. I honest to God thought the guy was guilty."

Kozlowski looked at Finn, who nodded, and Kozlowski let Fornier go. The little man wobbled on unsteady legs and took two steps back from Kozlowski, still trapped in the alley. He still looked raw. The blood had mixed with the melting snow, painting a bib of bright pink on the front of his shirt. His jacket was ripped, and his hair was wet and tamped down in the front. "What now?" he asked nervously.

Finn thought about it. "Where's your apartment?"

Fornier trembled. "A few blocks from here. Why?"

"Because," Finn said, "we're all going to go there right now, and you're going to write everything out that you just told us. Then you're going to sign your name to it."

"No." Fornier shook his head. "Mac will kill me."

Kozlowski grabbed the man by the lapels and threw him into the brick wall. Fornier's head slammed against the unforgiving, uneven surface. "Listen to me, you little shit," Kozlowski said. "Because of your lies, the best woman I've ever known is lying beaten in a hospital room. Another man was hacked into dog food with a machete, and our client has been pacing an eight-by-ten cell for over a decade for a crime he didn't commit. All of this because you didn't do your fucking job. Make no mistake about it—I don't give a shit about you. But if I was in your position right now, I'd be a little less worried about Mac and a lot more worried about me, you understand?" Kozlowski was holding Fornier off the ground against the wall. The little man's feet dangled like a marionette's as Kozlowski pushed him hard enough into the bricks to make it visibly difficult for the man to breathe.

Fornier nodded as he struggled to stay conscious, and Kozlowski let him drop to the ground. Fornier crumpled into a ball as he hit the cement.

Finn walked over and looked down at him. "Cheer up, Fornier," he said. "At least I can assure you that you won't have to worry about Mac."

"Why not?"

Finn looked at Kozlowski, and the former police officer looked back at him. There was no hesitation in Koz's eyes. "Because," Finn said to Fornier, "we're going to see him next."

Finn read over the statement that Fornier had scribbled out in his apartment. It had taken three tries, and the man's hand hadn't stopped shaking throughout. Only with the aid of a second glass of vodka had the effort been successful, and it was barely legible, but it was all there, down on paper. Together with Steele's statement, it was probably enough to get Salazar out of jail. Add in the expert report from Smitty and the report from the DNA testing, which was expected at any moment, and there was little question that Salazar would be opening presents with his family at his brother's house on Christmas morning.

But that wasn't enough anymore. Now this had become personal.

"It's worthless," Kozlowski said, interrupting Finn's ruminations.

Finn looked over at Kozlowski. They were sitting in Finn's car outside of Fornier's apartment. "What?"

"Fornier's statement. It wasn't signed under oath. Plus, it's hearsay. A court shouldn't even consider it."

"It's a statement against his own interest, which is an exception to the hearsay rule," Finn said. "Judge Cavanaugh will look at it."

"He could still claim he signed it under duress. He wouldn't even be lying; we beat him up pretty good."

"He could, and he'd be right. But I don't think he will. I just wanted to get this down in writing to lock him in a little. That's the best we could do under the circumstances. At least it will give us something to confront Macintyre with if he gives us trouble."

Kozlowski scratched his head. "Oh, I'm guessing he'll give us some trouble. You sure you even want to be involved with this? It might make more sense for me to go alone."

Finn started the car. "Where does he live?"

"Okay," Kozlowski said. "Just remember, I gave you fair warning. He lives in Quincy." Finn pulled out onto the street as Kozlowski reached down to his ankle, sliding a .38-caliber revolver from an ankle holster. "You should have this, at least. It's my spare."

Finn looked at the gun, then reached over and grabbed it, stuffing it into his jacket pocket. "You really think this could get that ugly?" he asked.

Kozlowski shrugged. "You never know."

Chapter Thirty-four

MACINTYRE'S HOUSE was just off Wollaston Beach in a quiet, traditional area of small, neat houses on small, neat streets. The residents were generally hardworking, law-abiding folk who spanned the virtually imperceptible social gap between Catholic union Democrats and blue-collar, family-values Republicans. It was not a neighborhood that tolerated disturbance well.

Macintyre's house was easily identified. All of the lights appeared to be off—both inside and out—and on a street bedecked with Christmas lights and holiday cheer, it stood out like a rotten tooth.

Finn parked the car a block and a half down the street. He and Kozlowski climbed out and walked quietly down the sidewalk, turning at the unshoveled walkway leading to Macintyre's front steps. Finn was acutely conscious of the revolver in his pocket, weighing down the side of his coat. He wondered how anyone could get used to carrying around a weapon like this on a regular basis, and questioned whether it had been wise for him to accept the gun from Kozlowski. It had been a long time since his rough-and-tumble youth on the streets of Charlestown, and he felt little nostalgia for the violence of his past.

They stood on the stoop in silence before Kozlowski reached out and pressed the buzzer. It sounded from deep within the house like a giant, angry fly, harsh and shrill. Kozlowski waited a few seconds and then buzzed again.

When the door opened, Finn's first instinct was to pull out the gun. Macintyre's appearance was so transformed that Finn didn't recognize him initially. He stood before them with his bathrobe hanging loosely from his shoulders and nothing underneath it but a stained pair of khakis and a thin T-shirt, yellowed under the armpits. A thick, patchy shadow of beard covered the man's neck and face.

Macintyre stared at them, a flicker of recognition sparking his face. Then he withdrew without a word, leaving the door open for them as he drifted back into the house.

Finn and Kozlowski followed him, both of them turning the corner into the living room with caution, fearing an ambush. Once they'd rounded the corner, though, the fear abated somewhat, for it appeared that the man was in no condition to mount any sort of offensive.

It was clear that the living room was where Macintyre was spending most of his time. There were pizza boxes stacked unevenly in several makeshift towers, and an assortment of beer cans and bottles of booze spread out on the coffee table.

Macintyre sat on the sofa behind the coffee table, sinking into the upholstery. Kozlowski pulled a small chair over to sit facing him across the table. Finn remained standing. The only light in the room came from the television in the corner; the Celtics were playing the Lakers, and Finn noted that Boston was down by ten at the half.

"You bring your gun?" Macintyre asked Kozlowski.

Kozlowski reached into his jacket and brought his pistol out from its holster. He put it down on the table in front of him. "Where's yours?"

Macintyre produced his service revolver from the pocket of his bathrobe. He held it up, examining it. "This was my first," he said. "Got this when I went on the job. Twenty-seven years ago, you believe that? Still the most reliable piece I ever had. That's the way everything was back then, you know? Solid. Reliable. You remember?"

Kozlowski nodded. "I remember."

"Back then you knew who was who and what was what. The department was run by cops, not fucking bureaucrats, and we were the fucking kings. The cops . . . we knew how to do the job, you know? Keep people safe and beat the piss out of the bad guys. It was simple, and it worked. If it meant you had to bend a few rules, that was part of the job. Now you touch some perp the wrong way, and you're the one who ends up in jail. You believe that shit?" He was rambling.

Kozlowski pulled out a Dictaphone, clicked it onto record, and put it on the table between them. "I gotta record this," he said. "You understand, right?"

"You too, now?"

"We're here to talk about Vincente Salazar."

Macintyre waved his hand dismissively. "What a fucking cluster fuck that's turned into, huh? For all of us." Finn noticed that Macintyre was still holding his gun, punctuating his speech with it.

"It has," Kozlowski said. "You wanna tell me about it? What the fuck happened? How did it get this far?"

Macintyre reached up to his head with the hand that still held the gun, scratching his scalp with his trigger finger. Finn wondered whether he had forgotten that he still held the gun.

"Who have you talked to?" Macintyre asked.

"Steele and Fornier," Kozlowski replied.

Macintyre nodded in resignation. "Then you probably already know just about all there is to know." He looked long and hard at Kozlowski, but without anger, only sadness. "I always thought they were wrong to throw you off the force, Koz. Thought that was a bad move. Shit, we need more men like you out there, not less." He was pointing to Kozlowski with the barrel of the gun as he spoke. Finn reached into his jacket pocket and gripped the revolver Kozlowski had given him.

"Guys like us worked the job," Macintyre continued. "Shit, guys like us *were* the fucking job."

"I still need to know the rest," Kozlowski said. "And I need to hear it from you."

"Yeah, yeah, I know. All business to the end, right? Before that, though, let's have a drink." Macintyre reached over and felt his way through the bottles on the table until he found a half-empty bottle of bourbon. Then he located two dirty glasses and pulled them over, pouring them to the rims. "I'd pour one for your friend, there," he said, nodding toward Finn without looking up, "but he looks like a pussy."

"Thanks, I'm good," Finn said.

Mac picked up one of the glasses and handed it to Kozlowski. "What should we drink to?" He was smiling like a jackal.

Kozlowski held up the glass. "To truth, justice, and the American way?"

The smile disappeared from Macintyre's face. He thought for a moment. "How about just to the job?"

Kozlowski said, "To the job," and the two of them drained their glasses. Kozlowski put his down and looked at Mac. "So what happened?"

Macintyre leaned back into the sofa and closed his eyes. "I don't even remember how it started." He rubbed the butt of his revolver against his forehead. "It starts small, y'know? Fuckin' spics invade the country in waves, right? You can't fight it. Not really. There's too many of them. They come in and they take up space, and they take up jobs, and they fuck up the system, and they don't pay their taxes or nothing like that, so we gotta pay for them, right? But there's too many of them to kick them all out; it'd be like trying to empty the Atlantic with a fucking spoon. So you see a chance to make a buck or two off 'em, and you figure, what the fuck? Ain't like you're cheating real Americans."

"You were on the take," Kozlowski said.

"Not for much." Macintyre laughed. "Back in the early nineties, VDS started bringing in the illegals. Smuggling them across the border and trucking them up here and dumping them. So what, right? Shit, it's the land of opportunity, right? So yeah, they were giving me a piece in exchange for a little protection. Everybody wins, right?"

"Wrong," Kozlowski said.

Macintyre looked despondently at his navel. "Yeah, wrong. Very wrong. Not with these people. They're nasty fuckers. Nastiest I ever seen."

"Why were they smuggling illegals? Wouldn't drugs have been more profitable?"

"Not even fucking close. Don't get me wrong; occasionally, they'd bring in drugs, too. And guns. But the real money was in smuggling human cattle. Anyone with a little bit of money south of the border will give it all for a trip to the promised land. I swear to God, people down there must think we shit money and everyone is given a Corvette just for living here. They give a little bit of money, and the gang takes an IOU for the rest. When they get them up here, VDS sells them to employers who pay the illegals almost nothing for the worst jobs. The gang gets an up-front payment from the employers; plus, because the poor immigrant suckers aren't making any real money, they gotta keep paying the interest on what they owe for the trip up here. It's as close to slavery as you can get without chains—and sometimes they use those, too."

"Why don't the immigrants just take off?"

Macintyre's expression grew serious. "You don't know what these VDS fuckers are capable of. No one crosses them. Their leader is this sick fuck named Carlos. They call him the Padre, for Christ's sake. The Father. He's got tattoos all over his body—I swear, every single inch— and I've never seen such a cold, sick bastard. A couple of people tried that. Just took off. They were found later, hacked into tiny little pieces.

Carlos left the heads alone, so they would be recognized and everyone else would know exactly what happened to anyone who ran."

"What happened with Steele?" Kozlowski asked, leaning in.

Macintyre shrugged. "Just bad luck for her. Everything was fine until she got assigned to that fuckin' INS task force. She was all gung ho on showing her daddy how good a cop she was, and she started getting too close. Before she came along, everyone just assumed that the illegals made it up here on their own. Anyone who knew about VDS's racket pretended they didn't. Not her, though. She started pushin' her fuckin' snout into other people's business. I guess they decided she needed to go."

"You guess?"

"You think they'd actually admit to me they were involved? But I knew. And I also knew that if the investigation ever got any traction, it would lead back to VDS and Carlos. He's not the kind of a guy who would take that very well. At a minimum, my involvement with them would've been discovered, and I'd have lost my job—maybe even gone to jail. I had an ex-wife and two kids to support back then; I couldn't let that happen."

"So you framed Salazar."

"Yeah. I knew Steele was assigned individual illegals to target for deportation. I did a little checking to find out who was high up on her list and who she had been focusing on. Salazar's name popped up, so I figured, what the fuck? Good as anyone else. So I went to Fornier and told him that Steele had said he was the guy, but without fingerprint evidence, we'd never get the guy. Once Fornier had done his magic, I went to Steele and told her that we had a match on a fingerprint but that it wouldn't be enough unless she testified, too. Like that, bing, bang, boom, we had an open-and-shut case. Solved all my problems, right?"

"It's never that easy," Kozlowski said.

"For fifteen years it was just that easy. The only downside was that now Carlos and his boys had more on me than I had on them, and they're not the shy, retiring types. As they expanded their operations, they wanted more and more from me, and there was nothing I could do about it. Now that all the shit's coming down, they've decided they don't need me around anymore. So I'm sitting here in the dark, waiting for them to come. I feel a little like Butch Cassidy and the Sundance Kid, sitting in that shack at the end of the movie, waiting for the entire fucking Mexican army to open fire."

"It was the Nicaraguan army," Finn said.

Macintyre looked up at Finn for the first time. Then he turned to Kozlowski. "Where'd you find this fuckin' guy?"

Kozlowski shook off the question. "What about Dobson?"

"The other lawyer?" Macintyre put his head down again. "I tried to warn him off, but he wouldn't listen. Somehow he found out Carlos and his boys were operating out of this little church down near Logan in East Boston, and he went there." All of the blood was gone from Mac's face. "I was there, Koz. I've never seen anything like it. You don't want to mess with these people."

"Will we still find them at this church in East Boston?" Kozlowski asked.

Macintyre nodded. "They would've moved on, but they've got a major delivery coming in tomorrow night, and they couldn't get a whole new operation set up in time."

"Major delivery?"

"Yeah, they've expanded their smuggling. They used to bring in just your average everyday illegal looking for a better place to live. In the last few years, they've discovered a tidy little business in smuggling in Arabs."

"Terrorists?"

Macintyre shrugged. "Don't know for sure. It's not like they wear uniforms, but I've got to assume."

"And they're bringing in some of these people tomorrow night?"

"Yeah. Along with a few others who were 'lucky' enough to scratch together the money to buy a ride up here into bondage."

Kozlowski thought hard about this. "How many men does Carlos have?"

"I don't know, exactly," Mac said. "For a delivery, he usually has four or five guys with him."

"Armed?"

"Heavily."

"How many illegals will there be?"

Macintyre squinted, trying to remember. "I think he had four Arabs and maybe five or six regular suckers."

"Will the Arabs be armed?"

"You kidding me? Carlos'll do business with these guys, but he doesn't trust them enough to give them guns. He's smarter than that."

Kozlowski sat there staring at Macintyre, as though making up his mind about something. Then he switched off the Dictaphone. "I have one more question, Mac," he said.

"Like I haven't given you enough?" Mac said. "Not that it matters; I'm a dead man already."

"It matters to me," Kozlowski said. "Were you involved in the attack on Lissa Krantz last night?"

"Who?"

Kozlowski watched the man closely, and Finn knew he was trying to pick up any tells. "Lissa Krantz. She works with us, and she was attacked last night. You know nothing about it?"

"Look around, Koz," Macintyre said. "Does it look like I've been spending much time out socializing over the past few days."

"Did you?"

"No."

Kozlowski stared at him for a few more moments before he stood up.

"What now?" Macintyre asked.

"Now we go clean up your mess," Kozlowski said, heading to the door.

"No, I mean for me. What the fuck do I do now? They're coming to kill me; you know that."

"Yeah," Kozlowski said. "I know that."

"I can't go to the cops."

"I know that, too."

"So what the fuck do I do?"

Kozlowski gave Macintyre a cold stare. "You dug your own grave, Mac. If I were you, I'd make peace with it." He started to open the door and then looked back. "And Mac?"

"Yeah?"

"I wouldn't waste any time."

Walt Piersall was walking his wife's Scottish terrier down the block of his quiet Quincy neighborhood. It was freezing outside, and he rued the day he'd allowed her to get the stupid pooch. He was too old to be walking around outside in December with a plastic bag in his hand, waiting for the annoying little creature to take a crap.

As he passed the darkened house up the street, he saw two men emerge. One was a hard block of humanity with a thin raincoat flapping off his back. The other was tall, thin, well dressed, and at least ten years junior to his companion. There was something foreboding in their demeanor as they trudged across the snow-covered walkway, heading up the block toward an old European convertible. Walt watched them get in the car and sit talking to each other.

Suddenly, the sharp, unmistakable crack of a gunshot rang out from within the house, making Walt jump. He took a few quick strides toward the place, unconscious of the fact that he was dragging the dog behind him. Then he stopped, thinking better of it. He was too old to get involved; he'd call the police from the safety of his kitchen.

He looked down the block again. The two men had started the engine and flipped on their headlights. If they had heard the gunshot, they gave no indication that they cared. Then the car was slipped into gear, and the two men pulled away from the curb and onto the neat little street.

Chapter Thirty-five

FINN AND KOZLOWSKI were back at the tiny office in Charlestown. It had started snowing again, and a quiet had settled over the city as its residents huddled in their homes and apartments, waiting for Christmas to begin in earnest. Colored lights blinked on and off in windows up and down the street, and muffled strains of Christmas carols could be heard coming from many of the buildings.

Finn sat at his desk; Kozlowski was in the chair against the wall at the conference table. "You're crazy," Finn said.

"Maybe," Kozlowski replied. "I don't care. I'm doing this."

"He said there'd be five of them. Heavily armed. And that doesn't count the people they're bringing in. You like those odds? I don't like those odds."

"I'm going," Kozlowski said simply.

"Of course you are."

"As long as Carlos is breathing, Lissa's in danger. That means there's no decision to make."

"You wanna trade your life for hers?"

"That's not my goal. But yes, if it came down to that, I'd trade my life for hers in a heartbeat. I wouldn't even need to think about it."

Finn scratched his ear nervously. "We should at least tell the police. Maybe we could get some help with this."

Kozlowski laughed. "You think the BPD would listen to us? It'd be better for the department if we didn't come out of this alive. Less mess. Besides, these guys had Macintyre in their pocket, and they gave him up. They wouldn't do that unless they had someone else in the department already in place. If we go to the police, not only will we not get any help, we may tip Carlos off. You like those odds any better?"

"So what do we do? Just go in there shooting?"

"No, we take aim first. Shooting doesn't help unless you hit them."

"Funny. That's very funny." Finn put his forehead down on his desk. "This would take a fucking army; you know that, right?"

"Like I said, I don't have any options." Kozlowski stood up. "Look, this isn't your fight now. You don't have to come."

Finn looked up at him. "Not my fight? They put my client in jail. They tried to kill me, and they attacked one of the few people in the world who will speak to me with any sort of civility." He thought about Lissa. "Well, maybe 'civility' is the wrong word, but how can you say this isn't my fight?" He picked up the phone and started dialing.

"Who are you calling?" Kozlowski asked.

"I'm trying to get us an army."

Chapter Thirty-six

"How MANY?" Linda Flaherty asked.

"You asked me that already," Finn said. "Several times."

"And I'm asking you again. How many?"

"Five, we think."

"Five, you think. I should have my head examined." Flaherty, Finn, and Kozlowski were huddled in the back of a nondescript industrial van up the street from St. Jude's. Max Seldon, the head of the federal Homeland Security office in Boston, was in the front seat, loading a shotgun. Two similar vans were parked strategically on different blocks, close enough to the church to mount a rapid assault, but far enough away to be discreet.

"That's five of Carlos's guys," Kozlowski interjected. "There will probably be four or five of the al Qaeda types and another five or six South Americans. The South Americans shouldn't be a problem, but you never know about Osama's boys."

She frowned. "We don't know that they're al Qaeda," she said. "We just know they shouldn't be here. And you said they won't be armed."

"That's what Mac told us."

"Just before he blew his brains out?"

"Yeah. Pretty much."

She rubbed her hands together. "Like I said, I should have my head examined. What do you think, Max?" she asked the man in the front seat. "You could always pull the plug."

Seldon loaded another shell into the shotgun. "What, and miss a night out like this? I don't think so."

"Right," Flaherty said. She turned back to Finn. "So you're pretty sure there are only five of them who'll be armed, right?"

"You're really asking again?"

"Ease up on her," Kozlowski said. "It's part of the job."

"Annoying me is part of the job?"

"I don't know, you guys still dating?"

"Listen," Flaherty said sharply, "we've been keeping tabs on VDS for three years; these assholes are for real. Our information is that half of the terrorist cells active in the U.S. today have used these guys to enter the country. You call me up at one o'clock in the morning and give me eighteen hours to put together an operation like this on a Saturday three days before Christmas. Well, I'm here, but with me and Seldon and the two FBI teams in the other vans, we're going in with only six, and that means we're way understaffed for this kind of a raid, so you'll excuse me if I keep going over it."

"Can't you call in more agents?" Finn asked.

"Not on this schedule. And not when the only information we're operating on is from a dirty cop who ate his gun last night, a lawyer who's looking to free an attempted cop killer, and an ex-detective whose only goal appears to be to piss off every law enforcement officer in New England. If my boss finds out that I'm in the field on a lark like this, he'll put my ass in a sling. As it is, Seldon and the four others in the vans volunteered for this as a personal favor to me."

Finn kept his eyes on her face as she spoke. She still had the ability to mesmerize him; he felt a rush of excitement just being in her presence.

The fact that she also had the ability to annoy the hell out of him only made her more alluring.

"You've got seven going in," Kozlowski said.

She looked at him. "What?"

"I'm coming in with you."

"Eight," Finn joined in.

Flaherty rolled her eyes. "Koz, you're not a cop anymore. And you, Finn . . . hell, you've never been a cop before. A criminal once, but hey, why should we worry about that."

"That was when I was a kid," Finn pointed out.

"Great, I feel so much better. No, you two stay here. This has to be purely a law enforcement operation, which means you two aren't involved."

"I'm coming in," Kozlowski repeated. "You don't have a choice."

She frowned at him. "No?" She turned around. "Seldon, give me your radio." He passed a handheld unit back to her. "Blandis, Grossman, you in place?" she said into the radio.

The unit crackled two "Rogers" back at her.

"Okay, hold your positions. We may be aborting." She looked at Kozlowski. "Your call, Koz. Either you stay here or I pull our men out right now. What's it going to be?"

Kozlowski glared at her. Then he dropped his head and spat on the metal flooring of the van. "I guess you're the boss, boss," he said. "My, how the world has changed."

"Got that right," Finn said.

She picked up the receiver again. "Okay, we're on. Stand by." Just then two midsize cargo vans rolled by, through the intersection by the church. "Sit tight," she said quietly. The vans pulled into the church parking lot and disappeared around the back, down by the garage underneath the rectory. "This is it," Flaherty said into the radio. "Team two, you approach from the rear of the property; team three, you've got the side driveway. Seldon and I will come in from around by the church. Everyone wear your vests and jackets; I don't want us shooting each other."

The other teams acknowledged her order, and then the radio went silent. Flaherty looked at Seldon, who had already strapped on a Kevlar vest, and now pulled on a bright orange jacket marked FBI over it. He was holding the shotgun at the ready, and he nodded to her as he opened the door. Flaherty slid out and looked back at Finn and Kozlowski. "I mean it," she said. "You two keep your asses in the truck, or I'll have you arrested when this is all over, you understand?"

Kozlowski said nothing.

"Be careful," Finn replied.

She slammed the door and hurried across the street toward the church.

Flaherty moved silently. The church was on a corner lot, bordered in front to the left by a warehouse that ran barbed-wire fencing along the shared property line. At some point in the past, probably in an attempt to soften the industrial feel of the neighborhood, trees had been planted along the fence line, and shrubs had been grown along the front of the property. As a result, much of the church was hidden from the street view.

It made for a difficult approach, but from the information they had, it seemed as though most of the activity took place in back. There was always a chance that a guard would be watching from the front, but it seemed unlikely, given the small number of gang members involved. There was no way to be sure, though, so Flaherty and Seldon ducked through the bushes cautiously.

It was good to see Finn.

The thought jumped into her head, unbidden and unwelcome. Now was a time when she had to focus all of her attention on the task at hand; her survival, and that of the men she was with, depended on it. It was the wrong time to be thinking about her personal life.

But it was good to see him. She couldn't help admitting it to herself. She hadn't realized how much she had missed him until she was near him again, and now all of the feelings she had been suppressing for months came streaming back over her. It made her question her decision to pack up her life and move to D.C. There was more to life than police work, after all.

"You ready?" Seldon whispered.

She shook the thoughts of Finn out of her head. "Let's do it," she said. "Left side. Through the playground."

Then they were moving, keeping low, just inside the shrubs. There was a full moon casting a bright blue light over the unbroken field of white between them and the front of the church. Once they started in toward the buildings, there was no way to avoid being exposed, at least for a moment or two.

Flaherty and Seldon came even with the front of the church, then nodded to each other and turned a right angle, moving as fast as they could toward the corner of the building. Their guns were drawn, and their eyes searched the scene in front of them, looking for any sign that they had been spotted. The place looked and felt deserted, and it took only a few seconds before they were engulfed by the church's shadow, continuing to kick their way through the snow until their backs were up against the building. Flaherty motioned to Seldon, and the two of them raced along the side of the church, down toward where the troika of buildings met. They still had not seen a soul, and it felt wrong. Very wrong. Still, they had no other options now; they were committed.

Tucked behind the corner of the church, Flaherty nodded to Seldon, and the two of them dashed across the walkway that separated the church from the rectory; then they ducked around the outside of the little house toward the garage below them.

———✦———

"You're not staying here, are you?" Finn asked.

"No," Kozlowski replied as he checked his gun and slid it back into his holster.

"I didn't think so." Finn pulled out the revolver Kozlowski had given him and looked at it. It had been years since he had fired a gun.

"You can stay here," Kozlowski said. "I'm a big boy."

"I'm coming," Finn said. "And it's not you I'm worried about."

"Flaherty?"

"No, Seldon. He seems like a decent guy."

Kozlowski gave a humorless chuckle. "I didn't see a ring on his finger. I'm sure you two will be very happy." He slid the van door open and stepped out into the night.

Finn took a deep breath and followed.

———✦———

Kozlowski followed the tracks that Flaherty and Seldon had left in the snow. He stayed low and moved silently, as they had. Behind him, he heard Finn curse quietly under his breath as he tripped over a rock in the churchyard. When he got to the front of the church, Kozlowski crouched by the side of the building, waiting for Finn to catch up. Finn eventually slid alongside him, his shoulder bumping into the clapboard siding, making Finn groan ever so slightly.

"Your arm still hurting?" Kozlowski asked.

"Only when I'm awake," Finn replied. "It's fine. Between the fear and the painkillers I can barely feel it."

"You stay here," Kozlowski said to him.

"What?" said Finn. "Why?"

"This is police work, Finn. You're not a cop."

"Neither are you," Finn reminded him.

"Yes, I am," Kozlowski replied evenly. "Always was; always will be."

Finn just looked at him. "So you want me to wait out here?"

"You want to do something useful? Check out the church and make sure no one's in there waiting to ambush us. I don't want to take care of business around back only to get my ass shot off when I think it's all over."

Finn blew out a long breath, watching the steam rise from his lips. "Fine," he said. "But once I'm sure the church is all clear, I'm coming back there to help you out."

"Fine," Kozlowski said. "I'll be looking for you. Just be careful. You get yourself killed, and I have to find a new office to rent. I don't like change."

"You're all heart," Finn said.

———◆———

Finn peeled off and scrambled around the corner to the front of the church. There was some truth in what Kozlowski had said; Finn wasn't a cop and had never been one. This was a law enforcement operation, Finn told himself, and he had no training in that area. He knew he probably would be of little help in the raid and might even get in the way. Still, he didn't like that Kozlowski had pointed that out to him, and he liked even less the notion that he wouldn't be able to keep an eye on Linda.

Finn pushed on the front door to the church, and to his surprise, it opened with a low, tired creak. Gripping Kozlowski's backup gun, he stuck his arm through the crack in the door, pointing it around in the darkness. It made little sense; he could see nothing. But somehow it made him feel better to let the gun lead him in.

He slipped into the church and allowed the door to close behind him. He was lost in darkness, swimming in it as he waved his arms about, keeping his back to the door. His eyes began to adjust, and he could make out the shapes, if not the details, of his surroundings. In front of him was a row of what appeared to be heavy drapes, separating the entryway from the church's main hall. It was pulled fully across the entry, blocking out whatever moonlight might make it through the windows of the church. To his right, he could see a stairway leading up to the balcony at the back of the building.

As he turned to his left, he caught a glimpse of a tall figure against the far end of the wall, his arm raised, a gun pointing directly at Finn's head. Finn let out a shout and dove to the ground, rolling to his right and coming up on one knee, his own gun aimed instinctively at the man. "Freeze!" he yelled. "Put the gun down!"

The other man didn't flinch, and the gun remained aimed at Finn. Finn waited no more than a second or two before he squeezed off two quick shots. He was gratified to see that his aim was still good; even in the dark and after all the years, he could tell that the two shots took the other man directly in the chest. The man rocked back and forth twice, still holding his gun out, and then fell stiffly to the floor. As his body hit the ground, the entire church shook with an enormous rumble, and as Finn watched, the man split into three large pieces on the ground.

Confused, Finn stood and moved carefully over to the man he'd shot. Kneeling, he could see a face, etched in stone, its eyes open in an expression of hope and compassion. Around its shoulders, a granite shawl fell to an inscription at his chest. ST. JUDE THADDEUS: "HE WILL SHOW HIMSELF MOST WILLING TO GIVE HELP." Looking more closely, Finn could see that the statue's arm had been raised out straight to bestow a blessing on all those who would enter the church.

As Finn knelt over the broken body of the patron saint of lost causes, he whispered to himself, "Shit. That can't be a good sign." Within seconds, all hell broke loose in the echoes of gunshots from the rectory behind the church.

Chapter Thirty-seven

LINDA FLAHERTY was tucked behind a row of bushes that separated the low-slung day-care center from the rectory, looking out onto the driveway leading into the sunken garage. The greenery that ringed the property combined with the natural landscape to hide the scene from the street, but she had a clear line of sight into the garage doors. A dim light bled softly onto the edge of the driveway, and inside the building, a dozen or so people milled about in tense clusters.

There were three distinct groups she could make out. The first was of least concern to her: three disheveled women, a gaunt young man, and two girls who couldn't have been over seven or eight years old. They cowered at the back of the garage, watched over casually by a rough-looking man in his mid-twenties with tattoos, wielding an automatic rifle. There was no way to mistake them for anything but what they were: scared and helpless refugees, just arrived in what they assumed was a land of untold riches and opportunity.

The tattoos on the man guarding them placed him solidly in the second group: VDS. She could see five of them, and they were all heavily armed. They moved about with arrogance in the driveway, overseeing the operation. One of them, an older man—thin, wiry, and covered with tattoos over every inch of visible skin—was ordering them about, and the other four obeyed without question or hesitation.

The third group interested her most. There were four of them, also all male, but not visibly armed. They all had dark olive skin and heavy beards. The tallest one seemed to be the leader, talking with the VDS commander as an equal. His voice, heavily accented from the Middle East, drifted across the driveway. The VDS gang members were not guarding this group the way they were the refugees. Though the VDS men seemed to treat them with the respect of business associates, there was a wariness to the way the two factions interacted.

She glanced over at Seldon, concealed behind the bushes with her, and nodded. This was it. It was what they had been hoping for. She knew that the other four federal agents would be spread out along the perimeter of the property, just out of sight. It was perfect. They had their suspects caught in a cross fire, and more important, they would have the advantage of surprise. From the look of the men loitering about, they had no idea that any sort of raid was imminent, and as long as that didn't change, the operation would be a success.

She raised her fist to Seldon, giving him the ready sign. In a matter of seconds, it should all be over.

It was at that moment she heard the gunshots. They broke through the quiet with electric clarity: two loud, crisp reports from up by the church. She flinched, and her heartbeat doubled as she watched all those within the garage break into motion, unslinging their weapons and heading toward the safety and cover of the garage.

The advantage was lost, she realized instantly, and what had looked to be a swift, easy roundup had morphed into an inevitable siege. She cursed under her breath. Then she stood up from behind the bushes, raising her gun toward the men running for the garage. In a loud, clear voice, she yelled, "Federal officers! Put down your weapons!"

Kozlowski was easing his way down along the side of the rectory when he heard the first two gunshots. He looked back up toward the church, which seemed to loom over the other two buildings in the complex in dark judgment.

Finn!

Kozlowski hadn't actually been concerned about the lawyer's lack of formal police experience. Finn was smart and levelheaded, and Kozlowski had seen the way he responded under pressure. He knew that Finn would be a good man to have around in just about any fight. But not this one. In this fight, Kozlowski had only one objective—to kill Carlos. Kozlowski couldn't go back to Lissa and tell her that the man responsible for her ordeal was still breathing. And if killing Carlos required him to give up his own life . . . well, his life had always been about sacrifice, hadn't it?

Finn, though, wouldn't understand, and even if he would, Kozlowski didn't want him involved. It was his sacrifice to make, not Finn's, and that was why he had sent Finn into the safety of the church.

When he heard the gunshots, though, Kozlowski felt ill. In the process of pursuing his own vendetta, he had sent Finn into an ambush. He took two steps back toward the church, then looked around again toward the garage below, caught in indecision. Before he had the chance to think through his options clearly, he heard Flaherty's voice calling out, "Federal officers! Put down your weapons!"

In a matter of seconds, the real gunfire started in earnest.

———

Flaherty was on her feet for less than two seconds before a barrage of gunfire chopped at the bushes in front of her. She went down, gripping the snow as she tried to push herself deeper into the ground. She wished she had chosen a spot with better cover, but there was little she could do to correct that now.

Besides, she was confident that the assault wouldn't last long. The two initial shots had drawn the attention of those down in the driveway and the garage toward the church, and her shouts had redirected it toward the day-care center. That left the driveway entrance clear, and she knew that the other agents wouldn't hesitate to exploit that approach.

She turned her head and looked through the shrubs in front of her toward the driveway, breathing a sigh of relief when she saw that her assumptions were well founded. Three of her men were moving in quickly down the driveway, advancing on the VDS gang members from behind. They didn't even bother announcing their presence or intentions; they simply took aim, dropping two of the shooters without warning.

Three left, Flaherty thought as she took advantage of the break in the gunfire to stand up and motion for Seldon to follow her. As long as the Middle Easterners weren't armed—and she couldn't see VDS arming a bunch of al Qaeda terrorists, no matter how much they were paying to be brought into the country—she and her men had a two-to-one tactical advantage.

As she and Seldon moved down the hill toward the driveway, she could see that the other agents were already pressing their assault. All four of them were there, and they were trying to cut off the retreat into the garage. That was where the terrorists and gang members were headed: pulling back to mount a stand. Behind them, Flaherty could see the refugees huddled into a corner, trying desperately to find cover and stay out of the way. The terrorists, unarmed as they were, seemed to be searching for some way to join the battle, but they probably realized from experience how ineffectual rocks and sticks were against modern police hardware.

Flaherty heard Carlos, the leader, yell something in Spanish, and one of the two remaining VDS soldiers rushed forward from within the garage, reaching up to grab the overhead door and pull it down. Flaherty dropped to a knee and squeezed off two shots, taking him in the center of the chest and putting him down. The door slid halfway toward the ground and then caught on its runners. The man had failed to close the door entirely, but the line of fire was partially blocked, and it would make the siege even more difficult.

Flaherty and Seldon joined the other agents, who were using the vans for cover as they peppered the garage doors with their fire. "Down to two?" she called out, looking to confirm her count.

"I think so," one of the other agents yelled back. "Never can tell, though."

"All right," she said. "Let's be careful with our aim. We want prisoners if we can get them. Body bags don't tell us much."

"Sure," the agent responded. "You got any ideas about how to be careful with our aim and not get killed in the process, I'm all ears."

She thought about it. "You stay here and keep them pinned down." She looked at Seldon. "You feel lucky?"

He gave her a game smile. "Always."

"Good. Come with me."

———— ⊙ ————

Carlos had been talking to the tall Syrian when the first two shots were fired. He called himself Hassan, but Carlos knew that was not his real name. The man's real name had been lost over a decade ago and been covered carefully by his sponsors to make tracking him—or even identifying him—nearly impossible. Not that Carlos cared about his real identity; Hassan was willing to pay for the services VDS could provide, and Carlos was, at the core, a believer in rough capitalism. To the extent that Carlos had any reservations, they stemmed from the increased risks associated with bringing people like Hassan and his associates across the border. The smuggling operation VDS had established nearly two decades before was a profitable one, and Carlos was sometimes concerned that he was putting that at risk. But the Arabs paid twenty times what the refugees could, and that kind of money was difficult to turn down, no matter what the risks were.

When Carlos heard the shots, it occurred to him that his judgment might have been flawed. "*¡Adentro! ¡Adentro!*" he shouted to his men. His men were well trained, but when the woman on the hill announced her presence, they turned and engaged her. It was a fatal mistake, he knew "*¡No! ¡Al garaje!*" He ordered them back into the garage, but it was too late. Two of his men were killed almost instantly, falling in their own blood on the driveway, as more officers moved in from the street. It left them with only three guns, and he knew then that it was a losing battle.

"*¡Cierra la puerta!*" he yelled to another one of his men. Carlos watched from behind as the man reached to pull the door down, but before the task was completed, the center of the man's back exploded as one of the federal officers' high-velocity shells hit him in the chest and tore a pathway through his body, exiting with a spray of blood.

Carlos ticked off the options in his head and realized that escape was the only one that held even a modicum of hope. He turned to Hassan and held out his automatic rifle.

"What will you use?" Hassan asked, taking the gun without waiting for the answer.

Carlos pulled a pistol out of his jacket, holding it up for Hassan to see. "We need as many men as we have returning fire," he said.

Hassan nodded and moved up toward the front of the garage.

Now was Carlos's only chance. If anyone else saw him, they would be tempted to follow, and while a single man might slip through whatever perimeter the police had established, a group would be doomed.

He moved all the way to the back of the garage, into the corner opposite from the refugees, who were balled up like rats on the floor, each trying to dive to relative safety at the bottom of the pile. There, covered by a stack of cardboard, was the door to a stairway that led up to the rectory's kitchen.

Carlos backed up against the door, taking one last look around the garage. Pedro, a young soldier who had been with Carlos for over two years, was still firing his weapon, trying in vain to hold off the onslaught. He was a good man, well trained and loyal. It might be possible to save him as well, but the risk was too great. Without another thought, Carlos ducked through the doorway and was gone.

Finn froze when he heard the gunfire coming from the rectory. All he could think about was Linda Flaherty. There were so many things he hadn't said to her—so many things he needed to say. It took a moment for him to stand, and once on his feet, he was unsure where to go. His first thought was to head back out the front door of the church and hurry around the corner to join the fight. As he stood there, he realized there might be a more direct route: through the church. It might get him into a position to help her that much sooner, allowing him to approach the gunfire from the rear, which might provide a strategic advantage.

He took a few hesitant steps toward the heavy curtain that separated the entryway from the nave. Then, as quietly as he could, he pulled the fabric to one side and slipped through the opening into the unknown.

Kozlowski was still caught in indecision, considering whether to run back to the church to help Finn, when the shooting behind the rectory erupted. It took only another moment for him to react. It was clear that the real fight was down by the garage; only two quick shots had been fired in the church, and it seemed that whatever skirmish had taken place there must have been brief and decisive. Finn had either survived it or not, and it was unlikely that there was anything Kozlowski could do now to change that.

He slid the last ten yards down the side of the sunken rectory garage until he came to the corner of the building. From where he was, perched on the hill directly to the side of the garage doors, he could see Flaherty and her men in the driveway, and it seemed that they had the advantage. Two bodies lay on the hardtop, and looking closely at them, Kozlowski could tell they were not officers. He could also see that neither one was Carlos, as their tattoos, while prominent, left significant swaths of unpainted skin on their faces, necks, and hands.

Kozlowski looked down and to his right, and he realized that he could see directly into the garage through the top row of windows. It looked as though there were only two armed men fighting the battle from within, though they were both wielding automatic rifles, which meant that a full-frontal attack on the garage would be like walking into a wood chipper. A group of defenseless people was piled into a corner, seeking cover, and another body lay in a pool of blood near the far garage door. Carlos was nowhere to be seen.

Kozlowski looked back toward the driveway and saw the federal agents fire a concentrated hail of gunshots at the garage—covering fire, Kozlowski guessed—and then Flaherty and Seldon emerged from behind one of the vans, making a direct run at the garage.

It was hopeless, Kozlowski could see. Although the covering fire probably seemed overwhelming from the driveway, one of the shooters in the garage was well protected by the garage door and still had a clear shot at the two officers as they made their approach. He aimed and fired, and Seldon fell to the ground with a sickening thud. Kozlowski watched as the shooter shifted his aim toward Flaherty, his head down on the gun's stock.

Kozlowski reacted without thought, bringing up his own gun and firing in one swift motion. The window on the garage door shattered, and the shooter jerked upright, his eyes wide in surprise as a stream of blood flowed from his throat. He hovered, looking about in confusion, and then fell over.

Kozlowski was nearly as surprised as the man he'd shot. He stood there on the hill watching the man die, as if in a trance. He was shaken back into the moment only when another small window in the garage door crashed apart, and he heard the whistle of gunfire pass by his ear.

Kozlowski turned to see the last remaining gunman in the garage pointing his rifle directly at his head. He dove back into the snow on the hill as the ground exploded in puffs of white around him. The bursts of automatic gunfire were deafening, and Kozlowski knew that even with poor aim, the shooter would hit him eventually. Then he heard three sharp, distinct reports of a military-issue pistol, and the rifle fire went silent. The quiet was soon replaced by shouting as the entire federal team moved into the garage. By all indications, it seemed that the situation was well under control.

Kozlowski sat up and patted down his chest and arms, feeling for wounds. He held up his hands, looking for blood, but all he could see was the snow melting on his fingertips. He gave one quick glance down into the garage and, satisfied that the shooting was over, pulled himself to his feet and ran back toward the church.

Carlos was heading out the side door of the rectory when the shooting stopped. He cursed his men; he had hoped they might hold out longer. In the future, he would have to train them better. He paused at the door, looking around and listening for any sign of law enforcement. There was nothing, but with the shooting over, they could be coming after him any second. He couldn't stay out in the open.

He ran along the covered walkway, his gun drawn. As he came even with the church, sensing few other options, he turned and ran up the staircase to the back door.

The main hall of the church was bright compared to the entryway; Finn was thankful for that, at least. The glow from the full moon streamed in through the simple stained-glass window behind the altar, lending the place a dim, otherworldly glow. It might have seemed peaceful were it not for the gunfire exploding in the distance, rattling the colored panes in the montage of biblical characters looking down in indifference. The sweet stench of decay lingered in the air, and Finn wondered if a racoon had died underneath the floorboards.

Finn swung his gun around toward the corners of the nave and the chancel, making sure the place was empty. Once satisfied, he moved quickly down the center aisle toward the altar, looking for the back entrance as he ran. He had just located it when the shooting stopped. He paused, his hand on the doorknob. Was it possible that it was all over? It had been more than a decade since he'd been in a church, and he was not generally given to prayer, but he was suddenly overwhelmed by the dread that Linda Flaherty had been killed, and he had done nothing to protect her. He turned and looked up at the stained glass, focusing on the figure of Jesus Christ in the center, looming over him. *Please,* he thought, *I'll promise you anything you want—make any sacrifice you ask for—as long as she's alive.* Then, convinced that he had done what little he could within his power to ensure her safety, he reached for the doorknob again.

Chapter Thirty-eight

CARLOS WAS MOVING quickly but quietly as he swung open the church door with a hard shove. It opened in and then shuddered to a stop as Carlos slipped into the building and found himself face-to-face with a tall, dark-haired man in a good suit, holding a gun. The two of them regarded each other in shock, and then the other man raised his gun toward Carlos. Carlos realized that he had no time to get his own pistol raised, and stepped forward to throw an elbow into the man's arm as it was still coming up to take aim.

They were only a foot or two apart, and as Carlos's elbow knifed into the soft tissue on the interior of the man's upper arm, the gun snapped back, flying from the man's hand, hitting the floor, and sliding under one of the nearby pews. The man could do little but watch his gun disappear across the floor. Then he turned and saw the gun in Carlos's hand, and his face went white when Carlos smiled at him.

"Wait!" the man said, which only caused Carlos's smile to broaden as he pointed the gun at the man's chest. He'd always enjoyed the thrill of killing.

"Wait!" It was all Finn could think to say. His mind was spinning, searching for some flash of salvation. There was no time, though, and the notion of a coherent strategy was clearly a luxury he could not afford. So he did the only thing that came to mind in the split second before Carlos had time to pull the trigger: He put his head down and ran straight at him as fast as he could. Finn felt his shoulder sink into the man's sternum as he drove him back toward the chancel.

Carlos was taken by surprise, and Finn had at least thirty pounds on him, so there was little that the gang leader could do but allow himself to be carried backward. After ten feet or so, Carlos's feet hit the step that formed the dais of the altar, and they both toppled over. Finn heard Carlos's gun hit the altar, and he realized that he had a chance now. His optimism was short-lived, though, as the other man threw three hard punches into Finn's body. They were sharp, well-placed shots, knocking the wind from him. Finn tried to fight back, but the pain from his wound left him at a clear disadvantage, and he knew instantly that he had to get away.

Finn rolled to his side and scrabbled toward the door, still doubled over. He looked back and expected to see the man crawling for his gun, but he wasn't. Instead, he was reaching for something closer—a long metal object that was leaning against the wall at the side of the altar. As he picked it up, Finn recognized it instantly, and he struggled to move more quickly toward an escape. It was difficult, unable to breathe as he was, to make his legs fully obey. In front of him, just as he reached the door, he caught a glimpse of a moon shadow on the wall—Carlos's arms raised above his head, the machete held aloft, only feet behind him.

Finn grabbed at the door and pulled it open right as Carlos swung the blade hard and fast. Finn looked up, and there, standing in front of him, was Kozlowski.

There was no question in Kozlowski's mind that he had found Carlos. The face of the man behind Finn was an indescribable mask of anger and hatred and euphoric bloodlust. It was a painted mask, at that, the eyes burning out from a living work of art.

Kozlowski didn't hesitate; he grabbed Finn by the shoulder and pulled him hard to the right, throwing him to the ground as the blade came down. It hit off the metal of the doorjamb, showering a long string of sparks into the darkness. Kozlowski had his gun drawn, but he was off balance from shoving Finn to safety, and as Carlos brought the machete back, he turned the blade, catching Kozlowski on the knuckles. The blow wasn't solid enough to separate any of Kozlowski's fingers from his hand, but it was sufficient to cause him to drop his gun. He looked down and saw the blood.

Carlos was in full fury now, and his anger was concentrated on Kozlowski. He came again, wielding the machete like a deranged Saracen. He swung high, clearly looking to take Kozlowski in the throat with one quick blow. Kozlowski ducked and parried the thrust with a shoulder to Carlos's forearm. Locked in close, Kozlowski prevented him from using the giant knife to his advantage, and as Carlos struggled to gain enough space between them to take another swing, Kozlowski head-butted him in the face.

It would have been enough to put most men down, but it merely stunned the gang leader, and he stumbled backward. Kozlowski pressed the advantage, rushing him and grabbing his arm as he slammed the man to the ground at the foot of the altar. He worked quickly, holding Carlos's wrist with one hand to keep the machete on the ground, and punching the man in the face with his other fist.

Carlos's face erupted in blood as his nose split and shattered. He let out what sounded like a squeal of anguish, and Kozlowski, feeling a rush of vengeful gratification, hit him again and again.

He was sure that his advantage was irreversible until he swung at the man's face a fourth time; then the momentum turned. Carlos's hand shot up, catching Kozlowski's fist as it came down. Carlos was incredibly strong, Kozlowski realized as he struggled to free his hand. Suddenly, Kozlowski found himself on the defensive again, and as he looked at Carlos, he realized he had been wrong: The man was not screaming in pain, he was laughing. His face was a bloody, tenderized mess, and he was missing two teeth, but he was laughing harder and harder. Then the face swung toward Kozlowski at an impossible speed. At the last moment, it tilted forward, and Carlos caught Kozlowski in the forehead with a shattering head butt.

Kozlowski fell off of Carlos, rolling to his side as he released Carlos's hand that still held the machete. Carlos, still laughing, stood up, grabbing Kozlowski's arm and pulling it behind his back until the detective was sure it would break. He tried swinging at the smaller man with his free hand, but it was no use; Carlos was behind him now, bending him forward as Kozlowski knelt at the foot of the altar. Then Kozlowski saw the flash of steel out of the corner of his eye, and he knew there was nothing left for him to do. He was about to accept his fate when he heard a revolver cock somewhere in front of him.

"Let him go!" Finn's voice rang out in the cavernous church.

———◦———

Finn had hit his head on the ground hard when Kozlowski pushed him out of the way. He lay there, stunned. With his cheek to the floor, he looked over and saw the revolver he had dropped lying under the second row of pews.

He turned and saw Kozlowski locked in combat with Carlos, the machete still in Carlos's hand. Then Finn looked back toward the gun and started crawling toward it. He could see the dull glow of the tempered steel barrel. It was lying on the ground, wedged up against what appeared to be a loose mound of clothing.

Finn was on his knees, sliding across the floor and around the corner of the pews. All he could focus on was the gun, and it was not until it was within reach that he looked up and focused on the rags behind it. It was the smell that caught his attention first; the putrid stench that he had noticed when he entered the hall grew overpowering as he closed in on the gun. In the shadows of the moonlight underneath the pew, Finn had to stare hard before his eyes could perceive any details, and the first thing that came into shape was a hand protruding from one side.

The sight brought Finn up straight as he pulled back from the gun. His first thought was that one of Carlos's men was hiding there. As he raised his head and his position relative to the lump changed, he made out a face. It confused him, since it seemed to grow out from between the man's legs, and Finn couldn't imagine twisting a body so drastically. After a moment he realized that the body wasn't twisted at all—the head had been cut off and tossed onto the corpse's lap. Looking more closely, Finn recognized the face of the man who had attacked him in the alley in Roxbury—the man who had attacked Lissa in her apartment later that night.

Finn thought he might throw up right there, but he managed to keep his composure. "Serves you right," he whispered to the head as he grabbed the gun.

He got to his feet and came around the pews toward the altar, where Kozlowski and Carlos were still thrashing about on the ground. At first it appeared that Koz was getting the best of the battle, but then Finn saw the detective's head snap back violently, and he crashed to the floor in a heap. Carlos was on top of him immediately, raising the machete to deliver the final blow.

Finn took aim but hesitated to shoot for fear of missing Carlos and hitting Kozlowski. "Let him go!" he yelled.

Carlos looked up at him. His face was bloody but locked in a sick, gap-toothed grin. With the tattoos covering his face, he looked like a demon from one of the horror movies Finn had loved as a child. Carlos grabbed Kozlowski by the hair and pulled him up to his feet, using him as a shield. He put the blade to his hostage's throat. "Drop your gun," he said.

Finn shook his head. "Let him go," he repeated.

Carlos smiled as he pushed the machete into Kozlowski's throat. "Drop your gun, or he dies."

Finn looked at Kozlowski, who had a cut over his eye from where Carlos had head-butted him. The blood was dripping off the end of his nose. "Shoot him," Kozlowski said simply.

Carlos pushed the blade farther into Kozlowski's throat, drawing a gasp. "Shoot him!" Kozlowski yelled.

Finn took careful aim at the corner of Carlos's head that was visible from behind Kozlowski. He felt his hand shaking as he began to put pressure on the trigger. Suddenly, without warning, Carlos's head exploded. The top half of his skull shattered to the right, carrying a solid lump of blood and bone and brain matter against the wall to the side of the altar.

Finn looked down at his gun. It was still cold; he hadn't fired. He looked around in confusion and saw Linda Flaherty crouched by the doorway in a shooter's stance, her gun still pointed toward the space behind Kozlowski where Carlos had been standing only a moment before. "Is there anyone else in the church?" she demanded, her eyes scanning the interior of the building.

"No," Finn replied.

"Are you sure?" Flaherty pressed.

"The guy who tried to kill me and attacked Lissa is decomposing underneath one of the pews," Finn replied. "His head is upside down in his lap, so I doubt he's going to be much of a threat. I checked the rest of the place out; it's empty."

Flaherty stood up and walked over to Kozlowski. He hadn't moved, other than to turn and look at Carlos's body lying just behind his feet. "I told you to stay out of this, right?" she said to Kozlowski.

He nodded. "I saved your ass down there by the garage, though."

"You did. I'd say we're even now."

"And then some," he agreed. "You knew I was coming."

"I had a pretty good idea." She looked at Finn. "I was kind of hoping you'd be smart enough to stay back in the truck."

"Never overestimate my intelligence," he replied. "You should know that by now."

"It's a mistake I seem prone to." She looked at him, and he could see something in her expression. It was a look that told him she had been as worried about him as he'd been about her. It was a look that told him there was still something left between them worth saving.

Outside, the scream of approaching police sirens could be heard in the distance, growing louder by the second. "The cavalry?" Finn asked.

"Better late than never, I suppose," she said. "We're going to have a lot to clean up here. We took several of the people these guys were smuggling in prisoner. They stay with us, no matter how much the local police bitch about it."

"Who are they?" Finn asked.

"I can't comment," she replied. "It may be that, officially, they were never here. Do you understand?"

"Do we want to understand?"

"Probably not."

"Enough said."

"You two did a good thing here tonight."

Kozlowski said, "Lissa is safe. That's enough for me. I'll leave the rest of it to you to figure out what's good and what's not."

The sirens reached a crescendo as they pulled up in front of the church. Flaherty looked at Finn. "I'm on a plane back to D.C. tomorrow," she said. "And tonight there's going to be a lot to deal with."

"I understand." Finn didn't, though. Not really. He sometimes wondered if he ever would. "We'll make it work," he said. His optimism was real. "Somehow we'll make it work."

Chapter Thirty-nine

Kozlowski sat in a chair pulled close to Lissa's hospital bed. The plastic surgeons had practiced their magic on her the evening before, and she still slept heavily under the influence of the anesthesia. Her face was hidden under bandages, but the doctors and nurses had told Kozlowski that the operation had gone well.

Every part of him ached. It had been a long night at the police station, and he'd burned through the last drop of his body's adrenaline hours ago. There was a long gash on his forehead and several other more minor cuts and abrasions from his battle with Carlos, all of which the doctors had tried to treat before he growled them away. He felt limp and weary, and his muscles cried out for sleep, but he refused to give in. He could not rest until he was sure that Lissa was okay.

It was nine o'clock before she woke, and even then it was a gradual process. She shifted her head first, searching for comfort as the painkillers loosened their grip. Her fingers fidgeted next, as if searching for something.

He reached out and put his hand on hers, and she finally opened her eyes. She looked at him without saying anything for a while, peering out from behind her bandages. When she did speak, her words were labored and slurred, both from the drugs and from the obvious pain of the operation. "You look like shit," she said.

He smiled at her. "I do."

"What does the other guy look like?"

"He looks dead," Kozlowski said. "They all look dead."

She turned her head away from him, staring off into space as she digested the news. When she turned back he could see that some of the fear had left her eyes. "How are you doing?" she asked him.

"I'm good," he said. "Just looking at you, I'm good."

"I'm glad. How am I doing?"

He squeezed her hand. "You're beautiful."

He saw her try to smile underneath the gauze and wince in pain at the effort. "Really? I feel like shit." Her eyelids fluttered as she fought the remaining drugs in her system.

"They say it couldn't have gone better," he assured her. "Another couple of days and you can go home."

Her eyes watered at the thought. "Will you take me?" she asked.

He squeezed her hand again. "If you'll let me."

"Thank you." Her eyes closed, and it was clear that she was losing the battle to stay awake. "You're . . ." Her voice trailed off as her breathing became deeper and more even. She shook herself back to the edge of consciousness once. "I'm sorry," she said, her voice barely a whisper. "I'm so tired."

"It's okay," he said. "You're okay. You sleep. I'll be here when you wake up again." She let out a long deep breath and her body relaxed fully back into the bed. He watched her give in to slumber. "I'll always be here," he said quietly.

He leaned back into the chair and watched her for a few more minutes. Then he closed his eyes, and was asleep in a matter of seconds.

INNOCENCE

Finn sat in his office early in the afternoon. He was exhausted, both mentally and physically. He had been kept at the police station into the early morning, answering the same questions over and over again, until finally, sometime shortly before five A.M., they released him, convinced at last that his story was unlikely to change.

With nothing left of the night worth the effort to sleep, Finn had gone straight to the office. He had an enormous amount of work to do in order to be ready for Salazar's hearing in front of Cavanaugh the next day; before they appeared in court, he wanted to file an extensive brief explaining in detail exactly what had happened—both fifteen years ago and in the past two weeks—so the judge would enter the courtroom mentally prepared to let Salazar go free. In order to do that, Finn had to gather together all the pieces of the puzzle: the affidavits of Steele and Fornier; Smitty's report indicating that the fingerprint evidence had most likely been faked; and a transcript of Macintyre's tape-recorded confession. If properly presented, it would be more than enough to ensure his client's freedom.

Reading over the brief again, Finn was confident he'd succeeded. Another hour's work and he might even be able to break away and see Linda Flaherty before she headed back to D.C. The night before had been a mess; the tension between them had been unbearable, in both the good sense and the bad. No matter how much they disagreed and made each other crazy, there was an undeniable pull between the two of them that neither of them could resist. He knew that if he could just find a way to be alone with her, even for a brief time, he could make everything right again. He might not be able to fix all their problems, but it would be enough for the moment. After that . . . well, they would have to take it one step at a time.

The phone rang, interrupting his romantic musings, and he reached over to pick it up. "Finn here."

"Finn, this is Tony Horowitz over at Identech."

Finn smiled: It was the final piece of the puzzle. "Tony, thanks for calling. I'm sitting here just tinkering with the briefs I have to submit to the court, and I've left a little hole where I can plug in your findings. I'm not even sure we need them at this point, but we might as well use all the ammunition we've got. Have you finished running the tests?"

"I have." There was an odd hesitation in Horowitz's voice, but Finn was too tired to credit it.

"Excellent," Finn said. "This will seal the deal, then. Let me have it so I can finish this up and get out of here."

"I would have called earlier, y'know?" Anthony said. "I guess I've been procrastinating; I know how invested you feel in this."

Finn's heart went cold. "What are you talking about, Anthony? Let me have the results."

"I'm sorry, man. There's just no way around a positive match."

"A positive match for what?"

"What do you think? For your guy—Salazar. The DNA from under the woman's fingernails from fifteen years ago is a match with your client's DNA sample."

Finn felt dizzy. "That can't be."

"I know it's not what you wanted to hear, but trust me, it's true."

"No, you don't understand. The cops already admitted that they framed him. He wasn't the guy."

Anthony said nothing for a moment. "I don't know what to tell you, Finn. Science doesn't lie, and science tells me that the man Officer Steele scratched fifteen years ago in that alley was Vincente Salazar."

PART IV

Chapter Forty

Scott Finn was sitting at the table in the small attorney meeting room at Billerica when they brought Salazar in. It was late, past normal visiting hours on a Sunday, but Finn had explained to the guards that his client had a hearing the next day. When they hesitated, he threatened to have them brought up on charges for denying his client's constitutional right to adequate representation, and after a few phone calls up the chain of command, they relented and told him he could have ten minutes.

Finn had talked to Salazar earlier that day by telephone, and related everything that had happened in the previous two days. He had assured his client that Sunday night would be his last in prison, based on what they had learned—but that was before Finn knew about the DNA test results.

Salazar sat across the table from Finn, waiting patiently until the guard had retreated from the room. Then he leaned forward and grasped Finn's hands resting on the table. "Thank you," he said. He put his head down on the table, and when he lifted it again, his face bore the expression of the exhausted relief of an answered prayer. "Thank you for everything."

Finn pulled his hands away. "You all packed?" His voice was sharp, and he could see a hint of concern creep into the corner of Salazar's smile.

"There is very little from this place that I want to take with me," Salazar said.

"Did you call your family? Tell them you were coming home?"

"Yes. Right after we spoke this morning, though I told them it was likely, not definite. I am a superstitious man."

Finn lapsed into silence, unsure what to say.

"Mr. Finn, is there something wrong?"

"There is." Finn was watching Salazar's expression closely. It had turned serious.

"What is it?"

Finn laughed bitterly. "I don't even know where to begin. I don't really know anymore, about anything. All I know is that I was wrong— the whole time I was wrong. I was wrong to listen to Mark Dobson; I was wrong to get involved in this case; I was wrong to think I could make a difference; but most of all, I was wrong for believing in you."

Salazar looked almost frightened. "Please, Mr. Finn, I don't understand."

"Yes, you do. There's no need to keep up the act; I know. I know, and it doesn't matter, because I'm your attorney, so I'm the one person you don't have to lie to. I couldn't betray you if I wanted to."

"Betray me how?"

Finn sighed. "You really want to play this thing all the way out? Fine. I got back the DNA test results today. You know, the one that compared your DNA to the DNA taken from under Madeline Steele's fingernails? The one that was supposed to establish your innocence?"

"Yes? And?"

"And I know you did it. You were the one in the alley that night. You're the man she scratched."

"But that's impossible. I didn't do this. I swear it."

"You can swear all you want, but like the man said to me this afternoon, science doesn't lie. What happened? Did you really think you could avoid deportation if you killed her? Or is there more to this than I even know? Are you actually a member of VDS? Never mind. Don't answer. I don't want to know."

Salazar looked shaken. He leaned back in his chair and stared off into space. Then he looked back at Finn. "What do you plan to do?"

"I don't know," Finn said. "I honestly don't know. What would you do if you were in my position?"

Salazar thought about it briefly before replying. "When I took an oath as a doctor, I swore to treat the sick and tend to the wounded, no matter who they were, no matter what I thought of them personally. My understanding is that you took a similar oath when you became a lawyer, no? To represent your clients to the best of your ability, whether you believe in them or not?"

"I also swore an oath as an officer of the court and a member of the judicial system. I can't lie, and I can't allow you to lie if I know the truth."

"I am not asking you to lie," Salazar said. "I am asking you to represent me to the best of your ability—within the law. Are you still able to do that?"

"I don't know," Finn replied. "I know you're guilty, so why would you want me to represent you at this point?"

Salazar smiled sadly. "If there is one thing I have learned in my lifetime, it is that we always know far less than we think we do. And whether or not you believe in me, I believe in you. I think that is enough; and I am sure you have represented people you believed to be guilty before. Did that stop you from winning?"

Finn stood up and walked to the door. He banged on the glass to signal the guard to let him out.

"Well, Mr. Finn?" Salazar said, looking anxiously at him. "Are you still my lawyer?"

The guard opened the door, and Finn stood there, weighing his options. He looked back at Salazar. "Shave tomorrow," he said. "You won't be allowed to wear anything but your prison fatigues, but make sure you comb your hair and do your best to look presentable. It can only help our chances with Judge Cavanaugh." Then he walked out the door without looking back again.

Salazar was shaking when he returned to his cell. The freedom he had thought was so close at hand now seemed out of reach, and the life he had thought he would be able to build with his family seemed to be evaporating in front of his eyes. Sitting on his cot, he tried to regain his bearings, but all he could think about was his daughter. He remembered her as a newborn—remembered holding her in his arms at that moment when the pain of losing his wife was still a scream in his head that drowned out everything but his love for this beautiful, helpless creature. He had clung to her during those difficult first months, finding meaning enough in her existence to keep breathing. He had taken a vow on that day when she and her mother had passed each other so briefly: that he would always protect her. He had failed in that vow, and now, just as he thought he would have the rest of his life to make it up to her, it was all falling apart.

He reached into the crease of the mattress and pulled out the disposable phone, hoping and praying that this would be the last time he would use it. He dialed the number, and when the call was answered, he spoke quietly. "The DNA tests came back," he said. "They were positive. We both know what that means."

"I'm sorry," the voice on the other end of the line said.

"I'm sorry, too," Salazar responded. "Are you willing to do what must be done?" His question was met with a silence that chilled him. "Will you do what must be done?" he asked again.

"Will Mr. Finn go along?"

"I don't know. He no longer has faith in me. It won't matter, if you will not be strong."

The silence came again. Finally, the voice answered, "I will do what must be done. For you."

"Not for me."

"No, not for you. Because I must."

"Good," Salazar said, though he felt little relief.

"I am sorry."

Salazar could hear the truth in the voice. "I know." He closed the cell phone and slipped it back into the mattress. He lay down on the cot and stared at the ceiling. He would not sleep, he knew, and it would be a long night. But then he had always been a patient man.

Kozlowski stretched his legs under the table in Finn's office. "So you're still representing him?"

Finn sat at his desk, focusing on the stack of papers in front of him, pretending to prepare for the hearing the next day. "I guess. It feels a little weird, but what choice do I have?"

"None that I can see." Kozlowski scratched his head. "Ultimately, I wouldn't think it would be that hard, would it? I mean, it's not like you've never represented a guilty client before. Shit, I'm guessing ninety percent of the clients we work for are guilty in one way or another."

"That's different."

"How?"

"I never believed in any of them in the first place. But with Salazar . . ." Finn sighed heavily, looking for the right words, but they didn't come.

"You thought you were doing something good this time?"

"Yeah," Finn said. "I guess that's it."

"You thought you were getting yourself clean? Maybe even buying yourself out of a little time in purgatory?"

"I guess."

"Yeah, I can see that," Kozlowski said. "But you can forget it. The world doesn't work that way, and you know it. You're a good lawyer. That means nine out of ten people who come looking for you are going to be dirty. You start buying in to their bullshit, and you'll lose your mind. You're a lawyer; do your job."

Finn shook his head. "I just don't get it. Macintyre admitted that he framed Salazar. Steele and Fornier confirmed it. How can he be guilty? It just doesn't add up."

"Why? You think the cops don't frame guilty people? Look at O.J., for Christ's sake. Most of the time it's the guilty people who are the easiest to set up. It happens that in this case, Macintyre thought he was framing someone who was innocent. He thought VDS did this, and he was wrong. So, instead of framing an innocent man, he got lucky and set up the guy who actually did the crime. Make the most of it—as a lawyer. After all, it's still not a terrible case."

"I guess not," Finn conceded. "But what the hell am I supposed to do with the DNA evidence?"

"If Salazar was just another client—if you had never believed in him—what would you do with it then?"

"I don't know," Finn said. "I'd probably try to bury it. Horowitz hasn't actually finished his report, and I told him there was no hurry. I suppose I could file what I have now—the evidence from Macintyre, Smitty, Steele, and Fornier. I mean, guilty or not, the way they framed him still stinks to high heaven. It should be enough to grab the judge's attention, at least."

"So there's your answer."

"If Judge Cavanaugh asks me a direct question about the DNA evidence, though, I'm not going to lie. I'm not losing my license for this guy."

"Of course," Kozlowski agreed. "As long as you treat this guilty bastard the way you treat all the other guilty bastards you've represented.

You can't tank the case just because you're pissed at yourself for believing the man."

"I am pissed, though."

"I know, but you're a lawyer. If you haven't gotten used to the fact that your clients lie to you, you might as well get out of the business altogether. Maybe you could be a florist."

"Fair enough. It's just that—"

"It's just that nothing," Kozlowski pressed. "Either you can do the job or you can't. It's that simple."

Finn looked down at the papers he had carefully crafted earlier in the day. They were good papers. Setting aside the fact that his client was guilty, they might be enough to get Salazar out of jail. He wouldn't be the first guilty man Finn had saved from imprisonment, and he sure as hell wouldn't be the last.

"How's Lissa doing?" he asked, changing the subject to take his mind off the moral dilemmas of his work situation.

"She's getting stronger."

"She's resilient," Finn commented.

Kozlowski nodded.

"Don't fuck it up."

"I could say the same to you. Did you get a chance to see Flaherty today?"

Finn gestured toward the papers on his desk. "These briefs didn't write themselves. I didn't have time, and she caught an early flight back to D.C."

"She's resilient, too," Kozlowski said. He stood up and walked back toward his office.

"Yeah," Finn said once Kozlowski was gone. "I know."

Chapter Forty-one

IT SNOWED AGAIN on Monday. That made fifteen straight days in Boston with at least some snowfall—a new record, even in a New England city well accustomed to winter whiteouts. Walking to the courthouse, Finn stopped to watch a group of city kids sledding down the alley on the backside of Beacon Hill, which led down toward the Suffolk County Courthouse in the heart of Boston. Their laughter made him nostalgic for a childhood he'd never had. He wondered what it would feel like to have that sort of freedom.

The courtroom was crowded, particularly for a Monday on the day before Christmas. Cavanaugh was the only judge holding court, but the headlines from that Saturday evening's raid on St. Jude's—and the rumors of a connection with the Salazar hearing—had piqued enough curiosity to fill most of the seats with a combination of press, lawyers, and law enforcement personnel. Finn caught sight of the Salazar family sitting in the front row: Miguel, Rosita, and Salazar's mother, packed together in nervous anticipation. Finn felt bad for them. Whatever Vincente Salazar was guilty of, they did not deserve the pain they had been through. He walked over to greet them. "Good afternoon," he said politely.

They were quiet and seemed almost frightened. Finn couldn't blame them, considering their past experiences with the American judicial system. "Mr. Finn," Miguel acknowledged him. "It feels like a good day."

"With luck," Finn replied. "You never know what can happen once you enter the courthouse, though. How are you holding up?"

Miguel shrugged. "I don't believe you have met my mother and my niece, Rosita."

"I haven't," Finn said. "But Vincente has told me enough that I feel like I already know them." He extended his hand to Salazar's mother, who took it with both of her own.

"Thank you for all you have done for my son," she said. "I am praying for you."

"I appreciate it," Finn said. "We can use all the prayers we can get." He held his hand out to Rosita, but she remained still. It took a moment for him to realize that she couldn't see it. "It's a pleasure to meet you, Rosita," he said.

She held her hand out in response, and he moved his to hers. "Thank you, Mr. Finn," she said. "Is my father really coming home today?"

Finn felt wounded. "I hope so," he replied, wondering whether he meant it. "I'm going to do my best." That much, at least, was true.

Sitting next to the Salazar family was Joe Cocca, a lawyer Finn knew from around the courthouse. "Joe," he said. Surveying the courtroom, he raised his eyebrows. "I'm surprised at how crowded it is, with Christmas and all."

"Interesting case," Cocca responded. "Is it true you were involved in the fireworks this weekend over by the airport?"

"Don't believe everything you read in the papers," Finn cautioned. "You just down here for the entertainment value?"

"More or less," Cocca responded. "But Miguel's a neighbor, and I thought I should be here to support the family."

There was a rustle from the front of the courtroom as the court reporter and two clerks came in and took their seats. It was a sign that Judge Cavanaugh's arrival was imminent.

"Gotta go," Finn said.

"Yeah. Good luck," Cocca said. "They're a good family."

Finn found it hard to meet Cocca's eyes. "Thanks. I'll do my best." He turned and spread his notes and papers out on counsel's table. The real question was whether his best would be enough.

Chapter Forty-two

VINCENTE SALAZAR WAS LED up to the courtroom from a holding cell in the basement of the courthouse. He'd spent most of his morning in transit and processing. The processing had taken the most time, but it was a part of prison life he'd grown accustomed to. He was dressed in a bright orange jumpsuit and cuffed at the wrists and ankles. His restraints were released only once he was at counsel table, and two burly, heavily armed bailiffs remained behind him, watching him closely.

He turned to look at his family, giving them a nervous wave. "I'm here," he called to his daughter, and her smile revealed a sliver of hope that broke his heart. "I love you," he called. *It's all for her*, he reminded himself. Then he turned and faced Scott Finn. "I didn't know whether you would show up."

"That makes two of us."

"There is something you should know."

"No, there isn't."

"We have to talk, at least briefly."

The lawyer swung around on him, looking at him for the first time. "There's nothing I want to hear from you," he said. "The less I know, the better. The more I know for sure, the harder it will be for me to do my job."

"But—"

"No buts. I'm about two seconds from walking out of here and leaving you on your own. You want me to represent you? Fine. But I'm going to do this my way. I'm going to do my best to get you out without violating any of my own legal or ethical obligations, but don't push me on this."

Salazar watched in silence as Finn turned his attention back to his briefcase, opening it and laying out stacks of papers, briefs, and legal pads on the table. Salazar wondered whether he should press his luck and try to force the man to hear him out, but thought better of it. If the lawyer thought there was a plan of any sort in place, he was the sort who would refuse to participate. Worse still, he could inform the court and destroy everything. Salazar would just have to trust that Finn was a good enough lawyer to stumble onto the answer himself.

He was still second-guessing his decision when the door behind the bench opened. A short, heavyset woman waddled her way up to the desk in front of the judge's perch. She flipped open a scheduling folder and checked a few notes on the desk, then nodded to the bailiff standing to the side of the bench. He nodded back to her and faced the courtroom.

"All rise!"

———※———

Tom Kozlowski sat at the back of the courtroom. By the time he'd arrived, there had been no seats left up front. That suited him fine. He wanted to be there in case Finn needed anything, but he could do that from the cheap seats. From his point of view, his personal and professional involvement in Salazar's case had ended when Carlos's brains hit the floor in St. Jude's. Lissa was safe now, and Salazar's fate was in Finn's hands. Kozlowski was little more than a spectator at this point.

"Haven't seen you here before," a voice to his left said. Kozlowski looked over at a grizzled veteran sitting with an old newspaper on his lap. The man stank of stale booze and cheap cigarettes, and the fatigues he wore looked as though they hadn't been washed since they'd left whatever field of battle the man had seen last. Kozlowski said nothing.

"I'm here every day," the man continued, undeterred. "It's the best entertainment in town that don't cost nothing, particularly when that guy is up there." The man was pointing at Finn, and Kozlowski's interest was engaged in spite of himself. "He's the best there is. Rough around the edges, maybe, but he'll keep you guessing." The man gave a broad smile that Kozlowski found endearing, notwithstanding the dark holes where teeth should have been.

Kozlowski finally said, "I'll keep an eye on him, then."

The man laughed. "You do that! You just do that!" His eyes sparkled as if he were the only one God had let in on some great cosmic joke.

"All rise!"

Kozlowski took a last look at the man sitting next to him. He was smiling excitedly, like a young boy at the opening credits of a beloved cartoon. He looked over at Kozlowski and winked. "Enjoy the show!" he said.

———

The Honorable John B. Cavanaugh approached the bench with more vigor than he had felt in years. His back, stooped though it was, felt stronger and straighter than he could remember, and there was an electricity in his veins that he'd once thought would never return. He felt, as he had so long ago when he first donned the robe, like an instrument of justice. It had been a long time since he'd felt like much more than an ineffectual bureaucrat, feeding the basest of human conflicts through the broken sausage grinder of the judicial system.

He stepped up to the bench, ignoring the pain shooting from his shoulder blades down to the base of his spine. "Be seated," he bellowed. He, too, sat, looking down at the lawyers gathered before him. He took a particularly long look at Vincente Salazar, sitting next to

Scott Finn. Then he swiveled his head and looked at Albert Jackson, the assistant district attorney. "I've read Mr. Finn's briefs," he began slowly. "It appears that we have quite a mess here, don't we? Were these proceedings not being transcribed, I would be sorely tempted to employ stronger language, but to preserve decorum, I'll leave it as a 'mess.' Quite a mess."

Jackson rose to speak. "Your Honor, if I might—"

Cavanaugh cut him off. "No, you might not, Mr. Jackson," he said. "Believe me, I will get to you directly, and I assure you we will have quite a bit to talk about. Until then I want you to sit down and be quiet." He took some small satisfaction in the look of fear that engulfed Jackson's jowly face.

Addressing Finn, Cavanaugh continued. "As I said, Mr. Finn, I have read your briefs. They set forth a compelling tale. But I couldn't help noticing that there was nothing in them about DNA testing. As I recall, that was what this case was supposed to be about, no?"

Finn stood before him. "Yes, Your Honor. When this all began, we believed that DNA evidence was the only way we could demonstrate that Mr. Salazar was wrongly convicted. But as you know from our papers, as our investigation continued, we uncovered a massive conspiracy to frame Mr. Salazar. We feel that this new evidence is sufficient to overturn his conviction even without DNA evidence."

"And the DNA testing?"

"We don't have an official report at this time, Your Honor."

Cavanaugh scrutinized Finn closely. "Are you telling me that you would prefer to proceed without relying on any DNA testing?"

"Yes, Your Honor. We believe that the evidence we submitted is sufficient."

Cavanaugh gave a last look at Finn, like a rounder trying to sniff out a bluff. Then he flipped through the papers in front of him. "I can't say I blame you," he said. "The evidence here is overwhelming." He looked at Jackson, his face narrowing like a hawk's. "Mr. Jackson, can you offer me any reason why I shouldn't overturn Mr. Salazar's conviction and initiate disciplinary action against your office to determine who knew what when?"

Jackson stood up and cleared his throat. "First, Your Honor, as you consider the issue of discipline, I would ask you to take note of the fact that I was still in college when Mr. Salazar was convicted and the events described in Mr. Finn's brief took place." He gave a smile almost as weak as his attempt at levity.

Cavanaugh took off his glasses. "Son, look at me closely. Do you see anything in my expression that would suggest to you that I am in the mood for humor?"

"No, Your Honor."

"Do you see any indication that I find any part of this god-awful mess the slightest bit amusing?"

"No, Your Honor."

"If I were you, I would bear that in mind as I address this court."

"Yes, Your Honor."

"You may proceed."

"Thank you, Your Honor." Jackson seemed to be bracing himself like a firefighter about to enter a burning building. "First, I, too, have read Mr. Finn's papers, and I can assure the court that the district attorney's office has initiated its own internal investigation to determine whether anyone on staff was aware of any of the allegations that have been brought to light. I am also told that our office will be coordinating with the BPD's internal affairs division to determine whether there is an ongoing problem within the police department."

"Whether?" Cavanaugh's voice dripped with sarcasm.

Jackson took a deep breath. "Yes, Your Honor. In spite of this all, however, the district attorney's office is strongly opposed to overturning Mr. Salazar's conviction."

"On what grounds?" Cavanaugh demanded. "By all indications, Mr. Jackson, certain members of the law enforcement community fabricated the evidence used to secure Mr. Salazar's conviction. By what possible logic can you oppose this man's release?"

"Harmless error, Your Honor."

"What?"

"Harmless error. We believe that Mr. Salazar would have been convicted anyway."

"I know what 'harmless error' means, Mr. Jackson," Cavanaugh sneered, and he could feel his face run scarlet. "I just can't understand how you could possibly advance such an argument with a straight face."

"I can, Your Honor, because the DNA testing you yourself ordered demonstrates with absolute certainty that Mr. Salazar is guilty of the crime for which he was convicted."

Cavanaugh shot a look at Finn. "I thought Mr. Finn indicated that there was no report," he said slowly, his faith shaken slightly.

"That is correct," Jackson continued. "There is no report as yet. The tests have been completed, though, and the results are indisputable."

Cavanaugh shook his head in disbelief. "Do you have someone who can testify to this?" he asked.

"We do," Jackson replied. "With your permission, we would like to call Anthony Horowitz to the stand to testify."

Chapter Forty-three

Finn's heart was pounding as Horowitz took the stand. He'd hoped that the DA's office wouldn't follow up with the DNA lab to check on the test results, but he'd known there was always a risk. Without the DNA evidence, Cavanaugh would have little option but to set Salazar free. But once Jackson demonstrated that Salazar was actually guilty, there seemed little hope. Finn could feel the judge staring at him as Horowitz was sworn in. Finn refused to meet his eye.

"Dr. Horowitz, would you tell Judge Cavanaugh what you do for a living?" Jackson began.

"I am the chief technician at Identech Labs," Horowitz replied. "We specialize in DNA testing."

"And were you retained to perform such testimony in this case?"

"We were. Mark Dobson, the defendant's first lawyer, called us a couple of weeks ago and asked us to test DNA found in skin and blood samples pulled from underneath Officer Steele's fingernails against that of the defendant, Mr. Salazar. Mr. Finn followed up with me a week or so later." Horowitz shot Finn a look that seemed almost apologetic. Finn had some sympathy for the man; after all, he was a scientist and had little choice but to follow the evidence presented him to its logical conclusion.

"What did Mr. Finn say to you when he talked with you?"

"He said, 'This guy's innocent.'"

"And how did you interpret this?" Jackson asked. He was a good lawyer; Finn had to give him credit. The examination could have been conducted in three or four questions, but he was dragging it out, giving it an atmosphere of suspense. It was exactly what Finn would have done.

"I'm not sure what you mean," Horowitz replied hesitantly.

"Did you take that as a request from Mr. Finn to do whatever you could to make sure that the results came out negative and cleared his client no matter what?"

"Objection, Your Honor," Finn said, standing. He infused his voice with enough indignation to make it clear that Jackson had no basis for the question, but otherwise, he remained composed. This was all part of the game, and Finn knew it.

"Sustained," Cavanaugh said.

"No," Horowitz said, ignoring the judge's ruling. "Finn's not like that."

"Of course," Jackson said. "And you know that because you've done work for Mr. Finn in the past, correct?"

"I've done some work for him," Horowitz admitted. "He's had a couple of paternity cases we helped out with."

"And you depend on lawyers like Mr. Finn to keep bringing you business in order to make money, right?" It was a good ploy, Finn knew. The questions were objectionable, but they were effective at conveying the notion that Tony would, if anything, have preferred to deliver the results Finn had been looking for.

"Objection," Finn said again, though this time with less indignation. There was no point in playing the victim at this point.

"Sustained," Cavanaugh said. It was clear from his tone that he'd gotten Jackson's point, though.

Jackson continued, not letting the interruptions slow the pace of his questioning. "In any event, did you perform the tests in this case?"

"We did."

"And what did you find?"

"We found that Mr. Salazar's DNA matched the DNA from the samples taken from underneath Officer Steele's fingernails in all seven of the variable sites for which DNA could be isolated."

"In the jargon of your profession, Dr. Horowitz, does that constitute an exact match?"

"It does," Horowitz answered with some reluctance. Finn knew that he was trying to make clear that he wasn't happy to be giving his testimony, but the effect was to demonstrate that his sympathies were with the defense, making the evidence all the more powerful for the prosecution.

"Having come to this conclusion, did you run any additional tests to try to verify your results?"

"We did. We ran a mitochondrial DNA comparison as well as a DNA site comparison—or STR test."

"Can you explain what that test is?"

"Yes. This is a test that can be used on samples where, as here, there is some degradation in the DNA sample. It is not as conclusive as the STR tests that we initially ran, but it can be a good check on initial matches."

"And what was the result of this second test?"

"It also came back as a match for Mr. Salazar's DNA."

Jackson let that answer hang as he walked back to counsel table. He shifted his notes, but Finn could tell it was just for effect. Finally, Jackson looked back up at the witness. "Dr. Horowitz, based on these results, can you draw any conclusions regarding Mr. Salazar's guilt or innocence in the attack on Officer Steele fifteen years ago?"

"I can," Horowitz answered. He looked up at the judge. "From these tests, I can conclude that Mr. Salazar was the man Officer Steele scratched on that night, and he was, therefore, the man who attacked and shot her."

———✦———

Finn stood up. Having recognized the possibility that he would be in this position, he'd spent the first half of a sleepless night trying to work through ways to attack Horowitz's testimony if the DA's office found out about the tests. In the end, he'd come up with little, and he'd spent the second half of the night hoping the man would not be called.

"Mr. Finn?"

It was Cavanaugh. He was glaring at Finn with a hostile expression. Only a hint of sympathy for his former student seemed to keep his anger from tipping into rage. "Were you aware of these test results?" the judge asked.

Finn held his head up and met Cavanaugh's eyes, but not without some substantial effort. "I was, Your Honor."

"When you answered my question before about why you had nothing in your briefs about the DNA testing, you chose your words carefully."

"I did, Your Honor."

"My father used to say that carefully chosen words were the tools of the devil."

"He sounds like a wise man, Your Honor."

"Just be warned from here on out, Mr. Finn. I will be looking over these transcripts very carefully. Don't give me an excuse to refer you to the Board of Bar Overseers for disciplinary action."

"Yes, Your Honor. Thank you."

"You may proceed."

Finn took a deep breath. He approached Horowitz slowly, with his fingers locked together at his lips. "Dr. Horowitz, can you tell the court how you obtained the DNA samples that were taken from underneath Officer Steele's fingernails?"

"Mr. Dobson gave me the copy of the court's order requiring the police and the DA's office to provide the sample, as well as a letter of authorization as Mr. Salazar's legal representative. I took those to police headquarters and obtained the samples from the chief technical inspector. I signed for the samples and took them back to the lab to run the tests."

"So you obtained the samples from the police department?"

"Of course. Who else could I get them from?"

"And this would be the same police department that falsified the original fingerprint evidence used to convict Mr. Salazar?"

Jackson rose. "Objection."

"Overruled," Cavanaugh answered without even hearing the grounds for the objection.

Horowitz shrugged. "I wouldn't know about that. All I know is what science tells me, and science tells me that the samples matched."

"But you don't really know where the DNA given to you actually came from, do you?"

"I'm not sure I understand the question." Horowitz clearly didn't like being challenged, and he was becoming defensive.

"It's possible, for example, that Mr. Salazar's DNA was placed there a few weeks ago, after the court ordered the police department to turn over the rape kit, isn't it?"

Horowitz considered the question carefully. "No, actually," he said after a moment. "That's not possible."

"How can you say that?" Finn demanded. This was his only decent line of questioning, and he wasn't going to let it die. "After they planted fingerprints fifteen years ago, after they committed perjury? How can you be sure that they didn't plant this DNA evidence as well?"

"Because I examined the samples myself," Horowitz responded. "No matter what their motivations, they can't change the laws of science. You see, when Officer Steele scratched the man who attacked her, the pressure and force of her hands drove the skin and blood into the crevices of her fingernails. When she was examined, her fingernails were clipped and placed in the rape kit. Over time, the skin and blood that were there fused to the cells of the fingernails themselves. So when we took the sample for testing, we actually pulled cellular material from two individuals—one was Officer Steele, one was Vincente Salazar. In both cases, the DNA and cellular composition showed clear deterioration consistent with the passage of a significant amount of time. It would have been impossible for this evidence to have been planted three weeks ago."

"It could have been planted fifteen years ago, though, right?" Finn was grasping now, and he was sure it showed, but he had no other angles.

"Not really," Horowitz said, his voice growing in confidence. "As I indicated, the skin and blood were impressed deep into the crevices of the fingernails. It would have been nearly impossible to achieve this if the evidence had been planted after the fingernails had been clipped."

"*Nearly* impossible?" Finn asked, emphasizing the modifier. It was weak, but it was all he had.

"I suppose anything is impossible if you push a hypothetical to its illogical end," Horowitz replied.

Finn stood there looking at the witness. He was out of ammunition, and he didn't feel like he'd even made a dent in Horowitz's direct testimony.

"Anything further, Mr. Finn?" Cavanaugh asked.

"If I could have a moment to go over my notes, Your Honor?"

"By all means. Be quick, though. My holiday cheer is running thin."

Finn walked back to counsel table. He had no notes there that would help him, but he needed to buy time to think. The case was slipping away from him. Notwithstanding the fact that he believed Salazar was guilty, the man was still Finn's client, and once the battle was joined, the notion of losing was anathema to him. He was a lawyer, after all.

Finn stood at the front of the courtroom, in front of counsel table, facing away from the judge, away from the witness stand, looking out toward the gallery. He could sense the crowd shifting in their seats, anticipating Salazar's imminent return to prison. Finn knew that if he hadn't convinced the crowd, he certainly hadn't convinced Cavanaugh.

As he looked out at those gathered in the courtroom, he caught sight of the Salazar family in the first row. Mrs. Salazar's head was down, and she was counting off rosary beads in her lap. Rosita sat still and straight, like a porcelain doll, her sightless eyes motionless. Miguel Salazar's face was drawn tight, and he stared straight at Finn. Finn looked back at him, feeling lost and helpless. He was struck by how much Miguel resembled his brother, and wondered what their lives might have been like if they hadn't lived through such hardship.

As he stared at Miguel, the shadow of a thought slipped across Finn's mind. It was fleeting and undefined, but he felt the substance behind it. He looked down at his client. Vincente was staring at Finn, too, his features set in stone. As he looked at Vincente, the shadow began to gain definition, and Finn found it difficult to breathe. He looked back and forth between the two brothers.

And then both brothers nodded. It was an identical movement, slight and subtle, too inconspicuous to notice unless, like Finn, you were focused on both at the same time. Finn felt the rush of revelation spread through him like a narcotic. He looked at both brothers, and confirmation was plain in their expressions.

"Mr. Finn?" Cavanaugh said testily, trying to push the proceedings along toward their inevitable conclusion.

"Yes, Your Honor," Finn replied. His mind was churning, trying to recall the information he had read in his research on DNA evidence over the past week. He turned and faced the witness. "Dr. Horowitz, you indicated that you were able to establish a match for seven variable points of DNA identification with respect to the samples in question, is that right?"

"That's correct."

"Can you explain what that means?"

"Sure. Although it's somewhat complicated." Horowitz looked at Finn as if to ask whether the lawyer really wanted him to continue.

"I understand," Finn said. "We'll take our chances."

Horowitz gave him a tired look. "Well, as most people know, DNA is the basic code—chemical code, if you will—of life that determines everything about what an organism will be. DNA itself is fairly simple; it is made up of four proteins that are lined up in a very specific order in pairs on strands called chromosomes. These chromosomes are made up of literally millions and millions of these protein pairs, and the differences in the order of the proteins is what creates differences between animals and plants, or two different species, or two different individuals. Because DNA is what makes us all different, we all have different DNA—it is unique to us, and that is what makes it so useful in identifying individuals when they leave their DNA behind, as Mr. Salazar did when Officer Steele scratched him."

"Thank you, Doctor, but if you could confine yourself for the moment to explaining how DNA identification works in general, I would appreciate it," Finn said. "We will get to Mr. Salazar's specific case shortly."

Horowitz frowned at being rebuked, but continued. "What is sometimes difficult to grasp is that, although everyone's DNA is different in some ways, on the whole, the DNA from two individuals is actually quite similar. When you consider the complexities involved in creating human beings, with hearts and lungs, and organs, and hands and legs—everything about the human body—the fact that we are all as similar as we are is really a marvel of chemical engineering. In that light, differences in height or eye color start to seem minor by comparison. Indeed, when you look at human DNA, over ninety-nine point nine percent of all human DNA is identical. You find differences only in a few limited, specific areas on DNA strands that are highly variable.

These spots are known as points of identification, and the FBI has recognized fifteen such spots that are used in DNA testing. If the patterns of the proteins on these spots match in two different samples of DNA, then you know that you are looking at DNA from the same person."

Finn nodded; the tutorial was bringing back much of what he'd read over the preceding week. "Right," he said. "There are fifteen such points of identification, correct?"

"That's correct."

"But you testified earlier that you were able to match only seven points of identification between Mr. Salazar's DNA and that taken from underneath Officer Steele's fingernails, correct?"

"That's true."

"Can you explain why you were unable to obtain a match for all fifteen sites?"

"Yes. You see, the DNA sample we were working with from the victim was over a decade and a half old. We were also dealing with very small samples—pulled from a tiny amount of tissue that had fused to the fingernail itself. As a result, there was an inevitable amount of degradation and contamination of the DNA, and we were not able to obtain clean samples for all fifteen sites."

"So," Finn said, "this is not a complete match."

Horowitz shook his head. "No, that's where you're wrong. You have to understand that these particular sites are highly variable between individuals, and they comprise thousands of protein pairs. The chances of someone else from the general population sharing the same patterns on seven sites is astronomical—in fact, the FBI requires a match at only five sites to establish an identification. This is an exact match by any scientific standard."

Finn was in dangerous waters, and he had to frame his questions carefully. "When you say that the odds of someone from the general population matching on seven points of identification are astronomical, how would you define 'astronomical' in these circumstances?"

"I'm not sure, exactly," Horowitz said. "Maybe one in a hundred million."

"And, Doctor, what are the odds that a sibling of Mr. Salazar's could match his DNA on seven points of identification?"

The question brought Horowitz up short, and it took him a moment to speak. "I don't know offhand," he said defensively.

Finn pounced. "You don't know *offhand*?" he demanded in an agitated tone. "Doctor, you are giving testimony here today that could put an innocent man back into prison for the rest of his life, and you are telling this court that you don't know what the odds are of this DNA matching someone other than the defendant *offhand*?"

"I didn't mean it that way," Horowitz sputtered. "Certainly, the odds would be greater, but I don't know exactly how much greater."

"How much greater, Doctor?"

"I just said, I don't know exactly."

"How about one in a hundred?"

Horowitz thought about it. "It's possible."

"Could the odds be greater than that?" Finn pressed. "Say, maybe one in fifty?"

"I don't know."

"One in ten?"

"No."

"How do you know that for sure? You just told the court that you don't know what the odds are, and now you tell us that you do know? What has changed, Doctor? Did you somehow conduct research as you were sitting here on the stand giving testimony?"

"No, of course not! It just seems too high."

Judging from the redness in Horowitz's face, Finn was approaching the point at which the man would never work with him again. There was no turning back, though. "It *seems* too high? You are willing to send a man to jail because the odds *seem* too high?"

"That's not what I meant, either."

"The truth is, Doctor, that you were telling the truth the first time, right? You really have no idea, as you sit here, what the odds are that a sibling of Mr. Salazar's could match on seven points of identification using the ASI test?"

Horowitz drew his lips together tightly. "That's correct." His voice was low and barely audible, but it was enough.

Finn turned and walked back to counsel table, making a note on a blank sheet of paper. "You ran a second test as well? A mitochondrial DNA test, Doctor?"

"Yes."

"Can you tell the judge what the odds are that one of Mr. Salazar's siblings would match his DNA using that test?"

"I just ran that test as a double check," Horowitz protested. "You know that."

"If you would, just answer the question, Doctor," Finn said.

"But—"

"Answer the question, Doctor," Cavanaugh instructed him. It was a good sign, Finn knew. At least he could be sure that the judge was fully engaged.

"That test involves an analysis of maternal DNA that resides in the cells. As a result, all siblings would have the same mitochondrial DNA," Horowitz explained.

"So," Finn said, "that sounds like the chance of a match between siblings is one hundred percent, no?"

"That's correct," Horowitz admitted wearily.

"Thank you, Doctor. Nothing further." Finn walked around counsel table and sat down.

"Redirect, Your Honor?" Jackson requested, standing. Cavanaugh nodded, and Jackson moved in. "Dr. Horowitz, are you certain beyond any reasonable doubt that the DNA you found under the fingernails of Officer Steele came from Vincente Salazar?" The ADA was going for broke. Finn knew he would try to rehabilitate his witness, but with this question, he was putting it all on the line, and he had no way of knowing how far Horowitz was willing to go out on a limb. Finn held his breath as the entire courtroom waited for the answer.

"How do you define 'reasonable'?" Horowitz asked, looking defeated. It might have been an attempt at humor, but Finn couldn't have asked for a better response.

"Please, Doctor," Jackson said, visibly shaken. "If you could just answer the question?"

"I don't know. Could it have been a sibling? I suppose that's possible. Beyond that, I'm sure it's Vincente Salazar's DNA." Horowitz looked as though he just wanted to get off the stand and be done with his testimony.

Jackson sat heavily. It was clearly not the answer he'd been looking for. "Thank you, Doctor." To the judge, he said, "Nothing further, Your Honor."

Cavanaugh sat on the bench, looking down at Horowitz on the witness stand, gauging his demeanor. "Mr. Finn?" he asked. "Anything further?"

"No, Your Honor, not for this witness. But I would ask your indulgence to call one witness of our own."

Cavanaugh looked over at Jackson, who looked like a puddle of defeat. "Mr. Jackson, do you have any additional witnesses for us today?"

"No."

"You may proceed, Mr. Finn."

"Thank you, Your Honor." Finn got back to his feet. "I would like to call Miguel Salazar."

Chapter Forty-four

VINCENTE COULDN'T WATCH his brother walking through the swinging gates at the front of the courtroom and making his way to the witness stand. Nor could Vincente turn around to face the rest of his family. His chest felt tight, and he found it difficult to breathe.

It was the right decision, he told himself. Fifteen years was enough; his brother had agreed. Miguel knew full well what he was doing, and yet after a lifetime spent protecting his family, Vincente could feel the guilt nestling into his stomach. He looked down at the table in front of him. *Just a little while longer*, he told himself. Then this would all be over.

Finn was violating one of the cardinal rules of trial law: You never put a witness on the stand when you don't know what he is going to say. In this case, Finn had no choice. He had to take the risk.

Miguel took the stand and was sworn in by the bailiff. He sat there quietly, looking at Finn, inscrutable. Finn couldn't tell whether the man regarded him as an enemy or as some kind of coconspirator, but he was about to find out.

"Would you please state your name for the record?"

"Miguel Paulo Salazar."

"Mr. Salazar, are you related to the defendant in this case, Vincente Salazar?"

"I am. He is my brother."

"Did the two of you grow up together?" Finn asked.

"In some respects, yes," Miguel responded. "He is more than ten years older than I am, but we were close. In some ways, he has been more of a father to me than a brother."

"Did you come to this country with your brother in 1991?"

"Yes. We had to come here. Otherwise, the death squads would have killed our entire family." Miguel's face betrayed no emotion.

"How old were you at the time?"

"Sixteen."

"Were you living with your brother at the time of his arrest, after Officer Steele was attacked?"

"I was."

"Did you know at the time that she was investigating your brother? That she was trying to have your family deported, and that you would be sent back to El Salvador?"

Miguel said nothing. He just kept staring back at Finn, and Finn could feel his heart pounding out a slow, anticipatory beat. Then Miguel's gaze shifted, and he looked at his brother sitting behind Finn. The two of them regarded each other across the courtroom.

"Mr. Salazar?" Cavanaugh prodded Miguel.

Miguel looked up at the judge. "I'm sorry, Your Honor." He turned back to Finn. "What was the question again?"

"Did you know that Officer Steele was trying to have your brother deported?"

Miguel Salazar took a deep breath. "On the advice of counsel, I decline to answer that question, and I assert my rights under the Fifth Amendment."

A gasp could be heard throughout the courtroom, and it quickly morphed into a buzz, then into a loud rumble. Cavanaugh pounded his gavel on the bench in front of him to regain order, and Jackson leaped to his feet. "Objection! Your Honor, this is obviously some sort of a cheap stunt dreamed up by defense counsel! You can't possibly allow them to get away with this."

Cavanaugh glared at Finn. "Counselor, are you telling me that you are representing both of the Salazar brothers? Because the defense you appear to be pursuing would put you in a direct conflict of interest—one so severe that disciplinary action would undoubtedly be called for."

"I do not represent Miguel Salazar, Your Honor. In fact, I wasn't aware that he was represented by anyone. This is all news to me."

Cavanaugh leaned over the witness box. "Mr. Salazar, who advised you to refuse to answer questions?"

A voice came from the gallery. "Your Honor, I represent Mr. Salazar." Finn turned to see Joe Cocca standing behind the balustrade. "Joseph Cocca, Your Honor. May I approach?"

The judge looked over at Cocca. "If you can provide some answers, by all means."

Cocca stepped through the swinging gate and stood between counsel tables, caught in a no-man's-land between the prosecution and the defense. "Your Honor, I can tell you that I have been retained by Dr. Miguel Salazar, and I have given him legal advice regarding certain of his rights. I can also tell you that I have not spoken with Mr. Finn about this matter; nor, to my knowledge, has my client."

Cavanaugh frowned, his nose rippling as though it had been assaulted by a foul stench.

"I still object, Your Honor," Jackson said, rising to his feet, his jowls shaking with indignation. "This is clearly a ploy to confuse the issues in this case."

"Mr. Jackson, sit down. The issues in this case have become confused only because your office put witnesses on the stand fifteen years ago who perjured themselves in order to assure a conviction. You should remember that when you start to feel holier than thou."

Jackson sat down, and Cavanaugh went back to scrutinizing Finn and Cocca. "Mr. Finn, do I have your word of honor that you have not spoken to anyone about Dr. Salazar's testimony prior to now?"

"My word of honor," Finn said.

Cavanaugh put his head in his hands, rubbing his eyes in consternation. Then he looked up. "You may continue with your examination, Mr. Finn," he said.

Jackson stood tentatively. "Your Honor?"

"What?" Cavanaugh snapped. "Mr. Salazar has the constitutional right to have his counsel ask questions, and Dr. Salazar has the constitutional right not to answer them. What, exactly, would you have me do?"

"I would ask that you weigh the credibility of this little farce when you ultimately rule, Your Honor," Jackson said.

"Don't presume to tell me how to do my job, Mr. Jackson. I will consider the entire record before I rule." Cavanaugh glared at Jackson until the assistant DA wilted back into his chair. "You may proceed, Mr. Finn."

Finn approached Miguel Salazar. "Dr. Salazar, you were aware, were you not, that Officer Steele was looking to have your brother deported?"

"On advice of counsel, I decline to answer at this time."

"You were angry about that, weren't you?"

"On advice of counsel, I decline to answer at this time." Miguel still showed no emotion, seeming to regard Finn as nothing more than a functionary.

"Can you tell us where you were on the evening Officer Steele was attacked?"

"On advice of counsel, I decline to answer at this time."

Finn walked back to counsel table. He stood in front of his chair at the table, readying himself to sit next to his client. "One final question, Dr. Salazar: Did you shoot Madeline Steele?"

The courtroom was silent. Everyone knew the answer that was coming, and yet the tension was electric. Reporters, who had been scribbling furiously into notebooks throughout the proceedings, balanced on the edges of their seats, looking alternately among Finn and the two Salazar brothers. Finally, Miguel Salazar sat forward in his chair and, leaning in to the microphone in front of the witness stand, he said in a clear, strong voice, "On advice of counsel, I decline to answer at this time."

Finn leaned against the wall in the courthouse corridor. Kozlowski stood next to him, hands in his pockets. The hall was crowded, though there remained a cushion of unclaimed space around the two men. The reporters and lawyers milling about threw furtive glances at Finn, as though he were some sort of dangerous wizard. After Miguel's testimony, the hearing had moved quickly. Cavanaugh had heard arguments from both sides but cut them short after a few minutes apiece. Then he'd stood and looked at everyone in his courtroom with unmistakable contempt. "I am going back to my chambers to consider everything I have seen and heard today," he'd said. "I will have a ruling for you in twenty minutes or so."

Now all Finn could do was wait.

"What do you think?" Kozlowski asked.

"I think I'm going to be sick." Finn's head was down. He was staring at the dingy tiled floor.

"You had a job to do. You did it."

"Nice fuckin' way to live my life, though, huh? My client may still be guilty, you know. They could both be lying just to get him out."

"You think the brother would do that for your client?"

"I don't know. I never had a brother."

Miguel Salazar sifted through the perimeter of strangers surrounding the two and walked over to them. "Mr. Finn, I'd like a word," he said. Cocca was behind him, trying to catch up.

"That's not a good idea," Finn said without looking up.

"Mr. Finn, I apologize if this puts you in an awkward position—"

Finn cut Miguel off and addressed his lawyer. "Joe, would you tell your client that he and I aren't speaking. Whatever he says to me isn't privileged, and I probably have an ethical obligation to report it to the judge."

"I saved your life in that alley," Miguel said.

"If you were the reason my life was in danger in the first place, I'm not sure you still get to call Yahtzee on that."

Cocca tugged at his client's elbow. "C'mon, Miguel," he said. "Finn's right; there are lots of conflicts of interest going on here. Plus, I don't want this to look like there's some kind of conspiracy involved."

"Good thought," Finn said. "God forbid any of us look sleazy in all this."

As Cocca dragged his client away, he said to Finn, "After the New Year, we'll grab a beer and swap stories on all this, okay?"

"Right," Finn responded. He watched the two men disappear into the crowd.

Kozlowski cleared his throat. "So, do they make you guys sign away your self-respect when they give out bar cards?"

"By that point, few of us would have anything left to hand over. The self-respect is gone long before the bar exam."

Kozlowski chortled. "Where's your client?"

"He's back in a holding cell."

"Should you be back there waiting with him?"

"Maybe. But I don't want to talk to him." Finn kicked at a piece of lint on the floor. "I'm not sure what I would say."

"Are you sure you're not just avoiding your own conscience?"

"Probably."

"Taking the easy way out?"

"You bet your ass." The piece of lint refused to give ground and instead drifted over in front of Kozlowski's foot. Kozlowski flicked his toe, and the lint popped up into the air, catching a draft and retreating into the loose web of people in the hallway.

"He was lucky," Kozlowski said.

"Who?"

"Salazar. Vincente. He was lucky."

"How do you figure?"

"He had you in there. Whether you still think he might be guilty or not, you fought damned hard. If I was in his shoes, I'd want you in there representing me, even if you thought I did it."

"Is that a compliment?" Finn asked.

"I don't know."

The door to the courtroom opened, and a clerk stuck his head out into the hallway. "Judge Cavanaugh will be back on the bench shortly," he said. He withdrew, and the tide of onlookers began to flow back into the courtroom.

"Moment of truth," Kozlowski said.

Finn looked at him. "I didn't realize you knew how to be ironic."

"It's a gift. I try not to overuse it."

"You succeed." Finn straightened up and threw his shoulders back, pulling his body off the wall. "I guess we'll find out now how good a job I actually did."

———◦———

"All rise!" The bailiff glared out at the crowd as he called the room to order, his eyes daring anyone to breach the sanctity of the tribunal. Finn heard the rustling of the spectators getting to their feet behind him as he stood next to his client.

Cavanaugh emerged from his chambers looking as though he had aged ten years in twenty minutes. His black robe contrasted eerily with the gray of his face, lending him the air of a weary grim reaper. He climbed the steps to the bench with visible effort, like an aged mountaineer on his last ascent. "Be seated," he said quietly enough that some in the crowd seemed uncertain of the instruction. "Mr. Salazar, you may remain standing." It was more than an invitation, and Finn stayed on his feet as well.

"There are times when this job is rewarding beyond comprehension," Cavanaugh began. He looked out over the crowd, pausing briefly on Jackson, then Finn, and letting his gaze settle on Salazar. "This is not one of those times," he continued, and the pit in Finn's stomach threatened to swallow him.

"Our system of criminal justice is firm—hard, even, at times. It must be. Stripped of the twin pillars of certainty and finality, the public would lose trust in our courts, and without the public trust, our entire judicial system would weaken, and our very democracy would be in peril. As a result, once a case has been decided and all appeals have run, that decision is considered final and cannot be challenged again." His glare at Salazar intensified. "You, sir, have been convicted of a heinous crime. There are few offenses as grave as an attack on the very people who have offered themselves up, and risked their lives, in the enforcement of our laws and in the protection of our citizens. Your conviction was handed down by a jury of twelve ordinary citizens, unanimous in their determination that you committed this crime beyond any reasonable doubt. You were afforded legal counsel, and there is no challenge here that such counsel was lacking in its effectiveness. While it is clear that there were significant breaches of procedure in the prosecution of your case, it is not clear that it was beyond the power of your counsel to expose those irregularities. In addition, evidence obtained more recently—at your lawyers' own request, no less—tends to indicate that you are, in fact, the man who committed this crime. Putting aside the little morality play staged by your brother and the attorneys, I am not convinced that you are innocent in this matter, and I admit only a minuscule possibility that the DNA testing does not conclusively establish your guilt."

Cavanaugh let his words sink in, and if the silence in the courtroom was any indication, he hadn't overestimated the impact of his oratory. "It must also be acknowledged," he continued, "that while our system of justice must be firm, it should not become so hard that it risks turning brittle. Without some degree of flexibility, our courts would lose an element of humanity that is at the core of their strength. In this case, there is evidence—indeed, overwhelming evidence—of an active conspiracy to secure a conviction through the falsification of evidence and the presentation of perjurious testimony by the police. As important to the public trust in the criminal justice system as the notions of certainty and finality are, so, too, are the concepts of fairness and truth. For if the government is permitted to rig the system against those it has chosen to accuse, none of our citizens can feel safe from the dangers of tyranny."

Cavanaugh rested his elbows on the bench, reaching and taking off his glasses. "These are the competing equities I must balance today. So where does all that leave us?"

Finn searched Cavanaugh's expression, but it revealed nothing, and he steadied himself with his hand against counsel table. No one was breathing in the courtroom, and Finn was sure that his legs would fail him at any moment. For the first time since the judge had retaken the bench, Finn allowed himself a brief sidelong glance at his client. Salazar stood frozen at the divide between two very different futures, and for the first time in twenty-four hours, Finn felt real compassion for him.

Cavanaugh took a deep breath. "Unfortunately, it leaves me with no choice. You have been convicted, Mr. Salazar, and I believe that you are guilty. Those undeniable realities, however, are not enough for me to uphold your conviction in the face of the blatant police misconduct used to procure your conviction. Mr. Finn has convinced me that there is a shadow of a doubt still remaining, and in these circumstances, I will not substitute my own judgment for that of an unbiased jury presented with all of the evidence fully and fairly. That is not how our system of justice was designed to work."

No one seemed to know for sure what the judge had done. No one moved, and the entire courtroom remained transfixed on the old, tired, robed man facing them. As if to dispel any doubt, Cavanaugh spoke again. "I hereby order that the conviction of Vincente Salazar in this matter is vacated, and Mr. Salazar shall be released."

The courtroom erupted as reporters streamed toward the back door, eager to deliver the news first. "It gives me no joy to do this," Cavanaugh continued, "and my decision is without prejudice. The district attorney's office is free to refile charges and retry Mr. Salazar as it sees fit." No one was listening anymore, and his final words drifted unheard into the commotion. "May God forgive me if I am making a mistake." He brought down the gavel, stood, and walked off the bench looking utterly defeated.

Salazar, who hadn't moved since Cavanaugh began speaking, stood with his mouth open, still staring at the tall black leather chair the judge had vacated. Then he turned and looked at his family. He took two steps toward them and grabbed his daughter over the bar, holding her tightly as the tears ran down both their faces. A bailiff tried to separate them, explaining that they still had to process Salazar's release before he would officially be free, but neither of them would let go. Finn suspected that neither would for a while.

Finn took his notes and laid them in his briefcase, closing the lid and snapping the locks shut. He took one last look at Vincente and Rosita Salazar trying to soothe the pain of fifteen years' absence with one embrace. Then he picked up his briefcase and left the courtroom without another word.

Chapter Forty-five

CHRISTMAS BROKE OVER Boston like salvation. The sun pierced through a crystal-blue sky, and for the first time in a fortnight, the meteorologists were predicting a day without precipitation. Across the city, children scrambled out of their beds in a frenzy, tearing down stairs and into living rooms awash in the glow of colored lights reflecting off red and green and gold wrapping paper. Even in the homeless shelters, the aromas of special breakfast feasts of pancakes and ham chased away the sad realities of life, if only for a few hours. It seemed as though the world had been released from its slate-gray captivity, and those waking from their nightly slumber greeted a day filled with possibilities.

Finn didn't wake up that morning. He didn't need to; he hadn't slept. At five A.M., after leaving his third voice-mail message for Linda Flaherty, he showered, dressed in a sweater and sport jacket, threw on an overcoat, and went out walking. He had no destination in mind and felt only the need to be on the move. He walked down off Bunker Hill and out the backside of Charlestown into Cambridge. He walked up the Charles River on the north bank, past the great dome of the Massachusetts Institute of Technology, through the brick thicket of

Harvard University, and then back across the river through Boston's Fenway, Back Bay, and Beacon Hill.

As he walked, he evaluated the city through new eyes—eyes that were considering abandoning the city for the first time. He had spent his entire life in Boston, never making it farther than a hundred miles from the place of his forgotten birth. And as he walked through the city, he realized something. He loved it. He loved it the way he supposed the fortunate love their parents—forgetfully, selfishly, taking for granted the splendor and warmth, the faults and failings, until the possibility that they won't always be there feels like more than hypothetical musing. He knew then that he would never leave. He existed only here, and there was nothing that could be done to change that.

At ten o'clock he arrived back in Charlestown and ambled his way up Warren Street to his office. He was surprised to find the door open and Kozlowski sitting at the conference table. In front of him were a box of donuts and two large coffees. "Been looking for you," Kozlowski said.

"You're a detective. I'm not that difficult to find."

Kozlowski shrugged. "Didn't say I was looking very hard. You took off pretty quick yesterday. I figured you probably wanted a little time to yourself."

"Good-looking and sensitive, too. Lissa's one lucky girl."

Kozlowski pushed one of the coffees toward him as Finn sat down. "That one's yours."

"Thanks."

Neither of them said anything. They just sat there and let the coffee warm them. "Santa bring you anything good?" Kozlowski said after a while.

Finn shook his head. "Just a big fat chunk of coal."

"You must have been naughty."

"Goes without saying, doesn't it?"

Kozlowski leaned back in his chair. "Look at it this way—given enough time, coal turns to diamonds, right? So maybe this is Santa's way of making a down payment."

"It takes like a million years for coal to turn to diamonds."

"Right. Maybe it's just a lump of coal, then."

Finn got up and walked over to sit behind his desk and put his feet up. "So, what are you doing down here?"

"Nothing, really. I had to clean up a few loose ends in the office, and I wanted to make sure you hadn't jumped off a bridge or anything."

"And people say you have no Christmas spirit. Go figure."

"You know what I mean."

"Yeah. I do."

"You good with everything?"

Finn felt like Kozlowski was analyzing him. Kicking the tires to make sure everything was still working. "Everything? No. But I'm good with enough."

"I guess that'll do."

"I guess it'll have to."

Just then the door opened. Vincente Salazar stood at the threshold. He nodded to both men. "Mr. Finn, may I come in?"

It took a moment for Finn to answer. "Yeah," he said without conviction. "Sure, what the fuck." He looked over at Kozlowski.

"Well, I'm sure you boys have lots of lawyer-client-type stuff to discuss, so I'll be back in my office if you need me." Kozlowski stood and walked to the door of his office.

"Detective," Salazar said.

Kozlowski turned around at the door. "Yeah?"

"Thank you. I know you risked your life."

"I didn't do it for you."

"I know that, too. Thank you anyway."

Kozlowski nodded and disappeared into the back of the building.

"I didn't get a chance to thank you yesterday," Salazar said to Finn. "I turned around, and you were gone."

"I'm like the wind. Eerie, isn't it?"

Salazar sat down in a chair across the desk from Finn. "You're angry. I understand that. I was hoping to have the chance to explain things."

Finn waved him off. "No big deal. It's my job. I did it. It's who I am. I'm fine with it. You don't owe me anything."

"I would like for you to understand that you did a good thing."

Finn laughed quietly. "Good and bad don't play into it. I'm a lawyer."

"You aren't curious at all?"

Finn shrugged.

"Are you still my lawyer?"

"If you want to tell me anything? Yes. For the purposes of this conversation, I am still your lawyer. Once you leave here, though, I think you'd be better off with new counsel."

Salazar looked away as though considering his options. "In my country, in the old days, there was no law. Not really. There was only what the landlords decided—that was the law. They had the guns, and they had the power. Sometimes one of the workers would break the landlord's law and would have to be punished. This created a dilemma for the landlord. If the worker was jailed or beaten, he wasn't working, and the landlord would lose money. Often, as a result, someone in the worker's family was chosen to suffer the punishment instead—maybe a wife or a favored son or daughter. In some cases, even, it would be a brother."

Salazar let what he was saying sink in. "When we fled to this country, it was the second time Miguel had his life ripped away. The first was when our father died and Miguel and my mother came to live with me. He was sixteen when we arrived here—young and passionate and angry."

"Not a great combination," Finn commented.

"No," Salazar agreed. "When Miguel found out that we might be deported—sent back to El Salvador to face the death squads—something snapped. He wanted to scare her, and he thought if he used a machete, the police would assume that VDS was responsible."

"He thought right. That's exactly what Macintyre assumed. That's why he framed you."

"God has an ironic sense of justice," Salazar observed.

"Apparently, he's not alone. Even if Miguel only meant to scare her, do you really think that justifies the fact that your brother attacked Madeline Steele?"

"No. Nothing justifies what he did. It does explain it, though. As young and foolish as he was, he saw it as self-defense. More than that, he saw it as defending his family."

"Did you know?" Finn heard the accusation in his own voice.

"No. I didn't really know until you told me about the DNA tests. But I think at some level, I always suspected."

"You spent fifteen years in prison for a crime he committed."

"I did. But perhaps that was the right thing. He was like a son to me. He was forced to come to this country because of my mistakes. Perhaps I was more responsible for his crime than I would like to admit. In any case, he is my family, and if I had the choice, I don't know that I would have changed the outcome."

"Why not?" Finn asked. "In this country, you are not responsible for the crimes of your family."

Salazar smiled. "That is a uniquely American and strangely naive point of view. In any event, my brother has spent the last fifteen years atoning for his sins. He has raised my daughter. He has cared for our mother. He has healed the sick, and he has even saved the life of a promising young lawyer, no?" Salazar raised his eyebrow at Finn. "And now he has willingly put his freedom in jeopardy to secure mine."

Finn shook his head. "I doubt it will ever come to that. The DA's office has already convicted you once. Even though the judge threw that conviction out, you still haven't been acquitted or exonerated. The DNA evidence matches both of you, so there is no way to prove which one of you did it. Ironically, that means that neither one of you will ever be convicted, because there will always be a reasonable doubt that it is the other one who is really guilty. Plus, given the scandal and the way the police framed you the first time, I would be surprised if the DA's office wants to open up this fifteen-year-old can of worms. Better for them to let the furor die down and be done with it. Let the two of you go on with your lives."

"What if they run more DNA tests? If they can isolate more points of comparison, they may be able to prove that Miguel was responsible."

"It's unlikely," Finn said. "They were small skin samples, and I'm not sure there are any left."

"It's possible. The technology used in DNA analysis is advancing rapidly."

"You could be right," Finn said. "Maybe that's an uncertainty that will hang over Miguel's head for the rest of his life." He took some satisfaction in the notion.

"Perhaps that is his punishment. Perhaps it is enough."

"You spent fifteen years in jail. Do you really think uncertainty is enough punishment?"

"I don't know," Salazar admitted. "It is enough for me—for my sense of justice. Have my brother and my daughter and I together not paid sufficiently for my brother's crime?"

"It's not my job to make those calls," Finn said. "I'm not a judge, and I'm not a jury. I'm a lawyer. My job is to represent my clients."

"Yes," Salazar agreed. "You are a lawyer. A good lawyer." He stood and extended his hand. Finn sat still, looking at his client; then he stood and shook the man's hand. "Thank you, Mr. Finn," Salazar said. "On behalf of my family, thank you."

Finn nodded but said nothing. Salazar turned and walked out the door. He didn't look back.

———◆———

Kozlowski stood out back behind the tiny brick office building. The temperature was still below freezing, but the sun was heating the asphalt shingles on the roof, causing a steady drip from the eaves protecting the back doorway. He had remained in his office for a few minutes, but in reality, he had no work to do, and he thought a breath of cold, fresh winter air would do him good. He was looking out across the street when he heard the door open behind him. Finn stepped out without saying anything.

"You believe him?" Kozlowski asked.

"I think so," Finn said. "It's easier to, I suppose." He took out a cigarette and lit it.

"Celebratory smoke?"

"I guess," Finn said. "Doesn't really feel like a celebration, but I'll take what I can get."

Kozlowski turned and looked at him. "Got an extra?"

"You don't smoke."

"I smoke cigars every now and then. How much worse can this be?"

Finn slid the pack out of his pocket and slipped a cigarette out, handing it to Kozlowski. "Careful. I hear they're addictive." He tossed Kozlowski his Zippo.

Kozlowski put the cigarette between his lips and flipped the lighter open. It took him two tries to get it lit, and when he held up the flame to the tobacco and inhaled, a rush of smoke attacked his lungs through the frigid air, forcing a muffled cough.

"It's good, huh?" Finn asked.

Kozlowski gave the lighter back. "Did you and Flaherty get things worked out?"

Finn shook his head. "Not yet. We'll keep trying, though, I hope."

"You could always move down there with her."

"No, I can't."

Kozlowski took another drag and managed to keep this one down.

He exhaled a long stream of blue smoke. "No, I guess not. But she's an appointee, right? So I guess you can always hope for a change of administration. She might come back."

"She might. You never know." It was clear that Finn wasn't in the mood to talk about his love life. "How about you? Everything okay with Lissa?"

"I suppose. It'll take time, but she'll get through it."

"It's Christmas. Shouldn't you be with her?"

"She's Jewish. Turns out Christmas isn't such a big deal when you're Jewish."

Finn grunted. "Who knew."

"She gets out later today, and I'm going to pick her up and take her home. We'll see where it goes from there." Kozlowski looked at Finn as he thought about Lissa. He remembered what she'd said about how much Finn needed him, and he looked away again. He felt uncomfortable when he thought about putting his feelings into words, but he also knew that she was right. More than that, he was coming to recognize that he needed Finn as much as Finn needed him. "I'm gonna say something," he said. Then he went silent, trying to formulate the words.

"Good to know," Finn replied after a moment. "Keep me updated."

"I don't want you to think it's weird or make a big deal out of it."

"Okay. I suppose it depends on what you're planning on saying, but I'll keep that in mind."

It took another drag off the cigarette before Kozlowski spoke again. "What would you think if I told you I cared about you?"

Finn said nothing. He stood there, inhaling his smoke. "I don't know," he said at last. Then he smiled. "I guess I'd think you were going queer on me."

"Right."

"Not that there's anything wrong with that. The world takes all kinds."

"Point made. Thanks."

"Does Lissa know?"

"Fuck you."

Finn's smile widened.

Kozlowski took another drag, and his body was racked with a coughing fit. "I don't know how you suck on this shit."

"It's an acquired taste."

The two of them stood there for a few more minutes, saying nothing. The sun was low in the sky, and it felt good on Kozlowski's face. "O'Doul's stays open on Christmas," he said.

"Trust the Irish to make sure everyone is shitfaced for the Lord's birthday."

"You got plans, or you wanna go over and grab a drink?"

Finn looked at him. "You buying?"

"Yeah."

Finn raised his eyebrow. "A good drink?"

Kozlowski closed his eyes as he let the sun warm his face. "Yeah," he said. "A good drink."

Afterword

Innocence is a work of fiction, and any similarities between any characters in the novel and any actual people are purely coincidental. The premise of the story, however, has its roots in fact and experience. Over the past ten years, nearly two hundred individuals in the United States have had their convictions vacated after DNA testing established that they were innocent of the crimes for which they had been convicted and imprisoned. David Hosp, the author of *Innocence*, is a trial lawyer at the Boston-based law firm of Goodwin Procter, LLP. For the past two years, he has worked with a team of attorneys representing Stephan Cowans in civil lawsuits resulting from Mr. Cowans's 1997 wrongful conviction for the shooting and attempted murder of a Boston police officer. Mr. Cowans was exonerated and released in 2004 through the work of attorneys and staff at the New England Innocence Project ("NEIP").

Based on information developed during an internal investigation following Mr. Cowans's release, the Boston Police Department's Latent Fingerprint Unit was shut down from 2004 through 2006 due to the inadequate training and expertise of the police officers serving as fingerprint experts. Since its reopening last year, the Fingerprint Unit has been staffed exclusively with civilian technicians and experts.

AFTERWORD

NEIP is a charitable organization dedicated to providing pro bono legal services to individuals seeking to prove their innocence of crimes for which they have been convicted. NEIP works to redress the causes of wrongful convictions, and is coordinated on a pro bono basis by attorneys and staff from Goodwin Procter's Boston office.